Nancy Thayer is a *New York Times* bestselling author who has written twenty-four novels to date, including *Beachcombers, Heat Wave, Summer Breeze,* and *Island Girls.* Her work has been translated into many languages, and her novels are enjoyed by readers the world over. She lives year-round with her husband on Nantucket Island.

You can find out more about Nancy by visiting her website at www.nancythayer.com.

Praise for Nancy Thayer:

'Nancy Thayer is one of my favorite writers . . . Here is a book to be savored and passed on to the good women in your life'

*New York Times* bestselling author Susan Wiggs

'Full of emotion . . . this novel is delightful'      *Romance Reviews Today*

'Nancy Thayer's gift for reaching the emotional core of her characters is captivating'                    *Houston Chronicle*

'Thayer has the knack of creating likeable characters who grapple with problems that will strike a chord with many readers'

*Boston Globe*

*By Nancy Thayer*

★ Available from Headline

# Nancy Thayer

## Nantucket Sisters

headline

First published in Great Britain in 2014 by
HEADLINE PUBLISHING GROUP

First published in paperback in Great Britain in 2015 by
HEADLINE PUBLISHING GROUP

1

Cataloguing in Publication Data is available from the British Library

ISBN 978 1 4722 1598 7

Typeset in Bembo by Palimpsest Book Production Limited,
Falkirk, Stirlingshire

Printed and bound in Great Britain by CPI Group (UK) Ltd, Croydon CR0 4YY

Headline's policy is to use papers that are natural, renewable and recyclable
products and made from wood grown in sustainable forests. The logging and
manufacturing processes are expected to conform to the environmental
regulations of the country of origin.

HEADLINE PUBLISHING GROUP
An Hachette UK Company
338 Euston Road
London NW1 3BH

www.headline.co.uk
www.hachette.co.uk

For Charley
again, and always

# Acknowledgments

I want to thank my agent and friend Meg Ruley for championing this book from the beginning. Linda Marrow, my angelically astute and gentle editor, coaxed and cajoled me through many drafts, changes, deletions, insertions, and improvements. The debonair Dana Isaacson helped so much with his insights and deft touches. Much thanks to him and to the perceptive Anne Speyer.

It is an honor and delight to work with the entire Ballantine group. I'm extremely grateful for the support of Libby McGuire and Gina Centrello. Kim Hovey, Ashley Woodfolk, Alison Masciovecchio, Quinne Rogers, and Penelope Haynes have been a delight to work with, especially as we all enter deeper into the computer world. For that, I also thank Christina Hogrebe at the Jane Rotrosen Agency, who has been enthusiastic and kind and never once called me an idiot. (As far as I know.) My gratitude also goes out to Paolo Pepe for working magic with my author photograph and for the gorgeous book covers.

I send my gratitude to Janet Schulte and Jascin Finger of the Maria Mitchell Association on Nantucket who helped me understand how the Natural Science Museum operates. Many thanks to Amy Jenness and Nancy Tyrer of the Nantucket Atheneum and to Wendy Hudson and her dynamite staff at Nantucket Book Works and

Mitchell's Book Corner. Thanks to the wonderful group at Titcombs Book Shop in Sandwich, and to Jody Levine of the Pelham Library, and a general hoorah to all libraries and independent book stores.

Thanks also to my wonderful friends who have brightened my life during the writing of this book and helped me believe I was not just hiding in my study talking to myself. When I say friends, I mean those I have had coffee with and all those with whom I would love to share coffee, my dear, funny, brave, inspiring friends from Facebook.

# Part One
# The Secret Garden

# Chapter One

It's like a morning in heaven. From a blue sky, the sun, fat and buttery as one a child would draw in school, shines down on a sapphire ocean. Eleven-year-old Emily Porter stands at the edge of a cliff high above the beach, her blond hair rippled by a light breeze.

The edge of the cliff is an abrupt, jagged border, into which a small landing is built, with railings around it so you can lean against it, looking out at the sea. Before her, weathered wooden steps cut back and forth down the steep bluff to the beach.

Behind her lies the grassy lawn and their large gray summer house, so different from their apartment on East Eighty-sixth in New York City.

Last night, as the Porters flew away from Manhattan, Emily looked down on the familiar fantastic panorama of sparkling lights, urging the plane onward with her excitement, with her longing to see the darkness and then, in the distance, the flash and flare of the lighthouse beacons.

Nantucket begins today.

Today, while her father plays golf and her beautiful mother, Cara, organizes the house, Emily is free to do as she pleases. And what she's waited for all winter is to run down the street into the small village of 'Sconset and along the narrow path to the cottages in Codfish Park, where she'll knock on Maggie's door.

First, she waves back at the ocean. Next, she turns and runs, half skipping, waving her arms, singing. She exults in the soft grass under her feet instead of hard sidewalk, salt air in her lungs instead of soot, the laughter of gulls instead of the blare of car horns, and the sweet perfume of new-dawn roses.

She flies along past the old-town water pump, past the Sconset Market, past the post office, past Claudette's Box Lunches. Down the steep cobblestoned hill to Codfish Park. Here, the houses used to be shacks where fishermen spread their nets to dry, so the roofs are low and the walls are ramshackle. Maggie's house is a crooked, funny little place, but roses curl over the roof, morning glories climb up a trellis, and pansy faces smile from window boxes.

Before she can knock, the door flies open.

'Emily!' Maggie's hair's been cut to an elf's cap and she's taller than Emily now, and she has more freckles over her nose and cheeks.

Behind Maggie stands Maggie's mother, Frances, wearing a red sundress with an apron over it. Emily's never seen anyone but caterers and cooks wear an apron. It has lots of pockets. It makes Maggie's mother look like someone from a book.

'You're here!' Maggie squeals.

'Welcome back, Emily.' Frances smiles. 'Come in. I've made gingerbread.'

The fragrant scent of ginger and sugar wafts out enticingly from the house, which is, Emily admits privately to her own secret self, the strangest place Emily's ever seen. The living room's in the kitchen, the sofa, armchairs, television set, and coffee table, all covered with books and games, are just on the other side of the round table from the sink and appliances. In the dining room, a sewing machine stands on a long table, and piles of fabric bloom from every surface in a crazy hodgepodge. Frances is divorced and makes her living as a seamstress, which is why Emily's parents aren't crazy about her friendship with Maggie, who is only a poor island girl.

But Maggie and Emily have been best friends since they met on the beach when they were five years old. With Maggie, Emily is her true self. Maggie understands Emily in a way her parents never can. Now that the girls are growing up, Emily senses change in the air – but not yet. Not yet. There is still this summer ahead.

And summer lasts forever.

'I'd love some gingerbread, thank you, Mrs McIntyre,' Emily says politely.

'Oh, holy moly, call her Frances.' Maggie tugs on Emily's hand and pulls her into the house.

Maggie acts blasé and bossy around Emily, but the truth is she's always kind of astounded at the friendship she and Emily have created. Emily Porter is rich, the big fat New York/Nantucket rich.

In comparison, Maggie's family is just plain poor. The McIntyres live on Nantucket year-round but are considered off-islanders, 'wash-ashores,' because they weren't born on the island. They came from Boston, where Frances grew up and met Billy McIntyre and married and had two children with him. Soon after, they divorced, and he disappeared from their lives. When Maggie was a year old, Frances moved them all to the island, because she'd heard the island needed a good seamstress. She's made a decent living for them – some women call Frances 'a treasure.'

Still, it's hard. It isn't that kids make fun of Maggie at school. Lots of kids don't have fathers, or have fathers who live in different houses or states. It's a personal thing. The sight on a television show, even a television ad, of a little girl running to greet her father when he returns from work at the end of the day, or a bride in her white wedding gown being twirled on the dance floor by her beaming, loving father, can make a sadness stab through her all the way down into her stomach.

Plus, her life is so cramped by their lack of money.

When a friend asks her to go to a movie during summer at the Dreamland Theater, Maggie always says no, thanks. She can't ask her mom for the money. In the winter, when friends take a plane off island to Hyannis, where they stay in a motel and swim in the heated pools and see movies on huge screens and shop at the mall, they ask Maggie along, but she never can go. She *hates* the things her mom makes for her out of leftover material saved from dresses she's sewn for grown women. Frances always tries to make the clothes look like those bought in stores, but they aren't bought in stores and Maggie and everyone else knows it.

Frances *never* makes Maggie's brother, Ben, wear homemade stuff. Ben always gets store-bought clothes – and nice ones, ones that all the other guys wear. Their mom knows Ben would walk stark naked into the school before he'd wear a single shirt stitched up by his mother. Ben's two years older than Maggie, and bright, perhaps brilliant – that's what his teachers say. Everything about him's excessive, his tangle of curly black hair, the thick dark lashes, his deep blue eyes, his energy, his temperament.

During good weather, he's outside, his legs furiously pumping the

Nantucket Sisters

pedals of his bike as he tears through the streets of 'Sconset, or scaling a tree like a monkey, hiding in the highest branches, tossing bits of bark on the heads of puzzled pedestrians. He's a genius at sports and never notices when he skids the skin of both knees and elbows into tatters, as long as he makes first base or tackles his opponent.

During bad weather, Ben becomes the torment of Maggie's life. When the wind howls against the windows, she'll be curled up with a book, assuming he is, too, for he does like to read – then she'll discover that while he was so quiet, he'd been removing her dolls' eyeballs in an unsuccessful attempt to give all the dolls one blue eye and one brown. One rainy summer day, he scraped the flakes of his sunburned skin into her hairbrush. Another time he put glue between the pages of her treasured books.

From day to day and often minute to minute, Maggie never knows whether she loves or hates Ben more. Emily says she'd give anything for a brother or sister. Maggie tells her she can have Ben anytime.

Emily is on the island only for three months in the summer, so Maggie doesn't understand why, during the school year, she misses Emily so much. It's not like she doesn't have friends. She has lots of friends.

Alisha is fun, but she's pure jock. Alisha's perfect day is going to the beach, running into the water, shrieking and jumping until a wave knocks her down. She comes up laughing, knees scratched from the sand, and runs back into the waves, over and over again. If Maggie suggests a game of make-believe, Alisha looks at her like bugs are coming out of her ears.

Delphine loves horses. Her parents have a farm. They sell veggies and plants in the summer and Christmas trees in the winter. When Maggie goes to Delphine's house, she spends all day on horseback, or helps Delphine curry the horses or muck out the stalls. Delphine doesn't like to come to Maggie's house – no horses there.

Kerrie reads and sometimes plays pretend, but Kerrie has an entrepreneurial mind. She started a summer newspaper for children that she writes, illustrates, and sells from a little newsstand she built out of crates and set up on the corner of Orange and Main. When she isn't selling her newspaper, she sells lemonade and cookies she baked herself.

Then there's Tyler Madison. He would be Maggie's best friend except he's a boy. Tyler will play pretend with her if no one else is around. He loves the island as much as Maggie does, perhaps even more, and she can often find him on the moors, painstakingly drawing in his own guide to landmarks, like the unusual boulders the glaciers left thousands of years ago. Using an ordinary scrapbook, Tyler is creating a fantastical volume of detailed maps, showing the names and locations of each salient feature. The cover is carefully pasted with calligraphed words: *Official Register of Secrets*. Inside, the first page is the *Table of Contents*. Next, Tyler has entered page after page of carefully sketched or photographed, imagined and described boulders and their locations: *Ocean Goddess. Island God. Pond Princesses. Lord and Lady Boulders.* Twenty-seven different elf communities. Twelve separate *Fellowship of Bushes* and the *Maraud Squad* of poison ivy, scrub oak, bayberry. It's so thoroughly detailed it seems as real as a chart of the stars. Maggie thinks the map is awesome and she adores Tyler, but Ben calls Tyler geekasaurus and four-eyes. It's too bad, but understandable. Pale, underweight, uncoordinated, too clumsy to do sports, Tyler's ostracized by most kids. Maggie suspects she's Tyler's best friend. Maybe she's his only friend.

Sometimes Maggie thinks that books are *her* best friend, her truest, most reliable friend. The fathomless, most treasured part of her own private self is her connection with books. She's happy when she's reading, and library books don't cost Frances a thing.

Maybe that's why she and Emily are so close. Emily reads as much as Maggie does. Like Maggie, Emily talks about the characters as if they were real people and she can enter a pretend world like a fish slipping into water. When Maggie met Emily, it was as if a gate opened in Maggie's life. Like a path curved into the future. Maggie began to believe having an imagination was a good thing, that somehow, even if she couldn't see it now, she could believe she had someplace to go, and knew with a wonderful sense of relief that she would have companions along the way.

Emily is the person who seems most like Maggie, who *gets* Maggie. Maggie's not an idiot. She knows Emily is rich while she is poor. Maggie *knows* rich and poor don't mix.

On the other hand, her favorite stories tell her they can.

They sit at the kitchen table, breaking off bits of gingerbread and munching it, washing it down with cold milk. Even now, in the middle of June, the heat and humidity are oppressive.

'Did you read *The Secret Garden*?' Maggie asks.

'I did. I loved it.'

'Oh, good! Because I have a surprise—'

The front door flies open and slams shut. A thirteen-year-old boy stomps inside, completely ignoring the girls as he rummages in a kitchen cupboard. He's got shiny black hair like a crow.

'Want some gingerbread?' Maggie asks.

Ben grabs a jar of peanut butter and a spoon. Tossing himself into a chair, he digs the spoon into the peanut butter and licks it off.

'Ben,' Frances says quietly.

'The jar's almost empty,' Ben tells his mother. 'I'm going to eat it all. No one else will get my cooties.' He's always got an answer for everything.

Ben wears nothing but swim trunks, and Emily thinks she sees some hair in his armpit. He's a teenager, she reminds herself, and the thought makes her stomach do flip-flops. She wonders when she'll grow armpit and pubic hair. She wonders if Ben has pubic hair. Emily and her city friends have all made bets on who will start menstruating first.

'Hey, Neanderthal,' Maggie says, 'could you say hello to Emily? She just got here for the summer.'

Ben jabs the spoon into the peanut butter again, then takes a bite and grins hideously at Emily, peanut butter hanging in disgusting clumps from his teeth. 'Hello, Emily.'

'Gross.' Maggie stands up. 'Come on, Emily, let's go outside.'

Emily follows obediently but reluctantly. She's never told Maggie, or anyone, that Ben, even with peanut butter teeth, is so gorgeous he gives her shivers. Maggie's just as good-looking; both have wavy, glossy black hair and deep blue eyes accentuated with thick black eyelashes. Beside them Emily, with her blond hair and freckled skin, feels colorless.

'I don't play with dolls anymore,' Maggie announces as they walk around the side of the house. 'You know how we made those Laura Ingalls Wilder dolls? Well, this year, I don't want to make dolls, I want to *be* Mary Lennox. Mom let me plant my own garden in the backyard, near the *rosa rugosa* and honeysuckle. I actually made a wall around the garden out of boards I found at the dump.'

'Wow.' Emily stops to stare, her heart filled with admiration and envy. It never occurred to her to build her own secret garden. Not that she could in her New York apartment, but she could have planned to build one in the backyard of their Nantucket house. Sometimes she thinks, compared to Maggie, she's *boring*.

'You have to crawl through here,' Maggie tells her, demonstrating. The doorway is made of bits of old trellis over which morning glory vines have grown. Inside, the floor is grass; the ceiling, sky. The air smells like flowers. Maggie has made a miniature dollhouse in one corner with pebbles and shells. In another corner is a plastic box holding a bracelet she's braiding out of yarn.

For a while they simply sit cross-legged in the shade, finishing their gingerbread, looking around.

'I like your secret garden,' Emily says. 'Except the grass itches my bum.'

They both giggle because she said 'bum'.

'Yeah, but you don't have chairs in a garden,' Maggie reminds her.

'Yes, you do,' Emily argues. Emily thinks of her Nantucket backyard. The caretaker has put out the glass-topped table and wrought iron chairs and several cushioned lounge chairs. Emily's not supposed to get them dirty; they're for the adults. If Emily tried to build something like this, a wall of boards from the dump around a secret garden, her parents would *kill* her.

Maggie looks around. 'This place is too small for chairs.'

'Yeah, I guess.'

Above them a bee buzzes and lands on a pink rose of Sharon flower. It's quiet, private.

'You know what?' Maggie whispers. 'Sometimes I hate my family.'

This happens all the time between Emily and Maggie. They think the same thought at the exact same moment. 'Sometimes I hate my family, too,' Emily confesses.

'You do?' Maggie's eyes are wide.

An unfamiliar excitement fills Emily, a kind of sharp danger and guilt. 'Sometimes my mother drinks too much. She bumps into things. She talks like this: "Em errr, whersh my purshe?"'

Maggie giggles. 'I've heard Mother do it with a man.'

All Emily's New York friends talk about sex, but no one's ever heard their parents do it. 'What does it sound like?'

'Oh, oh, oh, oh,' Maggie pants.

Emily's face grows hot. 'Who was it?'

'I don't know, I didn't see him, I only heard him. It was disgusting. I'm never going to have sex.'

'Me neither,' Emily announces loyally.

'Swear?'

'Swear.'

'Sometimes I think' – Maggie pauses, as a strange new sensation of guilt shoots through her like a quickly branching vine – 'that I don't belong in this family.'

Emily nods rapidly. 'I know! I feel that way, too. Sometimes I dream I'm adopted.'

'Me, too!' Maggie blinks with surprise at this coincidence. 'In the car, when I'm riding, sometimes I think my real family will see me and rescue me.'

'I do that, too,' Emily tells her. 'My parents are so . . .' Her voice trails off. She can't think of the words. She may not know the words. 'At least,' she continues thoughtfully, 'you have a brother.'

'Yeah, he makes it all better,' Maggie says scornfully, kicking the dirt. 'I don't want a brother. I want a sister.'

'Me, too,' Emily agrees. 'A sister would be fun. We could play together. Trade clothes.'

'Braid each other's hair.'

The two girls look at each other. Maggie wears rubber

flip-flops, blue shorts, and a yellow tee shirt. Emily wears red leather sandals, white shorts, and a striped red top. Except for their clothes, they look just alike, Maggie thinks. They're both skinny and tanned, although Maggie's hair is short this year while Emily's is pulled back in a ponytail. Still, Emily is blond with blue eyes, Maggie has dark hair and blue eyes. So they make a complete set, like salt and pepper.

'We're kind of like twins,' Emily decides.

Maggie's so pleased she giggles. 'Except, um, you're blond and I'm dark.'

'Yeah, but . . .' Emily bites her lip. 'It's not just the way we look. It's the way we think. It's the way we *are*.'

'I know.' Maggie cocks her head, considering. 'You're the closest thing to a sister I'll ever have.'

'Same here.'

'What if . . .' Maggie begins, then stops.

'What if what?' Emily prompts.

'I have an idea but I'm afraid you'll make fun of me.'

'Which would be so wrong because sisters never make fun of each other,' Emily teases.

'Okay, then. Here.' Maggie lifts the lid of the small plastic box in the corner. 'I'm making a yarn bracelet.' She holds it up, a few inches of blue, white, and yellow braided together.

'That's really pretty,' Emily says, a yearning note in her voice. She has bracelets at home, lots of them, but this one calls to her.

'Do you like it?' Maggie holds it out to her. 'You can have it. I mean, when I finish it.' Scooting around to face Emily, she directs, 'Hold out your hand so I can measure your wrist. I'll see how much more I need to do.'

An emotion swells inside Emily – a gratitude, a kind of love, and an astonishment that Maggie wants to give her this bracelet.

'And you make one for me!' Maggie tells her.

'I don't know how.' Emily's learning how to make knots for sailing, but she's never learned how to make a bracelet.

'I'll teach you. Right now. It's easy.' Handing the box to Emily, she says, 'Should I have the same colors or different?'

Emily's glad to be able to make a choice since the box, the yarn, and the idea are Maggie's. 'The same colors, of course.'

'Okay.' Maggie digs around in the box and takes out three skeins of yarn. 'You won't believe how easy it is. You know how to braid, right?'

'Duh.'

The two girls sit together, hands busy with the yarn, concentrating hard as Maggie shows Emily how to be sure the yarn is taut.

'Like this?' Emily asks after a while.

Maggie grins her irresistibly contagious grin. 'Right.'

They lean against walls on opposite sides of the little lair, braiding quietly in the quiet shade. It doesn't take long. Their wrists are small.

'Now,' Maggie instructs, 'I'll tie yours on your wrist, and you tie mine.'

Emily obeys. 'It's like a rope bracelet, only prettier,' she says.

'Only more important,' Maggie reminds her.

Emily smiles. 'Yes. It means we're sisters.'

Maggie proudly specifies: *'Nantucket sisters.'*

# Chapter Two

The next morning, Emily's mother drives Emily to the yacht club to sign her up for sailing lessons.

'You're going to have such fun!'

Emily wants very much to please her mother. She senses that Cara is disappointed with her because Emily looks like her father, who is big, muscular, and freckled, instead of like Cara, who is petite and slim. Emily does have her mother's blond hair and blue eyes, but they adorn a slightly long, horsey face, her father's face. Emily has overheard her mother say, 'Perhaps she'll grow out of it.'

Emily prays every night that her face and body will change. She can only wait.

But now, with her mother watching, she trots along with the other kids in their yellow life jackets, out of the echoing clubhouse, past the patio where tables are being set up for lunch, over the emerald green lawn, and down the wooden docks to the rainbows bobbing in the dark blue water. Their instructors are good-looking, private-school, private-college kids in deck shoes, white shorts, navy blue polo shirts, all tanned and good-natured, hearty and welcoming. Emily's glad they're so nice.

Five other kids are in her group, among them Tiffany Howard. A wiry, energetic redhead, she's obviously used to being on boats. Emily forces herself to pay attention to the instructors. She knows nothing about boats and is terrified of making a fool of herself. Her body feels stiff, made of sticks. She keeps bumping into things as the instructors point out the centerboard, rudder, tiller, hull, mast, bow, stern, boom. So much to learn. It's scary.

Once they're out on the water, actually sailing, Emily relaxes. The playful smack of the wind against the sail, the bob and glide of the boat, her hair blowing back from her neck, cooling her while the sun shines brightly down – all of it fills her with an unexpected, unaccountable happiness. Each student has a turn with the tiller and mainsheet, and when Emily feels the living tug of wind and sea, her heart leaps in her chest. She can't stop smiling. She wants to sail to India.

As they walk back toward the patio after their lesson, Tiffany says to Emily, 'You're a natural sailor.'

Emily blinks in surprise. 'I am?'

'Yeah, can't you tell? You should come out with us sometime on my parents' boat. It's an eighteen-foot Marshall cat.'

Emily doesn't know what that means and it seems odd because she's pretty sure cats don't like water, but she quickly responds, 'I'd love to!' She can't wait. And it will make her mother happy.

After that day, the summer slides by like honey, full of lazy sunshine, blue water, good friends. Some days Emily sails and afterward cruises town with Tiffany. Sometimes, especially on rainy or windy days, Emily tours the whaling museum and the Maria Mitchell house. If she has time, late in the day, she runs over to the McIntyres' to see Maggie, but Maggie is often babysitting.

In the middle of August, Tiffany's family leaves the island and Emily goes to Maggie's every day.

One morning, Cara comes into Emily's bedroom, her long tanned legs flashing against her tennis skirt. Emily has dutifully made her bed and put away her nightgown. Now she's sitting on the floor, buckling her sandals, in a hurry to run to Maggie's.

Cara sinks down on the white chaise longue next to the window overlooking the ocean. Emily hardly ever sits there – it's *white*! But now her mother pats the cushion next to her.

'Sweetie, come sit with me a moment,' Cara invites.

Pleased and wary, Emily sits. Her mother's perfume, citrusy, intense, envelops Emily.

'What are you doing this morning?'

'I'm going to the beach with Maggie.'

'I thought so.' Cara takes Emily's smaller hand in hers and runs her fingers up and down meditatively. 'Darling, Daddy and I wish you wouldn't become involved with the McIntyres.'

Emily stares at her mother, surprised. 'Why not? Maggie's fun.'

Her mother runs her soft hands down Emily's shoulders. 'Because, honey, I know you can't understand yet, but they're just not our kind of people.'

Emily frowns. 'Why not?'

Cara pulls Emily closer to her, keeping an arm around Emily's shoulders. She always holds Emily when she tells her something important. 'Baby, it's hard to explain. But you see, Daddy didn't buy a house on Nantucket and join the yacht club for you to

17

play with poor people.' Her diamond rings flash as she continues to stroke Emily's hand.

Emily considers this. She wants to please her mother. 'I met Tiffany Howard,' she reminds Cara. 'Her parents invited you for cocktails.'

'Yes, sweetie, and we're so proud of you for that. We want to meet more people like Tiffany and her family, you see?'

Emily doesn't understand but she nods as if she does. These few quiet moments within the aura of her mother's glow are precious.

Maggie has always been aware that her friendship with Emily is lopsided. Emily always comes to Maggie's house. She never invites Maggie to her enormous posh house on the 'Sconset bluff. Emily explained she can't have friends over because her father works at home on his investments, but during the winter Maggie has walked around the outside of the house, peeking through the closed curtains over the windows, and she knows the house is so big and has so many rooms that Emily's father couldn't hear them if they played drums in Emily's bedroom.

Emily also confessed that her mother's a snob. 'It's all about who belongs to what club and who went where to school,' Emily said once when she was mad at her mother. 'Honestly, she doesn't even know what this island is *like*!'

Today the two girls biked to the moors to have lunch by a hidden pond they can reach only by squeezing through the bushes along a deer trail. Water lilies blossom across the surface of the pond. Egrets and herons daintily step among the grasses sprouting on the island in the middle of the pond.

'She's such a phony,' Emily says. 'She's so pretentious.' She shoots a quick glance to be sure Maggie knows that word. They've made a pact to learn all the words they can, to use *precise* words, and when they read a book, they meet afterward to discuss the new words they've learned.

'She's very beautiful,' Maggie reminds Emily. She's only met Cara Porter a few times, when Emily's mother picked Emily up to take her somewhere, and Mrs Porter has always been cold and aloof, like Emily said, a snob. But she *is* beautiful, and her clothes are fancy, not homemade, like those of Maggie's mom.

Maggie's mom is such a disorganized mess, Maggie's too embarrassed to even complain about her.

Maggie changes the subject. 'See that boulder over there? Tyler calls it Neptune's Nephew. It oversees all the fish and other creatures in this pond.'

'Oh, *Ty-ler*,' Emily whines, and kicks a pebble into the water.

'You're jealous of Tyler,' Maggie singsongs, elbowing her friend gently. Maggie may not have money, but she does have this island they both love, and she does have a friend who thinks about the island the way Maggie does.

'Am not,' Emily snaps. 'He's funny looking.'

'He's already read all of *The Once and Future King*.'

'Well.' Emily sags. There's no topping that. T. H. White's fantastical tale has proven too complicated for Emily, while parts of it – the swans – enchant her and Maggie both.

Maggie experiences a tingle of satisfaction as Emily pouts. When Maggie's not babysitting or helping her mother with housework, and when Emily is at her yacht club, Maggie bikes to the moors. Tyler can often be found in his secret den near the hidden pond behind Altar Rock. Poor Tyler, who now has buck teeth! Part of every summer, he goes to visit his father, who lives in California. Tyler's parents are divorced, and he lives with his mom, who makes peculiar jewelry out of paper clips and screws.

Tyler's gotten kind of strange, in a cool way. He's obsessed with the island's Indians, the Wampanoag, who've all died off by now. He's developed his own bizarre mythology, a kind of Native American meets the Brothers Grimm. Wildflowers are different families of elves; shrubs and bushes are spirits and sprites and gnomes; the ponds are cousins of the ocean; and the ocean's Queen; the island, King. It's a complicated scheme that grows more complex every time Maggie sees Tyler, but it's clever and surprising and fun.

If she bikes to the moors and Tyler's not there, she still calls out greetings as she pedals past. 'Hail, Lord Boulder! Salutations, Princess Pond!'

In a weird way, having Tyler for a friend partly makes up for Maggie not having a father and for not having any money. Emily's friends can sail and play tennis, but they don't seem to have the spark of imagination that makes life much more vivid and colorful. Tyler's wicked smart, too, much smarter than Maggie and Emily put together.

For just a moment, Maggie enjoys Emily's jealousy. Then she nudges her with her shoulder. 'Emily. You know you're my best friend. You're my Nantucket sister, you dope.'

Suddenly Emily's face is sunshiny. 'You're mine, too.'

Maggie smiles back. 'Did you bring your list of words? Let's go over them.'

Emily digs in her backpack and pulls out her small pink notebook with the gold peacock on the cover. 'Spell "delirium."'

Maggie takes a breath and begins.

★　★　★

That night, a summer storm swats the McIntyres' little home like a cat with a toy. The next day, a newly broken gutter hanging just above the front door pours water down their backs, sending Ben off with a face like thunder and Maggie back into the house, dancing with the shock of the cold. The next night, through each long hour, gusts of wind slam the gutter against the wall.

The next morning, Maggie finds her mom already on the phone at breakfast, begging a friend for a recommendation for someone, anyone, to fix the gutter. Frances is in one of her mad moods, black hair snarled, pajamas buttoned crooked, eyes red. Emily's mother would never look this way. Of course, Emily's mother's house would never have a broken gutter.

'I didn't sleep one second all night!' Frances wails to her friend Bette. 'I'm going to lose my mind!'

'I'll fix the gutter,' Ben offers when she has hung up the phone.

'Don't even think about it!' Frances snaps. 'All I need is for you to slice your arm open with a piece of metal gutter pipe and fall off the ladder and break your leg!'

Ben's face darkens, and Maggie understands – when will their mother stop treating him like a child?

All that afternoon, Maggie dreads going home after babysitting. It's raining again, and the wind tosses and howls. *She* can curl up with a book, but what can Ben do? It would be misery to bike on the moors in this weather. She understands why Frances is so cranky, but if she doesn't get off Ben's back, he's going to blow worse than a nor'easter.

She pedals down the lane to her house and drops her bike inside the fence. To her surprise, the gutter's fixed. Racing into the cottage, she's brought to a standstill by a heavenly aroma

– Frances made Toll House cookies! When Ben skulks in at dinnertime, his mom calls, 'Help yourselves to the casserole. I've got to keep working on this slipcover.' So Ben and Maggie watch television while they eat, and Frances doesn't even yell at them about that. It sounds like she's humming as she sews.

Very strange.

The following day, Maggie and Ben come home to hear clanking noises in the bathroom. They peer in: the toilet's completely dismantled and a man who looks like a Viking warlord has his hairy red arms twisting down inside the tank.

He is Thaddeus Ramsdale. A large, beefy man with a face nearly as red as his beard and eyebrows and wiry hair, he wears dirty, indestructible canvas work pants, dusty work boots, and faded flannel shirts.

When he says he'll have to come back the next day, Frances *twinkles* at him.

He likes their mom.
Their mom likes him.
Maggie thinks: *Ick*.

The Ramsdales are native islanders. Frances jokes that they arrived in the New World before the *Mayflower*, having dismantled their British houses to build their own private ship, and blowing the sails westward across the Atlantic with their very own breath.

Frances also says Thaddeus Ramsdale's land-poor. He lives by himself in a dilapidated old house on his farm on the Polpis Road. He works as a handyman, whenever he's in the mood to work. If he wakes up one morning wanting to scallop or fish or hunt or fiddle around in his barn, that's what he does. Thaddeus's mother, Clarice, widowed and haughty, lives on the island, in a once-majestic old house on Orange Street.

Thaddeus comes to dinner once, twice, and then several times a week.

He doesn't talk much, but he's *there,* a big burly man smelling of sawdust and machine oil, who eats even more lasagna than Ben does, and whose brief, simple words invariably bring a smile and a brightness to Maggie's mom's face. His presence alters the delicate chemistry of their little triangular family life.

Maggie and Ben don't talk about him, because they don't talk to each other much these days, but they suspect things are getting serious when Thaddeus begins to bring them presents.

They're wonderful presents. He gives Ben a Swiss Army knife, and shows him how to use it. He gives Ben a catcher's mitt, a snorkel mask, and flippers.

Thaddeus brings Maggie books. Some are picture books, and he always takes care to tell her he knows she's too old for them, but these are special. And they are. *Time of Wonder,* about an island in Maine, and *The Little Island,* and *Treasure Island,* and *The Swiss Family Robinson.* Thaddeus didn't attend college and he's not impressed by anyone who has, but Maggie soon realizes this doesn't mean he's not smart. In his own way, he's brilliant. He knows everything about plants and animals, the land and the sea, and he reads, too, almost as much as Maggie.

Maggie approves.

# Chapter Three

'Listen to me, Emily,' her father says one morning as she eats breakfast with her parents on the patio. The green lawn lies like a quilt to the edge of the cliff and the blue ocean sparkles beyond. 'This is very important, please pay attention.'

It's so rare for him to talk with her, she sits up straight and looks as intelligent as she can.

'The neighbors tell us there are vandals in the neighborhood.'

'Vandals?' She tastes the word; it has an appealing kind of Robin Hood ring.

Cara hurries to reassure her. 'They're not hurting people, don't be afraid of that. But people's possessions are being destroyed. The tires on Roger Johansen's Mercedes were slashed. Someone put dog feces in Tigger Marlow's mailbox – this is not funny! It's disgusting, it's a cowardly form of violence, Emily, as you'll understand if it ever happens to you.'

'They come at night,' Emily's father says. 'You'll be safely asleep by the time the little bastards get up to their tricks, but if you see anything . . .'

'Or,' Cara continues, making her voice sweet, 'if the little McIntyre girl happens to mention anything, perhaps some of their friends expressing ill will for the summer people – we expect you to tell us.'

Emily stares at her mother, confused. Is she being asked to spy on her friends?

'You understand?' Cara raises her voice.

'Yes, Mother,' Emily replies, although she's not sure she does.

The Porters are invited to a fund-raiser for Sandy Willard's political campaign. The Willards are holding a lobster bake on the beachfront of their Dionis house. This is a *very important* event, Cara tells Emily at least a trillion times. This man might someday be the president of the United States.

So Emily allows Cara to tie her hair with a red, white, and blue ribbon, and she wears the white sundress and matching sandals Cara bought for the party. With her long blond hair, she looks pretty, really, not beautiful like her mother, but pretty. It's not that often she's invited to her parents' gatherings, and secretly, she's looking forward to it. Her life has become a walk on a tightrope between childhood and maturity. Maybe here she'll find something that will make her want to cross over into adulthood. After all, she is eleven.

But the party turns out to be, for Emily, what Cara would call 'the most dreadful bore.' The lawn is crowded with men in navy blazers and patchwork trousers, while thin women with face-lifts and false smiles and flamboyant Lilly Pulitzer dresses prattle and coo like a crazy jungle where the birds have gone bonkers.

After Emily meets her hosts and politely expresses her gratitude for the invitation, she's set free to wander around looking for anyone her age. Near the house, a group of nannies herd a bunch of toddlers. Stepping inside, she finds all the other kids gathered in the family room – four boys younger than Emily and three girls older. They glance at Emily dismissively before letting their bored gaze trail back to the television screen.

Emily collapses on one end of the sofa and stares at the television, too, until two hours have passed and she can't stand it anymore.

By then her parents and the other adults are well oiled and relaxed by liquor into peals and guffaws of laughter at just about anything anyone says. Her father's face is crimson, and her mother's weaving as she stands, a fresh glass in her hand.

Emily asks if she might go home – it's almost eleven o'clock. Sure, they say, call a cab, they'll see her in the morning.

Yawning in the taxi in spite of the heavy metal music blasting from the radio at volcanic volume, Emily rides through the night to her home. She tosses the driver a bill and steps out onto her driveway.

The cab roars off, leaving Emily alone in a sudden expanse of stillness. She can hear the slight sigh of the waves, but no birds sing, they're all tucked away for the night. The yards on the cliff are large, the houses on either side dark. Hydrangea bushes loom like people crouching.

Her parents won't be home for hours. Too bad Maggie's in bed. It would be fun to prowl the streets with her. They could pretend they were Nancy Drew and Bess, peeking in windows.

Suddenly, three people bolt from the privet hedge three houses down. Footsteps and muffled laughter race toward her. It's three teenage boys – it must be the vandals! Seized with a terrified delight, Emily stands paralyzed as they draw near. She doesn't stop to think that these guys could hurt her.

She doesn't hesitate when she recognizes one of them.

'Ben?' she calls.

The tallest boy screeches to a halt in front of her. 'Emily? What are you doing out by yourself?'

Emily stares at him, dumbfounded, while one of the other boys mutters, 'Ben! Damn it, you retard, come *on*!'

'Are you okay?' Ben asks. Out of breath, he braces his hands on his thighs and sucks in huge draughts of air.

'I just got home from a party.'

'What do you mean you just got home from a party? You're just a kid!'

'Okay, man, we're out of here,' the other boy growls.

They speed off toward town, disappearing in the night.

'What were you doing?' Emily demands.

'None of your business. Look, Emily, go on in the house now, okay? You never know—'

Before Ben can finish his sentence, a galaxy of lights blooms three houses down. Old Mr Pendergast charges out into the street, in a blue and white seersucker robe and leather bedroom slippers. He wields a golf club in his right hand and a croquet mallet in the other.

'YOU!' he bellows when he spots Ben and Emily. 'You there! Don't try to run! I've got you now!'

Mr Pendergast favors lime green trousers with little whales on them during the day, and Mrs Pendergast, Cara says, has had so many face-lifts she hears through her mouth. Last year they bought the old Marsh house, a dignified historic summer home. They tore it down and replaced it with a brand-new one.

'All right, you little hoodlums,' Mr Pendergast snarls as he stamps down the street toward them. 'You're coming back to the house with me while I call the police.'

Ben goes rigid.

Emily steps forward. 'Hello, Mr Pendergast, are you all right?'

The old man stops dead in his tracks.

'It's Emily Porter, Mr Pendergast.' She offers her hand.

Mr Pendergast narrows his eyes suspiciously.

Her voice is as sweet as sugar, as cool as ice. '*You* know – you and Mrs Pendergast had drinks here last week with my parents and a few of their friends.'

'Who's this with you?'

'It's Ben McIntyre, Mr Pendergast.'

'McIntyre? McIntyre. That's not a name I know.' He peers at Ben. 'You look like an island boy to me.'

Emily puts her hands on her hips and raises her chin. 'He's my friend,' she asserts stoutly.

'Is that so? Well, what are you two kids doing out here at this time of night?'

'We've been watching a video. We heard some noises and came outside to see what was going on.'

Mr Pendergast glowers as he weighs her words. Finally he lowers the club and the mallet. 'Did you see anyone run by just now?'

'No, sir.' Emily is pure innocence.

'It's those blasted island kids again. They've put a pair of goats in the yard.'

'Goats?' Emily bites her cheeks to keep from laughing.

'They're eating all the flowers and shitting everywhere.'

'You could call the animal control officer.'

'Yes, yes, of course I'll do that, that's not the point. Someone's got to stop these nefarious little assholes before they do real damage.'

'That's exactly what Daddy says,' Emily coos.

The old man mutters away back to his house.

28

Expelling a huge sigh of relief, Ben seizes Emily's shoulders and brings her close so he can whisper in her ear. 'Whoa, Emily, you were awesome.'

'Have you seen *The Last of the Mohicans*?' Emily asks.

'Huh?'

'In case the cops ask us what we were watching. We own *The Last of the Mohicans*.'

'Wow, have you got a cunning mind. Yes, I've seen it.'

'Good. That's what we watched tonight, right?'

'But what about your parents?'

'They're at a party. If they ask anything, I'll tell them I let you in after Maggie went to bed.'

'They'll kill you.'

'Yeah, they'll bore me to death with a lecture.'

'Well, you saved my ass.' Ben is all heat and intensity and sweat and male, his black hair flopping in his eyes.

His hands remain on her shoulders, warm and possessive. Her knees are going wobbly. 'Oh, well—'

'Look, don't tell Maggie, okay? She'll tell Mom and I'll get murdered.'

'I won't tell. But, Ben—'

'I know. I'll cool it for a while.'

'Good.'

He wraps a brotherly arm around her shoulders and steers her up the walk to her house. 'Go inside,' Ben commands. 'It really isn't smart for a girl your age to be outside alone at night.'

Emily doesn't want him to leave – but before she can shut the door, Ben is gone.

# Chapter Four

Ben's so excited he's out in the street kicking a soccer ball at six in the morning. Maggie, more composed, pretends to read, but the words float away into the air, and Frances seems to spend whole hours putting mascara on each individual eyelash. At last Thaddeus arrives in his old clanking Jeep. Everyone crowds in, and off they go along the Polpis Road.

They're going to visit Thaddeus's farm, twenty-five acres between the road and Polpis Harbor.

Hidden by a great overgrown wall of privet, a rutted dirt lane leads to Thaddeus's property, rolling out in all directions, as roughly unassuming and straightforward as Thaddeus himself.

As they tumble out of the Jeep, Thaddeus says, 'Let me show you the barns and the dock before we go inside.'

'Lead on, MacDuff,' Frances says happily.

'Well, there's the house.' Thaddeus points at a large, weathered, rambling structure with a wisteria trunk thicker than a man's thigh plaiting its elaborate path over the front door. 'I inherited all this from my father, which is only right. My sister, bless her soul, she died a few years ago, never had much interest in this wild chunk of land. She was one for the city. I helped Dad build additions to the house, and together we put up the boathouse and dock, two sheds, and the barn.'

Frances, Ben, and Maggie amble behind Thaddeus as he leads them toward the various buildings. After a few quick peeks inside, they exchange amused glances with each other. The sheds and barns are crammed with two-by-fours, pieces of metal, loops of rope, wooden crates, parts of engines, fish hooks, battered buckets, torn shirts, rusting cans of oil, and what seems like thousands of other indistinguishable items.

'I know, I probably seem like a crazy old hoarder,' Thaddeus remarks, as if reading their minds. 'But remember, after all, I live on an island. When I was a boy, I was taught to save everything, every extra piece of rotted wood, hubcap, shard of glass, all of it. We never knew when we might need them, and we never have had a Home Depot here and never will.'

'Oh, I understand,' Frances tells him, laughing. 'When we rented our cottage, we found three drawers in the kitchen marked: "Long String," "Short String," "String Too Short to Use." '

'Exactly,' Thaddeus says. 'Back then, we didn't have UPS or FedEx, either. Just a Sears office so we could order from the catalog. Now hop in the Jeep. We'll go down to the dock.'

With Ben and Maggie bouncing along in the back, Thaddeus steers the Jeep along a rough dirt track through low green brush and miniature wildflowers until suddenly they're at the dancing blue waters of the harbor. At the dock, a red rowboat is tied.

Maggie notices a boathouse with its worn gray shingles and white-trimmed windows, but Ben runs straight to the rowboat.

'Can we take her out?' Ben asks.

'Absolutely.'

Ben jumps in, claiming the middle seat where the oarlocks are. Thaddeus helps Frances then Maggie into the rocking wooden boat, and climbs in after them.

'Take her out,' Thaddeus tells Ben, who pulls on the oars with such authority they spurt far out into the water.

The sun pours down on them so that the oars drip sequins. The only sound is the splash of the oars. Ben rows while Maggie and Frances recline, dipping their fingers in the water.

'Thaddeus,' Frances says, 'this is lovely. It's as if we're right in the middle of a picture.'

Thaddeus's cheeks grow pink. 'Now that way' – Thaddeus points – 'you can glimpse the town. See, there's the Congregational Church steeple.'

'It looks like the cupolas are floating,' Maggie says.

'That way, of course I'm sure you know, is Pocomo.' Thaddeus waves his large hairy hand to the north. 'Good for windsurfing, I hear.'

'Oh, Lord.' Frances sighs. She's terrified of Ben windsurfing, certain he'll break his leg.

'I've done it,' Thaddeus announces. 'It's easy if you're strong, and Ben sure is strong enough.'

Ben grins widely and gives the oars another powerful pull.

Frances's lips crimp a little as they do when she's displeased, but Thaddeus catches her eye and winks at her and her mouth relaxes into a smile.

Maggie, observing this, googles her eyes at her brother, but he's too busy rowing to notice her.

'We should go back,' Frances says. 'We haven't seen the house yet.'

Maggie's the first one out of the boat. While Ben and Thaddeus tie up at the dock, she runs to peek into the boat-house window.

'Not much to see in there,' Thaddeus tells her. 'The only boat I have now is this poor old girl. That shack's been empty for years.'

It might be empty to Thaddeus, Maggie thinks, but to her it looks like a haven for dreams. She could turn it into a secret retreat. She could hide her diaries here, and her notebooks full of poems and stories . . .

'Maggie,' Frances calls. 'Come on.'

As she wriggles into the back of the Jeep, Maggie secretly decides that if her mother wants to marry this man, that's great with her.

When they set foot inside Thaddeus's house, Maggie has second thoughts.

Ben is thoroughly charmed.

They enter right into the kitchen. The linoleum flooring is cracked. The appliances are squat and ancient. A round trestle table covered with magazines, newspapers, books, mail, and a few dirty plates and cups sits in the center of the room. A black–and-white cat occupies the rest of the kitchen table, meticulously washing her face. She pauses to appraise them with sea green eyes, then continues her work.

'Pretty kitty,' Maggie says.

'Her name's Cleopatra,' Thaddeus says. 'You can pet her, but go slow. She's not used to young people.'

'Whoa!' Ben cries, running his hands along the wide window-sills. 'Cool stuff.'

Maggie stands next to him, taking the time to appreciate the glass bottles of deep indigo and pale turquoise, iridescent shells, striated pebbles, sea glass, and arrowheads.

'We have collections like this, too,' Maggie tells Thaddeus shyly.

'Yeah, but Mom makes us keep everything in boxes,' Ben grumbles.

Frances doesn't seem to notice. She's checking out a cobweb in the corner, the dust on top of the refrigerator.

'Here's the living room,' Thaddeus says, passing through a doorway.

Maggie and her family follow. The windows are twelve over twelve, hung with plain white muslin curtains. A handsome wooden mantel trimmed with beadwork ornaments the large fireplace. On the sofa, a hound, deeply sleeping, wakes to peer blearily at them from her nest.

'That's Susie.' Thaddeus touches her graying head with a gentle pat of his enormous hand. 'She's not a youngster anymore. I might get a new pup,' he murmurs, 'but maybe not. Susie's special.'

Thaddeus leads them through the rest of the house which wanders out and up and down in all directions from the two small original rooms. All the rooms are in need of sweeping and dusting, and the windows cry out to be washed. Heaps of twine and rope spill from the corners of the rooms, and the steps of the wide staircase with its frayed runner can hardly be tread upon for the books, newspapers, and magazines piled there. In the long hallway, the tables and windowsills are cluttered with turtle shells, deer antlers, and dried wildflowers laced with dust in an old glass milk bottle.

'This place could use a good sorting out,' Frances murmurs quietly.

'It would be a *cool* house for hide-and-seek,' Maggie gushes.

'Oh, yeah,' Ben agrees, pinching the back of Maggie's neck and laughing like a monster.

Frances puts her hand on Thaddeus's arm. 'It's a wonderful house, Thaddeus.'

'I'm glad you like it,' he rumbles, growing pink again.

Maggie and Ben roll their eyes.


Sunday morning Emily's nerves skitter under her skin when she enters the McIntyre house. She has a secret with Ben from Maggie. It's weird.

Ben's not there. Maggie's lying on the sofa reading Edgar Allan Poe. Over the past few weeks, the girls have started reading every ghost book they can find. They're scared all the time, but somehow they love it.

'Hello, Mrs McIntyre . . . Frances,' Emily says.

Maggie's mom looks up from her sewing machine. Her black hair's piled on top of her head, and she wears gold-rimmed glasses which, while she looks away from her sewing, she pushes up past her forehead. They nestle in her hair like an odd tiara.

'Hi, Emily.'

Emily climbs on the sofa, lifting Maggie's feet to make way.

'Almost done,' Maggie mumbles. A few moments later, she closes the book. 'Mom, there's no ice cream and we're dying.'

'Poor things.' Frances rummages in her purse and hands Maggie a ten. 'Here. Go to the market and buy yourselves each an ice cream cone. Buy some bread, too, will you?'

Maggie grumbles as they walk down the shady lanes, cutting through yards, but Emily enjoys it. It's a kind of adventure. The picturesque village of 'Sconset, with its narrow bridge over the street, the giant sundial on the side of a house, its mansions and cottages, tennis courts and chapel, seems like a play set.

They buy the bread and the ice cream cones, sitting on a bench outside the Sconset Market to lick them. A red pickup truck rattles down Main Street toward them. Emily feels Maggie tense up.

'Who's that?'

'Mr Draper. He's repellent.'

*Repellent,* Emily thinks. She likes the word. It's grown-up and exotic, unrolling like a snake. 'Why?'

'He fixed our sink last winter and charged us too much and Mom won't pay the whole bill and he says he might take us to court. Plus he smells.'

'He's the Jabberwock,' Emily decides.

Maggie looks at her. 'You're right. He *is* the Jabberwock! We'd better hide.'

Spooked by their own thoughts, they shriek and run down Front Street, past all the small rose-covered cottages and their hollyhock and seashell gardens. Breathless, they hide behind a fence covered with old lobster buoys, giggling.

'I left the bread on the bench!' Maggie exclaims.

'Let's go back and get it.'

'All right. He should be gone now, anyway.'

They walk around the last cottage to Broadway, and amble down the narrow one-way street, back toward the Sconset Market.

The red pickup truck noses around the corner, roaring and coughing like a dragon.

'It's him!' Emily screams.

Shrieking, the girls dash between two cottages, pressing themselves into someone's outdoor shower. Bravely they make their way back to the market bit by bit, hiding behind hydrangea bushes, darting from house to house, covered with goose bumps and wild with an exultant fear.

The loaf of bread lies there, innocent and passive. Maggie picks it up and links her arm through Emily's.

'Ready?' she whispers. 'Let's run.'

Before they take a step, Ben zooms up out of nowhere on his bicycle, slamming to a stop next to them. Both girls shriek.

Ben looks down his nose at them. 'Freaks.'

'No, Ben,' Emily says, her voice low. 'We're being chased by some guy in a truck.'

Ben studies Emily. 'I doubt that,' he scoffs, then, surprisingly, continues. 'But just in case, I'll walk home with you.' He climbs off his bike and begins to walk it.

'Oh, thanks, Ben,' Emily says.

'*Oh, thanks, Ben,*' Maggie echoes snarkily, her eyes narrowed suspiciously as she looks at her best friend looking at her brother.

As they walk along the shady lanes, Emily confesses, 'We're probably being silly. We've been reading Edgar Allan Poe.'

'Have you read Sherlock Holmes yet?' Ben asks.

'Not yet—' Emily begins.

'But we're going to!' Maggie interrupts bossily.

Emily glares at Maggie. *You talk about books with Tyler!* she wants to point out, miffed that Maggie butted in on her conversation with Ben. Before she can gather her wits to come up with something to say to him, Ben swings his leg over his bike and pedals away without another word.

At the end of the summer, only a few days before the Porters leave the island for New York, Maggie tells Emily her mom is going to marry Thaddeus Ramsdale.

'Do you like him?' Emily asks.

'I think so. Yeah, I do. He makes my mom happy. And his place is awesome, Emily, you've got to see it.'

With her mom's permission, Maggie and Emily bike along the Polpis Road to Thaddeus's farm. Dropping their bikes by the house, they run over the rolling moorland toward the harbor. Small stars of yellow, pink, white, and violet flowers glint along the narrow path winding through the sandy heath. When they reach the water's edge, Maggie thumps down the length of the wooden dock, grins over her shoulder at Emily, and dives into the water with her clothes on. Laughing maniacally, Emily follows. The shock of cold water exhilarates them even more – they dive deeper and deeper, then explode to the surface, spewing water like whales.

Later, they lie flat on the dock, drying off beneath the steady lamp of the sun, almost dozing in the heat.

'I have an idea,' Maggie begins, 'but I don't know if it will work . . .'

Emily sits up. 'What? Tell me!'

'Let me show you.'

She leads Emily over the grass to an old boathouse. Inside, the floor has been swept clean and Maggie has scavenged some of Frances's sprigged blue cotton to tack up over the window. She's dragged down an old wooden cable spool to use as a coffee table and some boxes to use as seats. On a hook that once held rope, Maggie's hung a clouded mirror.

'How awesome is this.' Emily walks around the space with a big grin.

'I call it Shipwreck House,' Maggie confides shyly.

'Why?' Emily protests. 'All the shipwrecks took place on the ocean side of the island, not here on the harbor side, plus there haven't been any shipwrecks for about a hundred years.'

'I know that!' Maggie's tone is sharper than she intends, but she's on the defensive. 'It's just that when I'm here, I'm cut off from the rest of the world.'

'Okay?' Emily draws the word into a question.

Maggie lets it all go. 'I'm writing a book.'

'Can I read it?'

Maggie hesitates. Seeing the light in Emily's eyes, she rushes on: 'I've only just started. I know it's about a mermaid who can come out onto land but only at night, and a boy who becomes a sea horse, but only during the day.'

'Ravenna,' Emily whispers.

'What?'

'The mermaid's name should be Ravenna.'

Maggie starts to object, then pauses. She repeats the name, tasting it, judging. 'Cool. So I think the story is during the day they swim together, swirling and flipping and arching up from the water, laughing and having fun, and at night, when they're both human, they talk and talk, walking the beach or sitting together, hidden away from the rest of the world in Shipwreck House. But they don't know how to find a way to be together *always.*'

Emily asks, 'Can they talk to the fish?'

'I don't know. I hadn't gotten that far.' Maggie flaps her hands like her mother does when she's talking. 'I've got more babysitting to do, and school starts in a week, and I don't know when I'll have time to write. But this place is so . . .' She can't find the right word.

'Atmospheric!' Emily offers.

'Right.' Maggie puts her hands on her hips, assessing the space. 'I've got plans to fix this place up. Just wait till you see it next summer!'

'Maybe I can help write it,' Emily suggests cautiously.

Maggie twists her mouth, surprised at the offer. 'Maybe you can.'

In the fall, Frances McIntyre marries Thaddeus Ramsdale. Thaddeus isn't much of a churchgoing man, so he asks the minister of the local Unitarian church to perform the ceremony on the boat dock at the back of his land.

Thaddeus wears a good gray suit and a starched white shirt, and has been to the barber to have his beard and hair trimmed. He looks very nearly civilized.

Frances wears a romantic dress of pale cream and a ring of fresh violets and lilies of the valley in her upswept hair. She buys Maggie a new blue dress for the occasion, and matching sandals; the morning of the wedding, Frances twines pale pink baby roses through Maggie's dark mane. Ben grumbles and groans like he's being tortured, but agrees to wear a new blue button-down shirt and khakis, although he refuses to have his hair cut.

It's a small wedding party. Thaddeus's mother, Clarice, is there, her pale face shielded from the sun by a straw hat banded with ribbons and flowers. Maggie's intimidated by Clarice, who appears strict and distant with her ramrod-straight posture and a talent for silence that rivals her son's.

Frances's two best friends, Sylvia and Bette, attend with their husbands, and Maggie's friend Delphine comes, because Maggie felt it would just not be right to ask Tyler, who probably doesn't have any decent clothes for a wedding anyway. Frances told her children they were allowed to invite one friend each, but Ben didn't invite anyone.

After the ceremony, everyone gathers at the house. Frances and Maggie have cleaned it until it's mirror-bright, each crystal glass catching and reflecting the light of this bright autumn day. Clarice, who loves to cook, has made a six-tiered cake and brought champagne, and on this occasion, Ben and even Maggie and Delphine are allowed a glass.

After they move into Thaddeus's house, Frances has no time to sew for her customers. She's too busy whipping the place into shape. She pays Ben and Maggie a dollar an hour to carry Thaddeus's accumulated junk out of the house. He won't allow it to go to the dump, but he does agree to let them store it in one of the barns.

Starting with the kitchen, Frances clears the rooms, scrubs the windows and wooden floors, paints the woodwork, buys new furniture or makes slipcovers for the furniture that remains, runs up curtains and drapes, and turns the place into a home.

At last Maggie has a bedroom she's proud of, decorated exactly to her specifications, with yellow walls and glossy white trim, a daisy bedspread and curtains, and two entire walls of shelves that Thaddeus built to contain all her books.

Ben wants nothing done to his room at the end of the hall, even though the wallpaper is faded sprigged flowers. 'And don't come in my room when I'm not here,' Ben growls at his mom, who retorts, 'Fine, I'll just throw your clean laundry on the floor outside your cave.'

Maggie discovers she likes having lots of space between herself and her increasingly grisly brother. She even explores the scary attic, crouching under the eaves when the wind howls, making the old boards creak as if they're alive.

At dinner one night, Thaddeus remarks in his gruff, gravelly voice, 'So you've been exploring the attic, Maggie.'

She freezes, her fork halfway to her mouth. Is she in trouble?

'See anything you like up there?' he asks.

Still wary, she nods.

'Make a list for me,' Thaddeus tells her. 'I know you're fixing up the old boathouse as your own place, and it seems to me a lot of those castoffs in the attic might be useful to you.'

Maggie's eyes widen. 'Really?' From the corner of her eyes, she spots her mom smiling. 'That would be awesome! I've found an old gateleg table and a couple of chairs I'd love to have.'

'They're yours,' Thaddeus tells her. He chews awhile, thinking. 'I believe an old sofa's up there, too. Stained and clawed up from the animals . . .'

Maggie's almost in tears of joy. 'I'd love to have that old sofa. But it's too heavy to carry to the boathouse.'

Thaddeus chuckles, sounding like a boat engine rumbling. 'Don't you worry about that. Your brother and I can carry stuff down to the yard, load up the truck, and drive it there for you. Carry it in, too.'

Her throat has clumped with excitement. 'Oh, thank you, Thaddeus.' Turning to her brother, she adds, 'Thanks, Ben.'

Ben rolls his eyes.

'Ben,' Frances admonishes calmly, 'be nice. You've already fixed up your lair in the old barn.'

Ben flinches, alarmed.

'Now, now,' Thaddeus says, 'don't look so anxious, son. Your mom and I haven't been up to the loft and we have no intention of doing so. I know every kid needs a private hideaway. Lord knows I did. We won't violate your privacy. Or yours, Maggie.'

'Thank you,' Maggie whispers. She'd like to throw her arms around Thaddeus in a grateful hug, but she's still a little intimidated by him.

'You're most welcome,' Thaddeus tells her, and his smile is as warm as a hug.

Some winter nights the power goes out all over the island for hours at a time. Then Thaddeus builds a roaring fire in the living room, and Frances lights lots of candles, and they shut the door to the cooling air in the hall and settle on the floor around a board game. Ben loves Scrabble. Maggie prefers Clue.

While the dog snores on the sofa and the cat drowses in the wing chairs, Thaddeus teaches them to play poker. Maggie finds it very satisfactory, somehow, the people on the floor, the animals on the furniture. She becomes even more fond of Thaddeus because of this, and because of the way he makes her mom smile.

Thaddeus is changing Ben, too. He picks Ben up after school and takes him along on jobs, and when he's not working somewhere else, he's got Ben out at one of the barns with him, pounding nails or sawing wood.

By summer, Ben doesn't look like a boy anymore. He's shot up tall, and so gawky and lean that his leather work belt, crammed with hammers and pliers and screwdrivers, is always sliding down his hips. His black hair is pulled back into a short ponytail, his zits have disappeared, and his jaw is peppered with bristles. Beneath his black velvet eyelashes, his eyes are a dark flashing blue, a blue jay's wing.

And he's nicer. He smiles at Maggie. He thanks his mom when she hands him a basket of freshly laundered clothes and praises her cooking. His grades and teachers' comments couldn't be better.

Maggie's glad, of course, and yet she feels oddly abandoned.

Ben is suddenly so much older. His voice is deep, his muscles hard, his eyes inscrutable.

Maggie's changing, too. She's twelve, only months away from being a teenager. She's eager for that, but also frightened.

# Part Two
# Nantucket Glossy

# Chapter Five

*Six Years Later*

By the time Maggie turns eighteen, Thaddeus's farm is her home and the sanctuary of her dreams. She dutifully does her household chores, keeps up with her homework, and babysits at every opportunity, even though the islanders never tip like the summer people. Otherwise, every free moment, she's outside, irresistibly drawn to explore the twenty-five acres stretching from the Polpis Road to the harbor.

When it's breezy, Maggie pulls on a fleece cap and an ancient sagging cardigan she wouldn't be caught dead in anywhere else, and sets out, striding briskly over the Ramsdale land, stuffing her pockets with pebbles and arrowheads, each incline and hillock mapping itself into her memory through foot, leg, heart, brain. The sandy soil's freckled with heather and bayberry, with bearberry and blueberry, with blue-eyed grass, thistles, daisies, and vetch. Small groves of tupelo, oak, wild cherry, and pine grow hemmed around with brambles. She returns to the house after the sun sets, navigating her way through the dark as if she has eyes in her feet, each rock and tuft a star for her internal compass.

On warm days, she tucks herself away among bushes, only her darting eyes betraying her presence. Rabbits and deer, snakes, voles, wild mice, and wild cats claimed this land as home long before Thaddeus's family. Spiders spin webs of geometric complexity among the leaves of the beach plum, and beneath the surface, insects of all kinds go about their lives. She's fascinated by their movements, content to watch any of them, no matter how small.

Tilting her head back, and if the weather's mild enough, stretching out on the warm bed of the ground, she looks up to gaze at the soaring hawks, squawking gulls, and the sparrows, robins, and wrens who nest in the trees and swoop through the air. The landed birds are here as well: quail, pheasant, and guinea hens who eat ticks and bustle out in front of cars as if they're late for church.

As the land warms, the white flowers of Quaker ladies and shad bushes bloom in bridal profusion. In the summer, pink *rosa rugosa* and scarlet wood lilies play like children in the breeze.

The land doesn't know who owns it. It was here before owners, and will be here after, content with itself in all seasons. The wind's passion is as welcome as the sun's heat, it loves equally driving rain and calm moonlight.

The land was here before people, thinks Maggie. It endures. It provides soil for the roots and tunnels and burrows, solid earth for the weight and thump of feet, safe ground for the tickle of the crawling beetle, and for the bird beating homeward with its wings.

Does it love Maggie? Does it sense her own feelings of kinship when she squats to run her hands over a boulder, as if reading a message? Maybe it does.

She is loyal to this land. She belongs to it. Yet even this ancient land changes, has seasons, weathers, buds, and blossoms. She's changing, too. At the end of the summer she's leaving for Wheaton College in southeastern Massachusetts, not so very far away . . . but far enough. Maggie dislikes how she feels more nervous than eager.

On the first Saturday of July, Maggie stands at the end of the driveway, waiting for Emily. A red Jeep goes by, and a gray pickup truck, and a figure on a bike comes into view, then sweeps on past – a guy in bright spandex biking gear. Will the summer come when Emily doesn't call? Everyone's changing. Most of Maggie's friends are having sex and leaving for college this fall. Ben is twenty, already in college in Boston. Maggie herself is leaving at the end of the summer. She knows it's time to put away childish things, but not yet. Not just yet.

A convertible whizzes along, skidding as it turns into the Ramsdale driveway. In pink shorts and sneakers, Emily flies from the car.

'Maggie!'

They hug, nearly jumping up and down as they always do the first time they meet after a winter. Standing back, they study each other. The first few moments after a winter's absence are like a Polaroid photo developing, slowly allowing their familiar selves to come clear through the year's changes.

'You're so tall!' Maggie exclaims. Emily has grown a good four inches taller than Maggie in the past year. She looks older, with her stylish, expensive haircut, and Maggie feels like a kid in her cutoff jeans and white tee shirt, her black braid hanging down her back.

'You're so tanned already!'

'Hello, Maggie.' Emily's mother slides out of the convertible and approaches the girls. She's wearing tennis whites, complete with a glittering diamond tennis bracelet on her wrist. Sunglasses hide her eyes, but she's clearly studying Maggie.

'Hello, Mrs Porter,' Maggie politely responds. She doesn't smile or gush; she knows what Emily's mother thinks of year-rounders.

'Look at you,' Cara Porter says. 'You've become a stunning beauty. My God, you're Angelina Jolie all over again.'

'Thank you, Mrs Porter.' Maggie feels the impulse to curtsy, then chokes back a snort of laughter at herself. 'Would you like to come in?'

Cara steps backward. 'Thank you, dear, that's sweet of you, but I've got to hurry along to the club for my tennis game. Perhaps another time.' She slips gracefully back into her Saab convertible. 'Have fun, Emily.'

Maggie takes Emily's hand, and just like that, they're best friends again. 'Come say hello to Mom.'

Emily follows Maggie inside. The air smells of flowers and baking.

'Emily! Sweetheart!' Frances hugs Emily. 'How lovely you've become,' she says, brushing a hand lightly over Emily's long blond hair. 'The first batch of cookies will be out in a minute.'

'Great.' Maggie leads Emily up the stairs and through the hall, ending up in Maggie's room, where they throw themselves on her bed and stare at the ceiling.

'Your mom looks fantastic,' Emily says.

'I know. She's really happy.'

They're getting to know one another again, their friendship is like a tapestry tucked away in a drawer. Today is the iron passing over the cloth, smoothing out the wrinkles, bringing out the pattern that makes it unique and beautiful.

'What about you? How's Thaddeus?'

'He's really nice. Mom's happy, and Thaddeus continues to teach Ben all the manly skills.'

'The manly skills?' Emily arches her eyebrows suggestively.

'That's not what I mean!' Maggie pokes Emily's arm. 'I mean about wrenches and hammers, not how to seduce women.'

Emily widens her eyes innocently. 'Why, Maggie, that's what I meant, too,' she teases.

Maggie slumps. 'I hate growing up.'

'Oh, get over yourself. Enjoy it.' Emily leans back on her arms in a sensual pose.

'You've had sex!'

'Not yet,' Emily confesses smugly. 'But almost. Karl? This dreamy foreign exchange student from Germany? We had a few dates . . .' Emily's eyes glaze with memory. 'But *everybody* was having sex with him and I didn't want to be everybody. Still, we came close. And I'm glad.'

Maggie feels her mouth primp like her mother's when Frances is miffed. 'I suppose you just want to hang out at the yacht club this summer, playing tennis and sailing with guys.'

'Maggie, you brat, is that what I did last summer, or any of the past twelve, shall I count them, *twelve* summers?' Emily demands. Maggie grins, abashed, and Emily answers her own question. 'I was here almost every day. Perhaps not for the entire day, but most of it. Right? *Right?*'

'Right,' Maggie concedes. 'Want to go to Shipwreck House?' She holds her breath. Any day now, any moment, Emily will think she's too old for such childish stuff.

Emily jumps off the bed. 'Let's go!'

The grasses are a sweet lush green. The harbor water winks blue and turquoise as a summer breeze sweeps over it. Shipwreck House looks slightly the worse for the winter, more paint missing from the door and window frames, a few shingles hanging sideways, but Maggie has already opened the door to let the sunshine warm the room.

'Ahhh,' Emily sighs, dropping onto an old sofa. 'I've missed this.' She scans the room. 'I know I didn't email much, Mags, but senior year was a killer. My parents had me taking so many APs I barely slept. And now I've got to get ready for Smith.'

'I know,' Maggie agrees. 'I was worried all year about getting the grades I needed for those scholarships. Plus I babysat five days a week for George and Mimi West. I'll be babysitting for them this summer, too. Their kids are cute, but I don't know when I'll have time to work on *Siren Song* . . .' She keeps her back to Emily as she fusses with an old curtain, tying it back to let in more sun. The novel they've worked on for the past six years seems really good when she reads it by herself, but she's worried about Emily's more sophisticated New Yorker's opinion.

'I don't know when I'll have time, either,' Emily says. Lifting a leg, she scratches a bug bite. 'I've been talking to Jascin about volunteering at the Maria Mitchell aquarium.'

'You have? I know how you love that place. What do they say?'

'They've been checking their schedules, and they need someone in the afternoon at the Touch Tank, showing things to the tourists. So I think I'm going to do it.'

'Awesome! But what about sailing and tennis?'

'I'll have time in the late afternoon for sailing. I don't care much about tennis. You babysit in the afternoons, right? We'll still have the mornings to write.'

Five mornings a week, while the day turns from cool blue to a sultry gold, they write *Siren Song,* really Maggie's book, with Emily's advice and recommendations. Emily is learning so much by volunteering at the aquarium that she has all sorts of cool information about sea creatures to add.

When the heat invades the shed, they run out to the dock and fly into the water for a long swim. Later, they head up to the house, gobble the lunch Frances has made for them, and speed off on their bikes to their different destinations. At night they phone each other to discuss new plotlines and details.

In some ways, it's like it's always been, the two of them together, Nantucket sisters, so attuned to one another they scarcely need words to communicate. Sometimes they collapse into laughing fits that last until they're gasping for breath. Sometimes they discuss sad movies and dissolve into tears.

Sometimes they don't go to Shipwreck House but stay up in Maggie's room, experimenting with eye shadow and blush, painting each other's toenails, singing love songs along to Sirius Internet Radio.

That summer, Emily realizes how much of a fantasy world Shipwreck House provides for her. Maggie wants to ignore all signs of impending adulthood, sex, and the difficult life choices streaming toward them in an unstoppable tide, but Emily can't. As the golden season nears the end, each day with Maggie becomes more poignant, more bittersweet. Emily feels as if she's playing games with a friend who's stranded in a world Emily's about to abandon.

Maggie would absolutely *scream* if she had any idea how much Emily thinks of Ben. Emily seldom sees him – he's always working or off with his friends, but when she does catch a look at him, she's nearly paralyzed with a mixture of terror, awe, and, in the pit of her stomach, a melting sensation that she thinks might be love.

More and more, Emily accepts Frances's invitations to stay to dinner so she can get a glimpse of Ben. The Ramsdales don't really sit down to dinner in the summer – Maggie's always rushing off to babysit, or Thaddeus is gone till late bluefishing, or Frances and Thaddeus go off to someone's house for a cookout – but somehow there's always plenty of good food, fresh berry pies, a pot of chili, cold salmon covered with chives from the garden, and delicious fresh sliced tomatoes. Emily and Maggie pile plates high and carry them in to eat while they watch a video. Sometimes Ben passes through, sending a squall of testosterone through the air as he shouts hello, stomps up the stairs in his work boots to shower and change clothes, and rushes back out through the house to slam into his Jeep and roar off into the summer night.

One day, toward the end of the summer, Maggie tells Emily, 'I've got a treat in store for you. If you're up for it.'

They're lying on the wood dock after a cooling swim in the harbor. The sun picks off, one by one, drops of water from their skin.

Emily turns to look at Maggie, whose nose is peeling. 'I'm up for anything.'

Maggie's dark eyes glitter with mischief. 'Want to see Ben's hideout?'

'You're kidding, right?' Ben could come home anytime, to fetch something he forgot or something for Thaddeus, and what would happen then, Emily can't even imagine. As much as she wants Ben to notice her, she doesn't want him to hate her.

'Thaddeus and Ben went off island today to pick up some supplies. They're taking the late boat back.'

'What are we waiting for?' Emily cries.

The girls spring up. Without stopping to pull on dry clothes or shoes, they race along the dirt path through the heathland back toward the house and barns. Small thorns scratch Emily's ankles as she runs, and she couldn't care less. She's like a bullet, focused, aimed.

Ben's retreat is in the loft of the newest barn. No one's in the house and all the cars are gone, so they slip through the barn door and stand for a moment, catching their breath. The air smells of straw and metal. An assortment of shovels, rakes, gas cans, buckets, and bags of fertilizer for the garden make a maze the girls slide through on their way to the ladder at the shadowy back of the barn.

'You go first.' Maggie giggles.

Eagerly Emily grabs a rung and starts up the ladder. The wood is warm and firm on her feet and hands, and the ladder gives slightly under her weight.

She looks over her shoulder down at Maggie. 'You're sure this is safe?'

'If you're scared, don't do it,' taunts Maggie.

'I guess Ben does it all the time,' Emily decides. She climbs.

The ladder ends a few feet above the loft floor, making it easy to drop off onto the old wide boards. Maggie scrambles up behind her and they stand for a moment, looking around.

It's a perfect guy's den, drifting with dust motes, populated by spiders spinning in glittery, elaborate webs. Yet another of Thaddeus's barely dependable wooden chairs leans in front of a desk fabricated from crates. A globe and a knife and a pair of pliers lie on the desk. On the wall a large map of Nantucket is tacked by its four corners. Makeshift bookshelves hold *Call of the Wild, The Great Gatsby,* and *The Silent Spring,* plus stacks of comic books and magazines. A bucket on a pulley is rigged to lift heavy items from the ground floor up.

Several bales of hay are stacked in a rectangle, sleeping bags spread over it, and a pillow without a case. The girls approach this warily. They both know what this is, because next to the bed is an empty six-pack of Budweiser and a small cardboard box which, when opened, displays an assortment of condoms.

'Ben's,' Maggie whispers.

Emily picks the box up, loving and hating the queasy sensation in her stomach as she peers into it. 'Your brother brings girls here,' she whispers.

'Well, duh. He's had girls after him for years.' Maggie squats, lifting up the sleeping bag to see if anything's hidden beneath it.

Emily quickly pockets one of the foil-wrapped condoms, shiny as a foreign coin, and quickly shuts the box. This doesn't count as stealing, she thinks. Anyone would understand that this is love, or infatuation, or lust. Sliding it into her pocket, she shivers, thinking of Ben.

# Chapter Six

Two evenings later, Maggie pedals steadily along the dirt path toward Altar Rock. Clear golden light from the slowly descending sun burnishes the deserted moorland. Only birdcalls break the silence. It's nice on the moors at this hour, everyone else is home eating or heading out to the beach for a party. Maggie won't go to beach parties; she's not into the whole drunken scene, and Tyler won't go because he'd be ostracized there like he is in school. Maggie's tired after her afternoon of babysitting, but she hasn't seen Tyler all summer, and he was so insistent on the phone—

She walks her bike up the steep, rutted, rock-strewn road to the summit of the hill. From here they can see the ocean and the long sweep of moors.

'Hey,' Tyler says. His braces sparkle, his glasses gleam. He's skinny and gawky and clumsy as a giraffe on roller skates.

'Hey.' Maggie knocks her kickstand down.

'I brought goodies.' Tyler settles in front of the small boulder called Altar Rock and sets out two Cokes and a bag of his mother's homemade caramel chip cookies. He's wearing a tee shirt and shorts. His attenuated arms and legs, covered with brown hair, make him look like a giant spider.

'Great. So, how's your summer been?' she asks, settling on the grass across from him.

'Okay. Yours?'

'Okay. I'm doing lots of babysitting. Piling up some cash. And the kids are great. Did you have fun at your dad's?' She knows he has to go off island most of the summer to live with his dad. It was part of the divorce decree. She waits for the same old argument: he hates leaving the island in the summer; Maggie says he's lucky, at least he's got a dad who wants to see him.

'Not really,' Tyler says.

Maggie senses something. She narrows her eyes at him. *'What?'*

'I'm leaving the island.'

Maggie snorts lightly. 'We're *all* leaving the island. I'm going to Wheaton and you're going to Stanford.'

'More than that, Maggie. I'm not coming back.'

'What are you talking about?'

'I'm gonna go live with my dad. I'll go there for holidays and summer vacation.'

'In California?' Maggie gawks at Tyler as if he's just said he's moving to the moon.

Tyler shrugs. 'My dad thinks I need to be near a hospital so we can really fix this eye thing. My mom's dating Clarence Able, you probably know that, and I think she'd like a little time with me out of the house. Anyway, Mom and Dad decided, then told me.'

'Didn't they ask you first?'

'You're kidding, right?'

'This sucks,' Maggie says, discovering she means it. 'Life's going to be so boring without you. Who's going to make me laugh?'

'Yeah, well.' He looks away from her, finds a pebble, throws it down the hill.

'I meant because you say such funny things,' Maggie clarifies, sorry to have hurt him.

'I know what you mean.' His voice cracks.

She hates him for being pitiful. 'For God's sake, we all get insulted.'

Tyler clutches his backpack and digs around in it. 'I want to give you something.' He pulls out his scrapbook: *Official Register of Secrets*.

'Wow, I'd forgotten all about this.' Maggie scoots closer to him, watching as he turns the pages. 'You know,' Maggie says, tracing a sketch of a pond with one fingertip, 'these drawings are really good.'

'Nah.'

'Yeah, they are. Oh, man.' She sighs, leaning back, looking up at the impartial blue sky. 'It was a lot of fun being little, wasn't it? I loved all those fantasy games.'

'You were the only one I knew who liked to play that kind of stuff,' Tyler admits. 'That's why I want you to have this book.'

'Oh, I can't have that! Why not take it with you?'

'Because it belongs here on the island.'

'Then leave it with your mom.'

'If she marries Clarence, they'll move into his house. She'll pack up my stuff while I'm living off island.'

'But—'

'Look!' Tyler jumps up, pacing angrily away, then turning back.

'This doesn't come with any kind of *obligation*. I won't *bother* you, Maggie. I won't be phoning you or writing you or expecting anything from you. It's just, my whole life is changing, I won't have any one place to call my own. You're the only person in the universe who knows about this stupid book, and the only one I can trust not to destroy it.'

'Okay, geez, take a chill pill,' she snaps. 'I'll keep it. You can come take it whenever you want.'

'I won't be back next summer. I don't know if I'll ever be back.'

'Oh, Tyler.' Maggie clutches his book against her chest. In a way she's hugging him, and in a way she's using the book as a shield. 'This is terrible.'

Tyler starts to say something, then changes his mind.

'I've got to go.'

'Oh. Okay.' Standing, she brushes sand off her jeans.

'Can you bike home, holding that?' he asks.

'I think I'm probably just about that coordinated.'

Tyler approaches her. 'Good-bye, then.' He holds out his hand.

Maggie feels absolutely freaking weird. She wants to kiss him, and at the same time, she knows if he tries to kiss her, she'll hurl. She loves him, or maybe she finds him repulsive, she doesn't want him to leave, she'll die if he kisses her. 'I'll take good care of your book.'

'Thanks.' Turning, he picks up his dirt bike, jumps on it, and pedals away.

# Chapter Seven

Emily's parents are at some yacht club dance. Maggie's babysitting. Emily's so bored she's actually considering walking all the way home to 'Sconset. It's not even seven o'clock on an early August evening.

She's dawdling along Orange Street, headed out of town, when a Jeep slides up next to her.

'Want a ride?'

Emily rolls her eyes as she turns to say something dismissive – but it's Ben. Her breath catches in her throat.

'Where are you going?' she manages to say.

Ben shrugs. 'Where do you *want* to go?' He's wearing a navy blazer that sets off his glossy black hair and flashing blue eyes.

He's looking at her as if she's a girl, not his little sister's friend.

'I don't know,' Emily says casually. 'I'm kind of bored.'

'Climb in,' Ben tells her. 'We'll go to Surfside.'

Her heart thumps. 'I'd like that.'

He steers the Jeep away from the lights of town, past the high school and the Muse, and down the long road to the south beach. Here they can hear the island's sounds: the breeze through the wildflowers bordering the road, and then the long exhalation of the ocean against the shore.

They park in the lot, half-filled with cars. The concession stand is closed until tomorrow morning but all along the beach four-wheelers are parked. Far out in the ocean, a fishing boat's lights wink.

Ben steps out of the Jeep, removes his blazer, yanks his tie off, unbuttons the top buttons of his shirt. Bending down, he removes his loafers and tosses them into the back of the Jeep. He rolls up his sleeves and the cuffs of his pants.

'Cocktail party,' he explains.

*Cocktail party,* Emily thinks. He's so grown-up. Following his lead, Emily slips out of her shoes. The gritty sand against her bare soles is rough, *real*. She is alone with Ben, at night. She wants to pinch herself.

Side by side they walk down the long path of the sloping dune to the long, golden expanse of shoreline. In the distance, a cluster of four-wheel-drive vehicles circle a bonfire. They catch drifts of music. The people dancing and drinking are black shadows against the silver air.

'Let's go this way.' Ben takes her hand, steering her in the opposite direction from the party.

His hand is firm and warm as they walk at the edge of the waves, their feet sinking in the wet sand.

Ben is holding her hand. She can't believe it's happening.

He stops walking and turns to her. The way he's looking at her now – right at her, his face studying hers, his eyes so serious, shining in the moonlight – she has never felt so grown-up. She has never been so afraid.

'Do you know I had a crush on you when I was younger?' He grins, but in spite of that, he looks almost sad.

'You did?' Something lights within her as if a match has been struck.

'You bet. I used to keep a photo of you under my pillow.'

'You didn't.' Heat rises within her.

'I did. I still have it.'

She can't keep the smile off her face. She tries to be teasing. 'Under your pillow?'

'Not anymore. It's in a drawer somewhere.' He turns away, scuffing his foot in the sand.

'Where did you get a photo of me?' They walk again and her heart slows to normal.

'Oh, Mom took one of you and Maggie, when you were on your bikes. You wore braces on your teeth. And the goofiest smile.'

Emily groans. 'I remember that photo. I can't believe you had a crush on me.' She wants to hear more. When he doesn't elaborate, she says, 'I was a little dink. I was a *kid*. I was afraid of you.'

'You certainly weren't afraid of Mr Pendergast.'

'Oh, *right*. I'd forgotten all about him.'

'I haven't. I never will. You were like Joan of Arc or something, a real little warrior princess. You backed him right down.'

She's amazed. He thought she was a *warrior princess*.

He leads her up the beach, away from the water. They sit against a dune, legs stuck out in front of them toward the white surf rolling up to shore.

'Why did you guys do it? Vandalize stuff, and steal?'

'You're kidding, right?'

She shrugs.

'Emily. I was poor in a place where everyone else had money. I was angry. I was trying to get some revenge.'

'Are you still — angry?'

Ben scoops up a handful of sand and lets it trickle through his fingers, making a sound like whispers. 'Somewhere deep inside, I suppose I am. But Thaddeus changed my life. He's taught me so much about the island, and my place on it. He taught me how amazing this island is, how fragile. He's taught me it doesn't matter where I started from. I can matter. I can really make a difference in the world. Now I know what I want to do with my life.'

Never has a guy spoken like this to Emily. She's covered in goose bumps, from being so near him, from the sight of his large, flexible hands lifting and sifting the sand, his watch catching the moonlight, his hairy ankles, his enormous, bony feet.

'What do you want to do?' she asks quietly.

'I want to learn everything about this island. I'm majoring in American history, and eventually I want to work for a historical society, even run it someday. I want to be part of the future of the island, and I want to make a strong stand for conservation. This is where I want to make my life matter.'

'You're so lucky,' Emily tells him. 'I mean, knowing what you want to do with your life.'

'Well, you're only eighteen, right? I didn't know what I wanted to do with myself then, except get drunk and get laid.'

Those words — she shivers.

'On the other hand,' he continues, 'Maggie knows what she wants to do.'

Emily doesn't want to talk about Maggie, she wants to keep talking about Ben. But she laughs. 'Maggie *would*.'

'She wants to be a writer.'

'How perfect for Maggie. She always loved reading so much.'

'You write, too.'

Her little blue dress was short to begin with. Now that they're sitting like this in the sand, the hem of the skirt has slipped up her thighs almost to her panty line. She's glad her legs are tanned, not that you can tell in the moonlight. She wriggles around, adjusting her skirt. 'Not really. I'm more into science, actually. I think I'll major in environmental biology in college.'

'Excellent, Emily. Then you could come work on the island.'

'Oh.' She's stunned that he would think of her, that he would envision her working on this island he loves so much. With a kind of timid hope, she looks into his eyes. She can only barely speak. 'Ben?'

He pulls her against him, and with his other hand he tilts her chin up so he can kiss her. Her head falls back against his arm. His hand is on her cheek. His kiss is soft, his breath smells like wine. She doesn't feel desire as much as astonishment, so she's surprised when he holds her tighter, and his lips press more urgently, and a groan sounds in his chest.

He releases her. 'I've wanted to do that all my life.'

'You have?' She's trembling.

'And this,' he says, putting the flat of his palm over her belly. 'I've wanted to do this.'

Through the thin blue cloth of her dress, her slightly rounded belly feels small beneath his large hand, and the side of his hand is almost touching the top of her thighs. If he slid his hand down— abruptly he pulls away. He stands, brushing sand off his slacks.

65

'It's late. I've got to work tomorrow.' He extends a hand and helps her up.

He's silent as they climb up the dune to the parking lot. He's gone into himself.

They step up into the old Jeep. He starts the engine. The headlights flare across the darkness, over the concession stand, the beach grass, the bike racks, the other four-wheel-drive vehicles in the lot. Ben turns on the radio. He hums to an old Beatles tune, but he still seems tense.

'Did I do something to make you mad?' Emily asks.

'No. *I* did.'

'I don't understand.'

'You don't need to.' He looks over at her, and his face softens. 'I'm sorry, Emily. I'm just tired. I've been up since five, and I'll have to be up at five tomorrow.'

Emily crinkles her forehead, she looks at him so hard. He stares at the road, his profile proud. For a long time they ride in silence down the straight, seemingly endless Milestone Road.

'Ben,' she begins, not sure what to say. 'Ben . . . I liked that. Being with you like that.'

Ben takes a deep breath, as if she's wounded him. After a moment, he says, 'You're going to college in a couple of weeks. I'm going back to Tufts.' He shakes his head. 'This was a mistake.'

'No.' She reaches over to put her hand on his arm. 'No mistake. I've been wishing for that for a long time.'

Ben remains silent. He pulls up in front of her house, her parents' big house on the bluff where she has never yet, in all these years, invited Maggie. He knows that. There is more than age between them, but age does matter.

Turning to face her, he carefully reminds her: 'Emily, you just turned eighteen.'

This means so much. She wants to do it right. 'I know that. And I've never . . . but I want this, Ben.' Summoning up all her courage, she says, 'I want anything I can have with you.'

He frowns. He takes a deep breath. He touches the side of her face, stroking a lock of hair back behind her ear. 'Can I see you tomorrow night?'

She restrains herself from throwing herself across the seat on top of him. 'Yes.'

'Six o'clock,' he says.

'Six o'clock,' she promises.

'The light will be good out on Coskata,' he tells her.

'I'll bring a picnic,' she tells him. 'We can eat on the beach, watch the sunset.'

'Nice.' Gently, he kisses her cheek. 'Tomorrow, then.'

Emily lets herself into the house. It's quiet and dark. She takes off her heels again and pads across the floor to the living room window facing the ocean. It's calm tonight, and the moon stripes the water with a trembling light.

# Chapter Eight

During her senior year at Nantucket High, Maggie had bucked up her courage and submitted some writing to the school newspaper, which was not such a stretch since one of her close friends, Kerrie, was the editor. People liked her articles, short witty pieces about 'Backstage at the School Play,' 'How to Buy a Posh Prom Dress Here in Sleepy Hollow,' or 'The Accidentals and the Naturals Do New York,' so she wrote one every month. It wasn't fiction, but it was still fun.

And in August it leads to the most amazing job.

Late one afternoon, the phone rings. 'Maggie, it's Marilyn O'Brien.'

'Mrs O'Brien. Hello.' Maggie has half-turned to call her mother when Mrs O'Brien says, 'I'd like to talk with you about writing an article for *Nantucket Glossy*.'

Maggie almost falls over. 'Really?' she says, then hits herself in the thigh with her fist for sounding like such a simpleton.

'Really. I've enjoyed your pieces in the school paper. You have a gift for seeing things that others miss. I'd like to hire you to write about some of the public fund-raisers taking place this month. You'll know most of the students who'll be working at them, and many of the guests, and I think it would be fun to have a young person's view of it all.'

Maggie forces herself to say, 'Um, I'd love to, Mrs O'Brien, but what about Kerrie Smith? She was the editor of the paper.'

'I know, dear, and I'm impressed with her editorials. She's more confrontational than you are. Your style is more suited for my magazine. Your writing has flair.' Mrs O'Brien adds the fee she'd pay Maggie for each article, continuing smoothly with other details: how long she'd like the pieces to be, the slant she'd like Maggie to take on her first piece, to stress the fun and glamour of the upcoming party.

'The Theatre Workshop is having its summer fund-raiser in Beverly Hall's garden,' Marilyn says, and Maggie gasps. Beverly Hall is a famous photographer with a house overlooking the water out on the western part of the island. Maggie's heard it rumored that Beverly has seven different gardens on her land, each landscaped in a different style. Maggie's yearned to see them – and now she's being paid to do it?

'The evening's theme is Shakespeare in the Garden,' Marilyn continues. 'For entertainment, some of Nantucket's actors will put on a scene from *Midsummer Night's Dream*. David Lazarus will be in it, I've heard.'

Maggie listens, eyes wide, thrilled.

'We'll want a full account of the guests, their clothes, the food, the decorations . . . this is an extremely special evening, Maggie, and it will provide you the opportunity to show us at *Nantucket Glossy* what you can do. If you want to do it, that is.'

'I'll do it.' Maggie gulps, trying not to sound like she's just swallowed helium.

As soon as she puts down the phone, she clicks in Kerrie's number and talks to her about the article. Kerrie, to her vast relief, has no interest in something so frivolous and is surprised Maggie would consider it.

'But the galas are to raise money for Nantucket charities,' Maggie stresses. *And for me,* she adds silently.

'Please,' Kerrie says. 'I'm happy for you. It is so not my cup of tea.'

'Well, honey, it's my cup of mead,' Maggie jokes. Next, she calls Tyler, who's somewhere on the road to the West Coast. 'You'll never guess what just happened!'

Tyler listens to her babble, tossing in the appropriate 'Wow' or 'Amazing,' but after a few minutes Maggie can tell he's not enjoying this conversation.

'Hey,' she says, 'what's up? Even if you are leaving the island, you're still my best island friend and I want to share this with you.'

'Sorry,' Tyler apologizes. 'It's a huge deal. Congratulations. I wish I could see you at the party.'

Maggie grimaces – glad they're not on Skype. Marilyn O'Brien told her she could bring a date, but would she want to ask Tyler?

Before she can speak, Tyler continues, 'It's great, Maggie. Absolutely. It's like you're on your way.'

'I know,' Maggie agrees, twirling in place. 'It's like Fate's giving me a go-ahead sign.'

The very next day, another astonishing thing happens.

After breakfast, Emily arrives on her bike, wearing a bathing suit covered with a long tee shirt.

'We're not going to write today,' Maggie tells her. 'You've got to help me organize myself for my first real writing job!'

'What? Tell me!' Emily demands.

When Maggie tells her, Emily screams, hugs her, and then shouts ten thousand questions in one minute.

'It's this Friday,' Maggie tells her. 'It's a gala for the Theatre Workshop. Everyone will look so fabulous, and I don't have anything to wear. I don't even know what kind of thing to try to find, and I'll probably have to go to the thrift shop to look for something. Clothes are so expensive here. Would you go shopping with me?'

'I'll do better than that,' Emily says. 'Come to my house. We'll find something in my closet for you to wear.'

Maggie nearly falls over flat on her face. This is the first time Emily has ever invited Maggie to her home. Why would Emily ask her now? Perhaps this gala gig will make Maggie more acceptable to Emily's snobby parents.

Before Maggie can speak, Emily rolls her eyes. 'I know what you're thinking. Yes, I'm ten feet tall, but I'm sure we'll find something that will work on you.' Without waiting, Emily climbs back on her bike. 'Come on.'

Maggie grabs her ten-speed and follows Emily along the bike path to 'Sconset and Emily's house on the bluff. When she was younger, during long boring winters, Maggie used to sneak around outside the Porters' house, standing on tiptoes to peek through a crack in the drapes into the rooms inside. Most of the furniture was covered with dust cloths. It was spacious, a symphony of seaside blues and sands. Now she'll finally get to see Emily's bedroom. What if Emily's mother is there? Will she look down her nose at Maggie as she always does?

When they reach her house, Emily carelessly tosses her bike against the front porch, so Maggie does the same thing.

'No one's home,' Emily announces over her shoulder. 'Let's get a Diet Coke before we go up.'

Maggie trails behind her friend, trying not to be too obvious about scanning the rooms. Thaddeus's house is as big as this, but it's messy, cluttered with the paraphernalia of active lives. This house is like a stage set.

Emily's bedroom faces the ocean, its wide windows raised to let the sea breeze float the sheer white curtains like sails into the room. Emily's got a canopy bed and, by the window, a white chaise next to the windowsill covered with books.

'Okay,' Emily says, throwing open her closet doors. 'Let's see. You don't want to be too glitzy, you need something sophisticated, which makes me think, what shall we do with your hair?'

Maggie's heart is thumping. She's somehow passed through into an alternate universe, and while she's trying to process it all, Emily starts yanking dresses off their padded hangers. Black crepe. Lime satin. A sleek crimson slip dress. A long coil of silver.

'Emily!' Maggie can't help exclaiming at such abundance.

'Oh, shut up,' Emily says. 'You know I have to go to all the yacht club dances. Try these on. All of them.'

For an hour Maggie and Emily concentrate on slipping the garments off hangers and onto Maggie's voluptuous body. They settle on the silver dress, which has a lot of give in the material and a boat neckline so Maggie won't be seeming to flaunt her bosom.

'If you think it's too tight around the hips,' Emily says, cocking her head, 'have your mother take it out a bit. The seams are generous, and your mother will know what to do.'

'But then it won't fit you,' Maggie protests.

'That dress looks awful on me,' Emily says. 'I'm so flat I look like a drainpipe in it. Now sit down here and let's think about your hair.'

Maggie's thick black hair falls past her shoulders in waves. 'A chignon?' she suggests, twisting her hair up.

Emily squints. 'No. No. Just' – sweeping Maggie's hair up with both hands, she pulls it back from her face – 'a high ponytail, I think. We'll straighten it. I've got a silver clip to hold it back.'

'And maybe my mom's rhinestone earrings?' Maggie wonders. She's always wanted to wear those earrings, long dramatic falls of sparkle.

'No. No, that's too much. This dress is already enough shine, and then the clip . . . and a touch of makeup.'

Both girls stare at Maggie's reflection in the mirror, the shape of her face, the slant of her cheekbones, the thick black eyelashes over arctic ice blue eyes, the fullness of her lips.

'You're so pretty,' Emily declares. Not giving Maggie a chance to object, she says, '*Now.* You'll need a date.'

'I know . . .' Maggie's still turning her head this way and that, studying herself in the mirror.

'I'm hungry.' Emily tugs Maggie's hair. 'Take off the dress, come downstairs, let's find a snack. We need energy to think about this. Come on, you must have a crush on some guy. Or are you weirder than I thought?'

Yanked back to reality, Maggie slowly admits, 'Well, there is Shane.'

'Shane? You know a guy named *Shane*?'

Maggie pulls the dress off over her head to hide her blushing face.

'Out with it!' Emily commands.

'Shane Anderson.' Maggie sighs.

Emily makes a hurry-up sign.

'He's eighteen. He's tall, played football in high school. Nice, too.'

'Handsome?' Emily asks.

Maggie blushes red.

'Wow. So does he like you?'

Maggie nods. 'He's part of the group I hang out with. He's really sweet to me . . . but, Emily, I don't want to start all that dating stuff. I want to be a writer. I can't do that if I get pregnant.'

'For heaven's sake!' Emily scolds. 'You're only asking him to a party with you, not having his babies. Sometimes you are absolutely unbelievable.'

'Not everyone's as sophisticated as you,' Maggie swipes back.

Emily hands her the phone. 'Call him. Ask him to the gala.'

Maggie chews her lip. 'What if he says no?'

Emily gives her the eye. 'Do you *think* he'll say no?'

Maggie blushes again and calls Shane.

# Chapter Nine

Wednesday evening Ben drives Emily over the rutted sand to a beach on Coskata at the head of Nantucket Harbor. No one else is there. The light is diffuse with moisture, like an Impressionist painting.

Ben sits cross-legged on a blanket, eating the cold chicken, potato salad, and lemon meringue pie Emily bought at Petticoat Row Bakery. While they eat, they talk about the men Ben works with, and Emily tells him about the kids she showed around the aquarium.

When they finish eating, Emily tidies things into the picnic hamper. Then Ben walks down to the water and stands staring out. Emily stands next to him.

The tide is low, exposing all the sandbars. Channels of water ripple like clear silk over the pebbles. The sun sinks downward in the sky, casting long shadows. For a few moments they don't speak. They walk around the white branches of a fallen tree, stripped smooth and polished to marble by the wind. Fiddler crabs scuttle to their holes. On a distant sandbar, a pair of dark cormorants stand, two capital letter T's, their wings extended to dry. It's very still. The lights of town are far away.

He picks up a flat rock and skims it over the water. 'Okay. I'll say it. What are we doing here?'

Emily's confused, and at the same time, she's suddenly, ecstatically, aware. 'Having a picnic?' she answers, her voice light.

'Slumming it?' Ben suggests, not looking at her.

'What?'

'Come on, Emily. You're rich. You're a city girl. You've been everywhere. You're out of my league.'

Emily studies Ben's face. In the fading light, his expression is almost impossible to read, but she feels an urgency and a gathering-up in him, like a swimmer about to dive.

'That's ridiculous, Ben.' She touches his hand. 'Come on.'

He doesn't move away, but he seems to contract, somehow, to withdraw tighter in an invisible shell. She sees the pulse beating in his neck. His skin is hot, he's like a crystal figure in a kiln. With a lightning bolt through her heart, she understands that her words could liberate him or break him.

The magic of the night gives her courage. Breathing the air, she fills herself with its clarity. She knows exactly what she wants – and what it is that she can give.

'Ben, don't you know? I love you.'

He stands as still as stone.

'I've never said that before to anyone except my parents,' she confesses. 'I've never felt this way before. It's not just that I think you're handsome, although of course I do think that. It's that – I'm so full of admiration for you. I think you've become – wonderful. I always sensed that you were powerful, but now – well, now you're powerful and *good*. I don't think I've ever known anyone like you. I would never hurt you, never. I feel privileged that you showed me this island. That you shared your love for it with me. I love you for that.'

At last Ben turns to her. His blue jay eyes are solemn.

'Are you going to say anything?' Emily asks.

He smiles. He says, 'Emily.' He pulls her to him, he puts his mouth on hers.

She's wealthy. He's not. She gives him all she has – she gives him her mouth, her body, her praise. She kisses him. They help one another take off their clothes, making a nest in the sand. When they're both naked, Emily presses her lips against his chest, his belly, his groin, his eyes. She has heard about what girls can do to boys – it's always seemed ludicrous – but caresses now come to her as if they're all her own idea, the first time on this earth. Ben's breathing hard, shuddering, beautiful in the moonlight, and his hands are on her breasts. He rolls her on her back and rises above her. The sand shifts beneath her as she opens her legs. He says her name.

Like a diver on the cliff, he holds back. She moves her hips and then, to her surprise, she sees the flash of his teeth – she sees him smile.

She feels him stay. He's waiting. He's taking his time. He's in control as he looks at her face, her neck, her breasts.

He is taking possession.

He moves inside her. He's a diver, she's a rising wave. She wraps her arms and legs around him. He is hers now, he is really hers.

When Shane Anderson agrees to accompany Maggie to the gala, she's pleased. Most island girls would be delirious to have a date with Shane. He's drop-dead handsome, a stocky guy, strong, muscular, athletic, and a serious fisherman when he's not working for his father's contracting firm.

He likes Maggie. A lot. She's aware of that, although she's never much cared. She's too busy thinking of the world beyond high school.

Tonight she tucks her tiny Canon digital camera and a small notebook and pen into the evening bag Thaddeus's mother, Clarice, once used, a shiver of excitement zapping through her as she does. She slips her feet into the high stilettos she found at the Seconds Shop, and studies herself in her bedroom mirror. Emily's silver dress is form-fitting on Maggie, but not vulgar. She's wearing just a touch of makeup – this gala is outside, and the sun stays out late into the evening. She doesn't want to overdo it.

Frances leans into the open doorway. 'You look stunning, darling.'

'Really?' Maggie peers over her shoulder. No, her bum doesn't look big in this dress.

'Really. You're a knockout. Now stop admiring yourself. Shane's RAV4 just pulled into the driveway.'

'I hope the seat belt doesn't wrinkle my dress,' Maggie worries as Shane drives his SUV along Madaket Road. 'I know I'm babbling, Shane, and I apologize. It's just that I've always been on the fringe of these summer galas. Last year I helped bus plates from the tables in the tent for the Boys and Girls Club. Have you ever been to one of these events?'

'Oh, yeah,' Shane says casually, casting a lazy smile at Maggie. 'Let's see, I've helped set up the tents for lots of parties, and I've opened oysters for Spanky's Raw Bar at some of the events, and—'

'I don't mean that!' Maggie interrupts. 'I mean as a guest. All snazzed up.' She pauses to take in Shane in all his glory, wide shoulders bulking out a navy blazer, white shirt setting off his gleaming brown hair and eyes, confidence simply steaming from his pores. 'You look good.'

'You look kinda nice yourself,' Shane replies. He's a man of few words.

But he's got a sensible head on his wide shoulders. When he sees all the cars parked in front of Beverly Hall's house, he insists on dropping Maggie by the front gate rather than making her walk the dirt road in her high heels.

'Oh, thanks, Shane,' Maggie gushes. 'I'm already nervous about walking on the grass in these shoes, I'm afraid I'll sink right into the sod.'

Shane smiles in a way that would make most women her age faint. 'I'll support you.'

When he returns from parking the car, Shane takes Maggie's arm and escorts her through a gate along paving stones into a magical world. Separate paths lined by fragrant greenery wind in various directions, toward the seductive musical song of the water garden, to the labyrinth, to the desert garden with its bell and stones. In the forefront the house spreads like no house Maggie has ever seen, long and brilliant with sliding glass doors, statuary, porches, and decks. At one end of the garden a bar is set up. Shane settles Maggie on a stone bench where she snaps photos while he fetches her a drink. They stroll toward the other end of the garden, where a stage is set beneath a pergola hanging with lush ripe grapes. Colorful shawls from India are draped over chairs set out for the audience to the play.

Dazzling people are everywhere.

'I'm a little nervous about interviewing this artistic bunch,' Maggie whispers.

Shane bends close to her ear. 'Our coach tells us to do twenty-five jumping jacks before running out to the field. That pumps up our adrenaline and chases off the jitters.'

'Well, thanks for that advice, but pardon me if I don't take it,' says Maggie, but she's grateful he's made her laugh. Seeing a couple she vaguely recognizes, she decides to dive right in.

'Hello, I'm Maggie McIntyre, I'm here for *Nantucket Glossy,* and I've been admiring your dress. I wonder whether you'd allow me to photograph you and your . . . husband?'

'Of course,' the woman says, quickly smoothing her hair. She leans into her companion while Maggie snaps shots. The woman quite happily provides their names. Maggie introduces Shane, and the two couples chat briefly about the weather, the summer, this party, before Maggie waggles her fingers and takes her leave to photograph others.

Here, at her first assignment, Maggie learns that most people love the thought of being in the magazine. The women adjust their dresses, their hair, and sidle sideways, exposing their best profile. Shane is the perfect date, keeping Maggie supplied with ice water – everyone else is drinking wine, but she wants to keep her wits about her – and holding her elbow when they cross the grass. Waiters, many of whom Maggie knows personally, glide past with trays of bacon-wrapped scallops, miniature quiches, fresh shrimp, and curried mussels, then disappear into the house when the gong is rung and the play begins.

The actors step out from behind the tapestries draped on screens. Their robes are sumptuous, velvet and satin set with opulent jewels. On this mid-August evening, this passage from

Shakespeare's comedy, wonderfully acted and articulated by island actors, easily draws laughter and applause from the crowd.

Afterward, Maggie finally summons up the courage to take a picture of the renowned photographer, their hostess, Beverly Hall, and as the setting sun draws the crowd to the water side of the house, Maggie whispers to Shane that she's ready to leave.

'My notebook is full and my feet are killing me,' she confesses.

Shane brings the SUV around and actually steps out to open the door for her and hand her in. Maggie sighs as she leans her head back against the seat.

'Poor you,' Shane says. 'Talking to the beautiful people, eating gourmet food, and receiving pay for it. What a job.'

'I know.' Maggie sighs. 'It's hard, but someone's got to do it.'

'I'm ready anytime you need me,' Shane tells Maggie.

Glancing over at him she reads his expression in the gathering twilight. She knows his words have at least two meanings.

**Sorry not called. Busy being glamorous. Shane v. helpful.
☺ xoM**

Emily scans the most recent text from Maggie on her cell phone. She's glad Maggie's so busy with her *Nantucket Glossy* evening work plus her day jobs. At some point, Emily knows she's got to tell Maggie about what's been happening between her and Ben. It will be difficult, because she knows the moment she says Ben's name, Maggie will hear in Emily's voice the dense heat of love Emily lives in now.

It's as if they're created anew. As if the whole world is created anew.

During the day, while Ben paints houses, Emily reads books

about oceanography, keeping diligent notes. She's headed to Smith, where she's decided to major in environmental studies. They have a field station on Nantucket, and courses that apply to the island. After college, she'll take a job at Maria Mitchell, until she and Ben marry and have their first baby. Emily and Ben discuss their dreams endlessly, as they walk on beaches, or make love in his barn loft, or in the back of his Jeep, or on a blanket in the dark moors. It's all so rich, extreme, sensual . . . they're not ready to discuss it with other people yet. Not yet. It is still their private treasure trove.

Marilyn O'Brien congratulates Maggie on her excellent photos and accompanying tidbits from the Shakespeare in the Garden party. She hires Maggie full time, for the next two weeks, to cover every possible event Maggie can attend. Thrilled, Maggie accepts.

One morning as she stumbles into the kitchen in her boxer shorts and tee shirt, hair mussed, last night's mascara smeared under her eyes, she catches Ben just before he leaves for work. He's clean-shaven and smells like soap. He seems to be in a good mood, so Maggie takes a chance. 'Hey, Ben, would you ever go with me to one of the events I have to cover for *Nantucket Glossy*?'

'Too busy,' Ben says, snatching one of their mother's cheese muffins to take out the door with him.

'But listen,' Maggie protests, 'these events are at houses like palaces! The nibbles are gourmet, the crowd is full of fabulous people—'

Ben laughs, an unusual sound for him in the morning. 'Thanks for inviting me, Mags, but I don't think gourmet nibbles are quite what I'm up for this summer.' He goes out the door, whistling.

Maggie follows him to the door, wildly curious. 'What's turned you into Mister Merry Sunshine?' she yells.

Ben doesn't answer, but he's still smiling as he drives away.

Frances is at the table, finishing her second cup of coffee. 'What about Shane?'

Maggie slumps in a chair across from her mother. 'I don't want to keep asking him. He's acting kind of romantic, and I don't feel that way about him.'

Frances lifts an eyebrow. 'You're the only girl on the island who doesn't.'

'I know. But I don't want him to get the wrong idea.'

'Do you have to bring a date?'

'I guess not . . .' Maggie pours herself a cup of coffee, adds sugar and milk, and leans against the kitchen counter, thinking. 'It's more fun with a friend.'

'Then have a talk with Shane,' Frances suggests. 'Tell him how you feel.'

Maggie wrinkles her nose. 'Maybe.' After a moment, she adds, 'I think there's something wrong with me. I'm missing the sex gene.'

Frances grins. 'I doubt that very much. You just haven't met the right fella.'

That night Shane accompanies Maggie to a round of art gallery openings. In Kathleen Knight's Gallery on India Street, she takes her time chatting with people – by now she's recognizing faces and remembering names. An older woman clad in several paisley shawls and a velvet turban catches Maggie's eye, so Maggie searches her out, snaps a photo – she's so colorful, she'll make a sensational shot – and interviews her. She's an artist, she tells Maggie, flashing bracelets and rings as she speaks about her glory days. Maggie takes notes, but she's beginning to wonder if the woman's tales are all true, when she notices that Shane has gotten himself trapped over by the food table.

Although *trapped* might not be Shane's word, because his eyelids are drooping in a sexy look and he's got a crooked grin on his face.

'Thank you,' Maggie says abruptly, leaving the flamboyant artist. She strolls across the large gallery, watching Shane. Yeah, she's right, she thought she recognized the woman talking to him and she does. *Woman,* Maggie thinks, her mind caught on the word. Clementine Melrose is exactly Maggie's age, eighteen, yet she gives off the aura of a sophisticated, elegant adult. A summer person whose parents have a house in 'Sconset near Emily's, Clementine is tiny, part French, a ballet dancer who no longer studies ballet but still carries herself with the beautifully erect posture of a ballerina. Clementine's not really pretty, but she's sexy, each movement suggestively erotic.

Maggie chews on a carrot stick, pretending to eye the rest of the food, watching Shane with her peripheral vision. He's responding to Clementine, and why wouldn't he? In all these weeks of accompanying her, Shane has never seen Maggie tilt her hips toward him as Clementine's doing now. Maggie has never put her hand on his arm, drawing her fingers down into the palm of his big hand.

Jealousy spurts through Maggie. She doesn't know if she wants Shane, but now she knows she doesn't want anyone else to have him.

Maggie understands it's time for her to grow up.

Tonight Maggie's wearing a simple black dress she's had for years. Her mother has cut the sleeves off so it's cooler in the summer air, and as usual, Maggie has her long black hair pulled up and back into a high ponytail. She's got on dramatic black eyeliner and heavy mascara, and she knows that even if she's a lot bigger than petite Clementine Melrose, she's bigger in all the right places.

Sauntering up to Shane, she slides next to him, leaning against the wall, her hip nudging his. 'Hey, honey.'

Shane draws a deep breath. Maggie knows there are so many answers he could give. She's never called him 'honey' before. She's never rubbed her hip against his. He looks down at her, his dark eyes serious, almost threatening. She can read the message. Quite clearly, he's telegraphing her: *Don't toy with me.*

With a cunningly innocent smile, Maggie reaches over to extend her hand to Clementine, at the same time managing to press her bosom into Shane's arm. 'Hi. I'm Maggie McIntyre. I'm taking photos for *Nantucket Glossy* and I'd love to take your photo if you don't mind. You're so gorgeous in that red dress.'

Clementine's eyes narrow. She's not certain what just happened, but she doesn't like it. Shane's attention now is completely focused on Maggie.

'I don't think so,' Clementine replies, flustered. 'I'm so tired. I only this minute arrived from France.'

'Oh, were you on a hiking trip?' Maggie inquires, subtly implying knapsacks full of unwashed socks.

'I live in Paris,' Clementine snaps, her eyes flashing. 'Paris, and Nantucket in the summer.'

'Lucky you!' Maggie coos. 'Is your dress from Paris?'

Clementine settles down, flattered by Maggie's question. 'Yes. Yes, it is.'

'You look so fabulous. Oh, please, I'd love to have a photo of you for *Nantucket Glossy*.'

Flattered and irritated, Clementine shrugs her bony shoulders. 'Fine.'

Maggie takes a photo of Clementine, writes down her full name – even though she's seen Clementine often enough over the past few years to know it – and thanks her.

'Do you have enough stuff?' Shane asks Maggie. He's intense, a runner at the starting line.

*All right,* Maggie thinks. She's feeling rather amorous, herself. 'I do,' she tells him. 'Let's go.'

Shane has moved his bedroom from his parents' house into an apartment above their garage, so he can play his music full blast – and have visitors. It's basically a large rectangle with unpainted drywall and all the electric works showing, but he's got a king-sized bed with clean sheets and a bathroom that is messy but clean.

'Nice,' Maggie says, looking around the room.

Shane's focusing on her. 'You're nice.'

She can tell he's nervous. She makes the first move, reaching up to touch his face, and quickly he has her in his arms. He kisses her fiercely, then lifts her and carries her to his bed. His passionate fumblings at her clothes and his heavy weight on top of her are too rough.

'Shane. This is my first time.'

Immediately he slows down. 'Sorry. Sorry.' He begins again, kissing her lips, her neck, her chest, stroking her arms.

She returns his kisses. Sitting up, she lifts the black dress over her head and tosses it to the floor. She's wearing an underwire strapless bra. When she unhooks it, Shane groans and nearly rips his own clothes off his large impatient body. He pushes her back down on the bed, shoving her legs apart with his knees.

'Gentle,' she tells him. 'Gentle, Shane.'

And he is gentle. Maggie can see in his eyes that this is special for him, and she likes him for that, but she's also sad, deep in her heart, because she knows she can't reciprocate his affection. She closes her eyes and allows herself to be in the moment. The moment is very good.

On a late August evening, Emily and Ben walk along the beach at 'Sconset, idly watching the waves lazily slap against the shore.

'I remember when there were houses here,' Ben remarks, sweeping his arm up the beach. 'The "No Name Storm" – that's what we called it, because the National Weather Service didn't predict it – wiped out an entire row of homes.'

Emily scans the empty beach. 'Will the shoreline build up again?'

'Probably. It's supposed to accumulate on this side of the island.'

Emily points. 'Look. A seal.'

'Yeah. More and more are coming down here. They used to hang out only at Great Point, but now that we can't kill them, they're populating like crazy. They have to spread out to find fish.'

'Seals are adorable,' Emily says.

'Sharks certainly think so,' Ben tells her.

'Let's spread our blanket here,' Emily says. 'I think we're hidden from sight by the cliff.' Once they have the blanket on the sand, Emily sits, arms on knees, staring out at the ocean. 'I've summered on Nantucket all my life, Ben. I've worked for the science museum here for quite a few years. I want to be part of this island. But I'm not sure what direction to take. These changes – the beach erosion, the seals – they're changing the water itself. Not to mention all the summer houses being built on the island and the landscapers putting pesticides and chemicals into the ground. That runs right into the harbor.' She looks up at Ben as he settles next to her. 'I wish I knew the best courses to take at Smith.'

'They'll provide you with good guidance. You've got to find out how adept you are with stuff like chemistry and math.'

'Yeah. I worry about that.' She bites her lip, frowning.

'Hey.' Ben puts his arm around her. 'Stop worrying about the future. Think about something more important.' With a grin, he lowers his mouth to within inches of her own. 'Think about me.'

Aroused, she wraps her arms around him. 'I can do that.'

The daylight is dimming, turning the blue sky violet, gray, indigo. The darkness covers them as they move together on the blanket, and all worries have vanished into the warm salty air.

'Whoot!' Emily runs down the path to Shipwreck House, a book-bag bouncing in each hand. She's wearing shorts and a tee shirt and flip-flops.

'Hey, you.' Maggie steps out of the boathouse to greet her. Like Emily, she's in shorts and a cotton tee, flip-flops on her feet. She gestures with her hand. 'Enter, madam, the feast awaits.'

On the rickety old table where Maggie used to write, a feast is laid out on one of Frances's unironed tablecloths. Crusty Portuguese bread, soft and hard cheeses on a cutting board, British and Finnish crackers, containers of oily, garlicky pastas with smoked veggies, stuffed grape leaves, and pungent wrinkled olives.

'I've brought the drinks,' Emily says. 'Beer in this bag, sparkling water in this one.' By Massachusetts law, they're not supposed to have alcohol until they're twenty-one, but in the summer the law is broken regularly on the island. Still, neither girl enjoys the sensation of being smashed.

'Let's go down to the dock,' Maggie suggests.

They sit on the end, their feet dangling in the water. For a few moments they simply stare at the pale sky, the lights of town so far away, the houses across the harbor becoming shadowy.

'So many of the summer houses are closed,' Maggie muses. 'Already, before Labor Day.'

'Everyone has to go back to school.'

'I know. I leave in two days.'

Emily asks, 'Are you excited? Nervous?'

'Both. I've never spent much time off island. But Wheaton's not far from here. When I interviewed there, I got to the college and back to the island in the same day. Lots of island kids go there. Plus, it's gorgeous, and I'm *so* ready to start reading and studying.'

Emily leans back and laughs. 'You little bookworm.'

'Always.'

'I loved your articles in *Nantucket Glossy*.'

'Yeah, that was fun. Marilyn O'Brien's great to work with. But it's fiction I want to focus on. I know I'll have to take science and stuff, but I've been drooling over the literature offerings in the catalog.'

Emily is quiet for a long moment. Then she says, calmly, 'I've been drooling over your brother.'

Maggie cocks her head, giving Emily a questioning look. 'Um, okay.'

'I've been wanting to tell you. *We've* been wanting to tell you. But you and I haven't had a chance to really sit down and talk like this. I mean, you've been working all summer . . .'

'What are you saying?'

Emily takes a deep breath. 'I'm with Ben. We've been together since early August. Eventually we're going to get married.' She cringes, waiting for Maggie's reaction.

'Well, thank God!' Maggie throws herself at Emily, hugging her tightly. 'You'll be my sister-in-law, not just my Nantucket sister! Oh, my God, Emily, this is fantastic!'

'So you're happy about it?'

'Happy? I'm ecstatic! Except, how could you keep it a secret from me? And Ben, that sneak, no wonder he's been so damn cheerful all summer. Oh, Emily, this is awesome! Oh, my mom will be over the moon!'

Emily throws back her head and laughs at Maggie's exuberance. What was she afraid of, that Maggie would be jealous? That Maggie would think Emily wasn't right for her brilliant brother?

And suddenly Maggie cries, 'Oh, no!' Her face goes tragic. 'This means you love Ben more than you love me!'

Emily laughs again and hugs Maggie. 'I'll never love anyone more than I love you, Maggie.'

'This calls for a drink.' Maggie runs up to the boathouse, grabs a couple of beers, and brings them back. Clinking her bottle against Emily's, she toasts, 'Here's to you and Ben.'

They drink.

'While we're talking about romance,' Maggie says in a sultry voice, 'I've got some news myself.'

'Do tell.'

'You know Shane, who's been taking me to all the parties?' Maggie grins wickedly.

'You didn't. You lost your virginity and you didn't tell me?' Emily pretends to be insulted.

'He's the sweetest guy, Emily. He's patient and reliable and so kind. Oh, and sexy as hell, too.'

'Thank heavens for that. Do you love him?'

Maggie wriggles uncomfortably. 'Oh, I don't know. I like him. And I like having sex with him. He's a good guy.'

'Do you want to be by his side for the rest of your life, do you want to take care of him when he's sick and have babies with him and melt right into his body?'

Maggie stares at Emily. 'That's how you feel with Ben?'

Emily nods. 'And more. I can't even put it all into words.'

'Then no. No, I don't love Shane.' For a second, Maggie looks sad. Recovering, she shouts, 'But I don't care! Literature is my true love! I don't need a man!' Jumping up, she extends a hand to Emily. 'Come on. I'm starving. Let's go into Shipwreck House and eat everything we see.'

Emily takes Maggie's hand and rises. 'You're crazy, you know.'

'Yeah,' Maggie replies, skipping ahead, looking over her shoulder at Emily. 'And aren't you glad?'

Two nights before Maggie leaves the island for college, Shane takes her out to dinner, a proper date, he tells her, dinner at a real restaurant.

Sitting across from each other at the Boarding House, one of the more expensive restaurants on the island, the couple pick at their food, constrained by a web of things they haven't said.

Finally, Shane reaches over to take Maggie's hand. 'We should talk.'

Maggie takes a deep breath. 'Okay.'

'Everything's going to change, isn't it?' He speaks lightly, but his dark brown eyes are serious. 'You going to college, me staying here, a working guy.'

She wants to be honest with him, but she doesn't want to hurt him, and she's not sure of her feelings. 'Things will change,' she agrees. 'Not because I'll be in college, but because we'll be separated for most of four years. But I'll be back for summers and holidays, to work for money for school, and I absolutely will return to live on the island when I graduate. I never want to live anywhere else.'

Shane withdraws his hand. Leaning back in his chair, he's obviously gathering his thoughts. He's not easy with words. He doesn't like to read, so his vocabulary doesn't provide for him all the nuances he'd desire. Finally, he says ruefully, 'That seems kind of cold.'

Maggie takes the time to study the handsome big man across from her. His shoulders are wide, his entire body muscular, hefty, solid. His deep brown eyes are fringed with the same dark brown of his hair. Already his hands are scarred and callused from working, and when he walks his hands curve inward, as if he's always carrying a hammer. He's unbuttoned the top two buttons of his white shirt, and she knows he hates wearing it. It chokes him. He prefers the loose hang of a cotton tee shirt over canvas work trousers. He prefers work boots.

Not that clothes matter. Maggie doesn't care what he wears. It doesn't matter that he doesn't like to read. Most of the couples she knows have different interests. He coaches Little League baseball – as her friends say, he'll be a wonderful father. He's not a drunk, he doesn't have a bad temper, he makes good money. If she married him, she'd be able to squeeze some time out of her day to write. Her girlfriends have pressed all these arguments and more on Maggie. But he deserves to know the truth.

'You're right.' Now she reaches for his hand. She has never said she loves him because she isn't sure that she does. 'It's just that I want so much to be a writer, Shane. I want that more than marriage and kids—' She hears him inhale at this. She's never been quite so blunt before. 'My parents are really struggling to send me away to college, and I need to go. I've got so much to learn, I'm so excited to hear lectures from professors who've read and studied—' His face tells her that she's gotten off track. For him, for *him* she's gotten off track. Best to hit him with it all at once. 'Shane, I don't know if I'll ever have the feelings for you that you want me to have. I think it's only fair for you and me to break off. Four years is too long for us to try to stay a couple. I want to concentrate on my studies, and you, my gosh, Shane, you'll have so many women hitting on you the second the ferry leaves the dock—'

Shane jerks his hand away. 'You don't have to humor me. I'm a big boy. I can deal with rejection.'

As often happens at moments like this, the waiter's timing is impeccably off. 'Would you like to see the dessert menu?' he offers eagerly.

'No, thanks.' Shane's voice is almost a growl. 'We'll take the check.'

They don't speak again until they leave, and when they go out the door, Maggie notices how several women's eyes caress Shane. He *is* a hunk. He is a good man. She is sorry for both of them that that isn't enough.


Early Saturday morning, Ben picks up Emily and drives her to the ferry. Her parents have sent all her necessities straight to Smith. Emily has only one bag and a backpack. Most of her summer clothes will remain here on the island.

'You look nice,' Ben tells her as she climbs into the cab of his Jeep.

Nancy Thayer

Emily kisses his cheek and snuffles around his face, smelling the lingering fragrance of Barbasol. 'You always look nice.'

'Better stop that or you'll miss your boat,' Ben warns her with a smile. Ben backs out of her drive and heads toward town. All around them the gardens, moors, bushes, and trees are still green and flowering, as if summer will truly never end.

'Tired?' Ben asks, reaching over to take her hand.

'Aren't you?' Last night they had made love and talked almost until morning, trying to postpone their parting. After a wide yawn, Emily says, 'I should have brought some coffee.'

'Have some of mine.' Ben gestures toward the Styrofoam container in the cup holder.

She drinks it, savoring the knowledge that his lips touched the rim as much as she's enjoying the taste of the coffee.

'So you'll phone me tonight?' asks Emily.

'Sure. But you know once I'm back at school I won't be able to call you every day.'

'I know. I'll come to Boston as often as I can, and once I'm settled, you'll come visit me at Smith, right?'

'Right.'

All too soon they arrive at the Steamship Authority parking lot. The *Iyanough* is waiting, a large-white catamaran hovering above the water.

'Do you have your ticket?' Ben asks.

'Right here.' Emily holds it up.

Ben joins a line of cars dropping people off at the departure shed. 'I'll park and come wait with you.'

'No. No, I'll be fine, Ben. Just drop me off and go to work. This is the way our lives will be for four years. Coming and

94

going, meeting and saying good-bye. I've got to learn not to become a soggy emotional ball of wimpiness every time.'

'This is all good,' Ben assures her as he sets the gear shift into park. 'We're going to get our college degrees, and learn how to help the island, and we'll marry and be together forever. Remember that.'

'God, I love you, Ben!' Emily throws her arms around him and kisses him hard, tears rolling down her face. 'I'm fine. I'll talk to you tonight. I love you!'

She jumps out of the Jeep, lifts out her suitcase and backpack, and rolls her luggage to the cart to be loaded. Before she takes her place in the boarding line, she turns back to wave at Ben, but he's had to drive off so someone else can unload. He's going one way, she another.

She is stepping into her future.

# Part Three
# Shipwreck House

# Chapter Ten

*Four Years Later*

Emily prefers taking the plane to the island, not because it's faster than the ferry, but because from this height the coastline, shoals, and reefs are all visible.

In many ways, over the past four years, distance has been good for her. It has allowed her to separate herself from Ben. It's made it possible for both of them – Ben at Tufts in Boston, Emily at Smith in Northampton – to concentrate on their studies. Their passion simmers while they're apart. Their phone calls and emails are a mixture of visions of the future when they're together and commonplace complaints about papers due, cranky professors, irritating classmates.

A year ago, Ben graduated from college and returned to the island to take a job with a conservation association. Emily flew down to the island with a bottle of champagne to celebrate.

This year, Emily has been honored with a fellowship to work

on a master's degree in water ecology at UMass Amherst, her own project focusing on preventing pesticides from polluting Nantucket Harbor. She'll be part of a team assembling a report for the state officials. This might actually, in time, lead to legislative change. She knows Ben will be pleased for her, proud of her. This news is too important for phone or email, so she flies down to Nantucket to tell him in person.

When Emily steps off the nine-seater plane that bounced her through the clouds from Boston, Ben is at the gate to meet her, tall and handsome, her gypsy lover tamed by a sports coat and tie. He works for a town organization now. He's not dreaming; he's doing.

'Emily.' He pulls her to him.

Wrapping her arms around him, she speaks his name against his lips as his mouth crushes hers. She presses her body against his. For a moment desire ignites between them, and the world falls away.

Then a woman with a duffel bag accidentally knocks Ben on the shoulder. 'Sorry,' she mutters, steaming toward the departure door.

Ben releases Emily. 'Let's go.'

'Yes, please,' Emily begs.

They walk out to his old Jeep, awkwardly, his arm around her shoulders, both of them lopsided with luggage.

'How was the flight?'

Emily shrugs. 'All right. It's November. Lots of clouds, but I could see the shoreline.'

Inside the Jeep, Ben turns to hold Emily against him. 'God, you smell good. I've missed you.'

'Missed you, too,' she murmurs against his neck. 'I want to be in bed with you right now.' His hand is on her leg, pushing her skirt up. She puts her hand on the crotch of his jeans.

'Stop.' He groans, pulling her hand away. 'I won't be in any condition to drive.' He starts the Jeep, pulls out of the parking lot, and heads toward town, presumably to Thaddeus's.

When he turns off onto an unfamiliar road, Emily asks, 'Is this the right way?'

'A friend's letting me have his apartment for the night.' Ben waggles his eyebrows humorously. 'All night. Just you and me.'

'Fabulous.' Emily's truly thrilled. They can't make love in Thaddeus's house where Ben still lives so he can save money, and she doesn't want to do it in the barn. They're not kids anymore. Ben's stupid pride won't allow him to use Emily's parents' house or let Emily rent a hotel room. Because of her father, she will always have more money than Ben does, but this is an issue the two of them keep avoiding.

The apartment is over the garage near a house on Hummock Pond Road. The lot is beautifully landscaped, the house and garage well maintained, so Emily's shocked when Ben unlocks the door and she steps into his friend's apartment. It's not a pit exactly, but it's basic, to say the least, and not particularly clean. The wide screen television is the only item in the large one-room studio apartment that was created within the last decade. Clearly the bed, sofa, coffee table, and kitchen table are from secondhand shop or someplace worse.

A vase of flowers stands on the bedside table and a bottle of inexpensive champagne waits in a tub of ice in the sink. The sheets on the bed are so clean and crisp they look new – probably they are new. Emily imagines that Ben bought them and brought them over just for this occasion. They haven't been together for a month.

She's grateful for these thoughtful touches. Yet . . . the room smells of dirty male laundry.

'What do you think?' Ben's voice snaps her out of her thoughts.

She focuses on him, on this tall, confident, proud man who makes her heart sing. He's so handsome standing before her in his white dress shirt, sports coat, and tie. She's infatuated with his black hair, his mouth, his body. 'Flowers, Ben, oh, sweetheart.' She presses up against him, wrapping him in her arms.

Ben makes love to her gently, slowly, touching her as if relearning her every curve and hollow. It's cool in the apartment, but as their passion stirs and builds, they ignite as their skin slides against each other's, slick with sweat and saliva and other hot, sweet fluids.

Afterward, they doze for a while. When they wake, they lie on their sides, gazing into each other's eyes.

'I love you, Emily.'

'I love you, Ben.' She skims her fingers over his chest, twining the curls of his black chest hair.

'I don't want to be away from you for so long again.'

'No. I don't, either.' She strokes the side of his face. Is now a good time to tell him about her fellowship? 'Ben—'

He turns his head to kiss the palm of her hand. 'We should get married in May,' he says.

'Oh.' His words are so unexpected, they knock the breath out of her. She's rattled. She's thrilled, yet terrified. 'Is this a proposal?'

Ben looks surprised. 'Do you need a proposal?'

Pulling her hand away from his, Emily sits up in bed, leans against the wall – no headboard on this bed – pulling the sheet up over her breasts. 'Every girl likes a proposal.'

'Oh, you're a girl?' Ben sits up, too, next to her.

'Of course. I'm hardly a guy.'

'Yeah, but – a *girl*?'

Emily's completely confused. 'I don't understand.'

'*Girls* live with their parents. They don't earn their livings. They don't have credit cards they pay off themselves. *Women* live with their husbands. They work and help pay the mortgage and pay off their credit cards themselves. They have babies and take care of them. They cook dinner.'

'I know all that,' Emily snaps defensively. 'I can be a woman. I am a woman. But that doesn't mean I can't expect other things I've always wanted.'

'Like what?' His voice is raspy with emotion.

'Like a proper proposal. Like an engagement ring. Like a church wedding. Like—'

'Stop.' Rising from the bed, he pulls on his pants and shirt, then pads barefoot to the sink. 'Let's sit down and talk about this.'

While Ben works the cork from the bottle, Emily opens her suitcase and takes out her robe, wrapping it around her as if the cloth were protection.

He pours the bubbly into mismatched water glasses and hands one to her. 'I meant this for a celebration,' he tells her, but his voice is mild. 'I guess I was premature.'

She sips the liquid. 'It's nice to have it, anyway. Anytime we're together is a celebration.' That is the truth, for her.

'Then we should be together permanently.' Before she can respond, he continues, 'But you know marriage can't be a continual celebration—'

She interrupts him. 'I'm not an idiot, Ben. I do know that. I know marriage means commitment and hard work and highs and lows and all that stuff, but isn't that one of the reasons people have wonderful weddings? So they can start with the high? So they have some romance to remember?'

'Go on,' Ben says. 'I'm listening.'

She stares into her glass, thinking. 'Well, first I think there's an engagement ring. I'd really like one, Ben. A big one, if I'm honest.'

'I'll be honest, too.' Ben sets his glass on the table. 'I want to buy you an engagement ring. I intend to do that, and I'd like you with me to help pick it out. I don't know about jewelry. But I can't spend too much on it, Emily, because I'm saving money to buy us a house. You know how expensive real estate is here.'

'But, Ben, you shouldn't be so worried. You know my parents will help us.'

Ben flinches. 'No. No, I won't take charity from your parents.'

'Don't be silly—'

'You think I'm being *silly*?'

They've been postponing this argument for months, if not years. 'Excuse me. I used the wrong word. I should have said, "Don't be an arrogant prick." Let's get it all out in the open, okay? My parents have a lot of money and you don't. I'm used to a certain standard of living. Do you expect me to lower my standards, to live . . .' She stutters to a stop. 'Ben, where do you expect us to live while we're saving money for this house of ours?'

Ben rises and walks away from her. Turning back, he admits, 'I don't know. One option is to live with my parents—'

Emily coughs to cover her laugh. 'Oh, sweetie, with your parents? Maybe in the bedroom where you were a boy? We could share a room? Gee, could we have our own bathroom?'

Ben flinches. 'Another option is that over the winter Thaddeus and I could turn the barn into an apartment for us. It wouldn't be large, but it would be separate.'

'But if you did that, Ben' – she slowly thinks out loud – 'that would use up a lot of your savings for the house, right? To put in plumbing and electricity and heating and so on?'

'Or we could rent—' Ben begins.

'Same problem.' She wraps her arms around herself, shaking her head. 'No, no, it won't work unless my parents help out. If my parents help out, Ben, it would be so much simpler.'

'I won't take your parents' money.' Ben's jaw is set.

'Okay, well, listen. Ben – there's something else.'

Ben frowns.

Going to him, Emily puts her hand on his chest. 'This is a good thing. Maybe it will help us. Ben, I've won a fellowship in water ecology at UMass Amherst. I'll study there for two years. I'll receive my master's degree. Then, when I come back to Nantucket, I'll deserve a better-paying job at Maria Mitchell. They know I want to work there, and—'

'So you're not moving here for two more years.' Ben's voice is flat.

'No. I'll be in Amherst. Come on, we've lasted for four years. It's the same. I'll come back as often as possible, and you can come up to see me . . .'

Ben sinks onto the bed, elbows on his knees, head in his hands. 'I don't know, Emily.'

She sits next to him. 'Honey, what don't you know?'

Without looking at her, he mumbles, 'I've been faithful to you.'

She blinks. 'And I've been faithful to you. Are you saying this is all about sex?'

Lifting his head, he turns his face to hers, and his beautiful blue eyes are dark with sorrow. 'Emily. Did you hear anything I said? I want to marry you. Have a home with you. Come home every day and make dinner with you, kick off our shoes and watch some stupid video with you, choose furniture, make babies . . .'

Tears fill her eyes. 'I want that, too, Ben. But not yet. I'm only twenty-two. You're twenty-four. We have all the time in the world.'

'Right. Plus, you want an engagement ring. You want a big wedding. You want to live in the style to which you have become accustomed. Emily, you have always known I'll never have the kind of money your father has. It sounds to me like we've been fooling ourselves. This has been all wrong from the start.'

'That's not true. And I don't need the kind of money my father has, but I won't live with you in a *barn* or with your parents. And I won't give up my education and my chance to make a difference in the world just because it might hurt your feelings.'

Ben's face closes up. He's gone into himself, pulled down the drawbridge, barred the doors and windows to his soul. He's done this before and Emily knows her only option is to wait it out.

She says, 'It's good it's all out in the air, Ben. We need to think about all this.'

'Right. I'll take you back to the airport.' Ben pulls on his shoes. 'You can still catch a flight back to Boston.'

'What? I just got here! Ben—'

'We'll both *think* better when we're not together,' Ben mutters. His face is stormy with repressed anger.

Emily understands that he's hurt. Over the past few years she's learned to read the signs of his wounded male pride. She makes one more attempt, speaking softly. 'Ben, please. Let's not part like this. We have so much to talk about.'

'I think we've said enough already.'

'Come on, Ben, I thought you'd be glad I won that fellowship. I thought you'd be proud of me. I thought you'd see that this would mean so much for our future.'

His face bleak, Ben turns to her. 'I am proud of you, Emily. I'm always proud of you. I understand what you mean. Why you want a master's. Perhaps I'm just being an obstinate male. But somehow . . . let's take some time off from each other, okay?'

'Do you mean we're breaking up?'

'I don't know.' He shrugs. 'Emily, I really don't know. We need to think about it seriously.'

'Well. Wow.' Her heart thuds with emotion – shock, sorrow, anger. Her hands shake as she dresses and organizes her suitcase.

Ben carries it to the Jeep for her. They drive in an anguished silence back to the airport.

As they pull onto the terminal road, Emily looks at him.

'Ben.' Saying his name is her offer, her flag of truce. 'Please.'

Ben doesn't answer. He pulls into the ten-minute loading zone at the airport. He doesn't offer to carry her suitcase. She steps out of the Jeep, lifts it out herself, and wheels it back into the terminal. She takes the next flight to Boston.

Your brother insane. I'm done with men. xoE

What r men? I'm dried up old spinster, years without sex, must pull hair back in bun. xoM

This summer u/me nuns. xoE

Amen! xoM

# Chapter Eleven

A s her own life expands, Maggie discovers a whole new world in herself, drawn out by her college reading list. During her four years at Wheaton College, Maggie majors in English literature. She's been warned that this will prepare her for absolutely nothing in the job market, but she doesn't care. She wants to be a writer of *good* novels, and she needs to learn from educated, thoughtful professors how they are written, what makes them good. She wants to live on Nantucket, too, and when she returns to the island, she plans to work at whatever jobs she can find to support her writing during the evenings and weekends.

Maggie's first week back on the island, Thaddeus's mother, Clarice, has to have a hysterectomy, which slows even this formidable woman down. It's only logical for Maggie to stay with Clarice in her elegant Greek Revival on Orange Street. Maggie cooks her meals, brings her books and magazines, and becomes nurse and companion for her step-grandmother. The arrangement suits them both nicely. As the weeks progress, Maggie moves her summer clothes, laptop, books, and other necessary belongings into Clarice's house.

Shane Anderson waits until Maggie's been home for a month before contacting her. While Maggie was in college, he stayed on the island, working with his father's contracting firm. For four years, he and Maggie struggled with an on-again, off-again romance, sometimes coming close to one another, sometimes moving far away. In her deepest secret heart, Maggie cherishes the hope that now that she is an adult, twenty-two, a college graduate, she'll open the door to her old boyfriend and the veil will vanish from her eyes and she will see – her heart will *know* – that he is her one true love.

Shane is admirable in so many ways. Maggie misses his companionship, the warmth of his touch, his ardent kisses. It was a very sweet experience, having someone love her. She felt less lonely.

So on the early June evening when she opens the door of Clarice's house to see him, Maggie gives him the biggest smile she's got. 'Shane!'

He's come right from work. He's wearing canvas trousers with pockets for hammers and other tools, an old tee shirt, and an unbuttoned blue-checked flannel shirt as a sweater, because the June evening is cool. His brown eyes gleam with hope. His brown hair has been brushed into a shine. His eyes adore her.

'Hey,' he says, huge and masculine, loving and shy.

All she has to do is step into his arms. Throw herself against him, hug him, kiss him, and her future is set. She could be married to him and still write. He's always known she wants to be a writer.

It's possible he's the nicest man in the world. Certainly he's in the top ten.

But her spirit doesn't leap at the sight of the man, her heart doesn't lift to the heavens with sheer happiness because he exists. Instead, her heart sinks. She won't lie.

'Come in,' Maggie invites, stepping back, holding the door open, and they both know exactly what this implies. She leads him to the front room, once the parlor, now the living room.

'Nice place,' Shane says, looking around the high-ceilinged rooms with their antique molding.

Maggie waves him to one of the old-fashioned wing chairs by the fireplace. 'It is. A little stodgy, perhaps.'

Shane's like a breath of fresh air in the stuffy room. He seems a bit nervous. He clears his throat. 'How's Clarice? I heard she had an operation.'

Sitting on the wing chair across from him, Maggie has to admit to herself that Shane wins extra points for his thoughtfulness. 'It's nice of you to ask about her. She's getting better every day. It was a hysterectomy. There's no cancer or anything, but she's older, and any operation makes a person tired.' The formality of the living room makes her sit up straight. 'I've been home for a month, but I haven't seen anyone or gone anywhere. I've really been her nursemaid.'

'How's that been?' He crosses his legs and uncrosses them, shifting on the uncomfortable chair.

'Really? Kind of cool. She's a bit of an old bat but she's also a massive reader. The first couple of weeks I sat by her bed and read Daphne du Maurier's *Rebecca*. Just this week I finished reading some of Arthur Conan Doyle's Sherlock Holmes stories, and then we watched a couple of the new TV series, *Elementary,* where Holmes is in AA and Watson's played by Lucy Liu. Clarice loves it.' Maggie knows she's babbling, trying to postpone the inevitable discussion with Shane.

'That's cool.' He leans toward her, elbows on his knees. 'So you're here for a while.'

'I am.'

He asks, almost desperately, 'Won't you have to get a job eventually? If you want to stay here on the island, I mean?'

She tries to be casual about her intention to live on the island, to live alone, or with friends or relatives, but not, ever, with Shane. 'Oh, sure, I've got some jobs lined up already. You know I've always helped Greta and Artie White with their catering, but most of that isn't until July and August. Next week I'm going to start helping Domestic Goddess open up houses for the arrival of their summer clients.'

'Good.' Shane looks heartened. 'That's a great group.'

'Yeah. And I'll babysit, of course, especially in the evenings. *Nantucket Glossy* hired someone else, but we're sharing the work. I'm glad about that, because babysitting money's better, especially for the tourists, who tip big.' She pauses for a breath. 'Shane. How are you?'

Ignoring her question, Shane asks, 'So do you have any time to go out, Maggie? For a bite to eat sometime? Dinner, even lunch?'

Maggie swallows the rock in her throat. 'Not yet. I've got to stick around the house for a few more weeks. I'd hate to be out if Clarice needed something.'

He's quiet, as if waiting for her to say something else. Slowly, he understands what she means. 'So, um, you probably don't want me coming here often, either.'

Maggie bites her lip. 'Clarice does come downstairs more and more often these evenings. I mean, you could come, but you'd probably be bored, playing cards or watching television . . .'

Shane stands. He's tall, massive, handsome, and he looks so sad. 'It's over, isn't it, Maggie?'

If she went to him now, and touched him, kissed him, asked him to be patient just a little longer . . .

She bows her head. 'I'm sorry. You deserve more, Shane, you deserve better—' Looking up, Maggie holds out her hands. 'We could be such good friends.'

'Don't, Maggie. That doesn't help.' Shane stalks from the room. Maggie hears the front door slam.

The terrible thing is that to her the slam sounds like freedom.

Emily and Maggie decide to celebrate the return of summer at Lola 41. In this chic upscale restaurant near Children's Beach, they order margaritas with salt and sit at the bar, swinging their long legs and allowing themselves to become a tad bit tipsy.

'Your brother is a pigheaded, shortsighted, intractable ass,' Emily informs Maggie.

'That conjures up quite the image.' Maggie grins.

'He deserves it. I've won a fellowship and he wants me to blow it off and come play Little Wifey. He should be glad I'm going to spend two more years studying.'

Maggie lifts her glass. 'Hear, hear.'

'What *is* it with men?' Emily demands. 'Shane didn't care about your writing. Ben doesn't care about my research.'

'You can't equate the two men,' Maggie tells Emily. 'You know that, Emily. For one thing, you and Ben absolutely, truly, do share common interests, a common love for the island—'

'Then why isn't he glad about my master's?'

'I don't think it's about that.' Maggie licks salt from the rim of her glass, gathering her thoughts. 'It's more about money.'

'Please.'

'Please nothing. Be honest. You two could get married now and you could go to Amherst and study and come home on long weekends and holidays, and if so, where would you two go for a good long screaming, wall-thumping lovefest?'

Emily sags in her seat. 'You have no idea how right you are. Maggie, I honestly don't understand why Ben won't live in my parents' house. They never come to the island anymore.'

'Because he's proud, Emily. He doesn't want to seem to be leeching off your parents. He absolutely doesn't want to appear like he's latched on to you so you can support him.'

'That's ridiculous. Everyone knows I love Ben, I've loved him forever. The money thing doesn't matter.'

Maggie levels her gaze at her. 'You can only say that if you have money.'

Summer hits. Clarice can make her way around the house. She's healing well, gaining strength, entertaining her many friends who come to visit, bringing gossip and casseroles. Maggie housecleans, babysits, and writes articles for *Nantucket Glossy*.

Once a week, Maggie and Emily meet for drinks, dinner, and a head-clearing, heart-to-heart talk. If it rains, they eat in a restaurant, but usually they make picnic dinners and head out to the beach and talk about everything under the sun until it sets.

Summer storms have breached the sandy barrier between the ocean and Sesachacha Pond. Erosion continues along the eastern coast of the island, causing much of the cliff to plunge into the water, putting ocean-view houses in danger. Fortunately the Porters' house is to the south, away from the devastation. Out at Great Point, more and more seals are congregating around the

113

island, eating up all the fish the fishermen want to catch – another point of contention. Farther away, between here and the mainland, a company wants to erect a cluster of windmills in Nantucket Sound. The residents of the island are divided about this, which is a green solution for energy but could harm wildlife and cause more problems for the fishermen.

Maggie tells Emily of the people she writes about and photographs at parties for *Nantucket Glossy*. 'Some of them are unbelievably gross and stuck-up, acting like I should kiss their rings. But most of them are nice.'

'Maybe you'll meet some fabulously wealthy man,' Emily suggests. 'He'll sweep you off your feet, carry you away to his castle, and you can write book after book while your staff cleans house.'

'Only if his castle is on Nantucket,' Maggie replies. 'So how are you and Ben?'

'To quote your brother, we are "seriously thinking."' Emily sighs. 'At least we talk on the phone. Once or twice we've met in town for coffee. I've invited him to dinner at my house – my parents aren't here yet – but he won't come. So I've refused to go out to dinner with him. I know, I know. It's so high school.'

Maggie asks, 'Can't you make up with him for just a week? Go out with him, seduce him, sleep with him? I'd appreciate it. It's like having the Headless Horseman at the table when he comes for Sunday dinner.'

Emily laughs. 'Sorry. I'm relinquishing physical urges this summer. When I'm not working I'm reading environmental management books, trying to prepare for next semester.'

'You know,' Maggie says gloomily, 'if you ignore Ben and he marries someone else, I'll have to kill her.'

'I would definitely visit you in jail every week,' Emily promises faithfully. 'Or at least once in a while.'

'Ha-ha.'

When autumn comes and the island empties out, Clarice is hale and hearty, cooking, playing bridge, attending church, and volunteering at her favorite organizations. Now in her late seventies, Clarice tells Maggie, with a rare and startlingly gorgeous smile: 'You can't keep a good woman down.'

At long last Maggie has the leisure to write. Clarice's house has many rooms, but Maggie loves the attic best, with its view of the harbor and the long narrow stretch of sand out to Great Point and the lighthouse.

Her writing space in the attic is eccentric but deliciously satisfying. She carries a creaky, scarred, cracked old wooden table up the stairs from one of the second-floor bedrooms and sets it onto the wide-board pine floors right in front of the window overlooking the harbor. Before laying out her laptop and notebooks, she takes the time to clean and oil the old table until it gleams like the lid of a treasure chest filled with secrets. Fortunately, there's an electric socket by the window. She can plug in her laptop and her cell phone to recharge them. She also drags an old brass standing lamp over near the desk. Its stained glass shade is missing one pane of color, so she turns that side to face the luggage, old paintings, and cardboard boxes leaning against the side wall. Maggie wrestles a small bookcase from the back of the attic to hold her papers, notes, pens, and steno pad; the bookcase leans sideways a bit but that hardly matters, nor do the looming masses of antiquated castoffs stacked in the attic space behind her. She has a straight-backed dining

115

room chair with some of the cane missing, and her printer sits on the floor like an obedient dog. All is silent around her. It is her own private world.

While she writes, she lets her eyes rest on the outside world – if she uses field glasses, she can almost see Thaddeus's land: his boat dock and Shipwreck House. She goes there every Sunday when she and Clarice are invited to the farm for lunch. Maggie leaves the older people to talk and takes the opportunity to walk the land, breathe deeply of the salty air, and refuel her spirit for her work. She's obsessed with her writing, and Sunday nights, back on Orange Street, with Clarice tucked onto the sofa watching *60 Minutes,* Maggie hurries up to the attic to write.

Clarice has her own car, an ancient Taurus she's owned for about twenty years and has put about twenty miles on, so after a year of saving money, Maggie buys herself a four-wheel drive, dented, rusted Bronco that looks like a junker but bumps over the beach with spine-snapping ease. With Clarice up and about, Maggie's free to go out in the evenings for a drink or dinner and some fun and gossip.

Most of Maggie's social life is dinner with her friends or a girly movie, which leads to the formation of a book club and potluck dinner twice a month and then, with some of the women, to a walking group. Many of her high school friends have stayed because they love the island: the moors, the sea, the dunes, the weather. They joke that it's more an addiction than an association. Over the winter months Maggie's walking group roams parts of the island too overgrown to enter in the summer.

Kaylie, who has become one of Maggie's closest friends, suggests they combine the book and walking groups and walk entirely around the island, keeping a recorded account of where they start and finish each time, mapping their paths, and reading books especially about the island: novels, histories, biographies, walking guides. Something about walking for two or three hours in the fresh air makes the group talk more freely about their personal lives. Maggie tells them, not entirely joking, that they're inspiring her writing. The group responds by presenting her with a tee shirt reading: 'Be careful, or I'll put you in my novel.' They all laugh, but Maggie almost bursts into tears. Her friends believe in her. They think because she's had articles published in local magazines she can actually write a whole book. She's more grateful for their faith in her than she can ever say.

# Chapter Twelve

In September, Emily begins work on her master's degree at UMass Amherst. She's focused, ambitious, and determined to make Ben part of her future without giving up all of her past.

Part of that past is her friend Tiffany Howard, who's getting married in New York on a Saturday afternoon in October at the Cathedral of St John the Divine, followed by a reception with dinner and dancing at The Plaza.

Emily pleads with Ben to accompany her. He refuses. He's got to manage a conference that weekend; there's no way he can get away. He wouldn't even if he could. His work is more important than some wedding, he tells her.

Please make Ben go 2 Tiffany's wedding with me. xoE

You think Ben will listen to me? I did try. He harrumphed. xoM

Ben insensitive and harrumphing. Only old Pooka Sahibs are allowed to harrumph. xoE

Come on. It's only a wedding. Ben's got a conference 2 run. Aren't you being a bit pigheaded, yourself? xoM

Well snort on u both. xoE

So on a gorgeous Saturday afternoon, Emily holds her head high as she walks alone into the cathedral. The usher seats her on the bride's side, and already so many people are there that she finds herself at the back, on the side, next to an ancient couple with skin and necks like tortoises.

The wedding is magnificent. The minister's robes gleam, the organ swells, the soprano's pure voice brings tears to everyone's eyes. The flowers are amazing, huge fat roses of every hue perfuming the air. The flower girls are cherubic as they sprinkle rose petals on the carpet, the twelve bridesmaids are resplendent in sleek satin gowns of rosy pinks, corals, and lemon, and then Tiffany steps forth on the arm of her triumphant father in his tuxedo. Tiffany's gown is heavy, creamy satin, perfectly plain, to show off the lacework of enormous diamonds spreading across her bosom.

Emily shares a cab with the tortoises to The Plaza. They're both deaf, and mystified that 'such a comely young lady' is by herself. She assures them she's joining friends at the reception, but when she arrives, she finds to her complete dismay that her name card is set at a table with the elderly couple and other people she's never seen before.

Determined to be cheerful, she seats herself, smiling brightly, turning to chat with the tortoises. Another ancient pair dodders up to the table and creakily sits down.

She has been cast into the outer circle of hell.

A voice comes at her shoulder. 'Hello,' a man says. 'I believe this is my place.'

Emily breaks into a helpless instinctive smile of delight at the tall, handsome stranger. He's somewhat older, perhaps thirty, blond, hazel-eyed, slender in a perfectly tailored suit. He politely introduces himself to everyone: he's Cameron Chadwick. With flawless manners, he shakes hands with the tortoises, then takes his seat next to Emily.

In a low voice, he confesses, 'When I saw where my table was I thought I was being punished for some unspeakable offense I've forgotten about, but now that I see you're here, I believe I'm being rewarded for something fantastic I must have done.'

Emily can't help but smile. 'How do you know Tiffany?'

'I don't, actually. Her husband, Matt, is my friend. We sailed together at Harvard a few years ago.'

'You're a sailor?'

Cameron cocks his head. 'Is that a gleam I see in your eye?'

'It is.'

'Where do you sail?'

'Off Nantucket mostly. My family has a house there.'

'Ah, the warm waters of Nantucket. Our house is up where the people have fortitude. Camden, Maine.'

'Cold water. But I hear there are beautiful islands around there.'

'You're right. It's my idea of heaven. In the winter we go to Tortola, which is great in its own way.'

'I've never been to Tortola.'

'Did you say Tortola?' The older woman on Cameron's left taps his shoulder. 'We have a place there.'

'Really?' Cameron smoothly turns his interest to the older woman. 'What did you say your last name is?'

'Cummings.'

'You don't have a son named Andrew, by any chance?'

The woman laughs happily, putting her hand to her lips. 'Aren't you something. I have a *grandson* named Andrew.'

'I think I knew him at St George's.'

For a moment Emily allows herself to study Cameron as he chats with Mrs Cummings. God, he is gorgeous. Floppy white-blond hair, hazel eyes, wide shoulders, but relaxed with it, comfortable in his skin. Such a gentleman, too; she admires him for his kind interest in Mrs Cummings. She turns to the older fellow on her right and engages him in a rather one-sided conversation. He's liver-spotted, mostly deaf, but amiable, nodding agreement to everything she says.

Waiters glide silkily around the room, setting out the first course. Cameron turns back to Emily.

'Did you have to come far for the wedding?' he asks.

'Not really. I drove down from Amherst. I'm working on a master's in water ecology.'

'Damn, that's the topic of the day, isn't it. What's your focus?'

'Pesticides polluting the harbor waters.'

'You're speaking my language,' Cameron says. 'I'm sure our problems in Maine are different so far north from Nantucket, but with global warming, everything's changing.'

'Do you live in Maine?'

'Wish I did. No, I live here in Manhattan. Work on Wall Street. Boring money stuff.'

Emily doesn't think Cameron's boring at all. That he's handsome and also conscious of the environmental matters that

121

concern her just about knocks her sideways. Unfortunately their conversation is constantly interrupted by Mrs Cummings or by the waiters with caviar, duck, sirloin, and salad, each course accompanied by a different wine. Emily's almost giddy, and she's not sure whether it's from the alcohol or Cameron Chadwick's charm.

After the ritual of cake cutting and toasts, the band starts up and the lights dim. The music is geared toward the older crowd, but Emily's delighted when Cameron takes her hand in his and puts his other hand on her waist and guides her in a lazy two-step around the room. He smells *good,* not of cologne, but of an expensively and subtly scented soap. When his eyes meet hers, a surprising *zing* shoots all the way through her body. She stumbles. He tightens his hold on her and smiles, as if he understands just what happened between them.

When the party ends, she's surprised and a bit disappointed that he doesn't ask her to have a drink with him – then surprised and pleased when he asks her to join him the next day for lunch.

They meet at one at a little French restaurant on Fifth. Emily has almost forgotten how much she likes this: stepping out of the crowded street through a discreet door into an inner sanctum of gentle opulence, the maître d' bowing his head to her before leading her through the glittering room toward a table where a handsome man awaits.

He rises at her approach.

'Emily. How nice to see you again.' He's casual today, in chinos, a polo shirt, a blazer, no tie.

'Nice to see you, Cameron.'

After they receive their menus, he leans forward. 'I'm starving. I think I spent more time staring at you than eating my dinner last night.'

Emily blushes. She hasn't been complimented so directly for – well, she can't remember. That zing from yesterday is speckling into a force field around them, as if they're captured in a snow globe filled with sparkles.

She can hardly think a sober thought when she looks into his eyes, then down at the menu. 'What's good here, do you think?'

'I like it all, though I confess I've never tried the quiche.'

Emily laughs. 'I'll try it, then, and give you a report.'

'Wine?' Cameron asks. 'Champagne?'

'No, thank you,' Emily tells him. 'I had more than enough last night.'

Cameron orders sparkling water for them both. When the waiter leaves with their orders, he turns to Emily with an exaggerated sigh. 'Alone at last.'

'That *was* a crush last night, wasn't it?' She can't stop looking at the man. 'I'm surprised I haven't met you before.'

'I wish we *had* met before,' Cameron tells her, sounding as if he means it. 'But we probably run with different crowds. I'm not Matt's friend, I'm his older brother Bob's friend. Plus I spent a couple of years after college traveling.'

'Where?'

'Switzerland, mostly. Well, Europe. I like to hike and ski.'

Emily grins. 'And sail, too. Sounds like you enjoy yourself.'

'True. And why not? Life's short and we go around only once.' Catching a shadow falling over her face, he immediately asks, 'You don't agree?'

'I suppose I'm a bit more serious than you are, that's all. I do like having fun.' Quickly, she adds, 'I'm not a *grind*. I'm not a recluse. But I have some, well, I suppose they're vaguely scientific abilities, and I want to use them to do something to keep people from destroying the world.' Stopping as suddenly as she started, she closes her eyes in embarrassment. 'God. I sound like such a nerd.'

To her surprise, Cameron responds, 'True. It's tragic really, especially because you're so beautiful.'

This stops her in her tracks. Has anyone called her *beautiful* before? Ben has, of course. She takes a sip of sparkling water.

'Tell me,' Cameron invites, 'what inspired you to become serious?'

He's not making fun of her. He seems genuinely interested. Emily gives herself time to pause and gather her thoughts. 'Nantucket. The light. The air is exhilarating. But the sea, the harbor, the water . . . that's what fascinates me. Always has, ever since I was a little girl. As long as people don't keep spilling oil into the water . . .' She stops, not wanting to get political.

But Cameron's eyes are steady and warm. 'Beautiful and green, as well? You're too good to be true.'

'I'm real,' she insists, holding out her hand. 'Feel.'

Cameron draws his finger lightly from the tip of her ring finger up her palm to her wrist. 'Yes, you're real,' Cameron says. 'I am, too.' He draws the lightest of arabesques over the delicate skin of her wrist, his eyes instant messaging her about what he could do to other delicate skin on her body.

The waiter clears his throat. They pull apart. A pulse thrums in Emily's neck. She stares down at her lap, confused. What is she *doing*?

She's skirting dangerous territory. At university, the male grad students are either tech geeky and gauchely earnest, or arrogant earthy-crunchy pilled wool-sweater types, in a hurry to save the world and to be the first and most famous for doing so. This guy knows how to enjoy life.

The waiter puts a quiche and salad in front of Emily. Cameron has fried quail. For a few moments they focus on their food.

'You,' Emily begins, clearing her throat. 'Tell me more about you.'

'As I said, I work on Wall Street, for Endicott, Streeter, and Towle. I'm another ordinary broker, brash and greedy.'

She narrows her eyes in doubt. '*Are* you brash and greedy?'

'My family certainly is. I try not to let money control me, like it does everyone else in my family. Although, I have to add in the interest of honesty, I do like what money provides.'

'Where do you live?'

'Upper East Side. You?'

'In an apartment in Amherst right now. My parents live on East Eighty-sixth, and I stay with them when I'm in New York. They've recently bought a place in Sarasota, so Dad can play golf in the winter. And, of course, there's our Nantucket house. That's where I feel most at home.'

'Lucky you,' Cameron tells her.

They eat slowly, drawing out their meal, not wanting to leave the table, the restaurant, this shining spell, but finally Cameron pays the check, and all too soon they're outside in the bright autumn sunshine.

Cameron puts his hand on her waist, escorting her a few steps toward the street. 'Do you know where I'd like us to meet next?'

'Tell me.'

'Nantucket.'

Oh, dear. She shakes her head to clear it. Nantucket means Ben. Not a good idea for Cameron to go there. 'It's rather boring in the fall,' she says. 'No one's there except people who rave about cranberry bogs.'

'Hmm. Well, then, what's the best season?'

'Summer, definitely.'

'I guess I'll have to keep in your good graces until summer,' Cameron says, surprising her by pulling her to him and thoroughly kissing her right on the street in broad daylight. He bends her back slightly, one hand on her waist, one on her head, and she has the delicious sensation that they're posing for a photograph: Rich Young New Yorkers in Love. Oh, she's not in love with him, but she does admire the brightness of his hair and the lightness of his disposition.

When he ends the kiss, he steadies her with his hands on her shoulders and looks at her frankly. 'I don't want to wait until summer to see you again.'

Shaken, confused, Emily stalls. 'I've got to be up in Amherst all fall, working on my master's.'

'Could I come up some weekend to take you away for a day trip? Think how good a change of scenery would be for your mind.'

Emily hesitates, then decides. 'Yes. Yes, please come up. I'd enjoy that.' After all, she tells herself, it won't be a date. It will simply be – fun.

# Chapter Thirteen

A number of published writers – Maureen Orth, Charles Graeber, Maggie Shipstead, Julie Hecht – spend part of the summer on the island, and Maggie often helps Greta and Artie White cater their dinner or cocktail parties. Most of the people are relaxed and unpretentious, so they chat easily with Maggie as she passes through with trays of champagne or shrimp.

Maggie could ask one of the writers to help her find an agent. Actually, some of the guests *are* agents. First, she has to finish her book. Seldom nervous around the wealthy, she becomes slightly breathless at literary gatherings.

She's not ready yet, she reminds herself. She's started a novel, but she's trashed more than she's kept. She tries to write short stories, but that's a completely different genre, requiring different pacing and structure. She's young, and she needs to take time to find her voice.

This fall a kind of gentle melancholy accompanies her as she goes through her days. Summer friends leave, Maggie's got less work, more time to walk and write, and yet she feels lonely and dull without the summer people. She's not depressed, exactly, but at odds with herself. She misses Emily but, in a fussy snarky way, she wants Emily to miss her more and to do something about it. Email and texting isn't enough. Ben's doing fantastic work for a conservation group, but at home he drags himself around like a dying slug.

Several times Maggie's been at the Box or Lola's with friends and seen Shane across the room with Paulina, his stunningly gorgeous Bulgarian girlfriend. They're obviously in love. They can't stop touching each other. She doesn't want Shane, but she'd still like to have what they have.

That autumn in Amherst, Emily dives into her studies with a renewed determination. Her work is challenging, forcing her to think about real-world problems with mathematical solutions. She visits the island often, sometimes to see Maggie, sometimes for a formal coffee-and-friends-only meeting with Ben, but mostly to spend time by herself walking along Nantucket's different water-fronts: the harbor, the sound, the ocean, the ponds.

Some Sunday mornings she rises early to go birding with Ben. Afterward, they have breakfast with the rest of the group, and then she feels so close to Ben, so much a part of a community, a *tribe*. These days she and Ben don't discuss the future. And they don't have sex. They don't even kiss. He's punishing her, or that's what it feels like.

At school, she works incredibly hard. Often she bikes away from campus into town where she strolls around, getting a latte, sitting at a sidewalk café watching the world go by. She needs to rest her mind from her studies and her eyes from the computer screen.

And if she occasionally thinks about Cameron Chadwick, what's so wrong with that? She doesn't want to go to bed with him, she doesn't! Really. But it sort of perked her up, that weekend in New York, his frivolous flirting, his easy charm, so different from Ben, who often carries a heaviness in his stance. Cameron doesn't worry about the future of the world, she's sure. She's not betraying Ben by thinking about Cameron any more than thinking about Leonardo DiCaprio. It's not as if she's ever gone down to Wall Street to find Cameron in his office. She hasn't even looked up his phone number.

Yet somehow she's not surprised when she answers her cell one Friday evening to hear Cameron's mellow voice.

'Hey, Emily! It's supposed to be a glorious autumn day tomorrow. Why don't I drive you into Boston and we'll check out the Museum of Fine Arts?'

She's already told Ben she won't come to the island this weekend. He's involved with work, as always, so he won't be coming up here. It would feel *so* good to escape the drudgery of statistics, graphs, and multisyllabic scientific words. And if they go to the museum, that makes it an intellectual outing, not a *date*.

'I'd love to,' she tells Cameron.

If Ben asks her about her day, she'll be honest. She'll tell him she met Cameron at Tiffany's wedding, and he called on the spur of the moment. Not that Ben will call. They don't even email every day. For all she knows, he could be dating someone else. But no – Maggie would have told her. Should she tell Maggie she's got a date with Cameron? Well, Emily doesn't have to tell her everything!

And it's *lovely* to be driven along the winding roads beneath canopies of scarlet and gold leaves. The sun is warm, the air cool, the breeze playful as Cameron speeds his black Mercedes convertible along Route 2 toward Boston. He sets the volume high on his music, and a wild, thumping bass line combines with the light flaming through the maples to ignite an elation in Emily's heart. She's still young, and today the world is bandbox bright, blazing clean, sparkling as if diamonds were falling through the air!

How has she allowed herself to become so serious, so boring and *sober*? She's a healthy young woman, with a body as well as a mind. Lifting her face to the sun, she laughs.

When they reach Boston, Cameron slows the car down, but Emily's euphoria remains. As they drive through the city, people stare at them enviously from the sidewalks, and Emily revels in the illusion she and Cameron cast, of two blond, wealthy young people who possess the world.

With Cameron, she feels like she *could* possess the world. It's a seductive feeling.

They go up the wide marble stairs and into the long galleries of masterpieces, past Monets, Manets, Picassos, and Warhols, past Turners, Constables, and Holman Hunts, pausing to study paintings that catch their interest. Bucolic scenes of sheep and shepherds, battle scenes with fallen horses and spears, women with beauty marks on their cheeks and feathers in their hair, fat cupids lounging on clouds, display themselves along the walls. Emily's pleased that Cameron doesn't insist they discuss every painting and share opinions; rather than following him, she prefers wandering around the room until she finds something she likes. He doesn't talk too much, although he pauses before a glass case filled with antique sterling silver sugar bowls, tea canisters, and pots. 'Richard Shaw,' he murmurs to himself. Glancing at Emily, he adds, almost apologetically, 'We have some of his.'

'Mmm,' she murmurs, but she's impressed.

After a while, Cameron says, 'My eyes are crossing. Let's go to the gift shop. Maybe they'll have a book on Shaw.'

In the gift shop, Emily helps him search the books. Cameron chooses a hardback on British silver. As they wait in line before the cash register, Emily idly surveys the jewelry in the glass case.

'See anything you like?' Cameron asks.

Emily smiles. 'Of course.'

'What about this?' Cameron taps his finger on the glass, indicating a necklace of moonstones and amethysts. 'That would be amazing on you.'

'It's beautiful,' she agrees, and for a moment she wants it with all her heart. She wants it more than anything she's ever wanted in the world. Of course, she could always buy it . . .

'I'm going to buy it for you,' he says.

Pleased, she protests, 'Oh, Cameron, that's sweet, but no.'

'Miss?' Cameron aims his smile at a saleswoman. 'Could we have a look at this necklace, please?'

Unlocking the case, she carefully lifts the necklace up into the air.

'Turn around now. I'll fasten it on you and let's see how it looks,' Cameron instructs.

Emily can sense the other shoppers watching her as she holds up her blond hair while Cameron clinches the clasp, his cool fingers touching her warm neck. It's heavier than it looks. The stones are big.

She's flushed with excitement, so the necklace is as cool as chips of ice against her burning skin. The necklace lies across her collarbone, but Cameron reaches out and unbuttons the top two buttons of her sweater, folding them back.

Nancy Thayer

'There,' he says. 'Now I can see it. Wow, the stones make your eyes look as blue as the sky.'

'The necklace is five hundred and forty dollars,' the saleswoman tells him.

'We'll take it,' Cameron decides.

'Cameron—'

'Please,' he says. 'I'd like to buy this for you.' He smiles at her so innocently, how can she refuse? It would be insulting to.

'All right,' she agrees. 'Thank you.' Leaning forward, she kisses him lightly on the cheek. 'I really do love it. It's beautiful.'

'So are you,' he says.

His breath is sweet, his lips soft, his face saved from being angelic by the mischievous fire in his eyes. What deal has she sealed by accepting such a present? Would she be so very bad to have a fling with him? He's wildly sexy, but also incredibly nonchalant about it. As he walks her to the car, he speaks of his great-great-grandfather who started hauling coal in Pennsylvania as a boy and worked his way up to president of his own energy company. Cameron's grounded, realistic, nobody's fool.

The sun is sinking as they drive back to Amherst in the swift little car. Emily feels young, carefree, privileged – and why shouldn't she? Is it so wrong to enjoy herself? Is it so terrible to prefer a Mercedes and champagne to a coughing old Jeep and cheap beer? Isn't that the American dream? Shouldn't somebody live it?

They arrive back in Amherst in the early evening. Emily's hair is tousled from the wind, her face slightly wind- and sunburned. She's deliciously exhausted yet also exhilarated, as if she's been sailing all day. Stretching her arms, she murmurs, 'Mmm, I feel so happy.'

'Well, I'm not.'

Emily's surprised. 'What?'

'I'm *starving*. How about Italian food with lots of garlic and wine?'

Garlic, she thinks, not what one would eat with seduction in mind. On the other hand, red wine . . .

As they are ushered into Angelo's, Emily can feel the stones of her necklace glowing like captured comets, and she knows her wind-pinked cheeks make her blue eyes brighter. And beside her is this tall, blond, gorgeous man, with his confident stride, his impeccable clothes, his understated and elegant manners.

Antipasto is served first, followed by a rich, subtle, satisfying osso buco, perfect for the fall evening. Cameron quietly orders a red wine by name, and they eat, drink, and talk until their lips are glistening with olive oil. For dessert, they have cannoli and espresso, and then, sated, they lean back in their chairs. They sigh simultaneously, and laugh at themselves.

'Cameron, this has been a *perfect* day.'

He reaches over to take her hand. For a moment he simply holds it, running his thumb along her palm, as if reading her future. Then he glances up at her.

'Does that mean the day is over now?'

She knows what he's asking, and she knows what she would like to say. But there is the possibility that this man could be . . . more than a passing acquaintance . . . more than a casual affair. The thought nearly splits her heart in two. She *loves* Ben.

Yet here he is. Her body is begging.

'Cameron,' Emily replies gently, removing her hand, 'I'm involved with someone on Nantucket. We're in the middle of – I guess it's a kind of a negotiation, or confrontation. It's a mess, is what it is. I don't want to go to bed with you' – Emily's not sure she can explain – *'experimentally,'* she concludes.

'I wouldn't mind experimenting,' Cameron jests, immediately adding, 'Emily, it's fine.'

She relaxes, both relieved and disappointed.

'I'll drop you off and make the drive back to Manhattan,' he tells her. 'I have work to do tomorrow anyway.' He signals the waiter. Turning back to Emily, he says, 'But let me say this. I knew the moment I saw you, you were special. Damn, that's trite, but – we really do seem to get along, don't you think?'

Overwhelmed in the glow of his charm and gorgeous, aristo-cratic face, stunned by his ease and his serious admission of attraction to her, Emily can scarcely speak. You don't have to have sex with another man to be unfaithful, she thinks. She could never, ever, tell Ben about this day. She manages to agree, 'We do have a good time.'

'Good. I'll leave it with you, then. If you want to see me, well, give me a call.'

Cameron drives her to her apartment in an old Victorian house in Amherst and walks her to the door. In the shadows of the streetlights, he takes her in his arms and pulls her to him. He smooths back her hair from her face. He bends down, and with lips silky with wine, he kisses her for a long time. Her body rises up to him like a flower to the sun.

'Thank you for today,' he says. 'I hope you'll call me.'

Emily can't speak. Her throat is tight with tears, her heart thudding with a guilty, insubordinate desire. But then she says good night, and goes inside, alone.

# Part Four
# Siren Song

# Chapter Fourteen

Emily steps off the little nine-seater plane that jostled her over the swollen gray waters of Nantucket Sound from Hyannis to Nantucket. She takes a deep breath. She's going to spend this special Christmas Stroll weekend entirely with Maggie. Maggie has no idea that right now Emily has no desire to see Ben.

'Emily!' The moment Emily sets foot in the airport terminal, Maggie's there in a flurry of black curls and emotion, squeezing Emily in a tight hug, glowing like the sun. 'You're here, you're really here, and Ben doesn't get you for one hour this weekend. You're all mine!'

Emily can't help but laugh. Maggie's good mood is contagious. She allows herself to be whisked out of the airport and into Maggie's Bronco.

'*Everyone* wants to see you. I've got so much planned for us. We're having dinner at Pazzo tonight with Kerrie, Delphine, and Robin. Tomorrow we'll do the Stroll, watch Santa arrive by Coast Guard, go shopping at the craft fair – fabulous stuff, I can't wait – and hear Robin Knox-Johnston read "A Child's Christmas in Wales" at the library. Then – oh, my God, this is so exciting – you and I are going to get glammed up and attend a cocktail party thrown by Stevenson Braig, the author who wrote the true crime book? I met him when I worked a cocktail party and Marilyn O'Brien told him I write, too, as if I really do, which I guess I do, and he's ancient, but incredibly nice and he knows *everyone* . . .'

Maggie's cheerful chatter passes over Emily like smoke from incense. Her spirits lift, her heart lightens. They agreed that this weekend they would focus only on the positive. They would be *young,* forget about men and marriage and all that, and have fun, two girlfriends at the holiday season.

Friday night they party with friends, eating, talking, laughing, until they fall into bed at Clarice's, thoroughly hoarse and exhausted. The next day at the craft fair, they buy each other matching cashmere scarves, Nantucket sister scarves, they say, only half-kidding. The weather is chilly, crisp enough to make them need their coats as they stroll the cobblestone streets, petting pooches decked out in antlers or wreaths, listening to the Victorian singers, lunching in the tent on hot dogs and cold beer. At the writer's cocktail party, they flirt with everyone, munch on shrimp, scallops, and lobster, drink champagne, and signal each other with their eyes when they spot huge ruby necklaces, emerald rings, diamond Christmas tree pins. It really is a *scene* here, and when Emily meets people, she listens carefully and files their names into her mind for the future when she'll work at the science museum and be involved in fund-raisers.

Ben doesn't know Emily's on the island. If she runs into him, she'll act terribly casual, and Maggie will be her buffer. But Emily doesn't run into him.

After the party, she and Maggie sit up in Clarice's living room by the fire, in their flannel pajamas, drinking hot chocolate and eating sugar cookies, talking until three in the morning.

It almost kills Emily not to mention Cameron. She can't help feeling like a weasel, keeping such an important secret from her oldest best friend, but they have agreed not to talk about men this weekend . . . And Emily hasn't slept with Cameron. She has gone out with him several times, to events she totally enjoyed, which Ben would have no interest in. The Metropolitan Opera. An art opening. A couple of dinners at new fusion restaurants. It's such a luxury to have these provocative hours out in the city, to steal away from her desk, her computer, her texts, notes, and schoolwork, to toss off her sweatshirt and jeans and slip into a little black dress and high heels. Cameron's a charming date, attentive but never possessive. A gentleman. He hasn't tried to seduce her into bed again. But he's definitely biding his time.

Will there be a time? Emily doesn't know. She knows Maggie has her own concerns. Maggie would like to be in love. She would like to be *with* someone. Maggie's worried about the island, too, the way it's changing in so many ways.

On Sunday morning, when Maggie drives Emily back to the airport, they're both tired and sleep-deprived.

'At least we're not hungover,' Maggie murmurs from behind the steering wheel.

'Right.' Emily nods. 'A sure sign of adulthood.'

'Emily, I know I wasn't going to bring Ben up, but . . . never mind. I'll phrase it another way. Are you coming here for Christmas?'

Emily's glad Maggie's asked this now, when it's almost time for her to leave the island. 'I'm going to spend Christmas Day with my parents in New York. Plus, I've got so much work to do, Maggie.'

'I thought the semester was over.'

'It doesn't work that way when you're a graduate student with a long-term project. I've got tons of research to do on water quality, reports to compile—'

Maggie interrupts. 'Poor you.'

'No, it's fine. My parents will do the tree, the big dinner, the whole celebration bit and I'll be free to work. It's all for a good cause, remember? When I finally return here, I'll have gained some expertise and some authority.'

'It's only another year, right?'

'Right.'

Maggie pulls the Bronco into the parking lot they were in just only two days before. Switching off the ignition, she turns to face Emily. 'I miss you. Ben misses you.'

'I miss you and Ben.' Emily dips her face down as she adjusts her cashmere scarf around her neck.

'I wish you lived here,' Maggie says.

'I will.' Emily reaches out to hug Maggie, this spontaneous, ebullient, warm, loving friend, her Nantucket sister. 'I promise.'

'How was your trip to Nantucket?' Cameron asks.

Emily runs her finger around her wineglass. They're tucked away in a quiet corner of a noisy Italian restaurant on Fifty-fifth Street.

It's Sunday evening. Emily phoned Cameron from the taxi coming in from JFK. He asked her to dinner, and she agreed to meet him. She feels guilty, of course, and slightly embarrassed to seem so keen to see him – but she also feels excited and wants to go.

*Slow down,* she advises herself. *Be truthful.* 'Exactly what I needed,' Emily tells him. 'I've tried to explain this to my parents, but they don't *appreciate* it, the connection I feel to the island. It was wonderful seeing Maggie again, and the Stroll is always a blast, but it's the *island* that lights me up. The way it's always the same yet always different. The colors on the water in the harbor – more shades of blue than there are names. The sense of safety, of being home, the way the boats blow their horns when they leave or arrive, the lights flashing from the lighthouses . . . I can't explain it.'

'I'm actually going to spend New Year's Eve on Nantucket,' Cameron tells her.

'You *are?*' Emotions shower down through Emily: surprise, jealousy, anxiety – not good emotions, and she can't decide whether she doesn't want Cameron on *her* island or whether she's worried that he'll be with another woman.

'Mmm.' Cameron swallows a bit of his Bloody Mary. 'Clementine Melrose invited me.'

'Clementine Melrose. I know Clementine.' Emily becomes terribly interested in her tilapia. Clementine is her age, spends half her year in Paris, is *très* petite and while she's not beautiful, she's chic and sexy.

'We've been friends for a long time,' Cameron says slowly. 'Clementine's broken up with her boyfriend and asked me to come so she won't be alone.'

'Nice of you.' Emily can't keep the wry tone from her voice.

Cameron leans forward. 'I didn't think you'd mind. Won't you be on Nantucket yourself, with Ben?'

141

Emily puts down her fork. She smooths the linen napkin in her lap. 'I don't think so, Cameron . . . Ben and I haven't been talking much recently. I think it's possible that Ben and I are over. We are so different . . .' As always, guilt flushes through her when she speaks about Ben to Cameron. 'I'll be here for Christmas with my parents. I've been invited to a bunch of parties on New Year's Eve, so I'll stay in Manhattan.' Looking up, she meets Cameron's eyes. He's watching her carefully, intent on her words.

'Do you mind if I go to Nantucket?' Cameron asks.

She clears her throat, then, in a low voice, she admits, 'You know, I think I do.'

Cameron leans back in his chair with a huge grin on his face. 'Good.' He lifts his water glass as if making a triumphant toast. 'I would change my plans, but Clementine's father is one of my clients, and I try to keep everyone who invests with me happy.'

'I understand,' Emily says, and she does.

After dinner, without discussing it, they slowly wander over to his apartment on East Sixty-third. The doorman's face remains stony with dignity as he bids them good evening, as if Emily isn't yet another of Cameron's conquests being led to the kill.

Emily's nervous. As they enter Cameron's apartment, she focuses on the décor, a masculine mixture of old and new: fat leather sofa, chrome lamp, enormous wide screen television, antique Persian rug on the living room floor.

'Would you like some wine?'

'Sorry, what?' Emily blushes, knowing she's been caught off guard.

Cameron slides her cashmere coat off her shoulders and tosses it casually onto the sofa. 'I don't think I want any more wine,' she says. 'I want to be totally present.' Taking her face in his hands, he kisses her. His kiss is slow and gentle. She wraps her arms around him. He slides his hands down her back, pressing her body against his. His kiss becomes more passionate, and he breaks away from her only long enough to capture her wrist and tug her after him into his bedroom. One sweep of his arm, and his down comforter falls away from the bed. They fall onto it, still clothed, too excited to stop.

She wants him as much as she's wanted anything, with an urgency she can't repress. She tugs up her skirt, kicks off her shoes, wrestles with her underwear. When he enters her, it's so fiercely good, Emily bites her lip.

# Chapter Fifteen

Two days after Christmas, Greta White phones Maggie.

'Honey, I'm cooking a zillion-course fancy meal on New Year's Eve for a party out at Clementine Melrose's in 'Sconset and my assistant, Diane, had a death in the family and had to leave for a week and I'm in desperate need of help. Can you work for me?'

'Clementine Melrose.' Maggie hesitates. She knows who Clementine is, stinking rich, pencil thin, and haughty. 'Is it going to be terribly formal?'

'Probably. I'll pay you thirty dollars an hour, plus they should tip us nicely, seeing as it's New Year's Eve.'

'I'll do it,' Maggie decides.

'God bless you,' Greta says.


At six-thirty on New Year's Eve, Maggie drives her clunking old Bronco out to Baxter Road. The big blue van with 'Greta's Gourmet' painted on the side is parked about four houses away from the Melrose house, because in the Melrose driveway are parked two Range Rovers and a Mercedes four-wheel drive.

Maggie parks behind Greta's van and steps out into the crisp night. As she walks toward the house, she hears the great black ocean rolling and turning in its winter sleep.

Maggie finds the side entrance to the garage and the door leading into the kitchen. Greta and Artie are already there, having arrived earlier to set up the bar, arrange the table, and organize the kitchen.

'Let me look at you,' Greta tells Maggie after she's hung her coat in the back hall.

Greta's completely in white, white shirt and slacks, white apron, white sneakers, and her short, practical white hair's tucked under a white chef's cloche. She runs a critical eye up and down Maggie and pronounces, 'Perfect. I hope you wore comfortable shoes.'

Maggie's glad Greta approves. She spent some of her hard-earned money on this ensemble, a plain black skirt with a discreet slit up one side, and a simple white shirt of cotton and Lycra, which fits her like a glove and looks as expensive as it was, one hundred dollars, half price at Murray's Toggery. Her mother's pearls lie cool against her neck and chest, they'll show only when she bends forward. Her curly black hair is tamed tonight, caught up in a French twist with a few strands spiraling down each side of her face.

She's not wearing comfortable shoes at all – let Greta, who's old and married, wear comfortable shoes. Maggie's wearing strappy black evening sandals that make her legs look long and her figure sleek. Well, as sleek as someone with her curves can look.

It's only a little after seven. Everyone's upstairs dressing for the evening.

Greta shows Maggie where she'll be serving.

It's a wonderful house. The living room and dining room stretch along the ocean side, with great expanses of plate-glass windows framing the view. Both rooms have fireplaces with flames flickering, casting a golden glow into the air, and on the mantels and window-sills and tables and along the mahogany sideboard, tall tapers wait to be lighted to cast their soft illumination over the guests. Sofas, armchairs, windows, all are upholstered in flowery summer pastels, the material slightly faded and worn, subtly announcing: You can relax here, settle back, put your feet up, enjoy life. Multicolored banners reading: HAPPY NEW YEAR! are draped over mirrors and paintings. Streamers and helium-filled balloons hang in the air like enchanted trees.

Artie has set up the bar by the living room window overlooking the front yard. Glasses and bottles glitter there, and dishes of cashews and olives.

Maggie helps Greta set the dining room table. The heavy white cloth has already been spread down the length of the table, and cut glass bowls of spring flowers – irises, roses, daffodils, tulips, a fortune of flowers – decorate the table, alternating with white-and rose-colored candles. The women lay out the heavy silver, fold the thick white napkins, place the water glasses and wine-glasses in perfect alignment with the rest of the table setting.

'We won't light the candles until they're coming in for dinner,' Greta tells Maggie.

Back in the kitchen, Maggie washes lettuce, spins it dry, tosses it into a large wooden bowl to wait for the dressing, and covers it with a damp paper towel. She's intent on her task – she doesn't want to disappoint Greta – so she doesn't hear the door from the dining room open.

146

'Hi, Greta,' a woman says, and Maggie turns to see Clementine Melrose standing there.

Clementine comes by her sophistication naturally. Her father, Dr Melrose, is a dapper, almost antique little man, a devout Francophile who speaks with a French accent because he and his family spend half of their year in France. Mrs Melrose has the tendon-strung scrawniness of a chicken's foot, but Clementine looks drop-dead chic. Clementine's only five feet tall, and tonight she looks like she weighs less than the gold jewelry hanging around her neck. Her dark hair, sliced in an asymmetrical cut, is set off by a jagged long-sleeved crimson crinkle of sheer chiffon that screams *Paris.*

Clementine's dark eyes whip over Maggie with the same frank assessing stare she gives the canapés waiting on their silver tray. 'Maggie, right?' She says the name as a challenge. They've run into each other briefly over the years, and Maggie's got a suspicion from the way Clementine's eyes narrow that she remembers the night at the art gallery four years ago when Clementine flirted with Shane only to have Maggie sidle up and steal him away.

'Right. Hello, Clementine.'

Clementine sniffs. She addresses her remarks to Greta. 'Everyone will be down in a few minutes. Wait until, oh, let's say eight-fifteen before sending Maggie around with the caviar and oysters, okay? And be sure, Maggie' – Clementine flicks a look her way – 'to carry napkins with you. No one wants sauce or oil on her dress.'

Maggie considers curtsying and saying 'Yes, Your Highness,' but restrains herself to a simple 'Of course,' which Clementine doesn't notice, because she's already on her way out of the kitchen.

From the front hall, a grandfather clock strikes eight mellow notes, and soon after that footsteps sound on the front stairs.

Maggie and Greta hurry. Greta broils the marinated oysters, Maggie puts the doilies on the silver platters, and places the cocktail napkins close to hand.

At eight-fifteen, Maggie slides through the door to the dining room, carrying a platter of succulent oysters.

The living room is crowded with people. Artie, wearing a tux, stands behind the bar looking blank-faced, an automaton waiting for his orders. Maggie composes her face into a similar pleasant mask that signals: *I am here only to serve. I cannot hear. I cannot see. I cannot judge.* Maggie passes through the room, offering the platter and a napkin to each guest, saying nothing – those were her instructions, not to speak, unless a guest asks a question.

Six women and six men, just her age, laugh and chatter and collect their drinks at the bar. The men are all in formal wear, their shoulders are broad beneath their jackets' black fabric. The women wear dresses in splendid colors: crimson, daffodil, azure, apricot. They look like goddesses.

Maggie presents her tray to a man whose blond hair flops charmingly into his hazel eyes.

'Thank you,' he says to Maggie.

She nods politely without speaking and starts to move on, but he lightly touches her arm. 'Excuse me, but have we met?'

'I don't think so,' she tells him, thinking she would definitely remember.

'Well, then, hello. I'm Cameron Chadwick.'

She's not sure what to do. At other island parties she's worked, lines blur, but here at Clementine's, she's uncomfortable talking to a guest. 'I'm Maggie McIntyre.'

He's holding her with his eyes. 'Do you live on the island?'

'I do. My family has a house on the Polpis Harbor—'

'Maggie,' Clementine snaps, wrenching Maggie's attention away from the man. 'I'll take one.'

Maggie turns to offer Clementine a canapé.

Clementine takes Cameron's arm with a possessive grasp. 'Let me introduce you to the other guests so you have someone to talk to.' She steers Cameron away.

Maggie makes the rounds with her tray. As she does, she feels Cameron's eyes on her. When she pushes the door into the kitchen, she looks over her shoulder. He's still watching her. And smiling.

In the kitchen, Greta says, 'Honey! You're as red as a lobster. Is it too hot in there? Should we turn down the thermostat?'

'I'm fine,' Maggie says.

'Yes, well, but we don't want the guests dropping dead from heat exhaustion!'

'No, it's fine,' Maggie insists. But her hands are shaking.


Dinner is served at nine. By now the guests are well lubricated with champagne, everyone talks and laughs, everyone is having a wonderful time.

Maggie moves around the table like a ghost, setting the first course, sliced duck breast in Grand Marnier and hot brown peasant bread and fresh unsalted butter before them. She retreats to the kitchen to help Greta lift the broiled swordfish steaks and beef filets onto a platter, peeks through the door – they've finished the duck – and hurries out to remove the plates. She removes, as she was taught, from the left, and when she carries the platter of meat around, she serves from the right. She sets the platter of meat on the sideboard, covers it with a silver lid, steps into the kitchen to take the bowl of roast vegetables from Greta while

Artie follows her with a dish of mashed potatoes – Greta and Clementine agreed that men love mashed potatoes. Artie glides around the room filling the glasses with red and white wine, while Maggie uses silver tongs to distribute piping hot rolls to the bread plate above the forks.

The conversation – vivid, colorful, fanned with laughter – darts around the table like hummingbirds. Clementine's guests exchange tales of friends who got in trouble for stupid pranks in college, and everyone's laughing. Maggie remains as remote and expressionless as a mannequin although she can't help noticing that Cameron's eyes are on her every time she's across the table from him, bending down to offer another steak of swordfish or filet mignon.

Most of the guests are sailors, although some prefer sport fishing. They compare locations where they've sailed in all corners of the world, two of the men becoming heated as they argue over the waters off Australia and those off California.

'Don't you have a rather famous race here?' Cameron asks. 'With a cup . . .'

'Oh, yeah, oh, yeah,' a man, thick-tongued from too much liquor, agrees. 'It's the, the, the . . .'

'God, who *knows*,' Clementine cackles from the head of the table. 'So many races . . .' She's had, perhaps, too much to drink.

'It's almost on the tip of my tongue,' a woman in black silk says, tapping her lip.

When no one else names the race, Maggie, standing at attention near the sideboard, provides it: 'The Opera House Cup.'

'Right! Right! I was just going to say that!' the drunk bellows.

*'Waitress.'* Clementine's voice is as heavy as lead. 'We're ready for our salads.'

Flushing, Maggie begins to clear the table of the dinner plates. Clementine knows her name but wanted to put Maggie in her place, and Maggie feels strongly that Clementine succeeded. Maggie can't wait for this evening to end.

As the partygoers bend to their salads, Maggie and Artie clear the buffet of the heavy serving dishes. Maggie slips back into the kitchen to help Greta load the dishwasher and deal with leftovers. Then it's time to clear. Maggie follows Artie back out into the dining room. They swoop around the table, silently removing the salad plates. Artie pours more champagne, while Maggie returns to the kitchen for the final course.

From the oven, Greta takes an enormous, glorious Baked Alaska, its swirls and tips of meringue browned to a delicate caramel. With delicate concentration, Greta and Maggie maneuver the concoction from its baking tray to the silver platter. This is no ordinary dessert. The cake base is Greta's own recipe, rich, dark chocolate laden with liqueur. Peaked and glossy, it's a work of art.

Artie twists the top of a bottle of Courvoisier and pours it over the golden dome. Greta lights a match and touches the brandy floating in the platter, and the dessert ignites.

'Is that too heavy for you?' Artie asks as Maggie lifts it in both hands. 'Would you like me to carry it?'

'I'm fine.'

Artie holds the door wide, and with ceremonial solemnity, Maggie goes through, carrying the flaming Baked Alaska before her like a servant making an offering to a monarch.

Around the table, all twelve people are flushed from alcohol and food. At the sight of the blazing dessert, they stir, becoming more animated, exclaiming, turning toward her, pushing their chairs back expectantly.

As she carries in the Baked Alaska, Maggie's aware of all the eyes at the table on her. She forces back a smug smile. The radiance of the flames makes her face glow, she knows from having watched others carry in these desserts. She feels more like a queen than a waitress, more like a goddess presenting an offering, and perhaps she strolls a bit more slowly, making her walk a bit sensual, as she approaches Clementine.

'Give it to me!' Clearly exasperated with Maggie capturing the spotlight, Clementine stands up, reaches out, and jerks the fiery platter out of Maggie's hands with such force that Maggie, on her sexy stilettos, falls backward with a cry.

She lands in Cameron Chadwick's lap.

Her arms flail as she tries to regain her balance. Cameron brings his own powerful right arm behind her back to stabilize her. With his help, she struggles to sit up, wrapping her arms around his shoulders briefly for support.

For a moment, she faces him, her white-shirt-clad breasts brushing the elegant black and white of his tuxedo shirt and jacket. For a moment, her dark blue eyes meet his hazel ones. He puts his hands on her waist to steady her. Maggie knows her cheeks are blushing from the heat between them.

'Oh,' she says, wriggling to get her feet firmly planted on the floor. 'I'm so sorry.'

Cameron Chadwick says quietly, looking at her, 'I'm not.'

There's no graceful way to maneuver off a man's lap at a dinner table, especially when the man's hands are cupping her waist. Maggie thinks she might burst into flame herself.

'You clumsy idiot!' Clementine scolds. She plunks the Baked Alaska down on the table, her eyes shooting spikes at Maggie, so irritated at having such disgraceful behavior by the help at her dinner party that she doesn't notice that the hem of her gauzy sleeve has swept through the flames and caught fire.

'Clementine!' one of the women screams.

Maggie, terrified for the hostess, seizes a glass of water and throws it at Clementine's arm, soaking the material and extinguishing the fire.

Clementine shrieks. 'Are you insane?'

Chaos erupts. Artie and Greta race from the kitchen to see what has gone wrong. Two of the male guests are blowing on the flames of the Baked Alaska, while one of the women has left the table to find her cell phone to snap photos.

'It's all right,' Artie tells the group. 'The flames will burn down by themselves. Look. They're going out.'

'She set me on fire!' Clementine cries, pointing at Maggie.

Maggie, at last stable on both feet, draws herself up straight and tall. 'No, you did that. I put the fire out.'

'She's right, you know,' Cameron tells Clementine.

'Well, you shouldn't have served a flaming dessert,' Clementine snaps, on the verge of tears.

'It was what you asked for,' Maggie reminds Clementine, who's trembling with anger.

'Here now,' Greta says calmly. 'Everything is quite all right. Maggie, please return to the kitchen. You have all those dishes to do.'

Maggie's jaw falls open at this – Greta has never spoken to her this way, as if she were a foolish servant. In the next instant she understands the wisdom of Greta's words; it's a way of Greta taking charge, a way for Greta to punish Maggie for whatever it is Clementine thinks Maggie has done, so that Clementine will be appeased.

Nancy Thayer

Nevertheless, it hurts her dignity. Maggie stalks off toward the kitchen, tears of humiliation in her eyes. Behind her, she hears Greta helping Clementine assess the damage to her garment while Artie takes charge of the dessert, cutting it, setting it onto the antique china plates, spooning brandy over it. In the kitchen, Maggie leans against the wall, her head buzzing and her heart sinking into her stomach. She's more upset than she would normally be, because of that handsome Chadwick man. *Why* did she have to land in his lap?

Why had that sensation of desire passed between them?

Shaking her head brusquely to whisk off her thoughts, Maggie strides to the sink and begins to do the dishes.

Later, the party moves back into the living room to engage in an uproarious game of charades that has them staggering, collapsing with laughter. Maggie sets out bowls of nuts, cookies, and macaroons, then discreetly clears the dining room table. Artie brings out several bottles of champagne, uncorked and ready in deep cushions of ice in buckets and places them on various tables, ready to pour.

The clock strikes twelve.

Greta and Artie exchange quick kisses. Immediately, kindly, they wish Maggie, 'Happy New Year.'

'Happy New Year,' Maggie replies.

'Let's each have a glass of champagne.' Artie finds three clean flutes, pours, and hands them around. 'Here's to a prosperous new year.'

They clink glasses together and drink. The champagne is delicious. Maggie leans against the kitchen counter, relaxing, savoring the liquid sliding down her throat. She closes her eyes, resting.

'Aside from the fireworks, it went well, don't you think?' Greta

154

asks. Her face is shiny with perspiration, and her short white hair lies limp against her skull.

'Your food certainly disappeared,' Maggie says. 'Clean plates all around.'

'Yes,' Artie agrees. 'Probably one of your best efforts, Greta.'

Greta pinkens with pleasure. 'Not many scraps, that's true, and very little to pack up and take home. Maggie, would you like any of the salad? There's plenty of that left.'

'Sure. I'll put some in a plastic bag.'

The kitchen door flies open and in strolls Cameron. He's undone his black bow tie, which hangs on either side of his shirt collar, which he's opened as well. His blond hair sticks out in all directions, as if he's been rubbing it with a balloon.

'Hello, everyone.' His smile is debonair, charming. 'That was a magnificent meal. I'd love to meet the chef.'

Blushing, Greta says, 'I'm Greta White.'

'Cameron Chadwick.' He shakes her outstretched hand. 'I don't know when I've enjoyed a meal more.'

Greta's so pleased she practically curtsies. 'Oh, well, thank you.'

Cameron turns to Artie. 'And thank you, sir, for being such a splendid bartender. I'm happy to report that you've gotten all of us most thoroughly plastered. As we should be on New Year's Eve.'

'You're welcome,' Artie says.

Maggie stands paralyzed, captured in his courtly spell.

'I'd like to ask a favor, if I may.' He steps closer to Maggie. 'I need a little walk in the cool air. Could I appeal to your kindness and ask you to join me?'

# Chapter Sixteen

Maggie's dumbfounded, and so are the Whites. This man actually glows, as the strong kitchen light hits his blond hair, and the gold and diamond studs in his pleated snowy white shirt. He looks like one of the natural aristocrats of the world, and Maggie feels, in comparison, clumsy, a peasant.

Awkwardly, she chokes out an excuse. 'I need to help Greta—'

'Nonsense!' Greta cuts in, her eyes bulging. 'We're almost through here, Maggie. You go on and have a nice little walk, you deserve it.'

Artie's head bobs enthusiastically. 'We've got everything under control.'

'But—' Maggie can hardly breathe. 'Your friends—'

'They won't miss me,' Cameron assures her. 'They're embroiled in a battle of charades.'

Maggie's forgotten how to move. She stutters, 'It's cold out – your coat—'

Greta volunteers, 'The Melroses always keep a few coats hanging on the hooks in the back hall by the door to the garage.'

'There you are, then,' Cameron says.

Maggie finds an ancient good black wool dress coat. Cameron puts on an L.L.Bean canvas hunting jacket in loden green. He turns up the corduroy collar and, finding a navy blue Red Sox baseball cap, slips that over his pale hair. He opens a door and they go out to the brick patio off the kitchen.

The air is cold but almost eerily calm, not a breath of wind. The grass, nearly black in the moonlight, lies as still as a quilt.

'Which way do we go to get down to the ocean?' Cameron inquires. 'I realize that if I walked straight out from the house I'd fall off the edge and roll down the bluff. Even drunk, I'd rather not do that.'

'There's a walk behind all the houses along here. It leads to a brick sidewalk down to Codfish Park, and then it's only a short distance to the water.'

She sets off walking over the cold grass toward the edge of the bluff, purposely skirting the long rectangle of light falling onto the lawn from the living room so no one in the party will see them.

'Slow down!' Cameron slips his arm through hers, pulling her close. 'You might be able to see in the dark, but I sure can't.'

'Sorry. I know this area by heart.' His slender body moving next to her sends her heart tripping in her chest.

'You do, do you? How so?' Cameron's voice is calm, conversational.

As they walk, the Melroses' huge house seems to retreat into the distance on a sea of darkness. The seductive whispering of the waves sounds stronger here on the edge of the cliff.

'I grew up on the island,' Maggie tells him. She wishes she'd worn a hat. The moist wind teases strands of her hair out of the chignon, corkscrewing them into spirals that dance around her face.

'You did?' He sounds as fascinated and curious as if she'd said she grew up on another planet. 'Did you go to school here? I can imagine you walking barefoot on the beach, your beautiful crazy hair blowing every which way.'

'Careful here.' She sounds more stern than she means to, but his compliment flusters her. His *presence* flusters her. 'It's odd about the public footpath. It runs along the very edge of the land from the village of 'Sconset out to the Sankaty lighthouse. Or it did, until several storms tore off great hunks of the cliff.' She's so nervous, she's babbling. 'This is on the side of the island that isn't supposed to erode, but Mother Nature changed her mind, I guess. So the footpath has been moving closer and closer to the houses.'

'The yards are huge,' Cameron observes, 'but is the footpath open in the summer when people are living in their homes?'

'Yes, legally it's still open then. I always hate to use it, though. It seems intrusive to walk through someone's yard when they're having a quiet game of croquet or a cookout. But a lot of people like to walk here in the summer for precisely that reason, to catch a glimpse of the kind of people who can afford to pay millions for a house they'll use only a few weeks of the year.'

'So is one of these bluff houses yours?'

Maggie bursts out laughing.

'What's so funny?'

'Would I be serving dinner on New Year's Eve if my family owned a multimillion-dollar house?'

'Well, I don't know,' Cameron replies. 'Maybe. I mean, why not help a friend?'

158

The cliff falls off sharply, a tangle of wild roses and beach grass holding the dirt to the cliff face. In the dark it would be easy to step too close to the edge.

'Watch out,' Maggie warns. 'One more yard and we'll be okay.' With a sigh, she admits, 'I did live in 'Sconset for a while, but not up here with an ocean view.'

'Show me.'

She doesn't speak until they've come off the dirt footpath and onto a narrow lane between small, picturesque cottages, all of their windows dark. 'During the last century, the Nantucket fishing families used to come out here to fish for cod. They built these little shelters low to the ground so they could throw their nets over the roofs to mend them. Now, of course, they're all summer homes.' She pauses. 'You should see these in the summer. Instead of nets, millions of tiny pink roses climb all over the roofs. This is my favorite place, with the little patio. There's always an orange tabby curled up on one of the benches.'

'So where's your house?' Cameron persists.

'We're almost there.'

They walk down the brick sidewalk from Front Street to Codfish Lane. 'This is steep enough to sled on!' Cameron says, clutching Maggie close to his side.

At the bottom of the hill, Maggie turns left, leading him back along the narrow lane. On one side the bluff rises steeply. 'In the summer, this is covered with Queen Anne's lace and all kinds of wildflowers.'

On the other side of the lane lie ten modest cottages, closed up and tucked away for the winter. Maggie stops in front of one.

'This is it.'

'Huh. It's small.'

'Yes. And you can't see the charm of it in the winter. My mom always had window boxes full of flowers, and roses climbing over the roof. She was divorced, and my father disappeared, and so the three of us, Mom, and me, and my brother, Ben, lived here until I was eleven. Then she married Thaddeus Ramsdale, and we all moved to his place on the Polpis Road.'

'Thaddeus Ramsdale. That's quite a moniker.'

'True. He lives up to it.'

Arm in arm they pass down the lane, turn a corner, walk one short block, and there, on the other side of the street, lies the beach, stretching out to the surging water. Their footsteps make crunching noises as they tramp over the frozen sand. Moonlight illuminates the white curls of foam edging each wave and riding the crest of the lazy, leaden ones rolling in behind. Somewhere in the distance, the darkness of ocean blurs with the darkness of sky.

Cameron bends down, stretches his fingertips out, and dips his hand in the ocean. 'As cold as our water in Maine.'

'You're from Maine?' Not certain what this walk is really about, Maggie hasn't wanted to pry.

'My family has a home in Camden. But I live in Manhattan.' Shaking cold beads of water off his hand, he dries it on the outside of his coat. He's so close to her she can see his eyes, even in the dim light. He looks earnest, and the attraction between them is so strong she thinks it could alter the rise and fall of the waves.

'You're Clementine's date, right?'

'I'm Clementine's *friend*.'

Sternly, she says, 'We should go back. They'll wonder where you are.'

They tread over the beach, their feet sinking in the sand, until they come to the solid level of the street.

'I'm here tonight,' Cameron continues, as if they've been

discussing this without interruption, 'because Clementine broke up with her latest boyfriend and needed a date for the evening. I've known Clementine since preschool. Our mothers are friends.'

He's from another world, Maggie tells herself. She walks faster. They reach the top of the hill and find their way along the unlighted lane between the cottages.

'I was available for this party because I'm not attached to anyone presently,' Cameron clarifies. 'I work on Wall Street, for a brokerage firm. I shout into phones and squint at computers all day, have too many scotches with the guys after work, and collapse with Chinese takeout at night. I was more than ready to come to the island for some fresh air.'

'I hope you enjoyed yourself,' Maggie says formally.

Cameron catches her hand. 'I'm enjoying myself right now.'

Maggie starts to pull away.

'Stop. Please.'

She stops. They stand on the cliff, facing each other, the winter wind buffeting them, their eyes catching moonlight.

Cameron says, 'May I ask you a personal question?'

Warily, she answers, 'Sure.'

'Do you have a boyfriend?'

She can hardly breathe. 'No.'

He gazes at her face. 'How is that possible?'

Proudly, Maggie lifts her chin. 'I work very hard. When I don't work, I read. I don't have time for men.'

His eyes meet hers. His breath puffs into the air between them, so near she can smell liquor. 'I wonder whether you could ever make time for me?'

*This can't be real*, Maggie tells herself. Carelessly, she says, 'I'm here now, aren't I?'

Leaning down, he brings his mouth to hers. Their lips are cold from the night air, and then warm. They press against one another, but their coats are bulky and cumbersome between them.

Maggie draws away. 'I have to go back to the house.' She walks so quickly she's almost running.

Cameron follows without speaking. All along the bluff path the dark mansions loom up like mountains, until they see the Melrose house shining like a ship in the night.

Stillness waits in the kitchen. The Whites and all their pans and bowls have left, and all the appliances and counters gleam. From the door into the rest of the house come noises of an increasingly raucous New Year's Eve celebration. Someone has turned on the television, and music is blasting away, and while they listen, laughter explodes from the living room.

Maggie says, 'You should get back to the party.'

'Yes, all right.' Cameron starts to take her hand, then stops. 'Can I see you tomorrow?'

He has no idea how brave Maggie feels when she says, 'I – I would like that. I'd like that a lot.'

'Okay, then. I'm staying here at Clementine's—' Hurriedly, he adds, '*Not* in her room. I'll catch some sleep, call you tomorrow, and you pick me up. How does that sound?'

'That sounds wonderful,' she says.

'I'll walk you to your car.' Cameron takes her hand now, drawing them together.

They hurry through the garage out into the dark night. Lights from the house fall over the driveway where various vehicles, sleek sports cars, powerful four-wheel drive Jeeps and Range Rovers, are parked.

'Is one of these yours?' Cameron asks.

'No. I'm down the street.'

The privet hedges stand high and black as stone walls. They pass through the arch on to the narrow lane where Maggie's old Bronco sits.

Cameron opens the door for her as if it's a gilded carriage. 'I'll call you later today.'

She squeezes herself onto the seat behind the steering wheel. Cameron leans in, cups her face with his hand, and kisses her softly, a seal of heat and promise. Dazzled, Maggie puts her key into the ignition and drives away.

'Good morning, Maggie. I hope I didn't wake you.'

Maggie laughs. 'It's after noon, Cameron.'

'I wonder, could I take you to dinner tonight?'

Maggie hesitates. 'What about your friends?'

'It's all under control. I've had a sudden change of plans, have to go up to Maine to see my uncle, so I won't be flying back to New York with everyone else. Instead, I'm doing taxi service.'

'Oh.' Maggie's still uncomfortable.

'Clementine leaves at three,' Cameron continues. 'I'll drive her to the airport in my rented car and drop her off, then hang out until my own flight.'

Maggie's so silent she thinks she can hear Cameron smiling.

'Or I might decide I like this island so much I'll stay another night. I have a reservation at the Jared Coffin House. I hear they have an excellent restaurant. I was hoping I could take you there for dinner.'

What a setup, Maggie thinks. Dinner in a hotel restaurant? So he can take her to bed later? She's surprised at how much the idea appeals. She wouldn't mind that at all, not even if it's only a fling. And maybe it could mean more . . .

'I'd love to have dinner with you,' Maggie tells him.

'I'll pick you up at seven,' Cameron says.


The main dining room of the Jared Coffin House unfolds in lush patrician pastel hues, the walls hung with magnificent oil paintings of nineteenth-century whaling ships. Swan white tablecloths, fresh flowers, flicking candles create an aura of private luxury, and Keyo Raith, who graduated from Nantucket High School two years after Maggie, takes one look at Cameron and Maggie, then leads them to the most intimate table in the far corner. As she walks away from them, behind Cameron's back, Keyo mouths, *'Wow.'*

Maggie has to grin. By tomorrow morning everyone will know where and with whom Maggie had dinner tonight.

She settles back in her chair, reading the menu. She's wearing a little powder blue knit dress, very plain, very expensive – one of her mother's discoveries at the Seconds Shop. It had been brought in with the store tags still dangling from the cuff of one sleeve; this often happened, summer people bought piles of clothes, then discarded them, tired of them before bothering to wear them. Her hair is loose, slightly subdued by violent measures with the blow dryer, held back with a blue headband. She wears no jewelry, and only lipstick. She knows her cheeks are flushed enough.

Cameron is wearing a camel hair blazer and a white shirt with gold links in the French cuffs.

'Explain, please,' he says. 'I thought you said your family lives on the harbor, but I picked you up at a house on Orange Street here in town.'

'I'm living with my grandmother, Clarice. It works well for

both of us. When I finished Wheaton last spring, I knew I wanted to return to the island. So I'm here, doing lots of odd jobs, writing in the summer for a local glossy mag, and . . .' She can't help it. She wants to impress him, and she feels somehow that she can trust him. 'And I'm working on a novel.'

'I see,' Cameron says, arching an eyebrow. 'You are what my grandmother would call a *bohemian.*'

Maggie frowns, confused.

'Artistic, you know. *Interesting.* I've always wanted to be a bohemian,' Cameron continues, 'but I'm just too dull.'

Maggie laughs. 'Hardly.'

The waiter sets their first course, smoked salmon, before them.

'Sorry, it's true, I work at an investment firm, and so do my two brothers. My father's a tax lawyer. Mother volunteers for the library.' He brightens. 'Although we do have two dogs, spaniels, and they're allowed to sit on the sofa.'

'Ah, well,' Maggie says, relaxing into the spirit of the evening, 'then you're *almost* bohemian.'

'I read books, too,' he offers.

'Doesn't everyone?' Maggie counters.

'You'd be surprised. The average American watches twenty-eight hours of television a week and reads three books a year.'

'You're kidding! How do you know?'

Cameron shrugs. 'I research stuff. I need to know what people like. So I hope you're impressed with me now, because I do read.'

Maggie gives him an assessing eye. 'How many books a year?'

'Probably, let's see, two a month, that's twenty-four. Not bad, don't you think?'

She loves this little game, this sense that she has the upper hand, that he's trying to impress her.

'What do you read?' she inquires as the waiter brings their swordfish.

'Thrillers. Love them, and you can't tell me they're inferior literature.'

'I wouldn't dream of it.'

Maggie can't believe how easily the conversation is flowing. She worried that she'd be too intimidated to eat in front of this cosmopolitan man, but by the time the waiter takes the dessert plates away, Maggie and Cameron are inclining toward one another across the table, comparing opinions. He can't believe she's never read *The Count of Monte Cristo*. They both love Arthur Conan Doyle's Sherlock Holmes books and argue fiercely over the movie adaptations.

They're the only ones left in the dining room. How can the evening have gone by so fast?

'I'll tell you one book that I'm definitely going to read,' Cameron says.

'What's that?'

'Your novel.'

She takes a deep breath. How nice of him to remember that she wants to write a novel. How kind of him to assume it will be published. She's tongue-tied.

The maître d' hovers near the door, pretending to be busy with a chart on his podium.

'We should let the poor man go home,' Cameron whispers.

Maggie gathers up her purse and rises, slightly unsteady on her high heels. In an instant, Cameron's next to her, his hand supporting her elbow. That touch sends a flash of fire through her blood. The intoxicating softness that she floated on all through dinner vanishes like a mist, leaving her hyper-alert.

Cameron leads her out to the reception room and finds their coats, helps her slide into hers, pulls his on, and taking her by the hand, leads her outside. They stand at the top of the steps for a moment, looking out at the town. Small Christmas trees march in rows up and down the streets, twinkling with lights. Above the shops, here and there, lights shine from windows shaped like fans. It's almost midnight.

'Would you like to see my room?' Cameron asks.

Standing on the steps, her hand in Cameron's, Maggie feels perched on the end of a diving board. It's her choice: to jump or to retreat.

She says, 'Yes.'

He leads her across Centre Street to the annex, and up the stairs. He unlocks the door and ushers her inside. The room is large and graceful, with a silky Persian rug spread over gleaming wooden floors. A tapestry fire screen stands in front of the fireplace, the fabric portraying a pineapple, a Nantucket symbol of welcome. The canopy bed, side tables, and chest of drawers are antique. The only modern touch is the television in the armoire. A deep crimson armchair is next to a window overlooking Broad Street.

'Beautiful room,' Maggie says.

'Beautiful woman,' Cameron replies, and leaning forward, he kisses her.

She falls back against the wall, surrendering. All she's thought about all day is Cameron. She's nervous, but he's gentle, telling her she's beautiful over and over again until she believes it, although he's the one who shines as his pale body arches over her, like a crescent moon spilling light.

★   ★   ★

167

When they wake, a bar of daylight lies between the drapes. Maggie stirs her limbs luxuriously among the tangled Egyptian cotton sheets.

Cameron opens his eyes, yawning. 'Good morning,' he whispers.

'Good morning.'

He starts to kiss her, but she pulls away. 'I need a toothbrush.'

'Use mine.' When she hesitates, he chuckles. 'I think we've gotten intimate enough for that.'

Brazen, she runs naked into the bathroom. The tile floor thrills her feet with its chill, and the minty tang of toothpaste makes her entire body feel fresh and clean. Her reflection in the mirror is flushed, full blown, like a rose. Her breasts seem fuller than they did yesterday, her whole body has ripened overnight. As she walks back to bed, she doesn't mind a bit that Cameron lies there feasting his eyes on her.

They snuggle together in the warm bed, intertwining their knees, hers, smooth; his, thick with downy hair. Plumping and folding pillows, they recline, staring at each other.

With the lightest of touches, he draws his fingers along her mouth, around her jaw, down her throat, along her collarbone. His hazel eyes follow his fingers, as if he's memorizing her. In turn, she gazes at him, fascinated by the milky hues of his skin. His narrow rib cage seems sheathed in an envelope of white silk, with fine, very blond hair curling over his chest. Near his left nipple is one small pink mole, but otherwise his arms and torso are unmarked by freckles or blemishes. Reaching out, she touches his chest, drawing her hand down to his hip. The silky linen duvet makes a shivery sound as she sits up.

He says, 'Tell me more about your family.'

'Well . . . let's see.' Maggie shifts her gaze from his body. 'My mother is like a magician. She used to sew for women, rich women, and she could make the most beautiful clothes. Now she's married to my stepfather, and she's turned his big old house from a kind of storage locker into a warm, comfortable, cozy home. She bakes. She's tamed the yard around the house and she's become an avid birder, so she's planted all sorts of bushes and put up bird feeders. Even in the coldest winter, we can sit in the kitchen and look out at cardinals, brilliant red against the white snow.'

'She sounds like a fairy-tale mother.'

'She's wonderful. Well, to continue the fairy-tale motif, Thaddeus, my stepfather, is the beast her love has transformed into a prince. He's huge and gruff, likes to pretend he's fierce but really he's softhearted. Then there's Ben, my brother. Two years older than me. So smart, and incredibly handsome – at least every female I've ever met starts drooling when he walks into the room.'

'Do you like him?'

'My brother? Of course I like him. Sure, we sometimes fight, but I adore him.'

'You're lucky to have such a family.'

'Tell me about your family.'

Cameron sighs. 'You understand, we had nannies and boarding schools, and all that. A lot less time together watching cardinals out the window, you might say. More time schmoozing with the right people. My brothers and I work for different brokerage houses. We're a bit competitive, and our father likes it that way. So family is kind of a profession for us.'

'Like the royal family.'

'More like a money-making system. Each person has a job to keep the mighty engine working. I want my own family to be different.'

'Tell me,' Maggie urges.

'I'd like a big house with porches all around upon which I can sit at night and watch my unruly brood of kids catch fireflies. I'll work in the city, commute home every night to my wife and children.' His hand moves along her arm, the side of his warm palm grazing her breast. 'I intend to love the woman I marry.'

He stops talking, and gently turns Maggie's face toward his. He tenderly kisses her. This is the most intimate connection she's ever had with any person in her life, and as she wraps herself around him, Maggie surrenders her body and her soul.

They have a delicious room service breakfast of cheese omelets and Nantucket beach plum jam on toast. When they're drinking the last of their coffee, Cameron says, 'I hate this. I've got to go back to the city.'

Maggie's heart sinks. So soon. He's leaving so soon.

'I wish I didn't have to leave today,' Cameron tells her.

'I know. I wish that, too.' Maggie turns to him so he can zip up the back of her dress.

'You think you could come down to New York any time?' he asks.

She's glad he can't see her face. Come to the city? Doesn't this imply a kind of commitment?

'Cameron . . .' She pauses, uncertain of her words. She wants to be straight with him. She wants everything between them to be honest. Turning, she faces him and says, 'You and I don't exactly run in the same crowd.'

Cameron also takes time forming his thoughts. 'True. That's why I want to see more of you, Maggie. You're a breath of fresh air. You're not old school, rah-rah, like everyone else. You're unique.' He smiles. 'You're *bohemian* and you make me believe I could be that way, too, with luck.'

Maggie laughs. 'What an ambition. I'd love to come in.'

'Good.' He pulls her to him in a tight embrace. Kissing the top of her head, he murmurs, 'I'll phone you.'

'Sounds like a plan,' Maggie says, carelessly. With his warm arms around her, and his steady heart beating powerfully against her chest, she feels a contentment she's never felt before.

# Chapter Seventeen

Emily phones Ben from the mainland to ask him to meet her on New Year's Day at her parents' home on the bluff. He agrees, but doesn't offer to pick her up at the airport. Good. This will make it even easier to break off with him.

Emily doesn't tell Maggie she's coming. This is between her and Ben. She doesn't intend to stay more than the one night, and she's only spending the night because no planes or boats leave after eight o'clock. Arriving at the Nantucket airport, she's dressed casually: jeans, cashmere crewneck, down jacket, and carrying only a small overnight bag. A taxi takes her to the house on the cliff.

Inside the giant empty house, she turns on all the lights and turns up the heat, then sets about making a fire with the cherrywood stacked next to the fireplace. She flips some of the dust covers off the chairs and sofa and unceremoniously dumps them on the rug. Ben won't notice the décor. Probably he won't stay very long. She imagines that when she tells him she's breaking off with him for good, he'll slam out the door.

It will be hard — it breaks her heart — but she has to do it. It's good to start the new year clean.

In the kitchen she digs out the coffee, sweetener, and container of creamer. After two mugs, she stops, realizing the caffeine is only making her jumpier and more nervous.

At six o'clock, the doorbell rings.

On the front porch, Ben stands very straight, shoulders back, looking handsome and serious and vaguely military — *at attention*.

'Ben.' Usually Emily would kiss him hello, but something in his expression makes her hesitate. She holds open the door. 'Come in.'

She leads him to the long living room where the fire is nicely blazing, warming the room. She sits in an armchair facing the sofa. Ben lowers himself to the sofa. For a long moment, they say nothing, both afraid.

Ben is clean shaven and smells freshly bathed, like pine-scented soap. His black curls gleam, but dark circles shadow his eyes.

'That sweater looks good on you,' she observes.

It was her Christmas present to him last year, a navy blue cashmere crewneck that sets off his vivid coloring. He and Maggie have always looked more *distinct* than other people. Emily always felt wan and anemic next to them.

'Thank you,' Ben says simply. 'It's a great sweater.'

She thinks her heart will split open with love and sadness. He is so *brave* to wear this sweater, to try to please her, to remind her of their profound connection, especially after all their discontent lately.

'Look, Emily, I have something to tell you.' Ben leans forward, clasping his hands together, elbows on his knees.

'All right,' she responds warily.

'I know you're worried about me and money. About my ability to support you.'

Emily cringes. 'I'm so sorry—'

He holds up his hand to stop her. 'I haven't come here to criticize you. I love you, Emily, I've loved you all my life. I'll never stop loving you, no matter what happens.'

Emily's heart is breaking as she looks at this lovely man with his clear, honest eyes, his open, trusting face. She does love him, too, but clearly they aren't good for each other. She clasps her hands. 'Oh, Ben—'

'Emily, I think we should end it.'

She feels as if a bolt of lightning has struck her, shearing her in half. *He* wants to end it? Confused, she touches her forehead, trying to make sense of what he just said. 'Ben, I'm not sure . . .'

'I am. We're making each other miserable, and it's getting us nowhere.' Rising, he paces the room, running his hand through his black hair. 'We've talked ourselves crazy. We haven't found a solution.'

'If you weren't so stubborn—' Emily starts to protest.

Ben turns and honors Emily with such an affectionate smile he takes her breath away.

'Yes,' she admits quietly. 'I'm stubborn, too.'

Ben nods. 'We've worked ourselves up into a truly unpleasant snarl of disagreement. We need to end it and move on with our lives. You should finish your master's degree. I'll focus on my work here.'

'Other people?' Emily's eyes fill with tears. The thought of Ben with another woman makes her feel first wild with jealousy, then weak with sadness.

Ben sits down next to her on the sofa. 'Other people.'

'Oh, Ben.' Emily's crying, and if she had to say why, she wouldn't be able to sort through all the reasons.

He puts his hand on her shoulder. 'You know I'm right.'

Does she? Does she know anything for sure? Almost frantically, she embraces him. 'Oh, Ben, I do love you.'

'I know you do.' He kisses her forehead.

'Ben—' She has never loved him more. She has never wanted him more. 'Please, Ben.' She doesn't even know what she's asking for.

Ben whispers, 'Hush. It's all right.'

His mouth finds hers. Their kiss is passionate, knowledgeable, dense with memories and sorrow. She pushes him away long enough to strip off her sweater, jeans, and underwear. He pulls his sweater off over his head, his black curls crackling with electricity in the dry air. He stands to unzip his pants and step out of them, then perches on the edge of the sofa for a moment to bend down and take off his shoes. He pulls her naked body against his. He is strong and powerful, his chest and thighs and forearms are meaty with muscle. He is no angel, no spirit, he is as real as the earth they walk on. He lifts Emily onto the sofa and rises above her, telling her with his mouth and eyes and his body that he loves her. He steals her soul, he forcefully melds spirit and body, making her whole. He cannot be breaking off with her, he *can't*. Emily clutches Ben against her as tightly as she can.

He shudders and subsides against her. When he tries to push himself up, she doesn't release him. 'No. I won't let you go.'

Ben lies with her while their breath evens out. She can feel the wrinkles of the dust sheet against her back, the whisper of his hair against her neck, the bulk of his body against hers.

He pushes up again, this time with enough effort to break her

175

grasp. He jumps off the sofa and goes into the bathroom. She pulls on her clothes, runs her hands through her hair, attempts to corral her thoughts into some order, but when he comes back, she can tell his mind is set. He's ready to leave her.

'Ben, can we at least talk on the phone? Email?'

'I don't think that would be a good idea. Better to make a clean break. It's a new year. Time for both of us to start over.'

She can't prevent the tears swelling her chest and throat and spilling down her face. 'Ben, I *love* you,' she pleads.

'I love you,' he replies evenly. Then he delivers the blow: 'And I wish you well.'

He goes out the door, shutting it quietly behind him. A moment later Emily hears the engine of his Jeep roar, and headlights flash across the front of the house.

Ben's gone.

Somehow this was not what she meant to happen.


'Hi, Maggie.'

'Cameron!' She almost leaps off her chair with joy. 'How was your trip home?'

'The trip was easy, but I arrived here to find a shit storm, excuse my language, of work waiting for me. Sorry I didn't phone last night like I said I would, but I had to go to the office. I was up half the night with John Endicott working on some tax problems for a client.'

'Oh, dear.' Maggie sighs theatrically. 'How terribly unbohemian.'

'Right. Dull as dirt and wickedly complicated. In fact, I've got to rush back to the office. I wanted to say hello and I'd like to talk longer. I don't know when I'll find a chance to call again. This is like trying to wrestle Medusa.'

'Don't worry about me,' Maggie tells him confidently. 'I'll be right here on the island whenever you have time to call.'

'That's good to know, Maggie, it really is.' Cameron's quiet for a moment, then says, 'All right. Good-bye for now.'

'Good-bye,' Maggie says, but she's not sure he's still on the line to hear her.

# Part Five
# Treasure Island

# Chapter Eighteen

Frances holds Maggie's head while she vomits into the toilet. 'Thanks,' Maggie says weakly. Slumping against the cool tile wall, she catches her breath.

Frances hauls Maggie up and walks her to her childhood room in Thaddeus's house. 'I'm glad you came home to be sick. I wouldn't want Clarice to catch this flu, and she's hardly up to taking care of you, anyway. Want some more 7Up?'

Maggie collapses on the bed. 'No, thanks, Mom. I want to lie here and be miserable.' She moans as she looks around the bedroom with its cheerful yellow walls, pristine white trim, and daisy-sprigged curtains. Such a sweet, optimistic place.

Frances pulls the daisy-spotted covers up over Maggie, then bends to kiss her forehead. 'Don't be miserable. Dream.'

Maggie obeys, curling beneath the covers. She hasn't seen Cameron since their romantic liaison in the Jared Coffin House. It's been six weeks since he phoned her from Manhattan. Since then, she's had only one brief, rather impersonal text from him:

*First of year crazy busy. I'll call soon.* But he hasn't called or texted since.

Next to her, the February wind rattles the bedroom windows. A blizzard heads over the island like a relentless unstoppable fate.

Emily returns to Amherst to work on her master's. She forces herself to concentrate on her research. She tells herself it doesn't matter if her phone doesn't buzz.

But by the middle of February, everything has changed.

Emily sits alone in her apartment. Her two roommates are in class. She told them she had the flu, but she's sure that's not what's making her nauseous. The past week she's kept saltines under her bed and munched a couple before sitting up.

She can't be pregnant, absolutely *won't* be.

New Year's night with Ben . . .

That December night with Cameron.

She picks up the phone and punches in Maggie's number. 'Maggie? Can you talk? I haven't heard from you in a while.'

'Oh . . . I've got the flu.' Maggie's voice is weak.

'I know exactly how you feel. I really do. I've got the flu, too.'

Maggie chuckles. 'Poor us. It's the season.'

'Listen, Maggie . . . not that I don't want to talk about *you*. I do. But I need to know about Ben. It's been a month now. He won't answer my phone calls. He won't answer my emails or texts. I don't know what to do.'

'Emily, a month isn't very long. Give him more time.'

'Is he seeing someone else?' Emily asks. Her heart stops when, for a long time, Maggie doesn't respond. 'Maggie? Maggie, answer me. Please. Oh, God, Maggie, Ben *is* seeing someone else!'

'Let's say he's seeing quite a few someone elses,' Maggie admits.

'Oh, Maggie, no.'

'Emily, it's better than if he were seeing one special woman. Don't you think?'

'I don't understand him, Maggie.' Emily stands up when she speaks, and a wave of nausea nearly knocks her to the ground. 'How could he start seeing other women so fast?'

'I think he really meant it when he said it was over between you two.'

'It can't be—'

'I know, Emily, I hate it, too. I've tried to talk to him, I really have. I've spent hours trying to make him change his mind, but he won't talk to me. He feels deeply, I know, but he shoves the emotion inside and it fuels him like a race car.' It sounds like Maggie's crying. 'Emily, you know I've hoped for years you two would get married. But now . . .'

Emily's weeping, too. 'Do you truly believe Ben is through with me?'

Maggie's quiet again before she says, 'Emily, I don't know what to say. Except, maybe, couldn't you allow him some time to sort this all out in his dim male mind? Give him a year or two?'

Emily almost laughs through her tears. Her call-waiting light blinks; the number comes up on her phone. Cameron Chadwick is calling her.

'No, Maggie,' Emily says sadly. 'I don't think I can wait that long. If Ben's made up his mind, well . . .'

Maggie interrupts in an urgent voice. 'Emily, I'm going to barf. I'll call you back.'

Emily puts down the phone and sits staring into space, lost in her thoughts, lost in her life.

Then she listens to her voicemail message. Cameron's going

skiing at his boss's ski house this weekend. Would Emily like to come?

Well, okay. Yes. She would.

At the end of February, Maggie's curled in a ball when she hears her mother come into the room.

'Good morning, sweetheart. How do you feel?'

'Awful.'

'Would you like to see the doctor?'

'No, Mom.' Maggie sounds more brusque than she means to.

'Maggie.' Her mother very carefully sits on the side of Maggie's bed. Lightly, she puts her hand on Maggie's shoulder. The warmth feels nice. 'Maggie. Do you think it could be something else?'

Dread flushes Maggie, as if she's inhaled dry ice and it's freezing her veins. 'No.' She rolls over. 'Oh, Mom. It can't be.'

'I don't mean to scare you, but when did you have your last period?'

Maggie presses trembling fingers to her eyes, trying to remember. 'I don't know,' she whispers. 'Maybe not since the middle of December. But, Mom – oh, my God.'

'Look,' Frances decides practically. 'Before you spin into freak mode, let's find out, okay?'

'Okay,' Maggie whispers.

'Tell you what, I'll go buy a pregnancy test.' When Frances rises, the bed creaks lightly, like a baby's whimper.

The ski lodge in Stowe, Vermont, is decorated in a rustic style, all open beams and fires in stone-faced fireplaces, but the rooms are luxurious and modern. Cameron's boss, John Endicott, and his wife, Cornelia, had seen on the snow report that Saturday would be a perfect day to ski, so they booked the firm's private plane, a nine-seater. The other partner, Clark Streeter, and his wife, Mindy, flew up, too. The Streeters are an ancient couple, so they choose to snowshoe around the grounds before cuddling up in front of the fire with books. Cornelia Endicott is fifty, but a tremendous athlete, a better skier than her husband. Emily is good, but it's been a while since she's skied, and she is grateful that Cameron matched his pace on the slopes to hers.

Her morning sickness faded the moment she stepped into the private plane and disappeared completely as she skied over the pristine white powder. Her legs felt strong and flexible, her heart pumped out energy, and her senses expanded with pleasure at the beauty of the world. She'd forgotten this, the exhilaration of winter sports.

Now as she stands under the steaming hot water in the glass shower, her sensation of delight continues. So many little, seemingly insignificant moments happened today, and Emily smiles smugly as she reviews them. The way Cameron introduced her to the Endicotts and the Streeters, subtly stressing her last name, Porter, which naturally led his boss to ask Emily if her father were Peter Porter, the financial lawyer. The glances the Endicotts and Streeters exchanged when Emily told them that yes, he was. When Cornelia Endicott told Emily she knew Emily's mother, Cara, from charity work, Cameron looked pleased. Emily's acquaintance is an asset to him.

But is that the only reason he invited her here?

Emily comes out of the bathroom wearing a fluffy white terry-cloth robe, her hair wrapped in a towel, her entire body flushed with the heat of a hot shower.

Cameron's waiting, stripped naked for his shower. His body is narrow and slender, and while not bulky with muscle, it is fit and firm. Elegant, a greyhound's racing body.

He sees her looking and grins. 'Uh-uh. You have to wait. We have to meet the others for drinks and dinner.' He brushes past her as he moves into the bathroom. 'I won't be long.'

Emily pulls on her black tights and Icelandic sweater. She pulls her hair back with a headband and applies the minimum of makeup. Her morning sickness has almost disappeared, and her belly's still flat. But her breasts are larger than normal, and they tingle. She won't think about that this weekend.

Steam rolls through the room as Cameron comes out. He dresses in corduroy trousers and a flannel shirt. 'So what do you think?'

'I think this is a perfect weekend,' Emily tells him, enunciating carefully as she applies her lipstick at the old-fashioned vanity table.

'Do you like the Endicotts?' Cameron brushes his blond hair, and he's ready.

'I do.' Emily gives herself one last assessment in the mirror and stands. 'The Streeters are a bit . . . old-fashioned . . .'

'Well, of course. Clark and Mindy are a million years old.'

'True. I do like Cornelia. She's fun, and she's a fabulous athlete.'

'Good,' Cameron says. 'I'm glad you like her.'

As he opens the door and ushers Emily out of the room, Emily wonders why Cameron's glad. She's had the sense over the past month that he's been vetting her, putting her through her paces in front of friends and family. Does he want to marry her?

Does Emily want to marry him?

She wonders what Ben is doing.


Frances and Maggie sit together on her bed, watching the second hand of Frances's watch click around the tiny round face.

When the time's up, they lift the indicator and read the color: blue.

'Blue as baby's booties,' Frances says.

Maggie covers her face with her hands.

Back in Amherst after their ski weekend, Emily strolls through a baby care store to see how it feels. To her surprise, the sight of it all enchants her: the sweet little furniture, the bassinets and cradles, the musical mobiles, and especially the miniature clothes, with the cotton as soft as baby powder. They're all the most seductive things she's ever set eyes on.

She has to be sure.

Emily goes to a pharmacy across from the public library, off campus, where she's not likely to run into anyone. She buys a pregnancy test, then hurries into the library and down the stairs to the rest-room. Here, in the silent basement of this majestic institution, she takes the test.

One last time she calls Ben's cell. This is it, Emily decides. Here we go, Fate, she thinks, she prays, I'm rolling the dice. You make the call.

Ben doesn't pick up.

She calls Cameron. He answers. Emily invites him to dinner at her parents' home in New York that Friday night.

Emily's parents have left for their Florida house, so Emily tells the other grad students she has a family emergency (well, she does), finds her little Touareg in the underground garage, and drives down from the university into the city.

Snow falls on Manhattan, transformed by the streetlights into powder puffs. Emily goes around the apartment's living room, turning on lights, pulling the drapes closed over the long windows. It's as if she's shutting them into a cozy, private little world. A luxurious world.

She's wearing a scarlet cashmere sweater that does an excellent job of displaying her breasts, swollen with pregnancy, for once a decent, commendable size.

Cameron steps off the elevator into the foyer, shaking snow off his fur hat. 'We've got a real winter storm going on,' he says. 'Good thing you wanted to eat inside. I don't think our chances of getting a taxi are high.'

'It's nice in here, too,' Emily coos, kissing Cameron's cheek. 'Let me take your coat.'

She hangs it in the closet, then leads him into the living room, which glows like a scene from *Masterpiece Theatre,* with the burning fire and the abundance of food spread out on the walnut table next to the window.

'I'm glad to see you again,' Emily says, sinking onto the sofa and patting the spot next to her.

'Same here.' Cameron sits. 'You look very attractive.'

'Thanks.' She's trying to be casual but inside she's trembling. 'Would you like some wine? I thought red because—' She gestures toward the table set with interesting cheeses, seedless red grapes, lime green Granny Smith apples, crusty French bread, and several different desserts from the local bakery.

'Looks like a feast.' Something has put him on guard. Rising, he says, 'I'll pour the wine. Red for you, too?'

She accepts the wine but only pretends to sip it.

When she stretches her arms above her head, he playfully asks, 'Are you trying to seduce me?'

'Of course, Cameron,' Emily replies smoothly. She takes a sip of wine after all, for courage. 'But I need to tell you something first.'

'Okay.'

Now that the moment has arrived, all the clever scenarios Emily has imagined have evaporated. She sets her glass down. She takes a moment to gather her nerve.

'It's very hard for me to say,' she tells him honestly.

Cameron waits, no longer smiling.

She crosses her arms, hugging herself. Protecting herself. 'Cameron, I'm pregnant.'

Cameron blinks. 'Well. Huh.' He scans Emily's body. 'How far along are you?'

'Six weeks.'

'Just before Christmas.'

'Right.'

'If it's mine.'

'What?'

'The last time I checked, you were "sort of going" with Ben.'

She's reviewed every word she remembers saying to Cameron. She's prepared for this. 'Yes, that was true. I said that, and then you said perhaps I ought to do a little experiment to see if I was really in love with him. And you and I made love and—' She flushes and looks down. She hopes she looks modest and vulnerable. Lord knows she really *is* vulnerable right now. 'And I haven't been with Ben since.' Speaking, she completely believes her lie.

'Really.' Cameron stands up and walks across to the window. Pulling open the heavy curtain, he stares out into the evening, into the darkness swirled with falling snow. 'And you're sure the kid is mine?'

She sees herself reflected in the glass of the window, and Cameron's reflection, too. Their eyes meet. 'Yes. That's what I'm telling you.'

Cameron shakes his head. 'I'm shocked.'

'I know. Sometimes contraception doesn't work.'

He returns to the table, standing next to her, his face serious, but calm. 'What would you like to do about it?'

Emily doesn't have to pretend a thing. He's being nice, and the truth is she's afraid. Tears stream down her face. Sobs wrack her chest, and her throat closes up. She can't speak.

Cameron nods, as if, wordlessly, she's told him. He knocks back his wine and pours himself another glass. Emily cries steadily, face buried in her hands.

'If it's two months, you can have an abortion,' Cameron states quietly.

Emily struggles to control herself. 'Cameron, I thought that . . . going to meet your friends, staying in Stowe with the Endicotts . . . I thought you might have marriage in mind.'

Cameron shrugs elaborately, almost like a man trying to shake off a backpack. 'Maybe I did. But this is a bit more rushed.'

She needs to appear slightly elusive. She will not beg. She keeps her voice cool when she responds, 'More rushed than I had in mind, as well.' Emily finds a handkerchief and dries her face. 'One way or the other, I can absolutely deal with it. But I thought you should know.'

Outside, a siren screams past.

'Yes. You're right.' Cameron walks to the window. In a mild, conversational tone, talking to the night as much as to Emily, he says, 'I'll be the first to admit that I've screwed around a good bit in my life, without necessarily thinking of the consequences.' He shakes his head. 'It's surprising this hasn't happened before now. But I don't intend to walk away from whatever I've done.'

Emily waits.

'I wonder,' Cameron muses, 'could we make it, Emily? Let's really think this through now. Do you think we could get married and have a child, live together and be happy?'

Emily knows he's not waiting for her answer. He's searching his own heart. Rising, she goes into the kitchen and pours herself a glass of water. She returns to the living room, composed.

Cameron strokes his chin as he thinks aloud. 'My boss likes his employees to be married and have children. Thinks it gives us stability and incentive. Still – I have to tell you, Emily, I *need* to tell you – I'm not in love with you.' His eyes become hooded. 'In fact, I might be in love with someone else . . .' Sadness shadows his face.

Fresh tears swell in Emily's eyes. He's more brutal than she thought he'd be.

Bluntly, he continues, 'And I'm not sure you're in love with me.'

'But I am in love with you,' Emily says, and it's almost true. For if she's not *in love* with him, certainly she *could* love Cameron.

He shakes his head sadly, but comes to sit on the arm of her chair. He puts a steadying hand on her shoulder.

'That's very nice, then. That'll be a big help to us, won't it? We should be able to make a good little family.'

'Cameron' – Emily smiles, and at this moment she does love him very much – 'is there anyone else like you in all the world?'

'Maybe,' Cameron says. 'Maybe there is, right in there.' And he gives her belly a little nudge.

Frances sits on Maggie's bed. 'Tell me.'

Huddled in misery in fetal position, Maggie says, 'I met a man at the New Year's Eve party I helped cater.'

'I remember.' Frances nods. 'You went out to dinner with him the next night. Clarice told me she met him when he came to pick you up. She said he was quite the gentleman, and extremely handsome.'

'He's nice, too, Mom.' Maggie struggles to sit up. 'He's in finance on Wall Street, whatever that means, but he's sweet, and kind, and – how can I explain it? For a very short time, it was like magic, as if something special existed between us after our eyes first met.'

Frances chuckles. 'You don't need to explain that, honey. I think I can almost remember.'

'We had so much to tell each other over dinner. We were the last ones to leave the restaurant . . . and I went to his room. I spent the night with him.'

Covering her face with her hands, Maggie says, 'I was such a fool. I'm the biggest sucker on earth.' Lifting her tearstained face to her mother's, she says, 'He said he was going to call me. He wanted me to come into New York. He had plans for us . . . Oh, God, how could I have been so stupid?'

Pulling her daughter against her, Frances pats her back soothingly. 'He hasn't called?'

'He called once, the day after he returned to New York. He told me he was slammed with work, he was thinking of me, he didn't have much time to talk, he'd call me – but he hasn't called again.'

'Do you think you could phone him?'

'No!' Maggie pulls away from Frances, the movement making her queasy. 'No,' she repeats, more quietly. 'It's been eight weeks. He's only texted me once in eight weeks. He hasn't called. No one is that busy.' Bleakly, she faces her mother. 'What am I going to do?'

'How about if Thaddeus takes his shotgun and goes into Manhattan . . .?' Frances has a twinkle in her eyes when she speaks.

'Oh, Mom!' Maggie can't help but laugh, and somehow the

bitterness evaporates in the face of her mother's love, and the realization that whatever her situation is, it's not *tragic*.

'We'll find our way through this,' Frances says. 'Does Clarice know yet?'

'Oh, Lord,' Maggie moans. 'Of course she doesn't. She'll be horrified.'

'I doubt it. She's older now, but she's always been a lovely woman. No doubt she had her share of what she would call suitors.' Frances smiles. 'I'll bet it would cheer up the old lady enormously to have a baby around the house.'

'A baby,' Maggie whispers. She can't take it all in. She has to throw up.

She runs from the room.

Emily wakes. Cameron's beside her, still sleeping. She sinks into her pillow, playing through last night: her announcement, his kindness, their decision to marry. It was emotionally exhausting. She was glad she'd brought food, because suddenly they were both hungry and devoured her little feast. Emily drank no wine but Cameron did, which relaxed him, and they ended the evening making love in her bed.

It seems unreal to her, though. A dream.

Beside her, Cameron stirs and wakes. 'Good morning.'

She kisses his mouth. 'Good morning.'

He glances at the clock. 'I've got to get to work.'

'I'll make coffee.' She pads barefoot into the kitchen and fills the Keurig, prepares coffee the way she knows he likes it, and carries two cups of it into the bedroom. He comes out of the shower and quickly dresses, his mind obviously on business.

She hands him his cup of coffee. Leaning against the counter, she stares down into her own cup, milky and sweet.

'How would you feel about eloping?' Cameron asks.

Emily tilts her head, considering. 'Would your family be terribly upset if we didn't have a big fat wedding?' Elopement's probably a good idea, given Emily's condition, but she wishes *he* had asked *her* if she'd like a big fat wedding.

Cameron shrugs. 'They'd probably be happy not to interrupt their busy schedules.' Carelessly, he adds, 'Anyway, if we elope, you won't be bothered planning a wedding and you can still finish your semester and get your degree.'

'Okay,' Emily agrees reluctantly. She pulls herself together. The man is going to marry her. Sweetly, she tells him, 'Then I want to stay home and take care of our baby and take care of *you*.'

He lifts his coffee mug and salutes her. 'Sounds good. How are you feeling?'

Grateful for his question, Emily nestles against him. 'I'm fine right now. The morning sickness seems to have faded.'

'Good. Because I've got piles of work.' Cameron moves away, to put on a tie.

'Of course.' Emily gathers herself. Almost casually, she adds, 'I'll find out about getting a marriage license.'

# Chapter Nineteen

In her bedroom at Thaddeus's farm, Maggie sits at her old desk, making a list. She must buy baby books. See a doctor. Talk with Clarice. She hopes Clarice will understand if she moves back to the farm when she has her baby. Maggie will need Frances then as she's never needed her before. Clarice is getting around fairly well these days.

She adds to her list: tell friends. Ha, won't they be shocked! Boring old Maggie who does nothing but clean houses and write. Check out the thrift shop for secondhand maternity outfits, although she won't need those for months. And baby clothes? Baby furniture? She is so unprepared.

A vision of a baby snugly tucked into a carrier on Maggie's bosom blossoms in her inner vision, and happiness washes through her blood. This baby will have everything – a family to love it, and this magical island floating in the sea, with its shorebirds and seals and shells and ferries, its sailboats and tugboats and fields of wild-flowers, its picture book town with—

A cry shatters her thoughts.

And then, a heartrending howl.

Frances!

Maggie runs down the stairs and into the kitchen. The sight before her waves like a hallucination. It takes a moment to come clear. To make its terrible sense.

Thaddeus lies on his back on the floor, a felled giant. Maggie's mother is on her knees, hitting Thaddeus in the chest over and over again.

'Maggie!' Frances cries. 'Call 911! I think Thaddeus has had a heart attack!'

Maggie calls for an ambulance. She phones Ben, who's in Vermont skiing with friends. He doesn't answer, so she leaves a message on his cell: *Thaddeus. Heart Attack.* Dropping to her knees on the kitchen floor, Maggie takes her stepfather's wrist in her hands and feels for a pulse. If one is there, it's so light she can't find it.

The ambulance arrives quickly. With swift, efficient care, the EMTs lift the big man's inert body onto a stretcher and slide it into the van. Frances steps inside.

'Go. I'll follow,' Maggie tells her.


The Nantucket Cottage Hospital is two stories high and, not counting the labor-delivery-room area, it holds fourteen beds. Thaddeus is in the emergency room. Frances paces the floor of the waiting room, wringing her hands, her face white.

'What did they say?' Maggie asks her mother.

'They're trying to save him.'

*Save him.* Very quietly, Maggie asks, 'Is Thaddeus *dying?*'

Her mother's voice shakes. 'They told me the situation is grave.'

'Oh, Mom, Thaddeus is too young to die.'

'He's fifty-five.'

'That's far too young. I mean, his own mother is still alive.'

'No one ever said life was fair, Maggie.'

A nurse comes down the hall. 'Why don't you come in?' she says, inviting them to see Thaddeus at last.

The lights are low in the room made intimate by white curtains. Thaddeus reposes on a hospital bed, long and straight against the white sheets like the mast of a capsized schooner lying on its sails. Machines wink and blink around him and tubes snake into his gigantic arms.

Frances stands by his side, holding his hand. He doesn't know it, he's sleeping, or so it seems. Frances's hair is sliding free of the clip, her eyes rimmed with shadows.

'Hi, Thaddeus.' Maggie puts her hand on his arm, an uncomfortable gesture, for she's seldom touched her huge, taciturn stepfather. His arm, muscular, hairy, hard as bricks, is reassuringly strong.

Thaddeus's jaw clenches, and his throat bulges as he swallows, but he doesn't make a sound.

While Frances sits with her husband, Maggie drives to the house on Orange Street to tell Thaddeus's mother. Maggie lets herself in to the house. Clarice is seated in her living room, dressed in slacks, cashmere sweater, and pearls, reading a biography of Thomas Jefferson.

'Hello, darling,' Clarice says when Maggie enters the room. Seeing Maggie's face, she puts the book in her lap and removes her reading glasses. She sits up straighter, steeling herself.

Maggie knows not to touch Clarice right now, but she kneels next to her grandmother's chair. 'Thaddeus had a heart attack. He's in the hospital. Mom's with him.'

Clarice puts her hand to her heart and turns away, shoulders bent. For a moment Maggie thinks the older woman will crumple to the floor. But Clarice straightens.

'Could you drive me to the hospital, Maggie?'

'Of course.' Maggie holds a coat for the older woman to slide into, awkwardly, as if she'd forgotten how it all works, these moving limbs, this clothing against the cold.

Thaddeus dies at midnight. Frances is with him, as are Clarice and Maggie. It happens so quickly Maggie feels *cheated*. She feels more angry than sad. She wants to say, 'Wait!' Ben has texted to say he's driving home from Vermont.

She stands at the end of the hospital bed while Clarice smooths her son's hair and bends to kiss his forehead. Clarice turns to Maggie and says, 'Let's give your mother some time alone.' As they leave the room, Maggie turns back to see Frances fall across Thaddeus's body, her face contorted with such grief Maggie has to look away.

They wait in the hall, Clarice and Maggie, not talking, while in the room Dr Anderson does his final ministrations to Thaddeus's body and talks with Frances.

When Frances steps out of the room, Dr Anderson is with her, his hand on her elbow. 'I'm sorry,' he tells Clarice. 'It was massive, unavoidable.'

Frances reaches for Clarice. The two older women embrace, heads bent, keening softly.

Dr Anderson puts his hands on Maggie's shoulders and takes her aside. 'I'm concerned for Clarice. And for your mother. They're both in shock right now, and I don't think they should be left alone. I'm giving you sleeping pills, one for each woman.' With his weary, wise eyes, he scans their faces, and hers. 'I'll give you an extra in case you need one, too.'

★　★　★

Maggie escorts the older women out to the car, handling them as gently as porcelain statues. Clarice is nearly comatose in the front seat, but as Maggie drives back to the farm, Frances rails, arguing with Fate as if she believes she can change the course of things.

'This is absurd!' Frances weeps. 'He was so *hearty*! He didn't smoke, his cholesterol was fine, there's no earthly reason this should have happened!'

'I know, Mom,' Maggie says quietly.

'He was a *fighter,* God damn it!' Frances hits her fist against the window. 'He was a fighter, wasn't he, Clarice? Why didn't he fight this? Oh, God, why didn't I sense that something had happened? Why didn't I know? I can't believe I didn't feel something!'

Maggie helps Clarice from the car and holds her arm as they enter the house. Clarice has gone so white she seems nearly transparent.

'Let's go up to bed, Clarice,' Maggie says. 'I have a pill for you that will help you sleep.'

'I don't want to sleep.' Her voice is weak.

Because Clarice doesn't look strong enough to manage the stairs, Maggie settles the older woman on the living room sofa.

'I'm cold,' Clarice whispers. 'I want to keep my coat on.'

'I'll make you a pot of tea. But take this now. Dr Anderson prescribed it.' She fetches a glass of water and watches Clarice take the mild sleeping tablet.

'I'm going up to bed.' Frances weaves slightly as she stands in the doorway.

'Did you take your pill?' Maggie asks. 'You need to, Mom. It won't knock you out. It will help you sleep.'

'The house is awfully cold. Has the furnace gone out?' Frances asks.

Nancy Thayer

'I'll check.' Maggie looks and sees that it's a comfortable seventy degrees, according to the thermostat. She turns it up to eighty.

As Frances slowly goes up the stairs, Clarice's eyes close. Her body sags. Maggie removes Clarice's shoes and lifts her legs onto the sofa, arranging her body so it's fully supported, tucking a pillow under Clarice's head, and covering her with two afghans that Clarice had knit herself. Clarice is soon deeply asleep.

What else can she do? When she goes to her room, she sees that Frances's door is shut. She leaves her own door open, in case someone calls, and falls onto her old childhood bed wearing all her clothes, too tired even to remove her shoes.

Wednesday morning, Emily drives back to her apartment at UMass to organize her clothes.

She checks her phone and finds a message. One message, from Ben. 'Emily. Please call me. Please.' His voice is thick with emotion.

Great timing, Ben, she thinks. *Now* you deign to return my calls. Tears fill her eyes and she puts her hand to her mouth, as if she could force back a sob and all the sorrow it carries. But they've been over this before, they've argued, they haven't been able to agree, and their sweet young love has been transformed by reality into something different, something somehow soiled.

She erases the message with tears streaming down her face. Ben was her childhood love. Perhaps he was the love of her life. But now – she is *carrying* the love of her life.

In the late afternoon, when Frances wakes from her drugged sleep, Maggie brings her breakfast in bed.

'How is Clarice?' Frances asks.

200

'Stunned,' Maggie says. 'She spent the night here, on the sofa. Now she's just sitting there. I got her to drink some tea.'

'Have you reached Ben?'

'He drove all night from Vermont. He should be here any moment.'

Frances closes her eyes against the pain. 'Poor Ben.'

'Mom, drink some tea. I know you don't want to—'

'Actually, I do. My throat is raw from crying.' Frances drinks slowly. 'Thank you, darling. It's soothing.' Tilting her head, she remarks, 'It's quiet in here.'

'Yes,' Maggie agrees. 'I took the phone off the hook. It was ringing nonstop.'

'Oh, God.' Frances rubs her hands over her face. 'People will be coming by soon, won't they?'

'And they want to know about the funeral.'

'The funeral.' Frances seems to age years right before Maggie's eyes. Then she tosses back her covers. 'I'll dress. We have a lot to do.'

The front door slams. Ben stampedes up the stairs, energetic even in his sorrow.

'Mom.' He kneels next to the bed, hugging his mother to him. 'Fucking shitting hell.'

'Yes,' Frances agrees, smiling wanly. 'I would agree with that.'

Ben looks up at Maggie. 'Where's Clarice?'

'In the living room downstairs.'

'I tried to phone but the line was always busy.'

'I took the phone off the hook. Everyone's calling.'

Frances straightens her back. She throws her legs over the side of the bed. 'Let me take a shower and change.'

'Come downstairs with me, Ben,' Maggie says. 'I'll make you some breakfast. You must be exhausted after driving all night.'

'That would be great, Mags.'

Ben follows Maggie downstairs. As she prepares scrambled eggs, bacon, and toast for her brother, she recounts the details of the past hours: Thaddeus on the kitchen floor, the ambulance, the hospital.

'He's already been taken to the funeral home,' she tells Ben.

'I want to see him.'

'You can. Eat first.' She sets a plate before her brother.

'Aren't you eating?'

'I'm not hungry. I'm going to see if I can persuade Clarice to eat some toast.'

But Clarice is asleep, resting against the pillow, mouth open, looking shrunken and extremely old.

Frances comes down, freshly showered, wearing a nice dress and a wool sweater. In the kitchen, they sit around the table, drinking tea and making lists of all they have to do, a little trio like it was long ago in the rented 'Sconset cottage, before Thaddeus came into their lives.

In Amherst, Emily quickly discovers online how to get a marriage license in Manhattan. She fills out the application online and pays the fee of thirty-five dollars. The only snag is that both she and Cameron have to appear to sign the application, but the city clerk's office is down on Worth Street, near Columbus Park, close to Wall Street where Cameron works. It won't be too much of a hassle and no blood test is required. She emails Cameron the details.

Pushing away from her desk, piled high with research documents, Emily decides to give herself a period of indulgence. And why not? She's going to be married to a wealthy man. So what if she's eloping? She should look breathtakingly gorgeous; then Cameron will see how fortunate he is to have her as a wife. Quickly packing a bag, she skips down to her car and drives into Manhattan where she parks in her parents' garage, then takes a cab to Bergdorf Goodman.

She finds a winter white suit, lined with silk. For the ceremony, she'll wear this with her large diamond ear studs.

In the lingerie section, Emily settles on undergarments of hand-made ivory Belgian lace and silk stockings which, when fastened to the ivory garter belt, bunch into small rosebuds of silk.

On a whim, she buys a gorgeous red wool coat. It's dramatic, glamorous. She buys a silk nightgown and a silk robe, fabulous high heels, and cashmere sweaters in spring pastels, and, oh yes, a wedding present for Cameron, a brilliantly thin Chopard watch.

Returning to her apartment, she kicks off her heels and spreads her bounty on the bed. The light is flashing on her answering machine, so she absentmindedly hits the Play button.

'Emily, it's Maggie. Would you call me, please? It's important.'

Emily closes her eyes. She had always thought Maggie would be her maid of honor, and she would be Maggie's. How can Emily ask her now, when she's marrying Cameron instead of Maggie's brother?

Yet how can she *not*? Her most profound, enduring relationships are with her parents and Maggie. And Ben.

Screwing up her courage, she calls Maggie.

'Oh, Emily.'

Maggie's voice is distressed – for a weird warped moment, Emily thinks Maggie somehow knows she's through with Ben, she's going to marry Cameron. But of course Maggie can't know yet. 'Maggie, are you all right?'

'No, Emily, I'm not. Everything's in a terrible jumble. Emily, Thaddeus died. He had a heart attack. It was awful.'

'I'm sorry, Maggie, oh your poor mother. Poor Clarice. Poor Ben.'

'Everyone's heartbroken, Emily. We're all completely *staggering* under this.'

'I wish I could do something—'

'Come to the funeral. Please. It's in three days.'

Shocked by the coincidence, Emily barks out a choked laugh. Maggie's silence rebukes her. Immediately, she says, 'Maggie, I'm getting married on Friday.'

'What?'

'I'm going to be married. I was calling to ask you to be my maid of honor.'

'How can you be getting *married*? Good Lord, I can't take it all in.'

'He's a lovely man. I've been seeing him for a few months . . .'

'Sleeping with him.'

'Yes. That, too.'

'Do you love him, Emily?' There she is, Emily's Maggie, her Nantucket sister, cutting through the stormy turbulence of death and Ben and shock and surprise to care if Emily loves the man she's marrying.

'Oh, Maggie, I never could love anyone like I love Ben. But Ben's broken off with me. He won't answer my calls. And Cameron is—'

'Cameron?'

'Yes. La-di-da name, I know, but he's truly nice. Cameron Chadwick.'

Maggie's laughing.

'What? Do you know him?'

'Sorry, Emily, sorry. I think I've gotten hysterical. My heart is overloaded. It's the crazy timing of everything. You married the day Thaddeus is buried. It actually *rhymes*.' Maggie's voice tatters into sobs. 'Emily, I can't talk anymore. I can't— Listen. Congratulations. I wish you all the happiness in the world.'

Abruptly, Maggie hangs up.

Emily falls back onto the bed, lifting one arm to cover her eyes. Ben adored Thaddeus. His stepfather was his mentor, his role model, his idol. Ben will be devastated by Thaddeus's death.

And Maggie will have her hands full. But she can do it, she can hold them all together. Maggie has the vibrant, enfolding warmth of a red tartan cape against a cold wind on the darkest day.

Emily would like to do something to help Maggie, to help them all through this devastating loss, but what can she do? Emily can scarcely make it through the day, she's always exhausted with this pregnancy, not to mention the approaching marriage. She wishes she had someone to talk to, to ask advice from. Maggie would be best, but Maggie's overwhelmed.

As often happens these days, suddenly sleep sweeps over her, blanking out her thoughts.

She wakes to Cameron's telephone call. 'Hey, Emily, I want you to come out to dinner with a couple of my friends tonight. I'll pick you up in thirty minutes, okay?'

'Okay,' she says, returning to her new life.

The funeral is in two days. Frances, Maggie, and Ben are numb and overwhelmed with all the details and complications: the flowers, the phone calls and food, the decisions about hymns and which friends – out of many – would speak at the service. The obituary for the local newspaper. Finding a photo of Thaddeus, a decent photo where he doesn't look like a gorilla in stained fishing gear.

Frances wants to have the reception at their house, because it so very much represents Thaddeus. Maggie and Frances and Ben attempt to create at least an illusion of order, but everything that needs putting away is something of Thaddeus's – a net he's been mending for months, a book he's left half-finished on the arm of his chair, the grubby, oil-stained down vest he always wore instead of a coat. Frances carries each possession off to her room, cradling it like a child, humming deep in her throat as she chokes back tears.

Maggie takes charge of Clarice, driving her to her house to pack up a bag of clothing and necessities, then bringing her back to the farm. No one wants to be separated. The diminished family senses a need to huddle in one place.

Friends stop by, bringing casseroles, flowers, old photos of Thaddeus from years past. By the afternoon, Clarice and Frances have somehow clicked into a social mode, calm and gracious and robotic, allowing their friends to weep while they sit listening, their own grief locked away deep in their hearts.

The funeral at eleven in the morning is crowded; the reception at noon at the farm almost festive. Maggie's swept up in the embraces and well wishes of so many islanders their faces blur. Frances and Clarice, both white as paper in their black dresses, stand at the door shaking hands as friends come and go. Finally, around two in the afternoon, Dr Anderson insists they both sit down and, on his orders, eat some of the food set out on the dining room table and drink a cup of strong tea.

Old Evelyn Story, one of Clarice's best friends, settles in next to Clarice, and a cluster of gnarled, weather-worn friends of Thaddeus come to lean against the living room walls. They talk about Thaddeus, his strength, his stubbornness, his love of the island. How he had such a terrible temper as a child. The tricks he got up to as a young man. How fortunate it was he met Frances, who made him happy, and how Maggie and Ben were the children Thaddeus never had. As the older people talk, their voices lighten, they laugh, they cry, they seem delighted to remember the slightest foolhardy thing Thaddeus ever did. They talk and talk until they're hoarse, and the clock chimes three. It really is time for them to leave.

And Frances and her family have an appointment at the lawyer's.

That morning Emily has her hair washed and set in an elegant French twist. She toys with the idea of wearing some kind of flowers in her hair for the ceremony, but decides against it. At three o'clock, in her childhood bathroom in her parents' house, Emily steps out of the shower, towels herself dry, and stands studying her naked reflection in the mirror.

She's never considered herself beautiful, but she understands her looks convey something else. With her long bony face and pale blue eyes, she looks like an aristocrat. Her long, rangy, narrow body is so thin now, from morning sickness, that it provides her with the emaciated, neurotic, edgy appearance of a catwalk model. Her breasts are enlarging with her pregnancy, but her long waist is still trim.

'So here you are,' Emily tells her reflection. 'Your last few moments as a single woman.'

Her reflection smiles.

Emily slathers lotion all over her skin, and sprays a light mist of perfume at her wrists and neck and the backs of her knees. In the bedroom, she opens the drawer and lifts out the exquisite new lingerie. Silk stockings, the light wool suit, the high heels – perfection.

She puts on mascara and lipstick. Her pregnancy has truly given her skin a glow. She had her nails manicured and French tipped; she wants her hands to be groomed for the exchange of rings.

Pulling on her new red wool swing coat, Emily takes up her gloves and her purse and flies out into the day.

Brilliant sunshine floods down. On the sidewalks, the snow glitters as pristine as a bridal gown, and the air is clean and crisp. Her friend Tiffany arrives at the curb in a yellow cab. She's agreed to be a witness for Emily.

'You look amazing, Em,' Tiffany tells her as Emily slides into the cab. 'Are you nervous?'

'More sick than nervous.' Emily has told Tiffany everything.

Tiffany laughs her trilling laugh. 'Well, I think you're the bomb, Em. Getting pregnant and married all at once. How efficient is that? And I've checked Cameron Chadwick out. He's *loaded*.'

'Oh, Tiffany, he's dreamy,' Emily insists as they ride downtown. 'Witty and gentle and decent. Right away we connected, really profoundly. I think in time he would have asked me to marry him. This just happened first.'

'You don't have to persuade me, hon,' Tiffany says.

'We're here,' the taxi driver says as they pull up to the city clerk's building on Worth Street.

Emily's heart thunders in her chest.

# Chapter Twenty

Ben drives Frances's Volvo station wagon. Clarice rides in the passenger seat. Frances and Maggie are in the back. They drive into town and park near the library, then walk over to India Street and up the stairs to the law offices of Thatcher and Mulroney.

A receptionist rises when they enter and immediately shows them into the office of Kevin Thatcher, the attorney who has handled all of Thaddeus's legal affairs. With grave courtesy, he shakes their hands and conveys, once again, his sympathy, then ushers them to a leather sofa in front of a wall of bookcases. The receptionist comes in with a tray of coffee. For a few moments, everyone is occupied with the details of arranging themselves for the reading of the will.

Kevin Thatcher is a tall, lean, bald man, so darkly tanned from vacationing in the Bahamas, his skin blends with his brown suit. As his lanky arms reach and pour and hand the coffee around, he looks rather like a giant spider.

At last he deems the party suitably settled for the reading of the will. Clarice folds her hands over the purse lying on her lap. Frances sits with downcast eyes, pressing a handkerchief to her mouth. Ben crosses his arms over his chest, digging his chin down toward his collarbone, a posture Thaddeus often took during a serious discussion. The palms of Maggie's hands keep wanting to lie against her belly – she clasps them together and lays them in her lap.

Kevin Thatcher clears his throat. 'Before we begin, again, may I offer my deepest condolences to you all. Thaddeus Ramsdale was an unusual man, a good man, and his death is a loss to the island and all of us on it.'

Clarice looks at Frances, who is unable to speak. 'Thank you.'

Kevin Thatcher smiles gently. 'Now.' He unfolds the legal document and begins. '"I, Thaddeus Devon Ramsdale, do solemnly attest that being in sound mind, this is my last will and testament—"'

He drones on. Maggie's eyes threaten to close. She has been less nauseous the past few days, but more sluggish. Between the heavy maroon drapes, a window displays the bare, nearly black limbs of a tree shuddering in the cold wind. The room is over-heated, stuffy – Ben kicks her leg; Maggie lifts her head.

'"—I leave all the property on Polpis Road, including land, house, and outbuildings, to my stepson, Benjamin McIntyre—"' the lawyer intones.

'What?' Ben yelps. 'Hold on! That's not right. Thaddeus left his Polpis property to the Land Bank. Or the Conservation Foundation. He told me so.'

'It's all right, Ben,' Frances said. 'He changed his mind.'

'You know about this?' Ben's voice is shrill with surprise.

Frances nods. So does Clarice. Maggie tries to keep her face in control – she's so jealous. She always knew Thaddeus loved Ben more, she never really felt comfortable with her rugged, taciturn stepfather. She's glad for Ben, and yet she feels hideously slighted. Thaddeus could have left her some furniture or something. *Anything* would have made her feel not so left out, so abandoned. Tears prick her eyes.

'Shall I continue?' Kevin Thatcher inquires. 'Very well. "I leave all the property on Polpis Road, including land, house, and outbuildings to my stepson, Benjamin McIntyre, with the provision that my wife, Frances, be allowed to live in the house as long as she wishes, or be provided another house of commensurate quality—"'

Simultaneously, Ben and Maggie snort out laughs, then flash chagrined looks at one another.

'Sorry,' Ben says.

The lawyer continues. '"I leave the house on Orange Street to my stepdaughter, Margaret McIntyre, with the provision that if my mother, Clarice Livingston Ramsdale, does not predecease me, she will have the right to live there as long as she wishes."'

Maggie's jaw drops. For a moment she's speechless, then she cries, 'Wait. I don't understand! He can't leave me that house, that's Clarice's house!'

Clarice speaks up. 'No, Maggie. The house belongs – belonged – to Thaddeus.'

'But—'

'Let Kevin continue,' Frances suggests to her children.

'"All the Ramsdale property has been passed down through the Ramsdale line for eight generations,"' Kevin Thatcher reads. '"With me, Thaddeus Ramsdale, the Ramsdale line dies out, and for years this has been a source of distress for me. I have no natural children. When I married Frances McIntyre, I did not assume that I would automatically love her children. As you are all aware, I do not love easily, and I have usually thought land more lovable than people.

211

But over the years, as I watched Ben and Maggie McIntyre grow up, I realized that I had influenced them, perhaps more than blood can influence, and I was proud of that, and proud of them. I came to believe that I had been fortunate enough to find my children, and so I leave my worldly possessions to these two fine young people, knowing they will take care of my mother, Clarice, and my beloved wife, Frances." Signed, "Thaddeus Ramsdale."'

'My God,' Maggie says, and bursts into tears. 'Mom, why didn't he tell us? Why didn't you?'

Frances smiles and weeps at the same time. 'Darling, you know Thaddeus. He was concerned that if you knew, you might feel obligated to act differently toward him.'

Ben says, 'He probably was terrified that we'd start hugging him or something.'

'He was a private person,' Frances agrees.

'I always thought he was like a big red baboon,' Maggie murmurs, then catches herself. 'Sorry, Clarice.'

'It's all right,' Clarice tells her. 'I've often had that very thought myself.'


'Emily.' Cameron's already at the downtown municipal building, drop dead handsome in a gorgeous black suit with a camel vest and white shirt and red tie.

Behind him stands the justice of the peace, an older woman in a simple dove gray suit wearing a benevolent expression. What she must have seen, Emily thinks. Cameron's best friend, Aiden, stands next to him in a navy blazer. Tiffany squeezes Emily's hand and steps back as Emily takes her place next to Cameron.

The justice of the peace clears her throat.

'Well,' Cameron says to Emily, 'last chance to change your mind.'

'I'm not changing my mind,' Emily assures him. Her eyes meet his, and wow, there it is, the connection between them. Cameron is handsome, but more than that, he really is a stand-up, responsible man.

Cameron takes Emily's hand in his and leads her to stand in front of the justice of the peace. Tiffany and Andrew stand behind clasping their hands in front of them. The justice of the peace begins to pronounce the simple, familiar words. Cameron looks at Emily with a smile, and she smiles back. A few minutes later, he leans forward to place a circumspect but firm kiss on Emily's mouth, and they are married.

For Maggie, the next few days pass in a blur. She finds within herself a surprising quality of tolerance, kindness, and emotional generosity as she subtly tends to the needs of her mother and grandmother. They all stay at the farm, and Ben helps, too, buying groceries, listening to the guests who drop by to pay their respects, washing up endless teacups and cake plates. Maggie's pregnancy makes her sleepy all the time. When each day is finally over, she falls helplessly in bed, not having a moment to think about Thaddeus's legacy and what it means. But the knowledge of it is like a golden net beneath her, to catch her if she falls, not only the security that she has a house to live in, but the surprising news that Thaddeus cared for her that much.

Thursday, the local weekly newspaper comes out. Maggie drives into town to buy several copies. The obituary she wrote for Thaddeus will be in it. Returning, she carries the papers into the living room, where Frances and Clarice sit watching Ben build a fire. She hands a paper to the other women and joins them, perched on the sofa, opening the newspaper wide.

'It's on page five A,' Frances says. 'With a large photograph.'

After a moment, Clarice says, 'Well done, Maggie. They didn't cut a word.'

'They shouldn't have,' Frances says. 'Thaddeus was an important member of the community.'

But Maggie's eyes have snagged on a small item under 'Marriages and Engagements'.

Before Maggie can comprehend the words, Clarice says, 'Why, look. Ben, didn't you date Emily Porter? She just got married.'

Ben freezes in position, kneeling with firewood in his hands.

'To someone named Cameron Chadwick,' Clarice continues. 'They were married in New York.'

'Ben—' Frances begins, but stops at the sight of Ben's face.

Clarice reads on. 'The bride's parents are Cara and Peter Porter of Nantucket, New York, and Sarasota. The groom's parents are Emeline and Charleston Chadwick of . . .'

Ben finishes building the fire. When the kindling catches, he rises and stalks out of the room. 'Going for a walk.'

'Oh, dear,' Clarice says.

'I'll go with him.' Maggie jumps up and runs after him, pulling on her down coat as she hurries out of the house. 'Wait, Ben!' she calls.

He doesn't slow down but strides toward the harbor, pausing only to reach into his pocket to yank out his wool cap and pull it on.

The air is arctic but there's no wind. The sky is a white sheet, devoid of sun or flecks of color. Brittle fingers of heath plants pluck at their jeans as they pass over the frozen ground. The grass is the color of sand. A few juniper bushes are the only green in sight, their needles browning. At the harbor, the water is flat dead, a mirror with no reflection.

214

Ben walks to the end of the wooden dock and stands looking out, hugging himself.

'Ben?'

'What?' He stares out at the water, his face haggard.

'There's something else.' Perhaps if Maggie tells him now, it will deflect him slightly from his pain.

Ben turns. 'What?' Already his face is hollow-eyed from grieving, but the cold has provoked roses into his cheeks.

'I'm pregnant. I had a one-night stand with someone, and I'm pregnant.'

Ben's face breaks with disbelief. 'I don't believe you.'

'It's true. It's almost kind of funny, isn't it?'

'No, Maggie. Not funny at all.' His voice is hoarse.

She gazes up at her brother with infinite pity. 'Ben, I'm telling you this because my life is going to change. And I'd like to help you, but I don't know how.' She touches his shoulder. 'I don't understand why you broke off with Emily.'

Ben croaks out a harsh laugh. 'I was always going to lose Emily. I was a fool ever to think otherwise. It's all about money. It really is all about money.'

'Ben, let's *do* something,' she urges. 'Let's fly down to Mexico for a few days, lie in the sun next to a pool.'

'Great idea. And how will we pay for it?'

'Charge cards.'

'And what will we give up to pay for such a trip?'

'I don't know. But it's not that expensive—'

'Yes, it *is* that expensive. *Everything*'s that expensive! If we go on a trip, that means we can't pay our car insurance or buy food. Hell, if I have to buy new socks, that means I can't see a first-run movie. It's all about money, Maggie, it really is. *It really is.*'

'I know it seems that way—'

'Seems? *Is!* I have been such an idealistic sucker. I'm going to save the island – bullshit! I'm not going to be able to accomplish one damned thing. I won't save anything. I won't *have* anything. I don't matter. Because I don't have any money, I'll never matter! Everything we've been told about how we can be whatever we want to be is a lie. It's all lies the rich tell the poor to keep us in line so we won't kill them.' Ben's sobbing now. His shoulders shake. He bends his head down and covers his neck with his hands. 'People like us can't do anything. We can't have anything. It's all rigged from the start. You and I are disposable people. That's all we are, and all we ever can be, disposable people.'

Maggie puts her hand on her brother's back, trying to offer some comfort. She's crying, too, for her brother, for herself, for all their shining hope they've seen destroyed. 'I know,' she agrees quietly. 'I know, Ben.' She gestures across the water toward the roofline of the town. 'So many people pay five million dollars for a house they live in just two weeks a year. We can't ever compete with that kind of money. And come on, you and I wouldn't want to be that way, that vulgar, that careless of the land.' Facing away from her brother, she says, 'I'll bet this Cameron person Emily married is like that, all about money, excess, superficial charm.'

'Of course he is,' Ben growls.

'Well, let them be,' Maggie counsels. She's advising herself as well. 'We have our own lives, and we don't want to ruin what we have with resentment over what we don't have. We can still be happy, perhaps even—'

'Oh *fuck!*' Ben interrupts with a shout. His feet thud against the planks as he stalks off the dock. In a few strides he's out of sight.

Shivering in the cold, Maggie picks her way over the frozen

sand to Shipwreck House. The lock is painfully cold, but as her fingers remember the combination, it turns and opens. Inside are the desks and chairs, the funny sofa draped with shawls. A memory of summer superimposes itself over the empty space, and Maggie sees herself at the desk drawing, Emily at the other desk, both of them laughing, improvising wild tales.

*Emily.*

She closes the door behind her. Pulling one of the ancient blankets off the back of the sofa, Maggie wraps it around her, ignoring the faint smell of mildew. Snugging up at one end of the sofa, she thinks about the past and wonders about the future until she's shuddering with cold. Leaving, she locks the door behind her. She returns to the house where her mother mourns the loss of her husband, and her brother grieves for his own lost love.

Maggie puts her hand on her belly. She has new dreams, new realities to plan for.

With such a rushed wedding, Emily and Cameron have no time to prepare for a honeymoon. Cameron's overwhelmed at work, and Emily's finishing her degree in Amherst, driving down to Manhattan on the weekends to search for an apartment. She finds one on Park Avenue with a doorman and sunny windows in what will be the baby's bedroom, and then she sets about furnishing it. Being busy feels good. It keeps her from second-guessing herself.

Not until the end of March does she take a deep breath, sit at her computer, and email Maggie.

Hey, Maggie, when's a good time for me to call? I've got news. I didn't want to tell you this way, I wanted to see you face-to-face, but who knows when I'll get to the island again. Anyway, guess what! I'm pregnant. And very happy.

The response comes within an hour.

Wow. Glad you're happy. Sorry, don't have much time to write these days.

Emily writes:

Hope you're happy, too. Hope you're working on The Great American Novel.

A reply from Maggie never comes.

Emily is pregnant and married to Cameron Chadwick. Maggie is not married at all, but she's also pregnant.

Her child and Emily's have the same father.

Maggie can't wrap her mind around what this means. She recovered from Cameron's cavalier treatment, from his romantic seduction and unexpected desertion, with an ease that surprised her. Friends told her a term exists for such behavior: Seduce and Abandon. Apparently there are men who enjoy the thrill of the chase, but once the prey is brought down, they find themselves bored, ready to move on.

No, she sheds no tears at the loss of Cameron in her life. It was a blow to her vanity but it also provided a wake-up call. She has to grow up. Well, she *is* grown up. She carries a new life inside her, a being she has already come to love and fiercely vows to protect. This is her responsibility. This is her child.

She has imagined what would happen if she told Cameron she was pregnant by him. If he insisted on a DNA test, he would know for sure that the child is his – and Maggie does not want that. He would be obligated, or believe he was obligated, to give Maggie money to raise her child. She doesn't want his money. She doesn't want Cameron to have rights over this child, whom he fathered so frivolously, whom he fathered by lying, if not in words, certainly by insinuating that he was in love with Maggie and that they had a future together.

So she won't tell him. My God, what if Cameron demanded rights to her baby? What if he demanded joint custody? It doesn't bear thinking about.

And Ben would be maddened, wounded, *broken* by the knowledge that his sister was bearing the child of the man for whom Emily had left Ben. It was too much of a mess. Ben wouldn't be able to love Maggie's baby.

These are not the Middle Ages. Maggie is not some hapless waif wandering pitifully through a blizzard with a shawl clutched over her bosom. She has a family who loves her, a place to live, a community to support her, and a new life inside her that she never asked for or expected, but which daily increases her happiness, her confidence, and her sense that this world is more complicated than she ever imagined.

She only wishes she could share this with Emily, this entire bizarre coincidence. How they would laugh. But of course, Maggie can never tell Emily. She will never tell anyone.

# Chapter Twenty-one

That August, the heat in the city becomes unbearable for Emily, who is almost eight months pregnant. She tells Cameron she's going to Nantucket for the month, to live with her parents in the bluff house. He'll fly up on weekends.

She's on Main Street on the island, standing by the farmer's truck, filling her recyclable bag with lettuces, carrots, and fresh, fat red tomatoes, when she hears a familiar voice.

'Emily?'

She turns. For a moment, the woman lumbering toward her seems only barely familiar. Then she gasps.

'Maggie?'

Clad in a loose sleeveless dress, shod in those clunky rubber Crocs everyone seems to wear, Maggie is almost unrecognizable. She's cut her long black hair short and let it have its own natural, rambunctious way, falling in ringlets from the crown of her head to the nape of her neck.

Maggie stops a moment to return Emily's assessment. Emily wears black maternity running pants, a white, sleeveless, tight-fitting tee that expands over her pumpkin-size belly, and white running shoes. Her long blond hair is pulled back in a high ponytail. She glitters with diamonds, big studs in her ears, rings on her fingers.

'Wow.' Maggie shakes her head in wonder. 'Look at you.'

'Look at you,' Emily shoots back. 'You're pregnant, too? How did that happen?'

Maggie widens her eyes innocently and jokes, 'The usual way, I guess.'

'Oh, Maggie!' Emily throws her arms around Maggie, which is not an easy accomplishment, given their two bellies.

'I didn't know you were on the island,' Maggie says.

'I just arrived. It's unbearably hot in New York.'

'It's hot here, too,' Maggie counters.

Other people nudge them in their attempts to reach the vegetable truck. 'Do you want to grab something to eat?' Emily asks.

'Sure. We can take it down to the harbor.'

Emily winces. 'Can't we sit on a bench right here? My feet are swollen and walking kills me.'

Linking arms, they cross the street and ask to be seated in the garden at Met on Main. The walled-in area, with its overhanging trees, is shady and cool and, at this hour, after breakfast and before lunch, occupied by only a few other people.

'Let's order something deliciously fattening,' Emily suggests, 'to celebrate seeing each other again.'

'Why not? It's for the babies, right?'

As the waiter takes their orders, they shuffle around, settling their purses on other chairs, getting comfortable, and then they stare at each other for a long time, smiling.

'All right. You go first,' Emily says.

Maggie grins. 'Okay. Well, first of all – I'm pregnant.'

Emily laughs. 'You don't say. Who's the father? I'm not seeing a wedding ring. What's the deal, Lucille?' When Maggie hesitates, Emily worries that she's been too cavalier about her question. But Maggie seems happy . . .

Finally, Maggie shrugs and admits, 'It was a one-night stand.'

'With . . .' Emily prompts.

'An awesomely hunky guy.' Maggie pushes her hair back from her flushed face. 'Damn, it's hot.'

'Go on.' Emily's not going to let Maggie off that easily.

'He's not from the island, he's no one special, he could scarcely remember my name. He doesn't matter.' Maggie shakes her head as if shaking away unpleasant thoughts.

Emily hesitates, waiting for more. Okay, she thinks, if Maggie wants to keep her secrets, there's nothing Emily can do about it. She asks, 'How's Ben?'

Maggie looks at her hands, folded on her belly. 'My mother and Clarice are doing all right. It's hard for them, but they're hanging in there. Ben's a different matter.'

'Maggie—' Emily doesn't know what to say and sighs with relief when the waiter arrives with their order of iced juice and pastries.

It appears that Maggie's not eager to talk about her brother, either, because after she takes a sip of juice, she says, brightly, 'In a way, it's all working out well, almost as if this baby was meant to be. You know I moved into the Orange Street house to help Clarice after her operation? Okay, well, now my mom has moved in with us. She cooks dinners for us every night, she takes Clarice out on little jaunts, and she's knitting, sewing, and embroidering constantly for the baby.'

'You'll have the best dressed-baby on the island.'

'True.' Maggie's smile fades. 'Mom's being brave and positive but I know she misses Thaddeus terribly.'

'Ben must miss him, too.' It pierces Emily's heart to think of Ben losing his beloved stepfather.

'He's destroyed. Truly. He's living alone in the big old rattling house on the farm. Sometimes he comes to Orange Street for dinner. He's lost weight, he looks miserable . . .' Maggie takes a deep breath and faces Emily. 'Of course he was devastated when you married someone else.'

Tears flood Emily's eyes. 'I never wanted to hurt Ben. I care for him enormously, in a way I'll never stop loving him, but come on, you must remember *he* broke up with *me*. Anyway, all we did was fight, there at the end. He's so stubborn, Maggie. He wouldn't give an inch, there was no compromising with him.'

Maggie doesn't argue but Emily senses how tense they've both become. Desperate to prevent an argument, Emily swerves into a new subject. 'Maggie, I have my degree. I've been volunteering at a conservation agency in New York. I see my parents all the time . . .'

'. . . and your New York friends,' Maggie inserts in a neutral tone.

'Yes, but most of all, Maggie, Cameron is totally a wonderful husband! I can't wait for you to meet him. He's gorgeous, not like Ben, but in a blond, sort of Scandinavian way, and he works on Wall Street and he's loaded with pots of money – let me make that clear, since I know you think I married for money. But he works *hard* for his money. He's *always* working, or flying somewhere to meet with clients.'

Maggie holds up her hands. 'Stop. Enough about Cameron, okay?'

Emily sits back in her chair. She did it all wrong; she didn't steer their conversation toward happier subjects. Reaching for Maggie's hand, she says, 'I'm honestly truly sorry I hurt Ben.'

Maggie stares steadily at Emily. 'I am honestly truly sorry you're not my sister-in-law.' She withdraws her hand.

For once a waiter appears at the perfect moment. 'Can I bring you ladies anything else?'

'God, if only,' Emily says. They both laugh, and their laughter bridges the crack in their relationship.

'No, thanks,' Emily says. The waiter drifts away. 'Maggie, we can still stay in touch, can't we? I want to know about your baby and I want to tell you about mine – it's a girl.'

Maggie's face brightens. 'So's mine! If the ultrasound is right – sometimes they make mistakes.'

'Are you going to do Lamaze?' Emily asks, then bites her lip. Who would be Maggie's partner?

'I am,' Maggie answers, without hesitation. 'Mom's going with me and she'll be in the labor-delivery room. I'd like to have the baby at home, with a midwife—'

'No,' Emily interrupts, 'don't. Too risky. You can have a midwife with you at the hospital but if the baby is stuck, or something goes wrong, you need a doctor nearby.'

'Are you having a spinal?' Maggie asks.

'You think I'm too much of a princess to endure pain?' Emily arches her eyebrow at her old friend. 'No. I'm going the natural way, but at the hospital. I'll have a midwife, too, Mount Sinai has a great system for women who want midwives.'

'Are you scared?' Maggie asks, then answers her own question. 'I am. Excited, too, of course, but this baby is big' – she runs her hands over her great basketball of a belly – 'and really, Emily, the, um, *exit* is small. I don't understand how it's going to work.'

'I know, right? Who thought of this system?' Emily leans forward. 'It's like squeezing a whale through a bowline knot.'

Maggie throws her head back and laughs. 'Now, there's a Nantucket metaphor!'

Emily lowers her voice. 'Cameron's terrified about this. He hates watching the birth videos – I've caught him closing his eyes! I don't know why he's so squeamish. He's fabulous in bed, we have the most amazing sex—'

Maggie shifts uncomfortably in her seat and focuses on her plate, empty of all but crumbs. She wets her fingertip and picks up the crumbs, paying careful attention to them.

Emily shuts up. She could slap herself. Of course Ben's sister doesn't want to hear what great sex Emily's having with another man.

'Stretch marks!' Emily blurts. 'Do you have stretch marks?'

Maggie looks ruefully at Emily. She knows exactly why Emily changed the subject. ' 'Course I do.'

'I've bought that expensive vitamin E cream to rub on, and I do it twice a day,' says Emily. 'I'm diligent about it, but honestly, I don't think it's making a bit of difference.'

'Do you pee when you sneeze?'

'I leak like a broken faucet!'

For a while they're back together, laughing like the little girls they once were.

Then Emily says, 'Maggie, Cameron's going to come here for a few weekends in August. Would you like to meet him? I'd really like you to. He's awfully nice.'

The air around Maggie seems to shift and chill. 'I'm glad he's so great, Emily,' Maggie says. 'I'm happy for you. But I don't think I could handle meeting Ben's replacement—'

'He's not *Ben's replacement!*' Emily objects.

Maggie takes a few bills from her purse and puts them on the table. 'Anyway, no thanks. I'm awfully busy with Clarice and preparing the house for the baby, and I haven't given up working on my book.'

Emily puts her hand on Maggie's arm. 'Don't go yet. Tell me about your book!'

Maggie gently shakes off Emily's arm. 'Another time, maybe. I really must go.'

Emily watches Maggie waddle away. She gathers up her own bags and heads out to her Range Rover. As she drives to 'Sconset, a mood of melancholy surrounds her like a summer mist, and regrets torment her heart. If she'd married Ben, she'd be on beautiful Nantucket all the time, she'd see Maggie every day, they could share every humorous and cranky moment of their pregnancies, and she would go to sleep at night at the side of the man she's loved all her life. The man she will always love.

It's ironic – *funny,* in a terrible, bitter way – how things worked out. If Emily had married Ben, and Thaddeus died, she and Ben would live in the house on the farm, and Emily knows Ben would have had to agree to let her refurnish and redecorate with some of her parents' money. That ramshackle house would become charming. Plus, then she could carry her daughter down to Shipwreck House, tell her the stories she and Maggie invented. She could . . . Sorrow overcomes her. Emily pulls the vehicle to the side of the road and sobs.

After a while, she regains her poise. Remember, she tells herself, her baby *could* be Cameron's. She probably is Cameron's. Their child will be safe, their child will have Emily's parents' Nantucket house *and* the fabulous city of New York.

She drives back onto Milestone Road, but instead of going directly to the house, she drives down to the beach at 'Sconset. Kicking off her sandals, Emily slowly trudges over the sand to the ocean's edge. Clusters of sunbathers and swimmers lie on brightly colored towels in the sun. Children build sand castles. In the warm Atlantic water foaming up to the shore, pockets of light flash and gleam, vibrant as beacons. Awkwardly, Emily kneels, placing her hand in the warm summer water, palm up, to feel the glitter on her skin. *This* will wait for her. *This* will always be here. She puts her hands on her belly and feels her baby move.

When she returns to the house on Orange Street, which she still thinks of as Clarice's house although, remarkably, it belongs to her, Maggie quietly sets the groceries in the kitchen and makes her way up the back stairs to her bedroom. She doesn't want to tell anyone yet that she ran into Emily. She needs to think about this. Anything she says about Emily will eventually work its way back to Ben, and he's unhappy these days – she's worried. He can't seem to *move on*. He's become secretive, hard-eyed, humorless. He used to join them for dinner once a week and stop by for a drink and a good island gossip several evenings, but since Emily married, Ben's become reclusive and sullen. His bitterness has driven a wedge between Maggie and her brother.

As for Cameron, she simply doesn't think about him much. She trained herself not to. She doesn't want to think unpleasant thoughts when her growing child is curled inside her body. With each passing day, Maggie's pregnancy works like an opiate. This is something Ben can't share.

# Chapter Twenty-two

One early September afternoon Maggie decides to drive out to Thaddeus's farm to walk the paths she remembers from childhood. The farm is officially Ben's now, but he won't mind.

'Mom? Clarice? I'm going out to visit the farm. Want to come along?'

'No, thank you, dear.' Clarice looks up from her armchair in the living room. 'I'm in the middle of a good book.'

'I'll come,' Frances decides. She hasn't been there since Thaddeus's death six months ago. 'I'd like to see it again.'

Frances is quiet as they drive out of town and along the Polpis Road. She puts her hands to her heart when they drive onto the land and park in front of the house where she lived with her beloved husband.

'You okay, Mom?' Maggie asks.

'I'm fine, dear. Give me a moment. Such memories.'

They leave the car and walk up the steps. The door isn't locked; most people on the island never lock their doors.

They knock anyway, and call out, 'Ben?' His car isn't in the drive, so they know he's not there. They step inside.

The kitchen is as messy as it was before Thaddeus married Frances. The dog, an adopted mutt, sleeps under the table. She opens only one eye when they enter, but doesn't move to greet them.

Frances murmurs. 'It doesn't look like Ben spends much time with the dog, but of course she probably sleeps all the time . . .'

'Mom.' Maggie points to the kitchen table. 'Look at this.'

Spread across the wooden surface, pinned down with salt and pepper shakers, a sugar bowl, and a coffee cup, lies a large map printed with the words: *Thaddeus Ramsdale Property*. The boundary line is outlined in dark black. The land has been divided several ways in different colors of pencil. In darker pencil, two roads cut through from Polpis Road to the harbor, winding around, and on each bulge of each curve a house is sketched in.

It's a plan for a development.

Frances collapses into a chair. Her skin has gone gray. 'No,' she whispers. 'He wouldn't.'

Maggie takes out her cell phone and punches in Ben's number. She hasn't called him in weeks.

When he answers, she says bluntly, 'We're at the farm. You have to come here now.'

'I don't have to do anything. And it's not *the* farm. It's *my* farm.'

Maggie holds her anger in and tempers her voice. 'Ben, Mom's here. She saw your map. And no, of course you don't *have* to do anything. But you should. Please. I don't think you ought to make Mom wait now that she knows.'

'I'm coming.' He clicks off.

'He's coming,' Maggie tells her mother. 'I'll make some tea.' In

229

a gentle voice, she suggests, 'Why don't you go up to your room and gather some of your cold weather clothing to take back to Orange Street with you? The other day you were wishing you had your blue cotton sweater.'

Frances nods numbly and leaves the room like an obedient child.

Maggie busies herself around the kitchen, making tea, washing cups and dishes, wiping off surfaces. She sees Ben's truck pull into the drive.

'Mom? Ben's here.'

Frances comes into the kitchen, her arms full of clothing. 'Is there a plastic garbage bag here I could put these in?' She seems surprisingly calm.

Maggie's holding the bag open while Frances drops in the garments when Ben opens the door and steps inside. For a moment the trio stare at each other in silence. He's lost weight, looks lean and rather startlingly grown-up in his striped button-down shirt, khakis, and tie.

Ben says, 'I didn't mean for you to find out this way.'

'When were you going to tell us?' Maggie asks.

'Is that tea?' Ben acts pleasant, totally fake, and pulls out a chair. 'Mom? Want to sit down?'

Frances sits.

Maggie sets tea before them and joins her mother and brother at the table. 'What's going on?' she asks Ben.

He doesn't flinch, back down, or appear apologetic. He doesn't hesitate. In his gorgeous blue eyes a kind of darkness gleams that frightens Maggie.

Ben says, 'I'm working with Sedgwick Realty. I'm going to subdivide this property. I'm going to work with a contractor and architect to develop the land. We'll build a few extremely fine houses here. The best one, Mom, will be yours. You can have a harbor view if you'd like. Or—'

'Stop.' Frances lifts a hand. 'Ben, you can't subdivide Thaddeus's land.'

'I can, you know, Mom.'

'But why?' The words seem torn from her heart.

'So I can be rich. So we can all be rich.'

'Oh, honey, don't talk like that. You love this land. You love it like Thaddeus loved it. Why, what would Thaddeus think?'

'Thaddeus is dead.'

After a beat of silence, Frances says, 'You're still indebted to him, Ben. You still must behave honorably.'

Ben shrugs. 'I think I am behaving honorably. I'm doing what I need to do to secure a prosperous future for all of us.'

'A prosperous future?' Frances puts her hands to her head, as if it hurts. 'What the hell does that mean? We're all right, Ben! If I need more money, I can work. That's what people do!'

'You're too old—'

'I'm fifty-three, for God's sake, I'm hardly decrepit! Don't sell this land because you think you need to take care of me!'

'But I do want to take care of you, Mom!' The little boy's longing rings in the man's cry. 'I want you to be safe. I want you to be secure. I don't want you to have to sew other women's clothes—'

'There's nothing wrong with work, Ben!' Frances's eyes blaze.

'I'm not saying that, I'm saying that this house is a sty about to collapse, it's a fire trap. I want to give you a beautiful new house, with new appliances, and a cathedral ceiling! I want to hire people to help you clean and maintain it. Landscape it. Give

231

you a water feature. When you grow older, I want to be able to afford more people to assist you if you're ill so you don't end up in some old folks' home. I want to live *well*. Jesus Christ, Mom, I want to have some *power*! I'm sick of sucking up to rich people, I want to be rich! If I make enough money, I can control what happens to the future of the island!'

Maggie snorts. 'Yeah, *develop* it—'

Frances rises majestically to glower down at her son. '*Control the future of the island?* Good God, Ben, if you develop this land, you'll kill it, and you'll kill part of your soul, you know that.'

'No, Mom. I'll be rich.'

'*Rich.*' Frances spits the word. Softening, she leans her hands on the table, pleading. 'Ben, I don't understand why you're changed like this, although I can guess. I think you've been badly hurt, I think you're feeling alone, and I'm afraid you've lost your way. You need to take some time to reflect, Ben, before you do anything as crucial as developing this land. Could you do that? Could you take some time, the winter, let's say, to consider your actions?'

'I'm sorry, Mom.' Ben's jaw clenches. His eyes are hot with emotion but his voice is cool when he speaks. 'I've made up my mind. I need to start this as soon as possible, while the market's good. You and Maggie are already living happily with Clarice. You'll want to be together when Maggie has her baby. Mom, I'm going to build a house for you and one for Maggie, near the harbor—'

'Stop right there.' Frances stands up. Her voice is cold. 'Just because you've made a pact with the devil doesn't mean the rest of us have. If you develop this land, Ben McIntyre, don't think for a second that I'll have anything to do with it or with the profit from it.' Frances blazes with anger. 'If you develop this land, you'll betray every value I've ever tried to teach you. You'll betray me, you'll betray Thaddeus, you'll betray the land. And I won't be part of it. If you do this, I will cut you out of my life!'

Maggie thinks her mother's magnificent. Expectantly she looks toward Ben, assuming he'll relent, not all the way, but certainly a little.

'Fine,' Ben says. His eyes have gone cold. Blank.

'Oh, *Ben.*' Frances is trembling. 'Maggie. Let's go.' She walks toward the door.

Maggie picks up the bag with her mother's fall clothing. 'We'll have to come back,' she says to Ben. 'To pick up our things.'

'Fine,' Ben repeats. 'Whenever.'

# Chapter Twenty-three

In September, at Mount Sinai, after a long labor concluding with a C-section, Emily gives birth to a baby girl. Her parents are over the moon to have a grandchild.

When Cameron sees the infant's thick black hair, he's not so thrilled.

'Now, how is it,' he asks, in the hospital room, with the nurse right there, 'that I have blond hair, and you have blond hair, Emily, and our child has black hair?'

Emily's heart thumps heavily. She's woozy from the medications and scarcely has the energy to speak. What can she say? Her parents are in the room, too, both blond, although her father's hair has gone silver. Perhaps, she wonders foggily, one of her grandparents once had black hair.

Fortunately, the nurse chuckles knowingly. 'That's newborn hair,' she informs them. 'It will fall out and then the blond hair will probably come in. Or who knows, perhaps red hair – our genes are complicated, and Mother Nature does love to spin the

234

roulette wheel. I've seen babies with blue eyes born to parents with dark brown eyes. My, that caused a fuss!' She continues to chatter as she bustles around the room, checking mother and baby's vital signs, scribbling on charts. Emily wants to grab the woman and kiss her.

A hurricane is forecast for the northeast coast the day Maggie goes into labor. Strong winds whip the ocean into a froth of white. The trees, still laden with green leaves, flail drunkenly, limbs cracking off, twigs littering the streets.

Maggie's friend Darcie, a midwife, stays with Maggie at the Orange Street house, trying to allay her fears, which do have a foundation in logic. If something should go wrong – there's no reason anything should, but *if* some dire emergency takes place – the helicopters that come from Mass General Hospital to pick up Nantucket patients won't be able to fly in this wind.

Usually Maggie finds hurricanes exhilarating. She likes to walk on the beach, listening to the ocean roar. But today she wants to be safe. It doesn't help that the old house is creaking around her or that Clarice reminds her it has stood for one hundred eighty years in all kinds of weather. Maggie had assumed that since she was healthy and active, the birth would be relatively quick and easy, but after fourteen hours of labor, she's weak with exhaustion and pain. She wanted to have a home birth; she felt she'd be letting her baby down somehow if she didn't, but at three in the morning she begs her mother to drive her to the hospital. A doctor is summoned. He turns the baby's head, which was caught on her cervix, and in minutes, Maggie's daughter is born.

Over the next week, Maggie's friends, Frances's friends, and Clarice's friends come by with casseroles and infant clothing and flowers. Maggie names the baby Heather, because she loves the heather on the moors. Heather is small, pale, and dainty, with glimmers of blond hair on her pink scalp. Maggie is completely in love with her baby, and she's grateful for the support of her mother and step-grandmother, happy to be celebrated by her friends. Yet in the small hours of the morning when Heather wakes with her creaking cry, Maggie weeps as she nurses her child. She knows what it's like to be a girl with no father. She can't believe she brought this upon her own daughter. The thought that her baby has no man to love her is a spear of grief in Maggie's heart.

Ten days after Serena's birth, Emily dozes on the living room sofa, her baby in a wicker basket next to her. When she hears the apartment door open, she snaps awake, sits up, adjusts the neckline of her robe, and runs her hands over her hair. The baby nurse they hired for a week has gone. Her parents have made their daily visit and left. Emily's put on lipstick, blush, and eyeliner for the first time since she returned from the hospital, and as Cameron enters the room, she arranges her face in a welcoming smile.

'You've been working terribly hard,' she coos. 'Did you get dinner?'

'We had it sent in.' Cameron goes to the drinks table and pours himself a scotch. 'What are you doing up this late?'

'I'd like to chat. I haven't seen you for days, it seems. And look, we have all these lovely baby presents to open.' She doesn't mention the fact that he hasn't come over to peer down at his child or to kiss his wife.

Cameron sinks into a wing chair by the cold fireplace. He rubs his forehead. 'I don't have the energy to deal with those tonight.'

'Cameron, are you all right?' Emily leans toward him, genuinely concerned.

His smile is rueful. 'I'm fine, Emily. But with every day that passes, I feel more like a fool.'

'What do you mean?'

'Emily. No one in the Chadwick family has ever had black hair. You played me, didn't you?'

'No!' Emily's maternal defenses ignite. 'Cameron – what . . .' She begins again. 'If you're talking about Serena, then no, I absolutely did not play you. She is your child. She's only ten days old, give her some time.' Cameron's face is blank, unresponsive. Rising, she moves across the room, sinking onto the floor next to his chair, putting her hands on his knee. She knows her robe has fallen open, exposing her lovely, large milk-filled breasts. 'Cameron. You and I scarcely know one another, it's true. This has all happened in such a rush. I remember quite clearly that you don't love me, but every day I love you more. We can create a wonderful life for ourselves and our daughter. We can be happy.' She feels him relaxing. Emily moves closer. 'I want to make you happy.'

Cameron shakes his head but smiles at the same time. 'Oh, Emily.'

She moves her hand up his leg. 'I could make you happy now,' she whispers, moving between his legs. 'Let me try.'

Later, after Cameron has showered and Serena has wakened for her nighttime nursing and they are all tucked away in the bedroom – Serena slumbering in her co-sleeper attached to the bed – Emily snuggles up to Cameron. She wraps her arms around him, spooning her front against his back.

'I do love you, Cameron. You are such a good, sweet man.'

Cameron's silent for so long she thinks he's sleeping. Then he says, 'And I'll try to be for as long as I can.'

What does *that* mean, Emily wonders, but she's tired . . . Right now she needs sleep more than anything else in the world.

When Heather is fourteen days old, Maggie lies on a cushiony lounge chair on the back screened-in porch, her daughter asleep in a basket next to her. The day is a return to summer, hot, humid, calm, drowsy. She's wearing maternity shorts and an old blue shirt that buttons up the front, or barely does. If her breasts were large before, they're massive now, full of milk. Clarice is napping. Frances has gone to the grocery store.

A man comes around the corner and up the stairs. 'Hello, Mags.'

She blinks, startled out of her doze. 'Ben.'

He's dressed like a summer person in khakis, rugby shirt, and loafers without socks, and Maggie starts to sneer. Then she notices his face. His black hair is styled long and sleek, but his face is sad. She remembers him as a boy, pedaling like a hellion on his bike through the dirt roads of the moors, escaping or running toward – *moving* – and he's her brother and she knows exactly what he wants. He doesn't want to be fatherless, either. He doesn't want to be poor. He wants to be anyone but himself. Now Ben's older. He doesn't want Thaddeus, the one man who loved him, to be dead, leaving him without a guide. He doesn't want the woman who loved him to be married to another man.

'I'd like to see your baby,' Ben says simply.

Maggie bursts into tears. 'Ben, I've missed you so much!' Awkwardly, she tries to move off the chaise, but Ben backs away slightly, as if afraid to be touched.

'Are you okay?' Ben asks. 'Was it horrible, the giving-birth thing?'

Maggie smiles. 'Yeah, it was. And wonderful, too.' Swinging her legs to the floor, she pats the end of the lounge chair. 'Sit down and I'll show her to you.'

Ben sits, his eyes on the small bundle in the basket. Because of the day's heat, Maggie's simply dressed Heather in a diaper and wrapped her in a light cotton blanket. She's sleeping on her tummy, which doctors advise not to let an infant do at night, but which Maggie lets her do when she's right there with her.

Maggie picks Heather up. She already weighs eleven pounds. Her face is angelic. She has the glistening perfection of a newborn.

Ben is mesmerized.

'Want to hold her?' Maggie asks.

Ben draws back. 'I might hurt her.'

'No, she's not that fragile. Here.' She settles her daughter in Ben's arms.

Gently, with his finger, Ben pushes back the blanket to expose Heather's two little fists, lightly closed, smaller than scallop shells.

'Her fingers,' he says.

'I know.'

The baby gives a shuddering breath and opens her blue eyes. She gazes up at Ben for a long time with that inscrutable questioning infant stare. Then she smiles.

Maggie feels a tremor move through Ben. 'Her name is Heather.'

'Hello, Heather.' Ben touches his niece's cheek and she turns her head toward his hand. 'My God, Maggie, she's amazing.'

'Yes. Yes, she is.' Maggie knows her brother's holding back a powerful emotion, perhaps enough to make him cry, which might embarrass him terribly, so she rises. 'I'm going to fetch myself some ice water. Want some?'

Ben looks terrified. 'You can't leave me here alone with her!'

'Don't be silly. Sit there and talk to her. She'll enjoy a male voice.'

Maggie goes into the kitchen, takes down two glasses, fills them with ice, and bursts into tears. It is not fair. Love is not fair. It is too hard. She is deeply attached to the farm, but she loves her brother, and seeing him with her child cracks her heart open with joy.

After a few moments she wipes her eyes, runs tap water over the ice, and carries the glasses out to the porch.

'Did you both survive?' she asks lightly.

Ben looks up at her. 'Maggie, I'm not going to sell the land.'

Maggie almost drops the glasses. 'What?'

'I've been thinking. I mean . . . this baby is a little girl.'

Cautiously, Maggie sits next to her brother, almost holding her breath. 'Yes, that's true.'

Heather has Ben's finger clutched tightly in her tiny fat hand.

Ben gazes with adoration at his niece. 'She should grow up there, on that land. She should learn about the island there, run to the harbor like you did, play in the boathouse, in the barns.'

'Ben, that would be wonderful for her. That would be paradise.'

Heather makes a strange face and a stranger sound. Ben glances at Maggie, slightly alarmed.

'She just filled her diaper,' Maggie explains. 'I think that's a sign of approval.'

Ben laughs, gazing down at his niece with pride in his eyes. 'I'm going to buy her a pony.'

Maggie laughs, too, at the same time choking back tears. 'Ben, she's too little for a pony. But oh, I would love it if she could grow up on the farm.'

'Then that's what we'll make happen,' Ben says. 'I'll find a way.'

★　★　★

In the Park Avenue apartment, in her exquisitely hand-painted nursery, Serena enjoys her late morning nap. She is four weeks old, healthy and active, a true bouncing baby. Cameron is at work. Emily's housekeeper has left to run errands. Emily's parents, having fussed over Emily and her daughter for an appropriate amount of time, are at brunch with friends. Emily wanders her large, elegant apartment, overwhelmed with a melancholy so painful it's almost like homesickness. She misses Maggie. Tiffany, not yet pregnant, isn't interested in discussing the details of life with a new baby, and her Manhattan mommy friends are vaguely competitive – which agency did Emily's nanny come from, in which preschool will Emily enroll Serena?

She wants to laugh. She wants to be at home. Finally she gives in, curls up in a chair in the living room, and picks up her iPhone.

'Maggie, it's Emily. I'm calling to thank you for the gorgeous Nantucket sweater and cap for Serena!'

Maggie sounds distant and slightly formal. 'Oh, you're welcome. And thank you for the silver cup for Heather. I'm planning to write you an official thank-you note—'

'Please, don't!' Emily laughs. 'If you don't, I won't have to write you. And I don't have time to. I don't have time to go to the bathroom.'

Maggie chuckles, and instantly, they're close again. 'I know! How do they sense it? Heather will be sound asleep and the moment I shut the bathroom door, she wakes up and wails.'

'Serena does the same thing! It's like she possesses some odd ESP telling her the second my focus is on something other than her.'

'And the laundry. Who knew one little baby's poop could ruin so many of her clothes and mine at one time? Thank heavens my mother helps. Is Cara staying with you?'

Emily hesitates. 'No, although she did come over almost every day the first week. But she's not great with babies. Or with thinking of anyone but herself, actually,' Emily adds with an easy laugh. 'I think I'll break down and hire a nanny, though. Honestly, it's been four weeks and I still can't accomplish a thing. Time is doing a strange warp trick, moving faster sometimes and wayyyy slower in the middle of the night when Serena's having a crying jag.'

'I know,' Maggie says. 'I'm learning a lot about late night TV. Heather likes being awake about three in the morning. It's her wiggle time. No chance I can persuade her back to sleep for an hour.'

'Cameron takes care of Serena then,' Emily admits. 'He seldom sees her during the day, he's working. He's asked to take over the early morning feeding. I pump and keep bottles in the fridge.'

'Lucky you,' Maggie says. 'I don't know when I'll ever sleep a full night again.'

Emily asks, 'What does Ben think of Serena?'

'Oh,' Maggie begins, then interrupts herself. 'Emily, Heather's crying and Mom's out getting groceries. I'd better go. Let's talk another time. Love you.'

'Love you, too,' Emily replies. Without Maggie's voice, the silence around her seems enormous.

# Part Six
# Hail, Lord Boulder!

# Chapter Twenty-four

*Four Years Later*

On a foggy November afternoon, Maggie and Heather sit together at the kitchen table with their colored pencils and pads of paper, drawing pictures of the island and its creatures, real and imaginary. Frances is baking cookies, infusing the air around them with the scent of cinnamon and sugar, and Clarice is in the living room, lying on the sofa reading, with a blanket over her and the cat Cleopatra on top.

The phone rings. Heather jumps up. At four, she finds answering the phone a constant adventure. 'For you, Mommy.' She brings Maggie the handset.

'Hi, Maggie. How are you?' It's a vaguely familiar voice, low, compelling.

'Fine,' Maggie responds crankily. She hates guessing games. 'I'll be better when I know who this is.'

A short burst of laughter breaks over the line. 'Same old Maggie.'

Who is this? She *knows* she knows but can't quite conjure up the name. 'Come on!'

'It's Tyler.'

For a beat she stands there with her jaw hanging open. 'Tyler. Tyler! Honey, how *are* you?'

'I'm great, as a matter of fact. I'm coming to the island. I might settle there.'

'Get out!' She's wracking her brain but she can't remember the last time they wrote or emailed or talked. It's been years.

'It's true. I'm coming on Wednesday. Want to meet for a drink?'

'Meet for a drink? Are you kidding? I'm going to meet your boat!'

Again, the low roll of laughter. 'Think you'll recognize me after all these years?'

'Are you nuts? Of course I will.'

It's a blustery day, the intermittent wind pushing and tugging at the clouds, turning cloud hills into cloud mountains, then blowing the peaks away. Nantucket Sound tosses restlessly, its blue, green, gold waves leaping, lapping, and crashing over the long jetties, as gray and rounded as the seals who will soon recline there throughout the winter. The ferry rumbles in, banging the dock as a wave slams its hull, then the engines subside and the ramps are maneuvered into place and the cars roll off and the passengers come down the foot ramp.

Maggie shields her eyes with her hand against the noon sun and peers up at the line of people coming out of the boat. She doesn't see anyone who looks like Tyler.

'Maggie?'

A man walks toward her. Tall, muscular, easy in his bones, he strides along in chinos, blue dress shirt, red tie, leather jacket. A mop of gleaming brown hair falls over his forehead and ears. Dark Buddy Holly glasses, retro and attractive, frame his dark eyes. He's *gorgeous.*

'Tyler?'

'The one and only.'

'Oh, my God.' She throws herself at him, hugging him, then standing back to check him out, every inch. 'Tyler, look at you! My God, you're absolutely *handsome*! You've become a hunk! Your smile, I could die! Why, it's a *miracle*!'

'Don't hold back, Maggie. Tell me what you really think.'

'Oh, stop it.' She runs her hands down his arms. 'Look at these muscles!'

Tyler's face is serious when he says quietly, 'You're looking extremely appealing yourself, Maggie.'

She has no idea what she's wearing. Certainly she put no effort into her appearance today; she was only meeting Tyler. 'Yeah, but *you,* just look at you!'

'Hey, you're making a commotion. Let's get in your car.'

'Do you have luggage?' she asks.

'No, I'm only here for the day.'

'But you're coming back, aren't you?' Maggie grips him by the wrist as she drags him to her car. She can't take her eyes or her hands off him.

'Yeah, I told you, I'm considering setting up an optometrist practice here.'

She has to let him go while they slide into opposite sides of the car, then Maggie turns to stare at him again.

'My God, Tyler. I can't believe it.'

He smiles, but he's changed, become an adult, and now he rolls his eyes. 'Enough. Tell me what you're doing.'

'Oh, nothing, cleaning houses. Living at the farm, which we might as well call The Convent – it's all women, my grandmother, mother, me, and Heather.' Her heart stops. 'Are *you* married?' A guy who looks like this? He's married.

'Nope.' Tyler's head is bent as he fastens his seat belt.

'No way. Engaged?'

'Nope.' Seemingly determined not to meet her eyes, Tyler focuses on untwisting the belt.

'Why not?'

'I've been too busy.' He clicks the seat belt fastened. 'How's your mom? How's Ben?'

'He's good. But he's changed.' She can't talk fast enough, she has so much to tell him. 'All he wants is to get rich.'

'And is he rich?'

'Oh, yes. He lives in the Orange Street house.' Seeing Tyler's expression, she admits, 'It's taken a long time, but we've finally sorted it all out: Mom, Clarice, Heather, and I have moved from the Orange Street house to the farm. Ben and I did all the legal paperwork, and now the Orange Street house is his, the farm mine. It was pretty difficult, convincing Clarice to leave her beloved home, but she's older now, and aware that it's better for her to live with us. She'd lived on the farm years before, when Thaddeus was born, and she loves it there, too.'

'But why does Ben live in the Orange Street house?'

'Ben is now – wait for it – a real estate broker. He tried working as a stockbroker for a while, but Ben will never be a desk man, and he wasn't any good at it. He considered selling the Orange Street house, which would give him a fat chunk of money, but he needs a house of his own – he wouldn't want to live with us at the farm, how could he bring home his thousands of women? So he got his Realtor's license, joined a brokerage firm, and is doing quite well. He insists he's working for the island as well as for himself, showing people places that are already built, not showing them land we all hope will be kept open.' Maggie stops to catch her breath. 'Tyler, how is your mother? I know she married Clary Able and they moved off island – was it to Boston?'

'Portland. Look, I have appointments to look at some apartments, but can you have dinner with me tonight?'

'Are you kidding me? I'm your chauffeur for the day.'

'Could I borrow your car instead? I want to concentrate on business, and you're interfering with my focus.'

'Can't let that happen to an optometrist,' Maggie jokes. She's light-headed.

Tyler drops Maggie at the farm before driving off to check out rental spaces, commercial and residential.

Maggie searches out Frances and finds her in her sewing room, embroidering.

'Mom, you'll never believe it! I just picked up Tyler from the boat, and he's *gorgeous*!'

Frances pushes her sewing glasses up onto her forehead, leans back in her chair, and closes her eyes. 'Tyler Madison. Smart boy. One of your best friends. His mother and father divorced . . . and then they both left the island, right?'

'Right. But Tyler's an optometrist now—'

'That's not surprising.'

'—and he's going to practice on the island!'

'Good for him. I'd like to see him.'

'I'll bring him in later. He's driving my car to some

appointments. He's picking me up for dinner at six.' Maggie clutches her hair. 'You can babysit Heather, right? She's at Kerrie's for a playdate with Marina. Kerrie can drive her home. I've got to do something about my hair.'

'A change of clothes might be good, too,' Frances suggests, smiling.

In her bedroom, Maggie pauses to check herself out in the mirror. Over the past four years, she's been too busy being what Virginia Woolf called 'the essential angel of the house' – meaning doing most of the grocery shopping, caring for her baby, caring for Clarice. She's hung out with girlfriends for fun, and she's written a few articles for *Nantucket Glossy* during the summer. On winter evenings, she works on her novel. All in all, not a lifestyle requiring any sort of glamour.

She showers, washes her hair, blows it dry, taming it with hot rollers while she applies eye shadow, eyeliner, mascara, blush, lip gloss, reminding herself that this isn't a *date,* this is dinner with Tyler, an old friend. Still, she pulls on her sexiest dress, the red one that plunges low over her bosom.

When she opens the door to Tyler's knock, he whistles. 'Wow. You're all grown up.'

'Come in. Mom wants to see you.' Maggie can tell she's blushing at his compliment. Blushing because of Tyler? *Whoa.*

While Tyler and Frances and Clarice chat, Maggie waits impatiently, trying not to wriggle. Heather has been asked to spend the night at Kerrie's. Maggie's disappointed because she wants Tyler to see her beautiful daughter, but also rather relieved, because with one more person to drool over Tyler, they'd never escape this house and be alone.

She clears her throat. Tyler glances at his watch. 'Sorry,' he says to Frances and Clarice, 'I've made a reservation for seven.'

'Have fun,' Frances tells them, eyes twinkling.

As they walk out to Maggie's Bronco, Tyler tosses Maggie the keys. 'Thanks for loaning it to me.'

'Did you have any luck?' Maggie asks as they drive into town.

'Great luck,' Tyler tells her. 'Dawn Holdgate showed me several places. I think I've found an excellent location for my office, on North Beach Street, within walking distance of town.'

'Which building?'

'Across from the Harbor House.'

'Oh, I know which one you mean.'

'The rent is reasonable, too.'

'Did you find an apartment?' As she drives, Maggie's aware that Tyler's angled in his seat so he can look at her while they talk. She can't believe how nervous this makes her. She has to concentrate to find the restaurant she's frequented for years.

'I found two that will work. One's more than I wanted to pay, but it's close to the office space.'

They park on India Street, walk to the Boarding House, and are ushered to a table in the corner. Other diners glance up as they come in, but to Maggie's relief, no one recognizes Tyler, so she can have him all to herself.

After they order drinks, Maggie says, 'Now. Tell me everything.'

His mouth (his beautiful mouth!) quirks up in a half-smile. 'Which everything?'

'Any serious romances?' she asks boldly.

'One. Penelope. Three years.' He smiles wryly. 'A college thing, you know.'

She asks, 'Where's Penelope now?'

'Australia.'

'Ah.' Maggie can't help smiling. 'Good place for her.'

He laughs. Does he find her attractive? Can he tell Maggie's going wild?

'You obviously had a serious romance,' Tyler remarks.

'I did?' She's so flustered she can't think straight.

'Well, you have a daughter,' Tyler reminds her.

Maggie throws her head back and laughs full-heartedly. 'Honestly, Tyler? It was a one-night stand. I was such a fool, but I got Heather out of it, and I'm glad. Heather is my pride and joy, sweet and smart – oh, I can't wait for you to meet her.'

'Weren't you dating Shane Anderson?'

'I can't believe you remember that. Yes. Yes, I did date him, and he's a nice guy. But not the one for me. He's married now. He and his wife have twins.'

Their meals are set before them. For a few moments they concentrate on their scallops and steak, but the mood between them changes.

Their eyes meet. Maggie feels her protective façade melt in the face of her good old friend. 'Tyler? I know this is weird, but I feel kind of shy around you. You're so handsome. I can't believe that you're you.'

Tyler leans back in his chair and considers her words. 'Maybe I'm not the me I used to be. Actually, I hope I'm *not* the me I used to be. I was awfully isolated, Maggie, when I was a kid. It was hard, being such a dork. Plus, with both my parents finding other partners, having other kids . . . I became a real loner.'

Maggie nods. 'You stopped emailing me. We lost touch.' She smiles at him. 'But you've *changed*.'

'The changes didn't take place overnight, Maggie. The eye operations were hard. Having surgery isn't fun, wondering if you'll be able to see normally is scary. I had a few years of real misery. Plus, braces. Damn, they hurt.'

'Could you tell me about your operations, Tyler? I'd like to hear about them. Really.'

His eyes are meltingly deep. Slowly he straightens and smiles. 'Sure. I'll tell you about them. But not tonight, not over this delicious meal. I want to enjoy myself.' He cuts off a bite of steak and chews it. 'Let's focus on you. What about your writing?'

The mood changes to a brighter, lighter tone. 'Oh, Tyler, I have such fun in the summer, going to galas for *Nantucket Glossy*. Some summer people are snobs who don't give a fig about the island, I know, but some are really nice. A lot of them are truly generous to the island institutions. I enjoy interviewing most of them.'

'And your novel?'

'I work on it in the off-season. But taking care of Heather has been my priority. The first couple of years I could hardly take my eyes off her. She's the most beautiful, magical, darling, and fast-moving thing I've ever seen.' Thinking about Heather makes Maggie glow. 'She is my one true love.'

'Really?' Tyler raises a questioning eyebrow.

'Really what?'

'She is your one true love?'

Maggie stirs her pasta with her fork. 'You know what I mean.'

'No grown-up, male one true loves?'

Maggie deliberately takes a bite of pasta and chews, giving Tyler an insolent look. All at once she feels flirtatious. Maggie's emotions are taking her on a carnival ride, one of those centrifugal force things; she has no idea what's going on, but she feels as if she's whirling around ten feet in the air. Such a mix of childish responses to this old friend, plus a tsunami of entirely new adult physical flashes.

'Maybe. Maybe I've had several grown-up, male one true loves,' she says mischievously.

Tyler responds by saying nothing, only staring at her with his beautiful, dark intense eyes.

'Okay, fine.' Maggie takes a sip of wine. 'No, I've never truly been in love. Have you?'

Tyler smiles enigmatically. 'Yes. For almost all my life.'

Maggie's heart skips a beat.

Tyler leans forward. 'I want to ask you something, well, personal.'

Maggie nearly stops breathing. 'All right.'

'Do you still have *The Official Register of Secrets*?'

It takes her brain a beat or two to switch tracks. 'Well, *of course* I do.'

His face lights up. 'That's great. But I'm surprised.'

'Why?'

'I thought since you had to move from Thaddeus's house, you might have chucked it out with any other miscellaneous junk.'

'Hey! That masterpiece? It was never *junk!*'

With a lopsided smile and a shrug, he says, 'We were silly kids when I wrote it.'

The waitress appears, setting the bill on the table. 'Whenever you're ready.'

'We're ready now.' Tyler looks at his watch. 'I'd better not be late to the airport.' Pulling a credit card from his wallet, he hands it to the waitress, who goes off. He leans forward again. 'Know what I'd like to do?'

*Kiss me?* Maggie thinks. *Go to bed?* Damn, she is *giddy*. 'What?'

'I'd like to go for a nice long walk over the moors, with *The*

*Official Register of Secrets,* checking out the old rocks and trees and ponds and stuff.'

'Oh.'

The waitress returns. Tyler scribbles on the credit receipt, takes his credit card, and sticks it in his wallet. 'I'm coming back this Thursday. I need to start organizing my move here. How about Sunday?'

Maggie blinks. 'How about Sunday what?'

'To spend a day with me on the moors? We could take a picnic.' He checks his watch, pushes back his chair, and rises.

He moves with such authority, Maggie thinks, he's become such a *man.* 'Lord Boulder,' she says, grinning. 'Princess Pond!'

# Chapter Twenty-five

Sunday afternoon, Maggie and Tyler spend hours walking over the moors, checking out boulders, rocks, ponds, and trees. Tyler scarcely speaks, and Maggie, understanding his silent communion with the sacred places of his youth, respects his need for silence.

By the time they return to the car, it's too cold to stay out any longer, and the light's fading, so they bump over the rutted dirt lanes back to the main roads and to Tyler's hotel room. They set out the bread, cheese, and wine left over from their picnic. Tyler moves a chair so they can both sit at the small round table while Maggie pours the wine.

'I can't believe how many new houses there are on the island,' Tyler says.

Maggie looks at his hands, pale and long, covered with fine brown hairs. His nails are long and rounded and clean. 'I don't mind the number as much as how gigantic they are,' Maggie tells him. 'And the way they're situated on the land, as if saying, *Forget about the beautiful land. Look at me!* But never mind.' She taps her glass against his. 'A toast. Good luck. I'm glad you're moving back.'

Tyler smiles. 'Because I respect the island?'

Something about the way he's looking at her makes her breath catch. 'Well . . . *sure.*'

'Is that the only reason?' Tyler asks, as if in jest, but Maggie believes she senses something in his eyes that assures her his question isn't frivolous.

'Tyler, you're confusing me,' she tells him, her voice louder than she means it to be.

'I am?'

'Yes, you are! I mean, we're friends, and we haven't seen each other for a long time, and here you are back again, and I don't feel *friendly* at all.'

He smiles. He reaches out and takes her glass, which is a good thing, because she's started to tremble so much she's about to slosh wine on the rug. 'How *do* you feel?' he asks.

'How do *you* feel?' she shoots back.

He sets his glass and hers on the table behind them. Then he turns his full attention on her. 'Right now I feel happier than I've felt in years. And absolutely terrified.'

She almost bursts into tears. 'I'm scared, too.'

Tyler takes her hand in his. 'Then I guess you and I are going to have to go slow.'

His hand is warm and firm, his voice steady, his eyes clear and honest, his aura purely good – she wants to unbutton his flannel shirt and crawl inside and curl up next to his heart. 'Yes,' she says. 'I guess we should.'

But he pulls her to him and brings his mouth down onto hers. At first his kiss is tentative, a breath of warmth on her skin. She turns toward him; moving closer, she puts her hands on his chest, and Tyler groans, his arms hug her against him, his mouth searches hers, and he finds the answer he needs.

They can hardly stop kissing long enough to reach the bed. Tyler pulls her down onto it, kissing her and unbuttoning her shirt, kissing her and unzipping her jeans, while she tugs his clothes away from him.

'Oh, my God,' Tyler says, when they're both naked. 'Oh, my God, Maggie.'

Tyler's long body is warm. He's inside her almost instantly, and she folds her legs and arms around him to bring him tighter against her. They kiss as they move, wet, salty, sweaty kisses with strands of her hair caught in their mouths, and when they climax they hold each other as close as they can.

He collapses on top of her, and she does not loosen her arms and legs, she wants to hold him against her like this forever, his muscular chest pressing hers, his face nestled against her neck. She has so much to learn about him, she wants to roll him over and search out every detail of his skin, find his moles, what kind of hair furs his chest and crotch, and yet she doesn't want him to move away from her, not yet.

Finally he rolls over, and she takes a huge breath.

'Was I crushing you?' he asks.

'Yes,' she murmurs.

'Should I do it again?'

'Yes, please.'

They turn toward one another, this time less frantically. They explore one another, caress and kiss one another. It's almost unbearably exciting to Maggie, to touch this man she knew when he was a boy, to find such intimate physical joys with the friend who knows her deepest thoughts. Nothing is missing. Nothing is held back.

His kisses lap against her skin like waves. He enters her, he rocks her, he whispers the sweetest words in her ear, and soon she's sinking, floating down. Light fades, darkness covers her, pleasure flickers against her and through her, then she rolls over and rides Tyler like a girl on a dolphin, casting her body against him, as they rise, then plunge. Her body seems to liquefy. Maggie is all ebb and flow, suds and whirlpool, salt wetness and briny surf. The gleaming treasure flickers at the seabed, golden, radiant, shimmering – she touches it, she reaches it – she merges into it, she is the gleaming treasure, lost, then found.

Afterward, they lie together. 'Tyler?' The word squeaks out of her mouth, squeezed by hope and fear. 'Would you like to meet Heather?' She knows he's aware of how important this is.

'As soon as possible,' Tyler replies. He smooths back Maggie's hair. 'Tell me. What have you told Heather about her father?'

Maggie's shoulders squeeze up to her ears in discomfort. 'She's only a little girl. Only four years old. I haven't had to talk seriously with her about it. I told her that her father is a traveler who hikes in the mountains on the other side of the world and never uses phones or computers. She's not sad. She doesn't worry about it, about not having a father. Lots of children don't, it's not a big deal among the children she plays with.'

'What about Ben? How often does she see him?'

'Oh, *Ben*.' Maggie rolls her eyes. 'When Heather was a baby and a toddler, he doted on her, but as he sold more properties and made more contacts, his life changed. Now he shows up whenever it suits him, bringing some fantastically expensive toy, spending half an hour with us all on a Sunday morning, then rushing off again. But she knows she's got an uncle. When she plays families in her dollhouses, she usually calls the man Ben. That's better than nothing, I suppose.'

'Well, good,' Tyler says decisively. 'That means there's plenty of room for me in her life.'

Maggie smiles.

'We should go,' Tyler says after a few more peaceful moments.

'Hmm,' Maggie murmurs. 'I know. I promised I'd tuck Heather in bed.'

They rise and shower – separately – before dressing and painstakingly arranging their hair and clothing to show no sign of having been tousled or touched. As Tyler drives them to the farm in his rental car, they're quiet, holding hands, allowing the glow to continue.

Maggie leads Tyler into the living room of the farmhouse where Clarice sits in her armchair watching Frances read a storybook to Heather.

'How was dinner?' Frances's eyes twinkle.

'Great,' Maggie replies, and can't help grinning.

'Heather,' Frances announces, 'this is your mommy's friend Tyler.'

Heather is ready for bed, already bathed, blond flyaway hair combed, wearing her teddy bear pajamas and pink cotton robe with a flower for a pocket. She sits on the couch with an interested gleam in her eyes.

Maggie holds her tongue. Heather can be a handful if she wishes; she's Bette Davis at four years old.

'Oh, yes,' Tyler says, and offers his hand to Heather. 'You must be Rapunzel.'

Heather stifles a smile. She sniffs. 'I am not Rapunzel.'

'Oh, right, I meant Ariel.'

Heather crimps her lips. 'Not Ariel.'

Tyler sits on the sofa, keeping a large space between him and Heather. He thumps his forehead. 'I was so sure – I know! You're Dora the Explorer.'

Heather breaks into a giggle. 'Of course not.'

'No? Well then – Madeline? The Cat in the Hat? But wait, you're not wearing a hat.'

'And I'm not a cat!' Heather yells triumphantly. 'I'm *Heather*!'

'Hello, Heather,' Tyler says formally, extending his hand. 'I'm Tyler.'

Heather puts her tiny chubby dimpled hand in his large, elegantly shaped hand. In her best voice, she says, 'How do you do?'

'I'm excellent,' Tyler says, 'now that I've met *you*.'

Heather's eyes widen. 'Are you the man who travels in the mountains?'

Maggie holds her breath.

'Yes,' Tyler says. 'Yes, Heather, but I'm coming home.'

Christmas morning at the farm, the little family of females shares a traditional breakfast of pancakes and strawberries, then gathers around the tree in the living room. Heather has already discovered the wooden easel, box of paints, sketch pads, and colored pencils that Santa brought her. Now she's old enough to enjoy the pleasure of giving her gifts to her mother, Nana, which is what she calls Frances, and Grand, which is Heather's name for Clarice. Ben has of course been invited to share the day, but he's gone skiing in Vail with friends. He's left a present for everyone, though

– a special one for his niece. Maggie goes into the locked study and wheels out a sparkling pink bike with training wheels and glitter streamers hanging from the handlebars. Heather squeals with surprise.

The day is cold but sunny and dry. Maggie runs alongside, holding Heather until she's steady, then watches her pedal like a mad thing up and down the driveway. Maggie's happy but impatient today – she wants the afternoon to arrive. She's waiting for Tyler to get there. He's been invited for a walk on the moors and Christmas dinner.

After Heather has a forced rest in her room, during which she can be heard babbling the entire time to her stuffed animals, a knock sounds on the front door and Tyler comes in, his arms full of gifts. During the past month his presence has become so normal, it seems he was always around. Maggie wraps an apron around him, he rolls up his sleeves and peels potatoes to be cooked and mashed.

Clarice sits at the kitchen table with a cup of tea. 'How's business?'

'Crazy busy,' Tyler answers. 'I have a secretary now – Joanne Post—'

'Oh, she's a friend of mine,' Frances interrupts. 'You'll like her. She's reliable.'

'Good to know. Because the appointment book is filling up. I need to hire another woman to help out with fitting and choosing frames.'

Clarice chuckles. 'I'll bet that's always time-consuming. The color, the style, studying your face in the mirror, do you want round frames or rectangular—'

'Do these frames make my butt look too big?' Maggie jokes.

'Why are you all in here laughing?' Heather stands in the kitchen doorway, rumpled and indignant.

Maggie checks her watch. 'You have ten more minutes of rest time.' She shoots a quick glance at Tyler.

'Maggie,' he pleads, as she knows he will, 'it's Christmas Day! Can't you let Heather get up now?'

'I guess so,' Maggie agrees.

Heather simpers with triumph and launches herself at Tyler. 'You're here! I knew you'd come today!'

Tyler dries his hands so he can lift the little girl to his shoulders. 'I think we should go for a walk.'

'I agree,' Maggie says. 'What do you think, Mom? Do you need us to help?'

'Everything's under control,' Frances assures them. 'We'll eat around six.'

'We'll be back before then. It grows dark about four.' Maggie stretches up to tug on Heather's coat, mittens, and cap, secretly bumping her body into Tyler's as she kits her daughter up for the outdoors. She pulls on her own coat and snatches the car keys.

'Let's go to the moors today,' she suggests. 'We haven't been there yet, not the three of us.'

They drive along a rutted sandy track into the moors and park near Altar Rock. As they stride along in the cold fresh air, they study the gray, dreary, dry foliage, which will be this way until June. To most people, this monotone landscape is faceless, but Maggie, Tyler, and now Heather know that deer, rabbits, and birds hide among the bushes. Occasionally they spot their tracks on the sandy path, or a tuft of rabbit fur caught on a thorn. The pines remain a stubborn green, and red berries shine in the thickets.

'Man, it feels so good to stretch my legs,' Maggie says. She's holding her daughter's left hand, Tyler's holding her right and every few steps they lift her in the air and she giggles. 'I love being curled up with a good book on a winter day, but I go crazy if I can't be outside for a little while.'

Tyler doesn't answer. She can tell that he's straining to see ahead. This is the first time Maggie's walked on the moors with both Tyler and Heather, and she knows what's around the bend. She knows what she hopes will happen.

And it does.

As they come to the turn in the path that leads them up a slight hill, Heather pulls her hands away and races up to a large boulder. She makes a pretty little curtsy. 'Hail, Lord Boulder!' she calls.

Tyler stumbles. He looks at Maggie. 'You told her about my maps.'

'I did. Long ago, Tyler, when she was a toddler. I showed her your maps, long before we knew you were coming back to the island.'

Tyler's eyes grow warm, his cheeks flush. 'Foolish.'

'Not foolish. It's your world, Tyler. It's always been your world.'

'You've always been my world,' he tells her, taking her hand.

'You guys!' Heather chides. 'Come on! Let's go see Princess Pond!'

# Chapter Twenty-six

On New Year's Eve, after Emily has tucked Serena into her pink canopied bed, she wanders their Park Avenue apartment in search of her husband. She finds him in his study, on the phone. She's wearing her fluffy bathrobe, preparing to shower before dressing for the corporate party, so she simply curls up on his leather sofa and shoots him a smile, letting him know she'll wait.

'Right. Bye,' he says, clicking off and tossing his cell on his desk. 'Serena's asleep?'

Emily stretches. 'After five stories, she couldn't keep her eyes open.' Readjusting herself to face him, she asks, 'Cameron, can we talk?'

He stretches. He's not ready for the party yet, but wearing a cashmere sweater and sweatpants after exercising. 'Of course. What's up?'

'Honey, I want to have another baby.' Quickly, she continues, 'Serena needs a brother or sister. A baby would bring us closer, I think.'

Cameron folds his hands together on his desk as if about to discuss a business deal. 'Emily, I know how you feel. You need to understand my point of view. I'm junior at the firm, working insane hours. Half the time I'm on an airplane and when I'm home, I'm too wiped out to play with Serena, let alone deal with another baby.'

'Cameron—'

'Please. Let me finish. I'm not saying *never* to another child. I'm saying not *now*. We've gone over this before, and – oh, Emily, don't cry. That's not fair.' Rising, he moves around his desk, coming to sit on the sofa and pull Emily into his arms.

'I really want another baby,' she cries.

'You'll have one,' he promises, kissing the top of her head. 'Be patient, okay? Give me some more time. I need more time.' When she continues to sob, he says, 'We rushed into this so quickly, we married in such haste.'

Emily takes a deep breath and composes herself. He's always a gentleman. It's what brought her to him, but now she wonders if she hates this civilized, restrained aspect of him. He's reminding her in the most subtle way possible that she gently forced him into marriage. She owes him. At least she owes him time.

'Okay,' she sniffles. 'I'll wait.' Gazing up at him, she strokes his cheek. 'Oh, Cameron, I wish I could do more to help you.'

'You can.' He smiles and holds her away from him. 'Glam yourself up for tonight so the senior partners will fall over with amazement when they're reminded what a babe you are. They'll think: If that man's smart enough to attract *her*, he's smart enough to be given the biggest, fattest accounts.'

'Okay, then, boss,' she says, standing up. 'I'm off to the shower.'

She calls over her shoulder as she leaves the room, 'Would you listen for the babysitter? She should get here around nine.'

Emily wears four-inch black Manolo Blahniks and a simple black dress that suggests she's not wearing underwear. She pulls her long blond hair away from her face into a high ponytail fastened with a diamond clip. She spends half an hour on her eye shadow, liner, and mascara, giving a smoky, mysterious look to her blue eyes.

'You look sexy as hell,' Cameron says when he sees her.

'You clean up nicely yourself,' she tells him. He always looks good in his tux.

When they enter the party at the restaurant, they're aware of all eyes turning to take them in, this sophisticated, gorgeous, fortunate pair. A waiter offers champagne, one of Cameron's bosses comes up to them, and a moment later, the boss's wife approaches.

Cornelia Endicott is not young, but she's powerful, and she wears her power like a crown.

'Darling.' They air kiss.

'I've been wanting to talk to you,' Cornelia says, taking Emily's arm and leading her off to a quiet spot in the room.

Three other wives gather around Emily like a coven of fabulously perfumed, extremely wealthy witches. They chatter at Emily, praising her clothes, asking about her darling daughter. They've been trying for the last two years to entice Emily onto the board of their favorite charity, which raises money for the squirrel monkeys of Peru. Emily knows very well from watching her mother's life that this means Emily – as the novice, the beginner – will have to do all the work of running the annual gala. In the past she's gently refused, pleading the necessary duties of mothering a toddler, but Serena is four now, in preschool, and besides, Emily could easily hire a full-time nanny.

Over Cornelia's shoulder, Emily spots Cameron. He's been cornered, too, by a petite young woman with a sweet face and curly black hair and a voluptuous body that reminds Emily of Maggie. Jessica Beckett, that's her name. Her dress is red, sparkling with sequins, off the rack, but stylish. She must be a junior executive. She's new, smart, and very lovely. She's certainly captured Cameron's attention. His eyes fasten on her face with ardor, and as Emily watches, Cameron puts his hand on her shoulder. *So what,* Emily thinks, but then the girl places her hand on top of Cameron's, her entire little body in its sequined dress yearning up toward him. If they are not already having an affair, they want to.

'What do you think?' Cornelia asks Emily, moving her face right into Emily's line of vision, moving in close, doing what people call violating personal space.

Emily has no idea what they're talking about.

'I'd co-chair it with you,' another wife offers. 'I did it last year, so I know the ropes. Plus I've got files and files on florists, bands, venues . . .'

Emily acquiesces. 'Yes. I'd be glad to do it.' She's joining the herd, she thinks. She must do this to keep her child safe.

On this crisp January night, a yellow moon rides high in the sky, and the stars are precisely etched in the black sky. Maggie reads Heather one more story before kissing her good night. Quietly she showers, changes clothes, and tiptoes down the stairs to the living room, where Frances and Clarice are watching television.

'I'll be back. Call if you need me,' she tells them.

Tyler has rented a low-ceilinged cottage on Darling Street. Maggie's been at his house before, often, while Frances and Clarice babysit Heather.

She parks her car on Fair Street and walks in the moonlight down the narrow lane, so narrow only one car can pass at a time. When she knocks on the cottage door, Tyler opens it at once. He pulls her in, slams the door, holds her tight. 'I missed you today.'

'I missed you.'

'Want wine?'

'Want you.'

They climb the steep stairs to the bedroom. Already the windowsills and tabletops are covered: books everywhere, rocks, shells, bits of beach glass, and driftwood. Heather's artwork is taped to the walls.

Quickly they discard their clothing and slide into bed. Tyler's long body is hot, hers still bearing the winter chill.

Afterward, they lie side by side, catching their breath, her back curled against his chest and belly and groin, his arm over her waist.

Tyler says, 'I have something to tell you.'

'Okay.' Her heart flips around like a newly caught fish. She and Tyler have been quite sensible in spite of, perhaps because of, their nearly insane physical passion for one another. They've taken the time to learn about each other again. They both want to live on the island forever. They both want families. In all their conversations, the topic of marriage sits in the room with them like a purring cat, patient on a cushion.

She feels his chest swell as he takes in a deep breath. 'Maggie, I want to marry you. I want to have children with you. I want—'

'Oh, Tyler.' Tears well in her eyes. She rolls over to face him, she wants to kiss him.

'Wait,' he says. 'We might have a problem.'

'Oh, God.' Maggie closes her eyes, clenching her whole body in anticipation. He's been married before. He has a child. He has five children. He has a disease. He's—

'Maggie, I have money.'

'What?' The words don't make sense to her.

'I have a lot of money.'

Warily, she asks, 'How much?'

'Well, I guess you'd say I'm well-off.'

She sits straight up in bed. 'Tyler, how can that be? Your mother – Clary Able – they don't have any money! I know them!'

'True. But my father does.'

Maggie studies Tyler suspiciously. 'Go on.'

'Dad works in Silicon Valley. He's made what you could call a fortune in the last ten years. He's already set up a couple of trusts for me and any children I might have, plus he's been generous over the years, giving me cash and stocks and so on.'

Pulling the sheet up to her chest, Maggie scoots backward to the edge of the bed, pulling her legs under her. 'Tyler, why didn't you tell me this before?'

'Because you're not always rational on the subject of wealthy people.'

'Oh, come on—' She's annoyed by Tyler's comment.

'Maggie—'

'Okay, maybe I am a bit *unbalanced* on the subject, but, God, Tyler, you've seen what's happening to this island, it's being ripped open to provide swimming pools and squash courts for people who spend less than two weeks here, it's—'

Tyler interrupts. 'Let's return to the more simple subject of you and me.'

Maggie tosses her head. 'It's not so simple anymore, is it?'

'Look. I'm not disgustingly rich. I'm comfortable. I have enough, for example, so we could buy a house.'

'I own a house,' Maggie reminds him. 'I own the farm.'

'Yes, well, shall we live there with your mother and Clarice and our children? Wouldn't you find it a little crowded?'

'You know what?' Maggie begins to pull her clothes on. 'I have to leave.'

'Maggie.'

Sitting on the blanket chest, she laces up her boots.

'Maggie, come on. Don't act this way.'

'I'm not *acting* any way, Tyler.' She stands up so suddenly she nearly knocks him with her elbow. 'I'm confused. I need to – honestly, I don't know what I need to do.'

'Are you coming back?' Sliding out of bed, he pulls on his trousers.

'I don't know.' Tears sting her eyes. 'Tyler, I love you. But – but now I don't know what to think.'

'Well, for one thing, you can understand that wealthy people aren't bad just because they have bigger bank accounts.'

'I know that.' Maggie's brow furrows. 'But money changed Ben. And Emily Porter, my first true best friend, was going to marry Ben, she loves Ben, but then Cameron Chadwick came along with his money and she married him. Really, Tyler, I *hate* this.'

'Do you hate me?' Tyler asks simply.

Maggie forces herself to take a deep breath. 'Tyler, I could never hate you.' She touches his face, and her anger vanishes.

He takes her hand and leads her to the bed. They sit side by side as Maggie calms down.

'You know how to be poor and good,' Tyler says quietly. 'Do you think you could be wealthy and good?'

Humbled by his question, Maggie bows her head. 'I'm not sure I'm good at all, Tyler.'

Tyler's smile is gentle. 'Why not, Maggie? Because you slept with a guy and got pregnant? Come on.'

'My one-night stand.' Maggie snorts and glances at Tyler. 'What an idiot I was.'

Tyler leans against the footboard, listening. Maggie leans against the headboard, her feet touching Tyler, grounding her.

'He came on strong. I honestly believed he was in love with me,' Maggie says very quietly. 'I still can't believe how deluded I was. How naïve.'

'Maybe he was an expert con artist.'

'Or I was gullible. I wanted to believe it,' Maggie murmurs.

'Was *he* rich?' Tyler softly questions.

Maggie sniffs. 'Yeah. Yeah, he was, Dr Freud.' She smiles wryly. 'The money didn't matter, but his manners . . . he was *smooth*. I was a fool.'

Tyler gives Maggie a few more minutes of silence. He says, 'And then?'

Maggie looks up. Her face tearstained, she meets his eyes. 'What do you mean?'

'I mean, and then what happened?' Tyler's energy is intense, urging her toward a realization.

Maggie wipes her eyes with the cuffs of her sweater. 'You mean Heather. Yes, then I had Heather, and all that came before was insignificant. I do love her with all my heart. You're right, I know what you're thinking, I've thought it before, too, that I have to accept what happened because through that muddle I found such joy. My little girl.' She looks at Tyler, suddenly frowning. 'But you, Tyler? How do you feel about Heather?'

Tyler leans forward and grasps Maggie's ankle, causing her to glance up at him. 'What if I adopted her?'

The simple question takes her breath away. 'You'd do that?'

'Maggie, love of my life, I would be honored to do that.'

'She's another man's child.'

'She's Heather. She's a small girl with golden curls and your deep blue gypsy eyes. She's as quick as a whip, as silly as a puppy, as sweet as ice cream.'

Maggie thinks her heart is going to break wide open. Her chest swells with all the love in her heart, and her throat aches with all the words she's too overwhelmed to speak.

'So you'd like it if I adopted her?' Tyler asks.

Tears rain down Maggie's face, spilling onto her sweater, onto the bed, onto her hands, onto Tyler's hands.

'So you'll marry me?' Tyler asks.

She throws herself at this man, she lunges at him with such huge affection, such an explosion of joy, that she knocks them both backward on the bed. She kisses him all over his face and neck, saying, 'Yes. Yes. *Yes,*' and Tyler is laughing and kissing her back and then they are hugging tightly, as if they'll never ever let each other go.

'Cameron, honey?' Emily coos. 'Wake up, honey. We need to talk.'

She couldn't say this to him last night, because she fell asleep before he returned home from whatever 'business meeting' he was having. Today he'll wake, dress, and be out the door for work without having his coffee. Emily's set a mental alarm clock to wake early. She needs to know.

Cameron lies flat on his stomach, rumbling the thunderous snore of a man in a deep sleep. Not even the aroma of the cup of coffee Emily sets on the bedside table wakes him.

She gently jiggles his shoulder.

'What?' His voice is muffled, his eyes still closed.

Sweetly, she whispers, 'Cameron, please wake up and talk to me.'

He mutters something unintelligible and flips his head the other way so she can't see his face.

Emily settles at the end of the bed, leaning against the carved mahogany footboard, folding her legs up so her knees almost touch her chin. She's wearing a white tee shirt and white underwear, her hair is mussed, her face bare of makeup.

'This is truly the only time I'll be able to talk with you,' she says in a normal speaking voice. 'Serena is still asleep, so she won't interrupt us. You seldom come home for dinner anymore. On weekends, we're always rushing to take Serena to see your parents or mine. The nights we do see each other we're always at one of your necessary corporate parties.' If the government can filibuster, so can she. 'I don't know how to reach you anymore, Cameron, I don't know how to find a space of time when you and I can talk about anything.'

Cameron slowly rolls over and sits up. He opens his bleary eyes. 'Are you all right?'

'My health is good, if that's what you mean.'

'And Serena?'

'She's fine.'

Cameron runs his hand through his tousled blond hair. 'Emily, it's six-thirty in the morning.'

'I don't think you came to bed until after two.'

He scrubs at his face with his hands, muffling his voice. 'I was working.'

Her voice shakes. 'With that black-haired intern?'

'Oh, Emily.' Cameron reaches for his coffee and gulps some down.

Emily struggles not to sound antagonistic. 'Are you having an affair?'

'Emily . . .' Closing his eyes, he leans his head back and takes a deep breath. When he opens his eyes, he looks very tired. 'Look. You and I are good friends. We have a good family life. But I told you from the beginning that I don't love you. I care for you, Emily. I appreciate what you're doing with the wives, all the committee work for those monkeys. It's helping me with the senior partners, absolutely no doubt about it. I don't want a divorce.'

She can't stand the rational way he's speaking, as if no emotion is involved between them at all.

'Do you love her?' Emily asks, as sensibly as if asking whether it's raining outside.

'I don't know.'

Emily stares at him steadily, but her heart is trembling.

Cameron drinks the rest of his coffee and contemplates his next words. Emily waits.

He repeats, 'I don't know. That's the truth, Emily, I don't know yet.' A shadow crosses his face. 'I don't want to hurt Serena. I don't want to hurt you. Give me some more time, okay?'

Emily hears the exasperation straining his voice. She backs off. For the sake of her daughter's happiness, she says, 'Okay, Cameron. But, please, won't you let me try to make you happy? We could leave Serena with your parents and take a trip somewhere. We could play a bit, enjoy each other again.'

Cameron nods. 'Okay, Emily. I'll try.'

Emily starts to speak again. She can see how exhausted Cameron is, and she wants to be kind to him. She wants to be a good wife. 'Thanks, honey. I guess the best way to make you happy right now is to let you go back to sleep.'

She slides off the bed and tiptoes from the room. She can hear Cameron sink back under the duvet.

In the middle of January, Tyler drives Maggie to the farm, kisses her soundly, and promises to phone her the next day. Maggie floats into the house, hoping she'll find her mother still awake. The light is on in Frances's bedroom, so Maggie taps lightly on the door, then opens it a few inches, peeking in.

'Mom?'

Frances is propped against pillows, reading, the lamplight casting a gentle glow over her face. She looks cozy in her yellow flannel pajamas.

'Maggie?' She pushes her reading glasses up on her forehead. 'Come in.'

'Look, Mom.' Maggie rushes in. Sitting on the bed next to Frances, she holds out her hand to show off the antique emerald and diamond engagement ring on her fourth finger. 'It was Tyler's grandmother's.'

'Oh, darling!' Frances and Maggie had discussed the possibility of Maggie and Tyler getting married, but Maggie wanted to wait until now, this moment, the ring on her finger. Frances leans forward and wraps Maggie in a warm hug. 'Congratulations! Oh, I'm so happy for you. And this ring, my goodness!'

'Tyler had to go to Boston to take it out of a bank safety deposit box.' Maggie tilts her hand this way and that, watching the diamonds spark in the light. 'It's not too big, not gaudy?'

'It's exquisite. Maggie, I'm over the moon.' Frances takes

Maggie's hand and gazes at the ring. 'When will the wedding be?'

'As soon as possible,' Maggie tells her. 'We don't need a big to-do. We want to be married and start our lives together. I thought something small here in the house—'

Frances drops Maggie's hand. 'Margaret Ann McIntyre, you can forget that right now. I've been waiting all your life to make you a wedding gown, and I'm not going to miss that opportunity.'

'Mom—'

'And if you think you can deprive Heather of having the prettiest dress a princess ever wore, you can think again. And Clarice? She'll have an occasion to wear her pearls. Not to mention all your friends, the ones you've been bridesmaids for.'

'The money—'

'Oh, stop it. We have enough money for a beautiful wedding and a fabulous reception. You're my only daughter, after all.'

'I don't want to wait a long time, Mom,' Maggie almost wails. 'I don't want to wait until June to have a fancy wedding.'

'Can you wait until April? If I set to work right away, I can accomplish it all easily.' Frances opens a drawer in her bedside table, takes out a notebook and pen, and begins to write. 'Church. Reception. Date. Invitations.'

'But, Mom, who will give me away?'

'Ben, of course, who else?'

Maggie hesitates. She doesn't see much of Ben these days, and she's not sure she likes him in his new overactive Romeo Realtor persona. But that thought doesn't dim the delight she feels as she kicks off her shoes, curls up on the bed next to her mother, and plans her wedding.

★   ★   ★

The next night, before going to Tyler's for dinner, Maggie stops by the Orange Street house. She's dreading this moment, but Ben's car, a Porsche, of course, is in the drive, so she sucks up her courage and knocks on the door, prepared to see some woman half-undressed giggling in the hallway.

Ben opens the door. 'Hey, Maggie. This is a surprise.' He's wearing jeans and a sweatshirt, and a book dangles from his hand.

Maggie's wearing her puffy blue down coat, fleece cap, and gloves, but she's still shivering, from the cold and probably from nerves. 'Ben, can I talk to you?'

'No.' Ben shuts the door in her face. Immediately he opens it again, laughing. 'Just kidding. Don't be an idiot. Of course you can talk to me. Come in.'

'You are such a jerk,' Maggie tells him as she enters the warm house and follows him into the living room.

'Sit down. Want a drink?'

The furniture is an odd mixture of Clarice's antiques and severe modern sofas and chairs. A fire burns in the fireplace, filling the room with the fragrance of apple wood.

'Are you expecting someone?' Maggie asks, sinking onto a sofa and unzipping her coat.

'Nope.' Ben takes the chair he was obviously reading in, with a standing lamp behind him and a cup of coffee on the table next to him.

Ben. Book. Coffee. Not what she'd imagined. For a moment, Maggie's thoughts derail from her own news.

'No drink, thanks, Ben. I came to tell you something and ask you something.' Happiness floods back as she pulls off her gloves and holds out her hand, diamond ring gleaming.

'Wow! Maggie, I saw Tyler in town the other day, I know he's opening an office on the island, but I didn't realize— Wow,' he repeats, his face bright with genuine delight. 'This is spectacular news. He's such a great guy. When's the wedding?'

'This April,' Maggie tells him. 'As you can imagine, Mom's taken over the entire affair, she's bustling around like a hen with twelve chicks.'

Ben laughs. 'Good for her. She could use something fabulous like this.'

Maggie takes a deep breath. 'Ben, will you give me away? Please?'

Ben blinks in surprise. 'Maggie, it would be an honor.'

Maggie can't stop grinning as she drives from Ben's to Tyler's. But when she arrives at his rented apartment, a thought clouds her mind. Who will be her maid of honor? She sits in the Bronco for a moment, thinking about this, keeping the engine running for the heat.

Emily? No. Maybe once upon a time, but she and Emily haven't been in touch, except for Emily's all-purpose Christmas card, for years. It makes Maggie sad to realize this, that Emily won't take part in this most wonderful event – and then she thinks that she certainly wouldn't want Emily's husband to come, and all her doubt vanishes. Kaylie will be her maid of honor. Absolutely!

On her wedding day, the first Saturday afternoon in April, Maggie sits in her mother's bedroom, in front of Frances's old-fashioned vanity table with the three-sided mirror. She's wearing only her white undergarments while behind her Kaylie performs miracles on Maggie's curly black hair.

'I've never seen such thick hair,' Kaylie says. 'And it's so *springy*. Are you sure you want to wear it up in a chignon?'

It's an hour before the ceremony, and Maggie's nerves are jumping around like popcorn. 'It worked when we did the trial fitting.'

'Yeah, well, you must have washed your hair last night. Could we just try it down?'

'Oh, all right,' Maggie relents. 'I want a drink. I want a Valium.'

'You'll be fine.' Kaylie takes about a hundred pins out of Maggie's hair and brushes it so that it falls down past her shoulders in long, wavy black locks. 'Now.' From the table she lifts the white headband, glittering with pearls and small white shells, and sets it in Maggie's hair, arranging the fingertip, two-layered tulle veil to fall behind. 'Maggie, this is way romantic. Please leave your hair down.'

Maggie studies her reflection in the glass. Clarice, Frances, Kerrie, and Alisha wait in the other room with Heather so Maggie can concentrate on dressing, and Maggie's glad, because she could sit here forever staring at herself. Her makeup is light, almost no eyeliner, and her eyes are huge. Her hair billows around her like a waterfall.

'Okay,' Maggie agrees. 'We'll go with this.'

Kaylie lifts the headpiece off. 'Good. Now let's slip you into your gown.'

'We have to have Mother for this.' Maggie rises and opens the door to the hall. 'Come on in!'

Heather skips down the hall, adoring each movement she makes in her fluffy pink dress. She wears a headband of pink roses in her blond hair. Kaylie's wearing a cocktail length peau de soie dress with bateau neck and cap sleeves in dark pink. The two bridesmaids wear the same style of dress in a paler pink. Frances wears a tea-length chiffon sheath with a sweetheart neckline in a gray-pink, and Clarice wears a sheath with a chiffon tunic-length jacket in gray, with her pearls.

The women crowd into the room, chattering away, peering in the floor-length mirror to adjust their dresses, their hair, except for Clarice, who takes the armchair by the window and coaxes Heather to come twirl for her.

Frances unzips the garment bag hanging on the closet door and takes out the gown she made for Maggie. It is snowy white silk, strapless, close-fitted to the knees where it flares out in a mermaid skirt. Frances has sewn dozens of seed pearls on the silk. Now she holds it for her daughter to step into. She zips up the back and smooths the gown over Maggie's hips. Tears glimmer in Frances's eyes.

'Ahhhh,' all the women in the room sigh.

'Mommy, you look pretty,' Heather says, bouncing in her excitement.

Maggie bends to kiss her daughter. For a moment she holds Heather by the shoulders, smoothing her hair, tweaking a rosebud, calming the child. 'You look pretty, too, Heather. We're about ready to go to the church. Do you need to use the bathroom one more time?'

'No, I don't have to,' Heather insists.

'Let's give it a try anyway,' says Alisha, who has three children under seven. She holds out her hand and leads Heather away.

Kerrie slides around the room, snapping pictures of everyone as they redo their lipstick and adjust the flowers in their hair. Frances settles the headpiece over Maggie's long black cloud of hair, and there Maggie is, ethereal, glimmering, sublimely beautiful.

'I can't stop looking at myself,' Maggie admits in a whisper.

Everyone laughs. 'You'd better stop,' Frances tells her daughter. 'It's time to go to the church.'

Their friend Robin, a florist, waits in the kitchen to hand them their bouquets of white roses and to pin a corsage on Frances's and Clarice's shoulders before they go out the door to the limo waiting in the drive.

Maggie assumed it would rain, gust, blow, and probably snow, but this early April day blooms clear and fine, with a high, cloudless blue sky and only a gentle breeze that ruffles their hair as they arrive at St Paul's Church.

Ben stands by the door, handsome in his Armani suit. 'Maggie, you are a total babe,' he whispers, and his irreverence makes her laugh, gentles her nerves.

She hears the crowd inside talking and whispering. She hears the organ sound out Pachelbel's *Canon* as her mother and grandmother are ushered to their seats, as her bridesmaids walk down the aisle, as Heather tiptoes over the red rug, scattering rose petals from Clarice's lightship basket. The organ changes to the song Tyler and Maggie chose: Elvis Presley's 'I Can't Help Falling in Love with You.' Ben takes her arm, and Maggie slowly walks down the aisle toward Tyler, handsome in his suit and tie, smiling as he sees her come to him. Then she is standing next to him, looking up at him, caught in a spell of love and happiness so powerful, so magical, she knows it will last all her life.

After the excitement of the wedding and the fun of the reception, reality returns in a rush. Tyler and Maggie look at houses, settling on one near the schools and the Polpis Road out to the farm. While Tyler works, Maggie furnishes and decorates the house, being sure to take Heather with her after school to visit Frances and Clarice on the farm. They appear to live quite happily together, grateful for their peaceful time alone, knowing they'll have Maggie dropping off Heather and her friends most sunny Saturdays so the little girls can play in the barns or Shipwreck House before returning to the main house for cookies and milk. But they have their own lives, too. Clarice belongs to a bridge club and a book club. Frances volunteers for the library, the hospital, and the thrift shop. She also belongs to a book club, a different one from Clarice's, and she's sewing for others again, because it's what she loves to do.

Heather has preschool, and often brings her friends home, but just as often goes to her friends' homes. Maggie would be glad to have another baby right away, but when she discusses it with Tyler, they decide to wait for a year at least, to give them time to settle in, to let Heather feel this is now her family, and to allow Tyler and Maggie to enjoy the kind of romantic, passionate, knock-the-lamp-off-the-bedside-table sex they've been waiting for all these years.

Maggie's kind of nervous with so much time and contentment. She's great at pulling herself up by her bootstraps and trudging onward, but being in love with a great guy who loves her and her daughter, too, is almost more than she can comprehend. When she confides her anxieties to Tyler, he grins knowingly.

'Ah, Maggie.' He squeezes her shoulder. 'You know what you have to do, don't you? You have to start writing again.'

'Gosh, I think you're right.' She's stunned by his insight. 'Now I really am anxious,' she tells him, only partly joking.

She begins a routine, writing for one hour in the late morning, after Heather's gone to preschool and the house is relatively tidy. She takes out the novel she was working on, and rereads it with a critical eye. She starts over.

# Chapter Twenty-seven

'Oh, Cameron! Come see!' Emily bends over her daughter to tweak the petal of one of the daffodils into perfect position on Serena's headband. Bending down to her daughter's level, she coos, 'Serena, you look like the princess of spring!'

Serena twirls away, watching her yellow and white net skirt flutter around her legs, which are covered in yellow tights. It's Daffodil Festival Weekend on Nantucket, and the entire family is going to take part in the parade, which starts on Main Street in town with an antique car display and finishes in 'Sconset with elaborate tailgate lunches.

Cameron has joined them, just for today, but he has come with them, flying with Emily, Serena, and Emily's parents last night from Manhattan to open up the Porter house on the bluff. He's agreed to wear the straw boater with a yellow seersucker ribbon, like the one Emily made for her father, and a yellow vest. With his chiseled face and his blond hair, he looks like he came right off a Wheaties box.

'Daddy's outside with Granddad,' Serena calls from the living room window. 'I'm going to show them.' She scurries away.

Emily follows. Her father and Cameron are in the driveway, decorating their un-antique Range Rover with huge yellow bows. One on the front grille, one on the back, and smaller ones hanging from the door handles.

'Daddy, look at me, look!' Serena calls, running to her father.

Cameron sweeps her up into his arms, spins her around, and sets her down on the driveway. 'Serena, you are as pretty as a daffodil!'

Serena giggles and poses. She adores her father and when he has time to be with her, no one else exists. Cameron squats down to readjust the yellow ribbon around her waist. Emily watches, her heart swelling with gratitude. Cameron is good with Serena. Their two heads are on the same level now, as Cameron turns her around in order to retie the big yellow bow at the back of her dress. Their two heads: Cameron's shining blond, and Serena's glossy black. People have remarked, occasionally, on the oddity of two blond parents having a daughter with such extremely dark hair, such vivid blue eyes, but the remarks are merely conversational. No one has expressed any doubt about Serena's paternity, not even Cameron's parents.

'God. I look like Big Bird,' says Cara.

Emily turns to see her mother enter the living room, wearing camel trousers, a yellow cashmere sweater, and the sweater Emily made for the three females out of feather boas she found at an accessory store.

'I was afraid you'd be cold,' Emily tells her mother. 'It can be chilly here in April. And you look fantastic like that, Mother.'

'No, I look fat.' Cara tosses the feathery garment off. 'I'll wear a jacket.'

'But I wanted the three of us to match—'

'Sorry, sweetie, but I'm not coming down with pneumonia for that.'

Emily starts to argue, then stops. All right. So what. She's trying to make everything *perfect,* because she's beyond thrilled that they are all here together on this traditional Nantucket holiday. Cameron's been preoccupied and aloof, not attending Serena's ballet recital, and flying off God-knows-where more often than usual. Work, he claims, always work; she knew when she married him he was a workaholic, he says. Emily has been patient and understanding.

And who knows, perhaps her patience actually paid off, because over the past two weeks, Cameron's been more available to her, more present in his family's life. He's been home several nights in time to have dinner with them and to bathe Serena, read her a story, and tuck her into bed. He's taken Emily out to dinner and asked her about her committees, and laughed at her description of some of his bosses' wives, and confessed he was sometimes awfully tired of this daily grind. That night, after dinner and a good bottle of wine, when they went home, they made love. Emily didn't have to seduce him; Cameron made the first move.

Now he's joined them for Daffodil Weekend on Nantucket. Maybe only for one night, but he's here for the big day, the parade, the tailgate picnic, and Serena can hardly bring herself to leave his side.

Watching from the doorway, Emily studies her husband as he unrolls a length of yellow ribbon to drape across the tailgate of their SUV. He's speaking with Serena, telling her where to hold the end of the ribbon, and he's so handsome with his gleaming blond hair and his aristocratic profile that Emily can't help but admire him. She does love him. She's not in love with him, but it's okay, more than okay. It may be that this sensible kind of love will weather better than the overwhelming and irrational passion she shared with Ben.

*Ben.* She wonders if she'll see him this weekend, accidentally. She could say hello as they pass on the busy cobblestoned street . . .

She emailed Maggie to ask if they could get together, but Maggie responded that she and Heather were involved in a whirlwind of parties and picnics. They'd have no time to talk . . . couldn't they meet sometime this summer, the four of them, all girls, when no one else was around and they could have a good old chat?

*How's Ben?* Emily had casually asked. Email was great for this sort of thing; no one could see her face, watch her cheeks flush, hear her voice tremble.

*Ben's fabulous!* Maggie emailed back. Maggie's words stung Emily's heart.

'Mommy! Mommy! Daddy says we're ready!'

Emily and Cara bring out the picnic baskets. Emily's father follows. Most of the necessities, folding chairs, folding table, table-cloth, flowers, dishes, silver, were already put in the back of the car this morning. The five settle into the car, Serena bouncing with such excitement Emily can hardly fasten her seat belt.

Main Street is roped off for the display of antique cars. They find a place on Union Street to park, and walk into town. Cameron carries Serena on his shoulders. Emily runs alongside, snapping photos. The weather has been kind this year. The yards and window boxes fountain with daffodils, narcissus, and jonquils, in all shades of yellow and cream. A pale green canopy of new leaves extends over the brick sidewalks, casting shadows that dance in the slight breeze.

Main Street is lined three abreast with amazing cars – antique Bentleys, well-tended woodies, '59 Chevy Impalas, old fire trucks, VW buses – all swathed with flowers and ribbons and bows and shining like the sun. Women wear tiaras, crowns, and necklaces of daffodils, and of course the dogs are the most decked out of all, with daffodil collars and yellow suede coats and banana-bright bandanas.

Cameron sets Serena on the pavement so she can skip along, giggling, pointing, petting the dogs, squealing when they lick her face. Hundreds of people throng through the aisles, bending down to look inside at the creamy yellow leather of an antique Jaguar, or standing on tiptoe to catch a photo of the yellow balloons tied to the antennae of an old police paddy wagon.

Emily doesn't see anyone she knows.

When the parade heads out to 'Sconset, they return to their Range Rover and gradually join the line of traffic, finding a spot on 'Sconset's Main Street at the end farthest from the post office and general store. By then many of the other tailgate parties have been set up, so Cameron takes Serena off to enjoy the display of daffodil-themed picnics, costumes, and cars while Cara and Emily set up the table and food. Emily's father sits in a folding chair reading the *New York Times*.

She spreads a yellow-and-white-checked tablecloth piped with green over the card table, while Cara uncovers the bowls and platters of food: salmon, rye bread, capers, and cream; shrimp on skewers; deviled eggs; endive stuffed with crab salad; curried chicken salad; sweet corn, tomatoes, and mozzarella salad; champagne, 7Up for Serena; and of course, a tall white cake swirled with yellow cream icing and decorated with flowers. Emily ordered it all from her corner deli in Manhattan yesterday and brought it out to the island in a cooler. Her mother brought forced forsythia, yellow roses, and yellow tulips in a low green vase, and Serena chose to add her yellow rubber ducks from her bathtub. They circle the vase, ducklings following mother's lead, and the arrangement is so adorable several people stop to take photos.

They have way too much food – everyone's brought too much food – and the aroma of grilled hamburgers and hot dogs fills the air. Emily's family settles into their folding beach chairs, eating off plastic plates, which caused a slight disagreement this morning when Cara wanted to bring china plates and Emily insisted on the yellow plates she brought because if Serena accidentally dropped a plate, she'd be horrified. Serena's a sensitive little girl; Emily wants today to be perfect.

It is perfect. Couples with dogs pause at their table, introduce themselves, allow Serena to pet their dogs, and happily partake of champagne, salmon, and cake. Everyone they meet lives somewhere else and has come for the weekend festival. For them it's a ritual beginning of spring. Emily meets more people who live near her in New York City than people who live on the island. She doesn't see Maggie, and she doesn't see Ben. Which is fine, of course. Emily didn't come here *hoping* to see them. They're part of the island.

The island weather is typically chilly in April. Emily's parents have insulated themselves against the cold with alcohol, but Serena's energy is running out after hours outside skipping, petting dogs, and twirling in her yellow skirt. She's whiny and cold, and starting to suck her thumb, a bad habit Emily tries to ignore. Time to go home.

Taking off her jacket, Emily wraps her daughter in it and settles her into her car seat. Cameron helps her load up the Range Rover and her parents stiffly unfold themselves from their canvas chairs and stalk to the car.

Nancy Thayer

'Nap time for Cara Mia and Serena,' Cara says to her granddaughter.

Emily tries not to roll her eyes at her mother's use of the Italian phrase for 'my dear', which Cara is attempting to get Serena to call her instead of 'Grandmother.'

The ride home is brief since they're already out on the eastern end of the island. Cameron unbuckles a dozing Serena and carries her into the house and up the stairs to tuck her into bed. Emily's father helps her unload the picnic paraphernalia, and once that's done, he disappears up to his room with Cara for their own late afternoon nap.

Emily finds Cameron in their bedroom. He's tossing clothes into his suitcase.

'Cameron? Your flight doesn't leave until seven.'

'I called for an earlier reservation,' Cameron tells her. He drops his straw boater and yellow vest on a chair. He won't need them for business. 'The fog's coming in. I can't risk being stuck on the island tonight.'

'Oh, Cameron.' Emily's shoulders droop. 'I'm sorry you can't give yourself one more day to relax.'

'Me, too.' He drops into a chair and bends over to unlace his island sneakers and put on wing tips.

It's no use trying to persuade him to stay. They've done this routine before, many times. It's part of island living, sudden departures or arrivals due to eccentricities in the weather system. 'I'll drive you to the airport,' she offers.

'Great. Thanks. I'll get my Dopp kit.'

Emily quickly scans the suitcase and on the spur of the moment slips a pair of her laciest panties deep into it. That will surprise him. That will remind him of the night they made love, and make him eager to return home.

'I'm ready. We'd better go.' Cameron grips his suitcase, and as they go out the door, picks up his briefcase. He's already in work mode, wearing blazer, khakis, and tie, his cell phone in his pocket.

Emily drives. They pass through the main street of 'Sconset, where stragglers from the Daffodil tailgate picnic linger along the side of the road. A group of young people have set up a rock band where a sexy tall man with his hair dyed yellow and moussed into a wild puff sings into a mike while people dance in the street.

'Ah, to be young again.' Emily sighs.

'Come on, we're not so very old,' Cameron protests.

'Yet here you are, leaving on a holiday weekend to work.' Her voice isn't petulant, and she tries not to seem resentful.

'You knew when you married me what I do, and how hard I have to work,' Cameron reminds her yet again. His voice isn't accusatory.

After a moment, Emily concedes, 'That's true. It's just that I'll miss you. Serena will miss you.'

Cameron doesn't reply. It's only a fifteen-minute drive from their house to the airport, too short a time for a serious conversation, and what could Emily say that she hasn't said before? They're both quiet on the way in. Cameron's fingers fly as he texts on his cell. Emily keeps her eyes on the road.

When she pulls into the airport parking lot, Cameron says, 'You don't have to come in. It will be chaos in there anyway.'

He's right. Weekends are busy travel times to and from the island. Emily pulls the Rover into a fifteen-minute zone and parks.

'Cameron,' she says.

'Emily,' Cameron says, at the same time.

They laugh. Cameron leans over and kisses her cheek. 'I'd better hurry. Thanks for driving me out.' He opens his door.

'Wait,' she says. 'What were you going to say?'

Cameron faces her, suddenly serious. 'We need to talk. Soon. What were you going to say?'

As he speaks, he's pulling his suitcase from the backseat. He's only half-focused on her. His mind is elsewhere. They need to talk? What does that mean? Emily wonders.

'I wanted to tell you it was a wonderful weekend with you, Cameron, last night and today, with Serena and the island, and everything. Thank you.'

Cameron waves absentmindedly and strides toward the terminal. The electric doors slide open. He's gone.

Sunday morning, Emily's awakened by light slanting through the guest room onto her deep queen bed where she sleeps on blue-and-white-checked sheets. She's not used to light coming from this direction, or coming across her face, or being this clear and luminous. Going to the window, she sees the clouds parting to display a pure blue sky. Raising the window, she hears gulls cry and the gentle swoosh of the tide gently sweeping up to the shore. The day is mild and fine.

She peeks into Serena's room. Her daughter lies flat on her back, her black hair spread over her pink pillow. Emily tiptoes past her parents' closed bedroom door. Pulling on her fleece robe, she pads downstairs, she quickly makes herself a cup of coffee, then slips out to the patio to enjoy the morning. The lounge chair she set out yesterday is damp with dew; she doesn't mind. She settles in, knees drawn to her chest, and lets herself breathe.

This side of the island faces the open Atlantic. The expanse of shining water, so calm this morning that it's almost glassy, hides a galaxy of secret lives. Seals lazily swim in the depths, and also, probably, sharks, who have been enticed by the prevalence of seals to explore these particular waters. Bluefish, sea bass, tuna, swordfish, cod, and other fish flick through the cold water, and squid, eels, and grouper squirm around seaweed, mussels, crabs, and clams. The Algonquians named this bluff area 'Siasconset.' That means 'Near the great whale bone,' and all her life Emily's been hoping for a glimpse of a whale breaching out in the sea. She hasn't seen one yet, but she has time. Of course Serena always keeps an eye out for mermaids.

'Mommy?' Serena's suddenly at her side, startling Emily from her thoughts. 'What are you doing?'

'Sweetie.' Emily pulls Serena onto her lap and wraps the sides of her robe around her daughter's thin body. 'You snuck up on me! Are you hungry?'

Serena shakes her head. 'I want to go to the beach.'

Emily laughs. 'Baby, it's too cold in April to swim.'

'I know that. I want to look for shells. Please?'

'Why not? Let's sip some orange juice and we'll be off. But let's be as quiet as fairies so we don't wake the grands.'


They walk through the sleeping town along Main Street and down Gully Road to the beach. Over the years storms have eroded this part of the island so deeply that an entire row of beach houses has been swept away. Now the ocean in its fickle wisdom has decided to build the beach back up again, which will present a dilemma to land owners: to build again or not? Is this still their land?

Emily thinks such adult thoughts while Serena, clad in a tracksuit against the chill but barefoot, like Emily, skips through the sand to the edge of the water. She plays a game with the sea that all children must play, daring the incoming waves to catch her feet as she skirts the shoreline, trying to figure out the tide's pattern.

'Eeek!' she shrieks, when the sea washes over her bare ankles. 'Cold!'

The summer people who own the houses facing the water haven't arrived yet. No lights shine from the empty houses. No cars pass, no pedestrian strolls past with a dog on a leash. The golden beach stretches empty and still to the left and the right. Serena and Emily could be the only people on earth.

'Mermaid's purse!' Serena calls, holding up one of the rather hideous black skate egg cases that litter the shore. The little girl drops down to her knees, absorbed by a particularly fascinating cluster of rocks and pebbles.

Emily takes her time catching up to Serena. 'Pretty,' she says, observing the design her child is making from the rocks. 'Why are you making a moon shell?'

Serena shrugs, as if to say, *What a silly question.* 'I like moon shells. They're whirly. Crabs live in them. And fairies could live in the ones the crabs are through with. They're like a maze.' Serena glances up at her mother. 'Like a mystery, going round and round and in and in.'

Emily sinks onto the sand next to Serena. 'I see.' Focusing on the varicolored rocks, with their stripes, streaks, blotches, holes, and bumps, she selects the ones that catch her eye and begins to make her own design.

Mother and daughter work for a while in silence.

'Mommy,' Serena says, not looking up from her pebble moon shell. 'I want to live here.'

'Oh, sweetie, you have to go to school.'

'But they have school here.'

'Well, Daddy has to work in the city.'

'Daddy's always working.' Serena places a gleaming rock polished by the sea in the center of her spiral. 'Why can't we live here and Daddy can come visit on the weekends?'

'Oh, darling.' Emily sighs, unable to come up with an immediate answer. She stares out to the blue water. The tips of the waves catch the morning sun and seem to be flashing a message. 'Daddy would be sad not to tuck you in bed at night.'

'But I like it here!' Serena protests.

'I do, too,' Emily agrees.

This makes it more difficult when it's finally time to return to the house to pack up for the flight back to the city. Nantucket's Daffodil Weekend is not a national holiday; Serena has preschool tomorrow. Emily has committee meetings.

Back at the house, she finds her parents at the kitchen table, drinking coffee. Morning has never been an easy time for her parents. Emily serves her daughter a proper breakfast and allows Serena to shower with her, both of them washing their hair. After she dresses Serena, she asks her to help pack her little suitcase and her own duffel bag in which she carries the tiny pink Game Boy she's allowed to play only when traveling. Her parents dawdle around the house, their suitcase at the door. Emily goes through the house, double-checking lights, blinds, window locks, the kitchen.

'Mommy!' Serena calls. 'There's a man at the door!'

*Ben,* Emily thinks. Her heart races. She looks in the mirror. She's back in city mode, wearing a loose black dress, high black boots, with a gray cashmere sweater. Her skin still glows from all the spring sunshine – she looks good.

She walks toward the door, knowing it doesn't make sense for Ben to be here, yet still unable to stop hoping.

It's not Ben.

'Mrs Chadwick?' A police officer is at the door, in a navy blue uniform. He's young, in his early twenties, and the expression on his face is grave. Next to him stands a young woman, also in uniform.

Emily freezes. Police at the door mean bad news. Serena senses Emily's distress and presses up against her leg, hanging on to her tight.

'Yes, I'm Mrs Chadwick.'

'I'm Officer Jimmy Patterson. This is Officer Kathryn Stover. May we come in?' His face is flushed; he's under stress. The woman officer squints sympathetically.

'Why would you want to come in?' Emily asks.

'We need to speak with you. Alone, if you don't mind.'

She doesn't want to hear whatever it is they're going to say. 'I don't understand.'

'We have some news for you,' the female officer says quietly. 'About your husband.'

'Well, he's in New York. You must have—'

'Mrs Chadwick? Please.'

'I don't think so.' Emily doesn't move from the door but she realizes she must protect her daughter. 'Serena, would you run and tell Grandmother to make a fresh pot of coffee?'

'Grandmother doesn't like to work in the kitchen,' Serena argues. She keeps one hand tightly fastened to her mother's sweater.

'Please do as I ask, Serena.' Emily uses her *serious* voice.

With a dramatic sigh and drooping shoulders, Serena slowly, slowly trudges down the hall to the dining room.

'What's happened?' Emily asks.

'We'd like to come in.' Officer Patterson steps forward.

Emily makes a sudden decision. 'I'll come out.' A force deep in her gut insists that this house, this happy house where she was a child, where her child plays and laughs and loves, should not be contaminated by whatever news these officers of the law are bringing to the door. She steps outside and heads down the slate walk to the street. Once on the pavement, she faces the officers, who look slightly unsettled. 'All right. Tell me.'

Officer Patterson takes a deep breath. 'We regret to inform you that we've received word that a private plane crashed early this morning in the Adirondacks. Mr Cameron Chadwick was on the plane. There were no survivors.'

Perhaps everyone's first instinct is to disagree. Emily crosses her arms over her breasts defensively. 'Cameron wasn't going to the Adirondacks. He's in New York.'

'Ma'am, we have the flight manifest. Cameron Chadwick was on the plane that left from LaGuardia at six-fifteen this morning, headed for the Adirondacks Airport at Saranac Lake. It crashed on landing.'

Emily's fingers are numb as her mind tries to compute their words.

The female officer interjects helpfully, 'The plane belonged to the Endicott, Streeter, and Towle investment firm, based in New York City. Seven people were on board. We don't have the cause of the crash yet, but it seems faulty landing gear was involved.'

These young people in their crisp uniforms look terribly uncomfortable delivering this news. Endicott, Streeter, and Towle *is* the firm Cameron works for. Still, Emily thinks they must be wrong.

She shakes her head, trying to figure it out for them. 'All seven people on board died?'

'Fire,' Officer Stover gently informs her. 'The fire consumed the plane before the rescue trucks could get there.'

Emily is silent for a long moment. Then she strains toward Officer Patterson and Officer Stover. 'But I was happy this morning. Serena and I were on the beach, happy to be here, to be on the beach. Cameron has never enjoyed this island like I do, and he was a good sport to join us for Daffodil Weekend, but what you're saying, let me be clear, Cameron's plane from Nantucket to New York didn't crash last night, it was another plane, a smaller plane, a private plane, probably the company plane that crashed. So that's all right, then. I mean, it's not my fault.'

'Mrs Chadwick?' Officer Patterson steps forward. 'You're shivering. Let's go inside and have some coffee, okay?'

'Yes, but—' Emily's head is all muddled. 'You see, my daughter is in there, Serena, you saw her, she's only five years old, and I don't want to upset her. I really don't think we should give her this kind of news until we know for sure.'

'Ma'am, we do know for sure.'

Emily smiles gently. Officer Patterson is young. Such a sweet fresh face. 'I don't see how. You haven't *seen* Cameron. Perhaps he wasn't on the flight, or he's still home—' Yanking her cell from her pocket, she punches his number. Unpleasant beeps meet her ear, followed by a robotic voice telling her this number is not in service at the moment. *Please try again later.*

But she notices several messages have arrived for her this morning, which is unusual. They're all from wives of the investment firm employees. And from Edward Towle, one of the partners. Edward never calls her. Why would he call her? She listens to his voicemail, which begins, 'Emily, we are grievously sorry . . .'

She drops the phone.

Behind her, the front door of the bluff house opens. Her mother stands in the doorway, holding the house phone.

'Emily, honey? A call for you. From a John Endicott.'

Oh, Cam, Emily thinks, with your golden hair and your gleaming smile, with your kindness, your courtliness, your determination to be a good husband and father, how can this happen, how can all of your shimmering brightness be gone from the earth?

She can't remember whether she told him she loved him when he left.

She doesn't think she did.

# Part Seven
# Warrior Princess

# Chapter Twenty-eight

E mily heard somewhere that during such tragedies, time blurs. For her, time progresses with a hyper-vivid jerkiness, like a clock with faulty batteries. Like scenes from 1950s Kodachrome home movies with lines through the middle and sudden blank patches. Telling her parents. Calling Cameron's parents, who have been informed. Speaking with John Endicott. Thanking him for sending a company plane, but advising him (with a completely regrettable lapse of manners as she began to laugh, slightly hysterically, at the situation) that she'd made reservations with her parents on the Cape Air Flight that was leaving for LaGuardia at three and she'd rather take that plane than a company plane. Allowing her father to take the phone from her so he could speak with Mr Endicott to give the conversation the solemnity it deserved.

The flight back is bouncy. Serena talks incessantly. Emily hasn't told her yet. She doesn't want to tell her until they are away from the island. Nantucket was never Cameron's place. His death should not be allowed to dim the luster of the island's magic for Serena.

Nancy Thayer

Plus, she doesn't want to tell Serena until after they're out of the plane.

Emily wishes time *would* blur. Instead, it becomes staccato, it drags, it seems to reverse itself, she checks her watch and it's 5:05 and when she checks it again minutes later, it's still 5:05. Eons pass as they wait for their luggage. Civilizations rise and fall as she sits in the car driving them into the city. Her head aches hideously. Serena sings a maddeningly high-pitched silly ditty. Her parents discuss their coming week, both of them fastening their eyes to their iPhones, comparing calendars, clearing calendars, making calls, using euphemisms so Serena will not be alarmed.

Her parents ask her to stay with them for a few days, and Emily is glad.

Finally they arrive at the Porter apartment. The doorman greets them cheerfully. Emily returns a rubber smile. As they walk into the apartment, Emily switches off her cell.

*Now,* Emily thinks. She has to do it now. A force is rising up within her, violently pushing its way out. She has nowhere else to go. It has to be done. She has to tell Serena the sad news about her daddy.

'Mom? I'm going to take Serena into the guest bedroom for a little while.'

'That's fine, dear. I'll make some drinks,' Cara offers.

'Serena? I need to talk to you,' Emily says, amazed that it was only this morning she and her daughter played on the beach. With her arm around Serena's shoulders, she leads her into the room and closes the door. They're alone, just the two of them, together.

★　★　★

Five days later, Emily's in her own kitchen, making another pot of coffee for the people in her living room – her parents, Cameron's parents, a couple of lawyers – when her cell phone rings. The number is one she knows by heart.

'Emily?' After all these years, Maggie's voice is as familiar to Emily as her own.

'Oh, Maggie.'

'I just read it in the paper. About your husband. I'm so sorry.' The honest warmth in Maggie's voice breaks open Emily's heart.

Voices rise in conflict in the living room. Emily opens the door to the broom closet, slips inside, shuts the door, and sinks to the floor. 'Maggie, it doesn't seem real. I can't believe it.'

'Are you okay? Do you want me to come?'

'No, no, don't come. It's crazy here. Cameron's parents. My parents. His colleagues, their wives. No room to breathe.'

'Come to Nantucket. Bring Serena.'

'Oh, God, how much would I love to do that.' Emily's silent. 'Maggie, I have such a lot of *stuff* to do. You know. Wills, legal crap, phone calls. Right now it seems endless.'

'How's Serena?'

'Okay. She's okay. I mean, she loved her daddy, but she didn't see him all that much, it's possible she hasn't grasped the – the *finality* of it yet. And people are being kind, Maggie. Preschool moms are having Serena over for sleepovers and taking her on little jaunts. We have enough food for a millennium, and flowers, you've never seen so many flowers, although I said in the paper no flowers, all donations to charity.'

'Are you having a funeral?'

'Memorial service tomorrow. Honestly? I don't know whether to take Serena or not. She's such a wiggle worm, she can't sit still for a minute, and she talks all the time. The three heads of Cameron's firm all want to speak, you know they'll drone on and on, I mean *I* don't want to go, isn't that awful? Then we'll all go to the club and they'll get drunk and maudlin, and how does that help? How does that possibly help?' Emily can hear a mild hysteria in her voice.

'They say it brings closure,' Maggie says.

'Cameron's closure came the moment that plane crashed,' Emily declares.

'But what about you?' Maggie asks, sounding sensible, almost brisk. 'I mean, what are you going to do after the service and the reading of the will and all that?'

'I haven't thought that far ahead. These days I consider it an incredible accomplishment if I don't walk into the walls.' Emily wants to cry, but she's exhausted, and she's sick of crying, so sick her stomach cramps, so sick her eyes and throat burn as if she has a terrible flu. Will she ever have anything in her life but weeping again?

Is she a horrible person, a wicked, unloving wife, to think that thought?

'When is the will and all that?'

'The day after tomorrow. I know what it says, of course, but I should be there.' Emily is caught in a small dark room, a room full of grief and obligation to Cameron's relatives, his co-workers, his friends . . . she giggles at her thoughts. She really *is* in a small dark room, she's in the broom closet.

'Have you been sleeping?'

'The doctor gave me some pills. Yes, I've had some sleep.'

'And eating?'

'Not much. The thought makes me gag.'

'Are you pregnant?'

'What? Surely you jest.'

'I don't see what's funny about that. You are married. Were.'

'Our sex life hasn't been the most . . . active . . . recently. No, I'm definitely not pregnant, Maggie.' An abrupt storm of tears sweeps through Emily. 'But I wish I were, Maggie. Oh, I wish I were. I wanted another baby.'

'You'll have another one someday,' Maggie prophesies. 'For now, you have Serena. Now listen to me. When I hang up, I'm making a plane reservation for you two on the noon flight from LaGuardia to Nantucket next Monday. Are you paying attention? I'll meet your plane.'

'Oh, Maggie—'

'You and Serena can stay with us, or you can stay at your 'Sconset house, wherever you feel more comfortable. You know I'm married now—'

'What?' Maggie's casual announcement shocks Emily out of her tears. 'Who?'

'Tyler Madison. Remember him?'

'Tyler Madison? That boy with the glasses? Jesus, Maggie.'

Maggie breaks out into a full-bodied joyous laugh. 'He's changed, Emily. Wait till you see him. He's dreamy.'

'Tyler Madison is *dreamy*?' Emily realizes she's standing up now, with her hand on the doorknob, ready to move.

'You have no idea,' Maggie is saying. 'I'll text you with the flight information. That will be easier than trying to reach you by phone. Okay?'

'I'll give you my credit card number.'

'Emily, I'll pay for the flight. You have enough to deal with.'

'You'll pay for the flight?' Emily's head is swimming.

Maggie laughs again. 'Emily. It's been five years. We have a lot to catch up on. See you Monday.'

'Yes. Maggie, thank you. I can't imagine why you're doing this.'

'It's the least a sister can do,' Maggie says.

Because she's six months pregnant, Maggie's had her hair cut short again, into the pixie cap she wore when she was eleven. She remembers all too vividly how Heather as a baby would grab strands of Maggie's long hair and tug. How strong the little girl was, and how red-faced and howling she became when Maggie struggled to open her fat little fingers and release the hank of hair.

She's sure Emily will recognize her anyway. She hasn't changed that much in five years, except that she's happier than she's ever been in her life.

For this first meeting, with all of the possible emotional scenes – for how can she and Emily not cry, seeing each other again on such a sad occasion? – Maggie sends Heather to a friend's house to play. Maggie will have enough to cope with, keeping her own tears in check. Poor Emily, and her poor little girl.

Maggie's not all sweetness and generosity, though. She's nervous, anxious about how she'll appear to Emily, who has been married to such a compelling, seductive, successful man, who has lived the life of a wealthy New Yorker for the past five years. Maggie isn't sure how to dress. Everyone on the island is casual, jeans or khakis, cotton tops, sneakers, and Maggie needs sneakers these days when she's becoming off balance as her belly grows. She settles on an old, loose navy blue cashmere pullover that sets off her bright coloring, and applies only mascara for makeup. No lipstick. She's always kissing Heather, who hates to get 'that red stuff' on her face.

So here she is. Plain and simple. She parks her beloved Bronco, which seems determined to live forever, in the airport parking lot and heads for the terminal. Her heart pounds.

She waits by the luggage rack at the arrivals door and watches a small blue and white aircraft angle down from the clear blue sky. It bounces as it lands, turns, slows, and sputters up to the gate. The crew unlatch the door, which becomes the steps, and passengers slowly file off.

Emily is last. She's thinner than Maggie remembers ever seeing her, dressed in a black tunic, low-heeled black shoes, her blond hair tied back with a black ribbon. She's holding a little girl's hand, guiding her down the steps.

Maggie's heart stops.

Almost exactly Heather's height, the child has curly, glossy black hair and dark blue eyes with thick black lashes.

This little girl is Ben's child. Has to be.

She swallows, as if absorbing this knowledge: her daughter is Cameron's child; Cameron's daughter is Ben's child. Are the little girls half-sisters? Cousins? Maggie's mind reels.

'Maggie!' Emily and her daughter come through the electronic doors and walk straight toward Maggie.

The two women look at each other for a long moment, taking it all in, what has changed, and what has stayed the same.

'Maggie.' Tears spring into Emily's eyes. 'Dear Lord in heaven, it is completely fucking great to see you again.'

Maggie's heart breaks. She takes Emily in her arms. 'Emily. Oh, honey, I'm glad to see you, too.'

Emily hugs Maggie so hard she can scarcely breathe.

Serena tugs on her mother's dress. Emily picks Serena up. 'Serena, this is my oldest best friend, Mrs – what is it, Maggie? Sorry, I only remember Tyler's first name.'

'Madison. I'm Maggie Madison now, isn't that cool?' Maggie takes Serena's little hand. 'Serena, you can call me Maggie.' She starts to pick up a suitcase.

'Wait, I can do that,' Emily says. 'I mean, you probably shouldn't . . .'

'Pick up heavy objects because I'm pregnant?' Maggie laughs.

'How far along?'

'Six months.'

'Lucky you. Where's Heather?'

'She has a playdate today. Come on, let's go.' Maggie leads the way out of the building. 'Have you decided where you want to stay?' She tosses the question over her shoulder.

'In 'Sconset,' Emily tells her. 'You're awfully kind to offer to let us stay with you, but Serena and I love the house and the beach. It will be exactly what we need, won't it, Serena?' She buckles her daughter into Heather's car seat.

'How long will you be able to stay?' Maggie asks.

'I don't know. Haven't decided yet. I'm going day by day.' Emily looks over at Maggie as she pulls out of the parking lot. 'You look fabulous. Beautiful, healthy, happy. Marriage becomes you.'

'It does,' Maggie purrs.

'Are you writing?'

'When I have time. But of course I'm busy decorating our house, and taking care of Heather, and hanging out with my mother and Clarice, oh, yes' – she smiles – 'and being with Tyler every night. Life flies by.' Maggie remembers why Emily's here.

'Serena? Do you see that bag next to you? The one with the butterflies on it?'

In the rearview mirror, she watches Emily's daughter shyly nod her head.

'Open it, sweetheart. Everything inside is for you. Presents from me and Heather.'

'Maggie. That's really sweet.' Emily turns in her seat to help Serena unpack books, a jigsaw puzzle, and a wooden cut-out game of dress-the-princess.

'Thank you,' Serena says politely.

While Serena studies her little books, Emily says to Maggie, 'You know we've come here now and then. In the summers, usually with my parents. Cameron didn't like Nantucket,' she finds herself over-explaining, 'so I had to find a time to sneak off with Serena.'

'And you never called?'

Emily lowers her voice. 'Part of it was that I didn't want to run into Ben.'

Maggie jerks her head toward the backseat where dark-haired Serena sits. 'Yeah, I can understand why.'

Emily ignores her. 'But it wasn't only Ben. The longer I didn't call you, the more I was afraid to call you.'

'*Afraid to—*'

Emily's words rush over Maggie's. 'Listen to me. Maggie, I love this island. I've always loved it here. Until I met Cameron, the only place I wanted to be was on Nantucket. I thought I would live my life here. I love you, and I did love Ben. I suppose I still do. But the island, with or without you and Ben, is a wonderfully special place for me.' Observing the change in Maggie's posture, the challenge in the lift of her old friend's

309

Nancy Thayer

chin, she leans closer. 'Listen, Maggie. This is not *your* island. It's *my* island, too.'

When Maggie turns her head to meet Emily's gaze, her own eyes are full of tears. 'Of course it is, Emily. I know that. I *want* that. Why do you think I called you and told you to come here?'

Emily laughs and cries at the same time. 'Oh, Maggie, sometimes I think I lost my way. All my hopes and dreams of saving the world. And when I came here to the island, sometimes I had to be by myself, to be free from other people's needs tugging and pulling on me. I needed to walk on the beach and breathe.'

From the backseat, Serena pipes up in her sweet high voice, 'Mommy, why are you crying?'

'Because I'm happy, sweetie,' Emily tells her.

'Oh. Happy tears.' Serena goes back to her book.

Maggie sniffs back her own tears. In a practical voice, the one she often uses with Heather, she informs Emily: 'By the way, I have some groceries in the back for you. They should carry you through for a few days.'

'How'd you know I'd want to go to my house instead of staying with you?' Emily asks.

'Because I know you so well,' Maggie replies. 'I would say I know almost everything about you, Emily, except—' Again, she tilts her head backward, toward the car seat where Emily's daughter sits.

'Please, can we talk about everything another time?' Emily asks. 'I'm exhausted. I want to walk on the beach and let the wind blow through my brain, isn't that what we used to say? I want to eat enormous amounts of ice cream and watch the most idiotic shows television has to offer.'

'You'll have a lot to choose from,' Maggie says wryly.

310

Milestone Road becomes Main Street in the small village of 'Sconset. Everywhere trees are budding, flowers are blossoming, and the sun casts shadows that dance in the breeze. As they turn the corner onto Baxter Road, Emily gasps.

'It's lovely! Thank you, Maggie, *thank you* for telling me to come here!'

'It's my pleasure,' Maggie says truthfully.

She pulls into the driveway of the Porter house, the house where Emily once dressed Maggie up for her first reporting job as a teenager. She carries bags of groceries up and into the house while Emily and Serena bring in their things. She watches Emily go around the house, raising blinds, pulling back curtains. She can tell that Emily has already gone into her Nantucket mode, into her 'I-am-one-with-the-island' self; it's a state of mind she knows well.

'Call me if you need anything,' Maggie shouts as she goes out the door.

Emily's staring out the window at the sea. 'I will, Maggie. Thanks!'

Children's Beach is a small strip of white sand curving between the Nantucket Yacht Club and the White Elephant hotel. Tucked safely on the harbor, it allows children to play in the shallow water and watch the ferries and sailboats glide in. Behind, in a grassy field, are swing sets and a concession stand.

It's the perfect place to play. The day is bright with strong spring sun, and the breeze is light and intermittent. The water is still too cold for the girls to swim in, but they can wade, and use buckets and spades to build sand castles.

This morning Emily phoned Maggie, asking if they could meet

here this afternoon, with their daughters. Emily had been awake almost all night, yet oddly enough today she feels as refreshed as if she'd slept for eight hours. Sitting up in the wide queen-sized bed she'd once slept in with Cameron – but not often, for Cameron seldom came to the island – she tapped To Do lists on her Mac Air, lists about groceries to buy, who she should phone at Maria Mitchell about interviewing for a job, items she could have Donna, her housekeeper in Manhattan, pack up and send to her and Serena, phone calls she has to make.

This afternoon is her free time, her take-a-deep-breath-and-remember-that-life-is-good period. The afternoon glows with spring sunshine, gilding the sand and the water. The moment they step out of the car, Serena takes her bucket and shovel and runs on her pink flowered flip-flops to the beach. Emily follows, her arms laden with beach chairs, a bag of snacks and bottled water, beach towels. At the far end of the small beach, two young mothers with toddlers kneel in the sand, chatting above their children's heads.

Emily goes to the other end of the beach, sets up the deck chairs, organizes the bag, and spreads the towels. She hears Maggie calling hello. Turning, she sees her old friend approaching, wearing maternity tights and a long, loose cotton shirt, holding the hand of a little girl with blond hair and blue eyes.

'Serena,' Emily calls. 'Come here a moment.'

Serena reluctantly leaves the hole she's begun to dig. She notices a very pregnant Maggie waddling their way, and her eyes widen when she sees a girl her own age holding Maggie's hand.

'Hi, Serena,' Maggie calls cheerfully. 'It's nice to see you again. This is my daughter, Heather.'

'Hello, Heather,' Emily says. She sinks to her knees, to be eye level with the girls, and puts a steadying arm around Serena's waist. 'This is my daughter, Serena.'

The two girls size each other up in silence. Serena wears a pink bathing suit with white polka dots. Her black hair is in pigtails held with pink ribbons. Heather wears a blue bathing suit with white polka dots and her long blond hair is tied into pigtails with blue ribbons.

Heather announces, 'I'm five.'

Serena grins. 'I'm five, too! Want to help me build a sand castle?'

'Sure!' Heather tugs Maggie's hand. 'Did you bring my pail?'

'Right here.' Maggie reaches into her voluminous beach bag and takes out several bright plastic beach toys.

In a flash, the two girls scurry to the edge of the water.

'Here,' Emily says to Maggie. 'I've set up a beach chair for you.'

'Thanks. Now if you'll allow me to hold your arm while I lower my enormous ass . . .' Awkwardly, Maggie manages to sit in the low beach chair, her legs stretched out in front of her.

Emily sits, too. For a few moments, they watch their daughters as they chatter away, patting sand tightly into the pails to mold for building.

'Heather's lovely,' Emily says. 'But she doesn't look a thing like you, Maggie. I mean, her coloring is quite different.'

'You're one to talk,' Maggie says, jerking her head in Serena's direction. 'I know Heather doesn't look like me, but I don't care. I adore her. She's amazing. I'm proud of the way my mother and Clarice have dealt with it, and my friends, too. No one's acted as if I should be shunned and live my life wearing a scarlet letter.' She shifts on her chair, arranges a strap on her shirt.

'What have you told Heather?'

'When she was very young, I told her her daddy was a man who liked to climb mountains. Then Tyler came, and she thought he was the man, and oh, my goodness, Tyler *is* the man. He's legally adopted her. As far as she knows, Tyler's her father.'

Emily squeezes Maggie's hand. 'I'm glad. You deserve this, Maggie. You deserve to be happy.'

'Oh, Emily.' Pregnancy hormones are making Maggie cry all the time.

'We're thirsty, Mommy!' Serena yells.

Both girls come galloping up to the blanket, their bare feet spraying sand on everything as they run.

Emily hands out the bottles of water. 'Do you want your snacks now?'

'Yeah,' Heather says.

'Yes, please?' Maggie reminds her daughter.

'Yes, please.'

The girls take two bites of their apple slices, then abandon them to run back to their castle.

When the children are out of earshot, Maggie whispers, 'So we both have daughters who don't share our coloring.'

Emily shifts in her chair. She knows what Maggie is getting at. Still, she hesitates. How much anger is she going to set off when she opens this particular Pandora's box?

'Is Ben Serena's father?' Maggie presses.

'Yes, of course.' She turns toward Maggie, puts her hand on Maggie's arm, and speaks low and urgently. 'When I married Cameron, I thought he possibly could be the father. I mean, I had sex with Cameron and with Ben in, um, the same general period of time.'

'Oh, my.' Maggie smiles ruefully. 'You wild thing.'

Maggie sees the girls wave at her and Emily. She waves back cheerfully.

Emily finds a stick and digs into the sand while she talks. 'Maggie, you *know* Ben and I had been fighting for months when he broke it off. We couldn't agree on much of anything.' Tears suddenly fill her eyes as she remembers that time – as she remembers Ben.

'Ben has no idea about Serena?'

'No.' Summoning her courage, Emily remembers the resolution she made in the middle of last night. 'I need to see Ben.'

Maggie nods. 'Will you tell him about Serena?'

'Yes. I want to. I don't know if he'll be receptive . . .' She holds her breath, waiting for Maggie's opinion.

'Emily, listen. He's changed. He's harder now.'

Emily puts her face in her hands. 'It wasn't only my fault.'

'I'm not saying it was. But I want to be honest. Ben loved you so much. I think he still loves you. He's rich now, if that interests you.'

'Oh, stop that,' Emily snaps.

'He inherited Thaddeus's farm. I inherited the Orange Street house. We made a legal trade and now Mom and Clarice live there and Ben's at Orange Street. He's a real estate broker now . . .'

'Yes, I saw his name in the newspaper.'

'He's made a ton of money. But he's kind of grown away from the family. He loves Heather and takes her out for ice cream or to a kiddie movie occasionally, but he doesn't spend much time with the rest of the family. Emily, it's like he's tormented. Don't interrupt. I want you to understand this. I know *he* broke off with *you,* but almost immediately' – she snaps her fingers – 'you turned around and married Cameron. *Wealthy* Cameron. That hurt Ben's pride, but more than that I think it truly somehow undermined his sense of what the world's about. I believe he thinks that it really is all about money, and nothing else matters. But he isn't finding any peace or fulfillment in that kind of life, either.'

'Maggie, I'm really sorry. Hearing this breaks my heart.' Emily wants to tell her friend how *her* Ben had been as steady and true as a compass pointing north. He had been a safe harbor. *Her* safe harbor, as unchanging as the earth, her refuge, joy, and home. Lifting her head, she bleakly asks Maggie, 'Do you think he could ever forgive me?'

Maggie can read the honest emotion on her old friend's face. She says quietly, 'Why don't you ask him?'

Emily nods. 'I will.' After a moment, she asks in a low voice, 'Am I terrible to be thinking of Ben this soon after Cameron's death?'

'With a daughter who looks like Serena, how can you not think of Ben?' Maggie's mouth quirks upward. 'Look at those two. They could be you and me.'

Emily studies the two little girls busily working on their sand castle. It's true, and it's odd. Except that Maggie's daughter looks like Emily, and Emily's daughter looks like Maggie.

Maggie clutches her old friend's arm. 'Emily. Serena is Ben's daughter. That makes her my niece. That makes Heather and Serena cousins.'

Emily's jaw drops. 'Oh, my gosh, you're right.' She takes Maggie's hands in her own. 'You know, this, all this right here and now – it makes me feel that everything that's happened was meant to be.'

'Yes, like destiny. Like the moment we met, a path unrolled, only we didn't know where it was leading us.'

'Back here,' Emily tells Maggie. She enfolds her in a warm hug. 'Right back here, Nantucket sisters on a beach.'

Maggie hugs Emily back. 'Okay, enough. I'm going to cry.'

'Mommy!' Heather calls. 'The tide's ruining our sand castle!'

'Time to go home,' Maggie calls back. 'Help me up?' she asks Emily.

Emily clutches Maggie's upper arms and lifts. Both women stumble in the sand, laughing.

'You mommies are *silly*,' Heather announces with surprise.

'Yes, Heather,' Emily agrees. 'We are silly. Sometimes being silly is good.'

'Well, I know that!' Heather says.

The women gather the beach things and herd their children back to the cars.

'Call me!' Maggie orders as they prepare to drive away.

'Oh, you bet I will!' Emily tells her. Her heart feels lighter, her mind buzzing with plans.

Tuesday afternoon Emily drops Serena off at Maggie's house on Meadow View Drive, where Heather waits impatiently to play with her new friend.

'Your house is great!' Emily tells Maggie, taking a moment to glance around.

'It is,' Maggie agrees. 'You'll see it all later. Stop procrastinating. *Go.*'

Emily shoots a pleading look at Maggie. 'Want to come with me?'

Maggie laughs. 'I'm taking care of the girls, remember? Be brave, Emily. You can do this.' She wraps her arms around Emily. 'Good luck.'

Emboldened by Maggie's spontaneous warmth, by both their

hopes for what could be, Emily drives into town. She parks across from the newly spiffed-up Nantucket Hotel and walks into a handsome small house now serving as a real estate office.

When the receptionist greets her, Emily asks for Ben McIntyre, proud that her voice isn't shaking and her knees aren't knocking together. She's doing her best not to hyperventilate. She wears a simple summer dress, nothing too low-cut, nothing that screams 'Seduction!' She was unable to leave the house without lipstick and eye makeup, though. She wants to take Ben's breath away. He's already taking hers, and she hasn't even seen him.

'He's upstairs, first right,' the receptionist informs her.

Emily walks slowly up the stairs, controlling her breathing, turns to the right, and stands in the doorway of a large bedroom transformed into an office. She sees the filing cabinets, the club chairs on either side of a small table, the fireplace mantel with photos of Heather, the long elegant chrome desk, a fresh note in this old room with its wooden floors and Greek Revival wood-work, and there, in a big leather desk chair, sits Ben.

Her legs buckle.

He looks older. Well, of course, he *is* older. He's wearing a suit, which somehow seems wrong, except it's a gorgeous cut and he looks quite sophisticated in it. His glossy black hair is parted on one side, very fifties chic. He's beautiful.

Sensing the presence of someone in the doorway, Ben raises his head. When he sees Emily standing there, he recoils as if shot.

'Emily.' He stands up. 'What are you doing here?'

'Hi, Ben.' She's pleased at how natural her voice sounds. 'Could I come in?'

Color floods up his neck to his cheeks, but he remains dignified. 'Are you selling your house?'

She wants desperately to go to him, touch him, embrace him. But it's too soon. Oh, Ben, her Ben, she knows him by heart, even though he's wearing a Ralph Lauren shirt and has a hundred-dollar haircut. She enters the room and stands in front of his desk.

Clasping her hands together at her waist to steady herself, she says, 'No, Ben, I'm not selling my house. I came here because I want to talk to you about personal matters.'

His shoulders stiffen. 'I'm afraid everything important was said about six years ago, Emily. Right before you married Cameron.'

'You know Cameron's dead,' she says.

'Yes. I know.' He has the courtesy to add, 'I'm sorry.'

'May I sit down?'

He gestures to the chair in front of his desk with an open hand.

Emily sits, crossing her long legs slowly. 'Cameron was a good husband to me, and a good father to Serena. Have you seen Serena?'

Ben remains standing. 'Of course not.'

'You should see her. She looks like you.'

He flinches as if hit. Emily can imagine his body beneath his elegant clothes. His heart accelerating as he comprehends the full impact of her words. His jaw lifting, as Maggie's does, when they're feeling attacked, when they're defensive. His fists clenching, ready for battle. His hurt boy's heart in his grown man's body.

She wants to take him in her arms. It's too soon, that would be presumptuous.

Keeping her voice soft, Emily says, 'Ben. Serena is your daughter.'

Ben's jaw tightens, but he doesn't speak.

Emily coaxes, 'I want you to see her. I want you to know her, I want *her* to know *you*. I'd like—'

Ben walks from behind the desk to stand in front of Emily. She rises to face him.

'It's always about what you want, isn't it, Emily?' He's not angry, but sad. His eyes are deep blue, black-blue, with remorse.

'That's not true. You were the one who broke off with me.'

Ben makes a noise in this throat like a low growl.

Emily persists. 'Remember those days? We were fighting, we couldn't find a middle ground, you wouldn't answer my phone calls. We were so *young.*' Tears fill her eyes.

Ben's whole body tightens as he restrains his emotions.

It's taking all her own self-control not to embrace him. She knows that if she could hold him, he would come back to her. 'I wish I had married you, Ben. Even if we had to live with Thaddeus and your mother and ten other people in a barn. But I married the wrong man. It's done. We were both unhappy, if that's any consolation. But, Ben, I had the *right daughter.* And Serena and I are here on this island right *now.* You and I have another chance. Please don't let it go by because of pride. Please, Ben, at least agree to meet Serena. Come for a drink, or for dinner—'

Ben rubs his hands over his face. She sees his shoulders rise and fall as he inhales deeply. He meets her eyes. 'Emily. I'm sorry. It's too late. Too much has happened. There's no going back.'

'Of course not. But we can go forward.' Gently, she says, 'Ben. I have never stopped loving you.' She reaches out a hand to touch his shoulder.

Ben steps away. Several steps away. 'Emily,' he says, his voice aching. 'I've moved on with my life. You need to move on with yours.'

'Ben—' Emily's paralyzed, uncertain what to do. She waits.

Ben doesn't speak. He doesn't look at her.

Emily asks, 'You want me to go?'

'Yes.' He's rigid, locked.

Emily leaves his office, walks briskly down the stairs, nearly tripping. She passes the receptionist without speaking, and drives quickly to Brant Point beach, a few blocks away, where she sits in her car and sobs.

When she's composed, she drives to Maggie's.

'The girls are in the backyard,' she tells Emily when her friend knocks on the door. Seeing Emily's face, she asks, 'So he didn't greet you with open arms?' Tugging Emily lightly by the wrist, she says, 'Come in. I've made iced decaf lattes.'

They settle in the family room with its wide sliding doors to the patio and lawn. At the far end, Serena and Heather bustle in and out of a charming child-size log cabin. They seem to be running a pastry shop.

'I like your house,' Emily says, looking around. 'It's new and clean and open.'

'I know, right? I told Tyler I'd had my fill of creaky old houses with slanting floors. And I love Meadow View Drive. It's the perfect neighborhood for kids.'

'I'm not sure what to do about my parents' house. I mean, it's mine now. They've signed it over to me. They live in Florida now, and prefer it there. I'm happy in our 'Sconset house, but it's isolated except in the summer. No children.'

Maggie's eyes are bright. 'You're sure you're going to live on Nantucket?'

Emily's spirits lift as she answers. 'I absolutely am! I called Janet this morning to talk about the science museum. They're not hiring staff, but I'm going to volunteer this summer, like I did when I was a teenager. Plus, she's going to suggest to the chair of the building committee and the water biodiversity committee that I be allowed to attend the meetings because of my degrees.'

'Emily, that's wonderful. And Ben?'

Emily's face falls. 'I went to his office. I told him about Serena. I did everything but lie on the floor hanging on to his ankles. No interest.'

'I doubt that.' Maggie tilts back her glass of iced latte. 'He's never stopped loving you, but your return is unexpected. It's huge. You need to give him some time, Emily.'

'You're right. But I'm not patient.'

'Guess you'll have to learn to be.' She watches the little girls who are now kicking a soccer ball back and forth, running, giggling, falling over in the grass. 'Tyler's teaching Heather soccer. We don't want her to be all girly-girly. But I can't resist the pink fairy stuff, either.'

'I know.'

'Emily, think about putting Serena in day camp. Sun and Fun. Jascin at Maria Mitchell suggested it. I've enrolled Heather. Some days I could pick up Serena and bring her to my house. Heather would love that.'

'That's really nice of you. Thanks, Maggie.'

'It's easy to be nice when you're happy.'

'Are you writing?'

'I'm playing at it.' Actually, Maggie has sent her finished manuscript to an agent. This is a secret only she and Tyler know. Someday, depending on what happens, she'll tell Emily. She might want Emily to read and critique it. But – not yet. Two events in her life she'll keep silent about with Emily. Certainly, she'll never tell her about Cameron. And her novel? She'll see.

Emily says, 'I'd love for Serena to see Shipwreck House – is it still standing?'

Maggie smiles. 'It is. Heather and I go there a lot.'

'Could Serena and I ever visit there?'

'Of course,' Maggie says. 'We'll take a picnic.'

Tyler and Maggie lie snuggled in bed, talking drowsily as they relax toward sleep.

'Emily's nice, Ty,' Maggie murmurs. His arm is over her waist; she lazily tugs on the dark hair on his wrist. 'Thank heavens, because Heather and Serena get along really well.'

'That's good,' he responds lazily.

'She says she went to talk with Ben but he refuses to see Serena.'

'Give him time.'

'That's what I said, but I'm not sure. He's too stubborn for his own good.' She snuggles her hips against him, intimate and comfortable. 'Life can be hard.'

Tyler shifts away from her a few inches. 'Not this quickly, it's not.'

'Stop.' She playfully slaps his hand. 'I'm talking about . . . life. About living with people who have hurt you or offended you. You've been off the island for years. You probably can't remember what a small community it is, how people can carry grudges across entire generations.'

Tyler rises up on one elbow. 'Are you kidding? How do you think it feels when someone who once tormented me, bullied me, called me four-eyes, knocked me around, walks into my office needing glasses?'

Worried, Maggie turns over to face him. 'How does it feel, sweetheart?'

Tyler guffaws. 'Great. They're at my mercy now. They need my help, my expertise, they have problems with their sight, and that's always scary. If I have to put drops in to dilate their pupils, or approach them with my tonometer, the strongest men usually sweat. Every now and then I've had a patient say in the middle of the exam, "Didn't you used to go to school here?" and I want to throw back my head and give out a mad scientist laugh.' Tyler cackles to demonstrate.

Maggie shoves him. 'You do not, you idiot.' She rests her head against his chest. 'Do you think I should go talk to Ben?'

'Who would that help?' Tyler counters.

'Oh, I don't know.' Maggie sighs. 'He is my brother, he's Heather's uncle, but he's different now. Aloof, remote.'

'People change,' Tyler says simply.

'Yes,' Maggie agrees. 'They do.'

'Give it time,' Tyler suggests again. 'Let it happen naturally.'

'How Zen of you,' Maggie murmurs, relaxing into sleep.

# Chapter Twenty-nine

It's a glorious Saturday morning, the first hot calm day in June, the first real *summer* day. Three weeks have passed since Emily went to see Ben, and he hasn't come to see Heather or called Emily or called Maggie to broach the subject with her.

Maybe Emily has patience, but Maggie doesn't. As she bustles around her kitchen, she tucks her smart phone between her ear and shoulder and calls him on his cell. 'Ben? Hey. We haven't seen you for a while.'

'I've been busy,' Ben replies, his voice cool.

'I know you have. Your sales are in the paper all the time. But you've got to relax now and then. Listen, I'm taking Heather out to 'Sconset for a picnic and a swim today, and we want you to join us.' She's already in her fetching maternity bathing suit, long tee shirt, and flip-flops.

'Maggie, could you possibly be any more transparent?'

In the family room, Heather is carefully packing her own picnic tote with her special mermaid beach towel and several flavors of Burt's Bees Lip Balm, which Maggie allows her to use as ChapStick and Heather considers lipstick. Watching her happy child makes Maggie cheerful. She attempts an innocent tone with her brother. 'About what? Chicken salad sandwiches? Your niece? Sunshine and a swim?'

'Is Tyler going?'

Ben and Tyler get along as well as can be expected when Ben is so cranky and aloof. 'No, his office is open on Saturdays in the summer. Busy – you know.'

'I'm busy, too.'

'I'm sure. Plus, you're a coward.' She drops the word sweetly into the conversation. One thing a sister knows how to do is ruffle her brother's feathers.

Sounds of huffing breath steam through the phone. Then Ben growls, 'Oh, for God's sake, Maggie.'

Ha! She's hooked him. 'What? You're not a coward?'

Grumpily, Ben says, 'I don't care about her anymore. I'm over her. The end.'

'Oh, okay. I didn't realize that.' Maggie's voice is treacly, syrupy sweet. 'Sorry I insulted you. But hey, since you're totally over her, it won't bother you if you come to the beach with us and run into Emily and her daughter – who's your daughter, by the way, and looks exactly like you.'

An irritated sigh fills her ears. 'Maggie. What do you think you're doing?'

In a deep little pocket of her heart, like a bump in a giant tree, an old childhood elf jumps up and down, giggling mischievously, still alive from those days long ago when Ben used to torment her and she used to tease him. Thank heavens she's having another child! Who but a sibling can you annoy with such delicious wickedness?

'What am I doing? Inviting you to come see me and Heather at 'Sconset. I'm taking a picnic.' She double-checks to make sure she has sunblock in her bag.

'No, thanks. Now go away, Maggie.' Ben clicks off.

When Maggie and Heather arrive at the 'Sconset beach parking lot, they find Emily and Serena already settled in the sand. Emily jumps up to help Maggie unload. Serena races to take Heather by the hand, pulling her down to the beach, both of them prattling rapidly about the sand house they're going to build. Emily lugs Maggie's cooler in her arms.

'I called Ben.' Maggie carries a load of beach towels and blankets. 'He said he's not coming.' Still, she wonders if he just might show up.

Emily glances at Maggie, but keeps a stiff upper lip.

'He went on the defensive instantly,' says Maggie. 'I don't think he'd be that way if he were really truly one hundred percent over you.' As Maggie and Emily prepare their spot, holding down the blanket from the breeze by setting coolers, baskets, bottles on the corners, Maggie sings, 'He's got you under his skin.'

Emily scans the water. 'The waves are fairly large today. We should have gone to Jetties.'

'Nah. It will be too crowded. This is fine. We'll keep an eye on the girls. Anyway, I don't let Heather swim out here unless I'm with her.' As Maggie lowers her bulk into a beach chair, she eyes Emily. 'A bikini. Wow. Look at you.'

Emily sits, too. 'I'd rather look like you.'

'You mean pregnant?'

Emily sighs. 'Cameron didn't want another child. At least not with me. We weren't exactly happy together when he . . . when the plane crashed. The truth is, I'm pretty sure he was having an affair.'

'I'm sorry.' Maggie can hear the pain in Emily's voice. How complicated love is. Emily has never stopped loving Ben, but in a way Emily loved Cameron, too.

'Her name was Jessica Beckett. She was an intern in his firm's office. She was lovely – actually, Maggie, she looked a lot like you. Cameron wanted to do the right thing, and so he married me when I told him I was pregnant. When he saw Serena's black hair, he was suspicious, angry, but he didn't want to embarrass me, send me out into the snowstorm clutching my babe like a Charles Dickens heroine . . . and we did care for each other. We worked hard, trying to love each other, trying to make a family.'

Watching the girls play, Maggie reminds Emily: 'You did make a family for five years. Serena is a happy child.'

Lost in her own thoughts, Emily muses, 'Jessica Beckett's name was on the manifest of the plane that crashed. The firm had a memorial service for all seven people on board. I met her parents. We sympathized with each other . . . of course they had no idea.' Emily puts her face in her hands. 'It shouldn't have happened, Maggie. The plane shouldn't have crashed. Cameron and I could have divorced, and Serena would have been fine, she hardly saw him anyway, and he could have married Jessica and been truly deeply sincerely loved. I could have come back here . . .' When she looks up at Maggie, her face shines with tears. 'It's not fair. That I'm here, in this place I cherish, and poor Cameron is dead.'

Reaching across the beach chairs, Maggie hugs Emily. 'It's not your fault. You didn't cause it. You couldn't have prevented it. We don't know *everything,* Emily. Perhaps Cameron is happier now in some other universe—'

Emily sniffs. 'I don't believe that stuff.'

'That's your prerogative. Lots of scientists do.' Pushing up off the chair, Maggie opens the cooler, takes out two Diet Cokes, hands one to Emily and keeps one for herself. 'The point is, you are not responsible for the plane crash. You *are* responsible for her.' She nods toward the edge of the water where the two little girls kneel industriously in the sand, creating their sand city.

Heather senses her mother looking and waves. Serena tells Heather something. Both girls run up the beach to their mothers.

'We want to swim!' They're silly together, clapping hands, jumping up and down, making a racket.

'Fine,' Maggie agrees. 'Let's put your water wings on.'

'I don't need water wings,' Serena boasts. 'I passed the test at the pool.'

'This is not the pool, Little Missy,' Emily assures her daughter. 'This is the ocean, and you're wearing your floaties.'

'I'm a water fairy! I'm a water fairy!' Heather lifts and drops her water-winged arms, pirouetting a slow circle in the sand.

'Whoever heard of a water fairy!' Serena scoffs, but she relents, allowing her mother to fasten on the water wings.

'I've *seen* water fairies!' Heather brags as the girls run toward the water.

'You mean *mermaids!*' Serena insists.

Emily glances fondly at Maggie. 'I wonder where Heather gets her imagination.'

'Or Serena,' Maggie grunts in reply, shoving herself to her feet. 'Are you going in the water?'

Nancy Thayer

'Of course. I never let Heather swim in the ocean unless I'm right next to her. She's only five. She's a great swimmer, but the currents can be wicked here on certain days.'

'Oh, really?' Emily responds with a tang of acid. 'I had no idea.'

'Stop. I realize you consider this *your* beach—'

'I swam here every summer, growing up.'

'Really?' Maggie teases. 'I did not know that.'

Emily links her arm through Maggie's. 'Seriously, you great big water fairy . . .'

'Water buffalo, more like,' Maggie jokes.

'*Can* you swim in that condition?'

'Honestly? Not far, simply because I can't catch my breath as easily. But the water's buoyant. I can float on my back like an otter. The girls won't go out very far. I'll be fine.'

The wind comes from the east today, puffing in intermittent gusts, rippling the surface of the white breakers that slowly roll in to the beach. Heather and Serena are wading into the water, shrieking with glee as the cold froth splashes against their ankles, knees, bellies. Maggie wades in up to her thighs, stretches luxuriously, then gently lies down in the water, surrendering her body to its rhythms. A few feet away, Emily walks out farther, then dives underwater, swimming parallel to the shoreline.

Maggie bobs on her back, lifting her head to check on the girls.

'Mommy looks like a seal!' Heather calls, pointing at Maggie, whose short black cap of hair gleams glossily in the sun.

Emily backstrokes to her daughter. 'Swim with me.'

'We're baby whales!' Serena yells, throwing herself facedown in the water, splashing along vigorously next to Emily.

'Fairy circle?' Heather paddles up to Maggie, her little body

330

appearing to be all flapping arms and legs, tiny, vulnerable, and energetic.

'Sure,' Maggie agrees, although she hesitates to leave the Zen-like calm of her float. Shifting her body around, she searches for the surface of the underwater sand with her feet. She's farther out than she'd thought. The water comes to her chest. 'Give me your hands.'

This is one of Heather's favorite games. Holding hands, arms stretched full length, Heather lies faceup while Maggie slowly twirls in a circle, singing a song with constantly changing words about water fairies who spin in circles in the ocean to make magic. Maggie changes the tempo, sometimes swirling slowly then suddenly whirling fast, and Heather screams with delight.

Beneath Maggie's feet, the firm wet sand is as familiar as a wooden floor, the wash of waves against her torso a cool rocking motion, lifting her up and setting her down. The sun pours down on the sea in a buttery light, igniting water, beach, hillside, town, cottages, dunes, sea grass, shoreline, water in a loop so bright she squints against such blaze. Had she ever thought she would be here, at this beach, with her own daughter, and with her childhood friend Emily, and Emily's own daughter? No, they had never dreamed of such abundance, such happiness, such treasure.

'Mommy, do that to me!' Serena pleads with Emily, who takes hold of her daughter's hands and begins her own revolution.

'Okay,' Maggie tells her daughter. 'That's all, Buglet. Mommy's tired. Let's go back closer to shore.'

She releases Heather's hands in order to wipe her face dry of the salt water that's splashed into her eyes, stinging and almost blinding her.

That's when it happens. Later Maggie will blame herself. She knows this beach, these waters, the ocean's fickle, sudden currents that shoot unexpectedly from nowhere, blasting away from the shore, out to the deep Atlantic. She should not have let go of Heather's hands.

A white-tipped wave, higher than any others she's seen this morning, rises up in front of Maggie and slams her down, smashing her into the sand several feet below the surface. Maggie struggles through the flooding, glistening water to stand. The constant shove and suck of the tide disorients her, dizzies her. She slips and with great effort rights herself.

Wiping her eyes, she searches for Heather. Her heart is thudding hard from her exertions, and it triple-times as she sees the heaving water empty of any sign of her child.

'Maggie!'

Maggie turns toward Emily, who is staggering as if drunk a few yards away. 'What the fuck!' Emily screams. 'What was that? It ripped Serena right out of my hands.'

'I've lost Heather!' Maggie screams. She sees color bobbing not far from Emily. 'There!' Pointing, she directs Emily's eyes. 'There's Serena.'

Emily heads off in a steady, determined crawl.

Maggie scans the water again and now she sees Heather, a streak of blond hair, a blotch of bright green water wing.

Holding her arm as high as it will reach, Maggie waves, yelling, 'I'm coming, Heather!'

As she swims toward her daughter, Maggie silently assures herself of Heather's skill. She's been swimming in this ocean since she was a toddler. She's been dunked and flipped and knocked down by strong waves plenty of times. She knows the ocean. She won't be afraid.

But she hasn't been caught in a current before, Maggie realizes, as her efforts to reach Heather tire her but appear to take her no closer. The current is frigid, much colder than the water near shore, propelling Heather aggressively south, carrying her tiny body, like a piece of flotsam, away from the safety of land. Heather flails with her small arms, her head bobbing up and down as the waves lift and drop her. Maggie's tiring. Her belly weighs her down, it is another force she has to fight against.

The current is inexorable, a roaring freight train of energy. Terror explodes in Maggie's chest. Redoubling her efforts, she battles on into the icy cold, into deeper water, where the sun's warmth can't penetrate.

'Go back!'

With salt-reddened eyes, Maggie sees Emily swimming next to her. 'Go back! I'll get her!' In a long ivory gleam, Emily shoots past Maggie, her strong arms carrying her out farther and farther from shore.

Maggie treads water, reluctant to give up the struggle to save Heather, seeing – when the waves aren't splashing her face – how quickly Emily is covering the distance to the child. Maggie's heart beats so fast it blanks a blackness over her eyes, signaling her to rest or faint. She treads water. She watches.

A glistening turquoise hill breaks over Maggie, thrusting her into the depths. She swims upward into the light. She sees Emily reach Heather, grasp Heather's wrist, tug her toward her. Another wave slams Maggie's face, blasting her entire body backward – and then she's free of the current. Waves rock her up and down as she watches Emily grip Heather faceup, in a lifeguard's head hold.

Calming, Maggie looks back at shore. Serena stands on the edge of the sand, her arms wrapped around herself. Maggie swims.

She will reach Serena, wrap her in a sun-warmed towel, and hold her tightly as they watch Emily tow Heather back to safety.

She staggers onto the sand, weak, shaking, gasping, trying not to throw up.

She hears voices.

She is on her hands and knees. 'Serena?' she croaks.

A man is with Emily's daughter. He's squatting in the sand next to her, handing her a towel, speaking to her softly. He's not touching her – he knows she doesn't know who he is, and he doesn't want to frighten her. Serena hurriedly wraps the towel around her shoulders. She's listening intently, nodding her head as the man talks. Her black hair gleams in the light, exactly like Ben's hair gleams as he speaks to her.

# Chapter Thirty

'Ben.' Maggie collapses on her bum, allowing herself to focus on catching her breath. After a moment, she says, 'Serena. This is my brother, Ben. Ben, this is Emily's daughter, Serena.'

Serena is still shivering. 'Is Mommy getting Heather?'

Maggie holds out her arms. 'Come here, honey. We'll warm each other up. Ben, would you please bring me a towel?'

'Sure.' Her brother stands and heads up the beach to their little nest, returning with a large striped towel, which he wraps around Maggie's shoulders.

Serena runs to sit in Maggie's lap. Because of Maggie's belly, she has to sit sideways, and her pointed knees jab into Maggie.

'I was scared!' Serena tells Maggie. 'The water swooshed me off away from Mommy. I couldn't see her, but then she found me, and she pulled me back to shore, then she saw you and Heather, and she ran into the ocean, she swam so fast. Did you see her swim so fast?'

'I saw her.' Maggie squeezes Serena tightly against her. 'I saw her swim so fast, Serena. I've never seen anyone swim that fast. Look, here she comes, I can see her face, I can see Heather's head. They're coming closer.'

Serena gawks at Maggie, alarmed. 'You're crying!'

'It's all right,' Maggie assures the little girl. 'They're happy tears.'

Ben sits next to them, his large, warm body's presence a comfort. 'Drink,' he says, handing them each a bottle of water.

Dutifully, they sip the water, although Maggie feels guilty taking this relief when Emily is still out in the ocean, fighting her way back. But Emily has reached the safety zone where an adult can stand on the sand, with her head above water, and Emily does this for a moment, resting, breathing, holding Heather, whose arms are around Emily's neck.

'Mommy!' Serena jumps off Maggie's lap and runs to the water's edge. 'Heather! Mommy saved you!'

Ben stands and extends his hands to pull Maggie up. 'You okay?'

Maggie can't speak. She runs to the water, to gather her little girl in her arms.

Emily sprawls facedown on the sand, her rib cage expanding as she wheezes, breathing in the air for which her lungs are starving. One hand still grips Heather by her wrist.

'Emily. I've got her.' Maggie pulls Heather to her, framing her face in her hands, checking the color of her skin, her eyes.

Heather is panting, crying, and shaking so hard her teeth rattle. But she's breathing, her color is good, she's not vomiting, she's not unconscious, she's only very frightened. 'Mommy!' she cries as she hurls herself against Maggie, hugging Maggie hard.

Serena runs to her mother. 'Mommy, Mommy, are you okay?'

Maggie can see Emily's back heaving as she regains her body's equilibrium. Emily rolls to a sitting position, reaches out, and brings her daughter onto her lap.

'Mommy, I was really scared,' Serena cries.

Emily's voice is low when she speaks to her daughter, low because she hardly has the strength to speak. Maggie can see this, how weak Emily is, how she's battling not to let Serena know, and she wishes she could help her, but she can't move, pinned down with her wet, rescued, shuddering daughter and her own lumpy, fright-weakened body. Maggie opens her mouth to say, 'Ben, help her,' but before she can speak, Ben goes to Emily.

'I'm going to pick you up, Emily,' he says. He turns to Serena. 'I'm going to carry your mother up to her beach chair. Run and find the biggest towel you can to wrap around her.'

While Serena scampers up the beach, Ben squats down, slides his arms beneath Emily's body, and stands, holding her in his arms. She submits, resting her head on his chest. To Maggie, they look like lovers.

Emily remains limp as her daughter bustles around her, tucking beach towels over her, lifting her feet to wrap the towel firmly, babbling excitedly, 'Mommy, that was scary! I couldn't see Heather! I didn't know what to do! I was crying, Mommy! When we swam way out in the ocean, I couldn't see you. I was *cold.*'

'Sssh,' Emily says. 'Sssh, baby. It's all over now. It's okay. Everyone's okay.' She pulls Serena onto her lap and cuddles her, kissing her head. Kissing her damp, gleaming black hair. 'See how smart it was to wear your water wings? They kept you and Heather floating, even in the big waves. Did you feel that, how they helped you?'

As she speaks to her daughter, soothing them both with her

voice and their mutual embrace, she's aware that Ben is standing awkwardly to the side, watching them.

*He came,* she thinks. He said he wouldn't come, but he did. He's here.

The rush of adrenaline that fueled her swim left her dizzy and nauseous when she first hit the shore, but now it's receding, leaving behind, in her body and heart, a powerful brightness of joy. Serena's okay, and Maggie's okay, and she, Emily, saved Maggie's daughter's life!

'Did you drink some water, Serena?' she asks. 'Can you reach that water bottle? Mommy needs a good long drink of unsalted water.'

She sees Maggie awkwardly maneuver herself into standing position. Maggie takes Heather's hand and they walk to Emily, where Maggie drops to her knees.

'Emily. Thank you. How can I ever thank you enough? You saved Heather's life.'

Emily scoots to the edge of her chair so her arms can reach around Maggie's bulk in a long, hard hug. Heather and Serena dance and jump around them, crying in their shrill voices, 'Mommy, don't be sad!' The rim of the aluminum beach chair cuts into Emily's bum. Maggie's low on strength and leaning on Emily more than embracing her, and the girls are as exasperating as mosquitoes, as precious as the sun.

Emily pulls away, croaking in a bad actor's voice, 'Honestly, can't a woman have a good honest sob around here?'

'Mommy,' Serena says, 'I'm *hungry!*'

Emily, Maggie, and Ben laugh. Probably their laughter is more explosive than it would be normally – they are all relieved, grateful, and exhausted. Emily lifts her arms away from Maggie.

'Hungry,' Emily says. 'Right.' But her brain is moving slowly and it can't come to a decision about food.

Maggie stands. 'Okay, Serena, here's what we're going to do. I'm taking you and Heather to our house. You both curl up on the sofa with the puffy puffy quilt and watch your favorite DVDs. I'm going to make you grilled cheese sand-wiches and give you all the chocolate chip cookies you want for dessert.'

Serena cocks her head. 'I thought we were having a picnic.'

Maggie is already gathering up her beach bag and blankets. 'No picnics when little girls have been swept away by the waves. That's a rule. After something like that, it's necessary to go home and *rest*.'

'Mommy!' Heather stamps her foot, spraying sand. 'I don't *want* to rest!'

'Doesn't matter. You need to rest. I need to watch you, keep an eye on your color, be sure you're drinking water, and you are tired, whether or not you think you are.'

'Mommy!' Heather argues.

'Heather? This is *non-negotiable*.'

Heather sags. 'Okay.'

Serena stares at her own mother questioningly.

'Serena, go with Maggie. I have to sit here and regain my strength. I'll be there soon.'

'What about him?' Serena points at Ben.

'This is my friend Ben. He's going to stay and help me. Then we'll both come to Heather's house.'

Serena shrugs, but willingly follows Maggie and Heather as they trudge up the sand to the parking lot.

After the others have gone, the beach is quiet. No gull flies overhead, and the waves, which roared around Emily with such drama, peacefully lap the shore.

'Ben,' Emily says, patting the beach chair next to her. 'Come sit down.'

He sits. For a moment they both stare at the rolling blue water.

'You came,' Emily says.

'Yes.' Ben clears his throat. 'Emily, thank you. You saved Heather's life.'

He is very serious, this man she has known since they were children. He wants badly to do everything right, and his earnestness pierces her heart. She does love him, still loves him, and she wants to make him happy. To lighten his heart. To make him smile.

'Well, after all,' Emily says, 'you once told me I was a warrior princess.'

'Wow,' Ben says. 'I'd forgotten about that.'

'No, you didn't,' Emily tells him, gently knocking the side of his knee with hers.

A small smile lifts his lips. 'Okay, maybe I didn't.'

Emily decides to go for broke: 'She's yours, you know. Serena. She's your daughter.'

'Certainly looks that way.' Ben's voice is hoarse.

Emily studies this man, this obstinate, wonderful, proud, deeply beloved man. His face is tanned, and lines extend from his eyes and gently etch the sides of his mouth. His long black lashes hide his blue eyes. She can't read his expression. But he's here. He drove out to be here, and he stayed here beside Emily.

'She's *our* daughter,' Emily says. She sees his Adam's apple move as he swallows. 'Ben.' Reaching over, she puts her hand on top of his. 'If I could change things, I would. I'm sorry if I hurt you.

I'm sorry I went through the charade of the marriage I had with Cameron. But I didn't feel I had any choice.'

'I was a total ass. I'm sorry.' Ben moves his hand away from hers. He stands up. He's wearing a faded blue bathing suit and a white rugby shirt.

Her heart stalls. He's leaving.

'Let's walk,' he says, extending his hand. 'I mean – can you walk? Have you rested enough?'

'I'm fine.' Emily's more than fine, she's delirious as she takes Ben's hand and lets him pull her up.

Together they go down the beach, walking parallel to the shore, for a few silent minutes as quiet as an old married couple taking a stroll. The sand is warm to their feet, the sun warm on their backs. The tide floods up in a white lacework of foam and retreats, the water sinking into the sand, making it shine like satin.

'I never stopped loving you,' Ben says.

'Oh, Ben.' All at once, the weakness from her exertions in the water, combined with the glorious shock of Ben finally saying he loves her, slams into the backs of her knees. She wobbles. She leans against his arm. 'Wow, I think you literally knocked me off my feet.'

He turns to face her, putting both hands on her waist to hold her steady as he looks down at her. 'Are you okay?'

His eyes are a deeper blue than the ocean, a more sober blue than the sky. They blaze at her with the intensity of cobalt, warming her, sustaining her, adoring her. *Adoring* her.

'I've never been better in my life,' she tells him, wrapping her arms around him. 'Hold me,' she says.

Ben pulls her closer to him. She rests against his firm body, hearing the steady beat of his heart, savoring the warm strength of his arms around her waist.

'Why are you crying?' he asks, lifting her face to meet his.

'Happy tears,' she tells him. 'Serena can explain what that means.'

His smile is like the sunrise. Gently, he touches his fingers to her face, wiping her tears away. 'Can I kiss you?'

She lifts her arms to his shoulders, resting her hands on his strong, warm neck. 'Please. Although you'd better hold me tight. I might fall down.'

She closes her eyes, and feels the soft warm huff of his breath, the tickle of his skin, the sweet urgent pressure of his lips on hers. She allows her body to press into his, she wraps her arms more firmly around him, she sighs as her loins, belly, breasts, and mouth remember the touch of this man. She kisses Ben back passionately, opening her lips, touching his lips with the tip of her tongue, squeezing her leg between his.

He pushes her away. 'Okay, stop that. I was trying to be romantic.'

'So was I,' she teases.

'No. You were being seductive, and I am not taking you here on this beach in broad daylight.' He begins walking again, holding her hand, gazing out at the water.

'Where are you taking me?'

'I'm not sure. Years have passed. Maybe I've become more conservative in my old age.'

'Ben. You're thirty.' It is all coming back, the give-and-take between them, the passion and the pleasure, the indestructible connection. It is as enduring as the ocean touching the earth. Sometimes stormy, always unfathomable, their love is lasting. Has lasted, will last.

'Yeah, I'm only thirty, but I want to do the right thing. I think I may not take you to bed until we're married.'

*Married*. Grinning like a child, she asks, 'How long do I have to wait?'

To her surprise, Ben stops walking. Taking both her hands in his, he drops to his knees. Looking up at her, he says, 'Emily Porter Chadwick, will you marry me?'

Behind him, the sun strikes the waves into an ocean of diamonds.

Sinking to her own knees to meet his deep blue eyes, she says, 'Yes.'

It's like a morning in heaven.

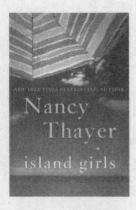

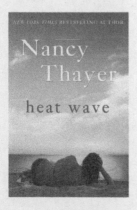
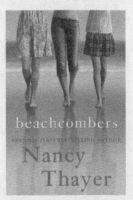